Praise for *Voices from the Street*

"Passion and paranoia drive this early novel by the visionary Philip K. Dick, prophet of a generation trapped between the atomic age and the apocalypse. Written at the dawn of his career, *Voices from the Street* is as fresh and tough as if he'd finished it yesterday."

—Kit Reed

"Unflinching, intense, and disturbing, *Voices from the Street* is a fascinating microcosm of the essential themes Philip K. Dick would unpack, novel by novel, in the decades following its completion in 1952. It is a necessary, unifying piece of the puzzle that was Philip K. Dick and further illuminates his kaleidoscopic exploration of the nature of reality and what it meant, for him, to be human."

—Kathleen Ann Goonan

"If Philip K. Dick's classic SF novels are gospels preaching of man's struggles with a hostile universe, *Voices from the Street* is their Q document."

—Michael Cassutt

"Remarkable...echoes of Dick's contemporaries such as Ralph Ellison, Richard Yates, Rod Serling, Raymond Chandler, and early Kurt Vonnegut Jr. resonate, and a bonus exists in Dick's impeccable eye for detail....Dick fans will be in rapture."

—*Publishers Weekly*

"Well written, it is a welcome addition to its author's large and brilliant canon."

—*Booklist*

"Despite its period context, *Voices* is surprisingly relevant to today. The rampant paranoia may no longer be about communists, the war may not be in Korea, but the symptoms are the same. Actually, the rejection of the evils of the military-industrial complex and American myths is even more relevant now than when Dick wrote this bleak novel of alienation....Dick predicted the moral landscape of the future, if not its outward technology, with frightening accuracy. Highly recommended."

—*Starlog*

Also by Philip K. Dick
from Tom Doherty Associates

Humpty Dumpty in Oakland

VOICES FROM THE STREET

PHILIP K. DICK

TOR®

A TOM DOHERTY ASSOCIATES BOOK
New York

This is a work of fiction. All of the characters, organizations, and events portrayed in this novel are either products of the author's imagination or are used fictitiously.

VOICES FROM THE STREET

A Tor Book
Published by Tom Doherty Associates, LLC
175 Fifth Avenue
New York, NY 10010

www.tor.com

Tor® is a registered trademark of Tom Doherty Associates, LLC.

Library of Congress Cataloging-in-Publication Data

Dick, Philip K.
    Voices from the street / Philip K. Dick.
        p. cm.
    ISBN-13: 978-0-7653-1821-3
    ISBN-10: 0-7653-1821-0
    1. Self-perception—Fiction. 2. Depression, Mental—Fiction. 3. Oakland (Calif.)—
Fiction. I. Title.

PS3554.I3 V65 2007
813'.54—dc22

                                                                    2006051496

First Hardcover Edition: January 2007
First Trade Paperback Edition: November 2007

Printed in the United States of America

0 9 8 7 6 5 4 3 2 1

To S. M.

They find it harder to locate their external enemies than to grapple with their internal conditions. Their seemingly impersonal defeat has spun a personally tragic plot and they are betrayed by what is false within them.

—C. WRIGHT MILLS

VOICES FROM THE STREET

PART ONE
Morning

Thursday morning, June 5, 1952, came bright and hot. Moist sunlight lay over stores and streets. Glittering from the lawns, the cold sprinkle of night steamed upward to the blue-glass sky. It was an early-morning sky; soon it would bake away and shrivel. An oppressive white haze would drift in from the Bay and hang lusterless over the world. But it was only eight thirty; the sky had two hours to live.

Jim Fergesson happily rolled down the windows of his Pontiac and, poking his elbow out, leaned to inhale vast lungfuls of damp summer-morning air. His benign gaze, distorted by a residue of indigestion and nervous fatigue, took in the sight of sunlight dancing from gravel and pavements as he drove from Cedar Street into the half-deserted parking lot. He parked, turned off the motor, and sat for a moment lighting a cigar. A few cars slithered in and parked around him. Cars swished along the street. Sounds, the first stirrings of people. In the quiet chill their movements set up metallic echoes from the office buildings and concrete walls.

Fergesson climbed from his car and slammed the door. He crunched briskly across the gravel and down the sidewalk, hands in his pockets, heels clicking loudly, a small, muscular man in a blue serge suit, middle-aged, face red with wrinkles and wisdom, puffy lips twisting the column of his cigar.

On all sides of him merchants rolled down their awnings with elaborate arm motions. A Negro was sweeping trash with a push broom into the gutter. Fergesson stepped through the trash with dignity. The Negro made no comment . . . early-morning sweeping machine.

By the entrance of the California Loan Company a group of secretaries clustered. Coffee cups, high heels, perfume and earrings and pink sweaters, coats tossed over sharp shoulders. Fergesson gratefully inhaled the sweet scent of young women. Laughter, muted whispers, giggles, intimate words from soft lips passed back and forth, excluding him and the street. The office opened and the women tripped inside with a swirl of nylons and coattails . . . he glanced appreciatively back. Briefly, he longed for one of them, any one of them. Good for the store . . . like the old days. A woman adds class, refinement. Bookkeeper? Better someone where the customers can see her. Keeps the men from swearing; keeps them kidding and laughing.

"Morning, Jim." From Stein's MensWear.

"Morning," Fergesson answered, without stopping; he held his arm behind him, fingers casually trailing. In front of Modern TV Sales and Service he halted and fished out his key. Critically, he surveyed his small, old-fashioned possession. Like a little old suit, the store steamed dully in the morning sunlight. The archaic neon sign was off. Debris from the night lay scattered in the entranceway. The TV and radio sets in the windows were murky, uninteresting shapes. Records, signs, banners . . . he kicked a pasteboard milk carton out of the doorway and onto the sidewalk. The carton rolled away, caught by the morning wind. Fergesson plunged his key in the lock and pushed open the door.

Here no life existed. He squinted and spat away the first stale breath that hung inside the shop. In the rear the ghostly blue of the night-light rose like marsh gas over a decaying bog. He bent down and clicked on the main power; the big neon sign spluttered on, and after a moment, the window lights warmed to a faint glow. He fixed the door wide open, caught up some of the sweet outdoor air, and, holding it in his lungs, moved about the dark damp store, turning on banks of sets, display signs, fans, machinery, equipment, intercoms. The dead things came reluctantly back to life. A radio blared, then a long row of TV sets. He advanced on the night-light and destroyed it with a single jerk of his hand. He ignited the listening booths that surrounded the dusty, disorganized front counter. He grabbed a pole and dragged back the skylight. He threw the Philco display into whirring excitement and carried it to the back of the store. He illuminated the luxurious Zenith poster. He brought light, being, awareness to the void. Darkness fled; and after the first moment of impatient frenzy, he subsided and rested, and took his seventh day—a cup of black coffee.

Coffee came from the Health Food Store next door. Under the front counter of Modern were piles and heaps of cups, spoons, and saucers. Bits of stale doughnuts and buns mixed with cigarette ashes, matches, Kleenex. Dust lay over them; years passed and new cups were added; the old were not removed.

As Jim Fergesson entered the Health Food Store, Betty dragged herself heavily from the back and lifted a tired arm to greet him. She carried a vast damp rag wadded and sopping under her arm; her face was lined with fatigue and her steel-rimmed glasses sagged.

"Morning," Fergesson said.

"Morning, Jim," Betty wheezed with a weary, friendly smile. She disappeared to get the Silex coffeemaker from the back.

He was not the first customer. A few middle-aged women, well dressed and chatting quietly, sat at the counter and tables eating cracked wheat and skim milk and drinking an all-grain beverage. To the rear a nattily dressed salesman from the gift shop was daintily nibbling at dry butterless toast and applesauce.

His coffee came.

"Thanks," Fergesson murmured. He got a dime from his vaguely pressed trousers and rolled it to Betty. On his feet, he moved toward the door, past the displays of sugar-free peaches and pears, nonfattening acorn-meal cookies, jars of honey and sacks of wheat meal, dried roots, bins of nuts. He kicked the screen door open, edged by the corner of a dried date-and-apple display rack upon which a poster of Theodore Beckheim rested, caught a momentary glare of disapproval from the stern-faced, beetle-browed minister, and then found himself free on the sidewalk, away from the heavy sickening odor of powdered goat's milk and female perspiration.

Nobody had entered Modern ahead of him. Olsen, the spiderlike repairman, was nowhere in sight. Nor were any of the salesmen. No elderly woman had appeared with a withered little radio to be fixed. No young couples wanting to finger expensive TV combinations. Fergesson carefully carried his cup of coffee down the sidewalk and into the store.

As he entered the store the phone began to ring.

"Damn," his mouth formed softly. The cup teetered as conflicting motor responses traveled up and down his arm. The thin black liquid sloshed over the edge as he set the cup hurriedly down and swept up the phone. "Modern TV," he said into it.

"Is my radio fixed yet?" a woman's voice shrilled.

Half listening, Fergesson groped for a pencil. The woman breathed harshly in his ear, a beast jammed up against him, muzzled by the phone. "What is your name, ma'am?" Fergesson inquired. A certain sweet kind of early-morning despair filled him: it had already begun.

"Your man took the insides out sometime last week and promised to have them back Wednesday, and so far I haven't heard a thing from you people. I'm beginning to wonder what sort of place you're running there."

Fergesson groped for the service-call sheet and commenced turning the stiff yellow pages. Outside the store the moist sunlight still filtered down bright and clear. Slim high-breasted young women still clattered by. Cars hissed sleekly along the damp streets. But there was no deceiving himself: life and activity were outside and he was inside. The primordial old woman was on the telephone.

Scowling, he gouged a few bitter words on the sheet—sharp jabs of disgust. The grinding wheels had begun devouring his soul. The reality of the workday had begun . . . for him, at least. The burden was on his shoulders; while his employees lay sleeping in bed or dallied at breakfast, Fergesson, the owner of the store, was reluctantly beginning the leaden task of looking up the woman's old radio.

That morning, at the other end of town, at exactly 5:45 a.m., Stuart Hadley woke up in a cell of the Cedar Groves jail. Somebody was banging on the metal bars; Hadley lay on the cot and cringed furiously to himself until the noise died down. Frowning at the wall, he lay waiting, hoping it had gone. But it hadn't gone. Presently it was back.

"Hadley," the cop yelled in at him, "time to get up."

He lay wadded up, knees drawn up against his stomach, arms wrapped around him, still frowning, still waiting, still mutely hoping it would go away. But now there was the jangle of keys and bolts; the door slid noisily back and the cop came inside, right up to the cot.

"Come on," he said in Hadley's exposed ear. "Time to get out of here, you stupid son of a bitch."

Hadley stirred. Gradually, resentfully, he began to unwind his body. First his feet extended themselves and groped for the floor. Then his legs stretched out, long and straight. His arms released their grip; with a grunt of pain he sagged to an upright sitting position. He didn't look at the cop; instead, he sat with his head down, staring at the floor, brows drawn together, eyes almost shut, trying to keep out the harsh gray light filtering through the window.

"What the hell are you?" the cop demanded, baiting him.

Hadley didn't answer. With his fingers he felt his head, his ears, his teeth, his jaw. Rough stubble scratched his fingers; he needed a shave. His coat was torn. His necktie was missing. For an interval he fumbled clumsily under his cot; finally he found his shoes and dragged them out. Their weight almost pulled him down on his knees.

"Hadley," the cop repeated, standing in front of him, legs apart, hands on his hips, "what's the matter with you?"

Hadley got into his shoes and began tying the laces. His hands shook. He could hardly see. His stomach gurgled and crept up in his throat. The pain in his head pulled his brows together in a thin, anxious frown.

"Get your valuables at the desk," the cop said. He turned and strode out of the cell. Presently, with infinite caution, Hadley made his way after him.

"Sign here," the sergeant behind the desk said, pushing a sheaf of papers at Hadley, and then a thick fountain pen. A third cop was off somewhere, getting the sack that contained Hadley's possessions. Two more cops lounged at a table, watching dully.

The sack contained his wallet, his wedding ring, eighty cents in silver, two paper dollars, his cigarette lighter, his wristwatch, his ballpoint pen, a copy of the *New Yorker,* and his keys. Scrutinizing each item intently he transferred them one by one to their proper places . . . except the magazine, which he dropped into the wastebasket by the desk. Two dollars. He had spent, lost, or been robbed of the rest. In all, about thirty-four dollars was gone. Now he noticed that the back of his hand was badly cut; somebody had put a Band-Aid on the groove. While he was examining it, the sergeant leaned down, pointed, and said:

"What's that in your coat pocket?"

Hadley felt in his pocket. A large crumpled piece of shiny paper came out in his hand; he opened it and spread it flat. It was a color reproduction of a picture: Picasso's *Clown Family with Chimpanzee*. One edge was jagged and ripped; probably he had torn it from a library book. He had a vague memory of wandering through the public library, as it was closing, its lights dimming one by one.

After that had come a lot of walking around in the evening darkness. Then the bar. Then another bar. Then the argument. And after the argument, the fight.

"What was it about?" the sergeant asked.

"Joe McCarthy," Hadley muttered.

"Why?"

"Somebody said he was a great man." Shakily, Hadley smoothed down his short-cropped blond hair. He wished he had his cigarettes. He wished he were home where he could bathe and shave and get Ellen to fix him some steaming black coffee.

"What are you," the sergeant said, "a Red?"

"Sure," Hadley answered. "I voted for Henry Wallace."

"You don't look like a Red." The sergeant studied the hunched-over young man. Even in his rumpled, filth-stained clothes, Hadley had a sharp-cut look to him. Blond hair, blue eyes, an intelligent but puffy face. He was slim, almost slender, with a slightly feminine grace. "You look more like a queer," the sergeant stated. "Are you one of those San Francisco queers?"

"I'm an intellectual," Hadley said dully. "I'm a thinker. A dreamer. Can I go home now?"

"Sure," the sergeant said. "Are all your things there?"

Hadley returned the empty sack. "Every one of them."

"Sign the paper, then?"

Hadley signed, waited a moment with leaden patience, and then realized the sergeant was through with him. He turned and walked soggily toward the stairs of the police station. A moment later he was standing out on the gray sidewalk, blinking and rubbing his head.

The two dollars got him a cab. It took only a short while to reach his apartment house; there were almost no cars out yet. The sky was hazy white, cold. A few people strode along, blowing pale breath ahead of them. Slumped over, hands clasped together, Hadley brooded.

Ellen was going to screech. As she always screeched when something of this sort happened. And the long-suffering silence that had grown, in the last month, until it was unbearable. He wondered if it was worth making up a complicated story. Probably not.

"Got a cigarette?" he asked the cabdriver.

"Smoking causes lung cancer," the driver answered, eyes on the empty street.

"That means no?"

"No, I don't, no."

It was going to be hard explaining the lost money. That was the part he hated. He couldn't even remember which bar it was; probably it was several bars. Only the memory of the two black-jacketed toughs, those two truck drivers, those two McCarthy supporters, remained clear in his mind. The cold air outside the bar as the three of them had stumbled out and tangled. The sharp wind, the fist in his stomach and in his face. The sidewalk, very gray and hard and cold. Then the police car and the struggling trip to the jail.

"Here we are, mister," the cabdriver said, stopping the cab. He ripped the receipt from the meter and clambered out, all in one busy motion.

Nothing stirred. The neighborhood was absolutely silent as Hadley unlocked the front door of the apartment building and made his way up the carpeted stairs and along the hall. No radios. No sounds of flushing toilets.

It was still only six fifteen. He reached his own door and tried the knob. Unlocked. Hesitantly preparing himself, he pushed open the door and entered.

The living room, as always, was dark, messy, smelling faintly of cigarettes and overripe pears. Ellen had long ago ceased exerting herself. The shades were down; he could hardly see as he passed through, already pulling off his coat and unbuttoning his shirt. The bedroom door stood wide open; he halted to peer in.

In the great rumpled bed his wife lay asleep. She was turned on her side, tousled brown hair piled over the pillow and around her bare shoulders, over the sheet and her blue nightgown. The sound of her low, labored breathing reached him; satisfied, he turned and stiffly made his way into the kitchen.

He was putting on the Silex of water when her voice came, clear and sharp. "Stuart!"

Cursing, he walked from the kitchen back to the doorway. She was sitting bolt upright, brown eyes huge with alarm. "Morning," he said drearily. "Sorry I woke you."

Nostrils quivering, face distorted, she gazed fixedly at him. He became uncomfortable as moments passed and still she said nothing.

"What's the matter?" he demanded.

With a cry, Ellen sprang from the bed and trotted toward him, arms out, hot tears dribbling down her cheeks. Uneasily, he retreated. But her vast, bulging form descended on him; her arms clutched at him fervently. "Stuart," she wailed, "where have you *been*?"

"I'm okay," he muttered.

"What time is it?" She broke away, looking around for the clock. "It's morning, isn't it? Where did you sleep? You're all—*cut*!"

"I'm okay," he repeated irritably. "Go back to bed."

"Where did you sleep?"

He grinned evasively. "In a thicket."

"What happened? You went downtown last night for a beer . . . and you were going to the library. But you didn't come home . . . You got in a fight, didn't you?"

"With savages, yes."

"In a bar?"

"In Africa."

"And you were in jail."

"They called it that," he admitted. "But I never believed them."

For a time his wife was silent. Then outrage and exasperation replaced alarm. The bloated softness of her body hardened. "Stuart," she said quietly, lips thin and pressed tight together, "what am I going to do with you?"

"Sell me," he said.

"I can't."

"You haven't tried." He wandered into the kitchen to see how his coffee water was doing. "Your heart isn't in it."

Suddenly she was behind him, holding on to him desperately. "Come to bed. It's only six thirty; you can sleep two hours."

"I'm coffee-oriented."

"Forget your coffee." Rapidly, she reached out and shut off the gas. "Please, Stuart. Come to bed. Get some sleep."

"I slept." But he was willing to go with her; his body ached with the need of sleep. Passively, he allowed her to drag him from the kitchen, into the amber-dark bedroom. Ellen crept back into bed while he stood clumsily removing his clothes. By the time he had his shorts and socks off, his body sagged with weariness.

"Fine," Ellen whispered as he sprawled against her. "That's fine," she repeated, pressing her harsh fingers against his hair, against his ear and cheek. This was what she needed: the immediate presence of him.

With a great yawning sigh he slept. But she remained awake, gazing ahead of her, holding on to her husband, pressing him tight, feeling the minutes slip away from her one by one.

In the absolute stillness of the bedroom, among the motionless half shadows left from night, the clock began to sing. With its tinny whirry metallic voice it hummed faintly, softly, thoughtfully to itself; then its noise picked up urgency. The noise of the clock stirred the room. The noise met the cold white morning sunlight that spilled in through the window, that filtered through the muslin curtains and spread out, pale and silent, over the icy asphalt tile of the floor, the fluffy scatter rug, the chair and dresser and bed and heaps of clothing. It was eight o'clock.

Ellen Hadley reached out her bare tan-fleshed arm and found the clock. She made no sound, no sound at all, as she shoved down the cold little stud protruding from its brass top. The clock hushed; it ticked on, but its noise was over. Sliding her arm back, away from the cold of the room, under the covers, Ellen turned a little on her side to see if she had wakened him.

Beside her, Stuart still slept on. He hadn't heard the clock; the faint tinny beginning of its noise hadn't reached him. Thank God for that. She wished he would never hear it. She wished she could keep it back until the metal wheels and springs had sagged into rust, and its dull hands were broken and gone. She wished—well, it didn't matter. Because soon he would have to wake up.

She had only delayed it. It would come, and nothing could be done about it.

A few birds stirred and crept outside the window; the rim of shrubbery danced violently as birds landed in it. A milk truck roared down the deserted street. Very far off the Southern Pacific train made its way up the track, heading toward San Francisco. Ellen drew herself up, raising the covers, holding them up, a shield between him and the window. Cutting off the sounds, the bright cold sunlight. Protecting him with her body. She loved him; his indifference, his gradual drift away from her, seemed to make her own hunger greater.

And still he slept on. In sleep, his face was blank and pale; his hair, dribbled across his forehead, was strawlike. Even his lips were colorless. The stain of gray beard around his chin had faded and blurred into the puffy whiteness of his flesh. Relaxed, mindless, he slept on, not knowing about the clock, not hearing the milk truck outside, the stirring birds. Not knowing she was risen up beside him, was hovering over him.

In sleep, he was ageless. Very young, perhaps, not quite a man, not even an adolescent. And certainly not a child; perhaps a very old man, so old that he was no longer a man, a thing left over from some archaic world, primordial, but cold and chaste as ivory. Something carved from bone, a tusk, shaped from passionless calcium: without rancor or excitement or knowledge. An innocent thing too old to care, alive but not yet wanting. Perfectly content to lie, attainment of something beyond activity . . . She wished he could always be like this, utterly peaceful, not needing, not suffering, not driven by any knowing of things. But even as he slept, the corners of his pale mouth twisted up into a tight, childish frown. A sullen, uneasy distaste; and with it a growing terror.

Perhaps he was dreaming out his fight, his shadowy ordeal with the enemy. The mist-dripping battlefield where dim shapes struggled, he and vague antagonists. Grappling with opponents he barely understood. . . . She had seen it before. She knew the blind, dazed, head-downward fight he put up. Mindless brawling for goals too tenuous to comprehend, or put into words.

He twisted; his head turned on one side. A tiny ooze of saliva slithered down his chin, onto his throat. There it glistened, thick and moist, a body fluid escaping from him, leaking from his relaxed mouth. Perhaps he was sleeping again on the hard cot of the jail. Perhaps he was dreaming of unconsciousness. One scratched hand came futilely up, batted and struck at an invisible presence. He was still dreaming of the fight. And of defeat.

"Stuart," she said sharply.

Beside her, he grunted. His eyelids fluttered; all at once his quiet, guileless blue eyes gazed up at her, wondering, baffled, a little frightened, startled to find her there. Not knowing where he was—he never knew where he was—and not understanding what had happened to him.

"Hi," she said softly. Bending down, she gently touched her lips against his timid, anxious mouth. "Good morning."

Color entered his eyes; he smiled weakly. "You awake?" He dragged himself up. "What time is it?"

"Eight."

Hunched over, scowling, he sat rubbing his stubbled jaw. "Time to get up, I guess."

"Yes," she agreed. Far off, a car honked. A front door opened and a neighbor came striding down his concrete steps. The muffled sounds of people . . . cold breath shimmering in the morning air. "It looks like a nice day," she said presently.

"Day. Nuts to day." With bewilderment, he examined his damaged hand. "What do you want for breakfast?"

"Nothing." He shook his head irritably. The whole episode of the bar, the fight, the police . . . it was all indistinct, dreamlike. Already, it was slipping away from him. "I've got a hangover," he muttered. "Christ."

"I'll fix coffee," Ellen said gently.

"No, the doctor says you can't." Dully, he groped for the covers, trying to get to his feet. "God," he muttered as his feet reached the floor. For a moment he stood by the bed, eyeing it with weary longing. Aimlessly, he began to scratch at his naked furry chest. Then, turning, he laboriously tottered out of the bedroom, down the icy hall, into the bathroom. There, pushing the door half shut, he stood slouched over the toilet, urinating. Finally he grunted, flushed the toilet, and somberly padded back into the bedroom. At the door, he stood.

"I lost some money," he told her wanly.

"That's all right." She smiled up briefly at him. "Forget about it and go wash."

Obediently, he got his razor and blades from the dresser drawer, and disappeared into the bathroom. Hot water roared in the shower, and he climbed gratefully into it. After that he systematically brushed his teeth, shaved, combed his hair, and came wandering out to look for clean clothes.

"Thirty dollars," he told her.

"We can talk about it later."

Nodding, he belched. "I'm sorry. Can I take something from the household money?"

"I guess so," she said reluctantly.

From the dresser Hadley took a starched white shirt. The smell of it cheered him up. Next came clean shorts, and then his carefully pressed and hung-up blue slacks from the closet. A kind of eagerness filled him; the joy of fresh fabrics and clean smells took away the staleness of night. But behind him in the dark, moist bed, Ellen lay watching; he could feel her avid eyes on him. Brown hair spilling over her shoulders, the swollen globes of her breasts. Her vast bulging middle stuck up grotesquely: not many more weeks now. The baby—ultimate burden. He would never get away then, and it was already oppressively close.

"I don't think I'll go to work," he said gloomily.

"Why not?" Anxiously, she asked: "Don't you feel better? After you've had something to eat—"

"It's too nice a day. I'm going down and sit in the park." His body stirred restlessly. "Maybe I'll play football with the kids."

"They're still in school. And it isn't football season."

"Then I'll play baseball. Or pitch horseshoes." He turned to her. "You want to go out in the country this weekend? Let's get out of here; let's get out where we can roam around."

Ellen touched her middle. "I shouldn't, you know."

"That's right." The great fragile tub of flesh . . . center of the universe.

"Darling," Ellen said, "do you want to tell me about last night?"

He didn't; but the firmness of her voice meant the time had come. "There wasn't much," he answered. "What I said already."

"Did you get—hurt?"

"It wasn't a real fight. We were too drunk. . . . We just sort of swung and cussed at each other." Reflectively, he murmured: "I think I got one of the bastards, though. A big one. The cops think I'm a Communist. . . . As they hauled me in I was yelling, 'Come on, you fascist bastards, I'll take care of all of you.'"

"Were there just two?"

"Four cops, two fascist bastards."

"It happened in a bar?"

"Outside a bar. It started in a bar. Or at the public library. Maybe it was a couple of librarians."

"Stuart," she said, "why did it happen? What's wrong with you?"

He got into his powder blue coat and halted at the mirror to examine his face, his hair, his teeth, his swollen eyes. Scowling, he plucked at a pimple on his smooth-shaven chin.

"It's Sally, isn't it?" she said.

"Yes," he said.

"You're tense."

"You bet your goddamn life I'm tense." It was today he had to pick her up.

"Do—you want me to go with you?"

"I'll pick her up alone," he said, starting toward the door. The last thing he wanted was to have Ellen tagging along, getting in the way, making the situation even worse. "Maybe you can clean up the apartment."

"Aren't you having any breakfast?"

"I'll catch it downtown." From the teapot in the kitchen he got all the money there was, ten or fifteen dollars, and crammed it into his pocket. The living room, as he strode through it, was still messy and still smelled of overripe pears. He didn't really expect Ellen to clean it up; she would start, perhaps empty the ashtrays, and then, exhausted, return to bed. It would still be this way tonight, when he brought his sister home. He was resigned.

"Wish me luck," he said at the door to the hall.

She had got out of bed; now she was tying on her heavy blue dressing robe. "Will you be home first? Or will you go directly up?"

"Depends whether I get the truck," he said. "I'll call you." Without kissing her good-bye he waved, grinned, and stepped out into the hall. In a moment he was outside on the sidewalk, on his way downtown.

Unless it rained he walked to work. But today the jogging bounce of his shoes against the pavement made his head ache. By the time he had turned onto Mason Avenue his vision danced with nausea; he wondered if he was going to make it. The hell with breakfast; in his condition he couldn't keep down a glass of tomato juice.

At the Lucky Market the Italian greengrocer was putting out his long trays of grapefruits and oranges. The greengrocer waved at Hadley, and he waved mechanically back. Out of habit, he nodded to the clerk in the jewelry store and to the little dried-up old lady in Wetherby's Stationery.

In the doorway of the Golden State Café the petite black-haired waitress stood lounging in her trim uniform, red skirt and blouse, pert hat buried in her dark curls. "Hi," she called shyly.

The sight of her revived him briefly. "How are you?" he asked, pausing.

"It's a nice day," she said, smiling coquettishly; Hadley was handsome and well groomed, a good catch for a girl . . . especially for one who didn't know he was married and about to be presented with a son.

Lighting a cigarette, Hadley said: "When are you dropping in?" He indicated Modern TV Sales and Service, which lay just ahead. "Come in and I'll give you a free TV demonstration."

The girl laughed cunningly. "A free *what* demonstration?"

Grinning, Hadley continued on down the sidewalk and into the dark shadows of the store. Into the familiar interior of silence and darkness, the place where he had worked since college.

Stuart Wilson Hadley sat hunched over his food in the back of the Health Food Store, picking irritably at his plate of tossed green salad and creamed chipped beef on toast. The clock over the counter read twelve thirty. He had twenty minutes left on his lunch hour. He had been sitting there forty minutes and he hadn't eaten a thing.

The Health Food Store was full of chattering women. They annoyed him; everything annoyed him. His stomach was queasy and his head ached dully. He began aimlessly ripping his napkin up and wadding it into a ball. Ellen was probably still asleep in bed. Sometimes she stayed in bed until three or four in the afternoon. He wished he were with her; this ceaseless shrill laughter was too much to stand. He should have eaten at Jack's Steakhouse; he could have got a plate of red beans and pork and rice and hot coffee.

His stomach gurgled sickishly. There'd be the smell of grease and dripping French fries oozing from the walls at Jack's Steakhouse. Drops of shiny fat like perspiration squeezed from the plaster, ignited by the fry cook at his sizzling grill. Clouds of cigar smoke manufactured from the dirty jokes of businessmen who squashed themselves together in booths like juries of vegetables. Jack's Steakhouse was a grotto of jukebox noise, an outhouse of smoke and bathroom grunts, a steam bath of *Chronicle* sporting-greens and toothpicks and spilled ketchup. Stuart Hadley didn't belong in its gymnasium of sweat and oniony hamburger smoke; could a sensitive man eat dinner in a locker room, surrounded by dirty underwear and athlete's foot?

Eating at Jack's Steakhouse was squatting in junior high school, in the perspiration and fatigue of his earlier youth. The fat, successful men in Jack's Steakhouse had belly-shoved their way directly there from gray shorts and tennis shoes and shower taking, had brought along Bicycle athletic supporters that had become dark strings of rot. The torment of Jack's Steakhouse maintained Stuart Hadley at the moment of climbing the rope suspended from the ceiling of the Cedar Groves Junior High School gym, the moment in which he had hung in agony, jeered by upturned faces, clinging piteously still not up to the knot—mark of accomplishment—and then falling exhausted, drained, to the polished floor. Stuart Hadley, swinging from the ceiling, a fly above mouths of many spiders . . . and after him the skinny little Jew boy Ira Silberman had swarmed up, Asiatic, competent, grinning. Jack, of Jack's Steakhouse, was Greek. Grinning over the cash register he palmed change with competent fingers; hand over hand it was taken in, the eternal ritual.

He wondered where the people hurrying past him were going. So fast . . .

no doubt it was somewhere important. Somewhere momentous, to do something vital. It was incredible that so many people could be abroad, all with significant errands, all gripped by purposeful goals. Involved in complex schemes and projects . . . cosmic doings.

Reluctantly, he turned and crossed the street. His steps dragged; he didn't want to return to the miserable little store. Anything to delay it. He could hide for a moment down in the crapper . . . but then—upstairs. Upstairs to the dull-faced customers.

In the window of the Health Food Store was a big glossy photograph of Theodore Beckheim, set in the middle of the date and nut display. He stopped before it for the hundredth time; it had been there since May. Beckheim was coming up the coast from Los Angeles, where he and his people made their headquarters.

The man's heavy dark face glared back at Hadley; vaguely, he felt uncomfortable. The man was incredibly commanding, powerful. His great black eyes and massive-ridged brow made him look like some primordial giant, a legend from the distant past. Under the photograph of Theodore Beckheim were the words:

> Will speak at the Watchmen Hall at
> 8 o'clock June 6, 7, 8. Admission free.
> Donations gratefully received.
> "Purity—the Bible Tells the
> World Order of Tomorrow." Lecture
> followed by discussion.
> Everybody invited!
>
> Society of the Watchmen of Jesus

Hadley gazed vacantly at the words and then back at the impressive face. The picture had been there so long he knew every line and circle of it. It was as if Beckheim were really someone he knew and not a remote public individual, a leader of a religious sect. There was its name on the poster: the Society of the Watchmen of Jesus. A worldwide society . . . pamphlets, a weekly newspaper sold on street corners. Followers in South America, Africa, in Iceland and Iran. Power of the Bible . . . healing by the Word.

The image of Theodore Beckheim seemed more and more familiar the longer he examined it. For a while it reminded him of Franklin Delano Roosevelt; then it was like his father, as he dimly remembered him, big and deep-voiced, strong. And somewhere in the heavy black brow was the stern gaze of a high school physics teacher, a man who had strode down the hall with firm step and steady gait, in a long white robe that billowed behind him like Saint Paul's. The image gave Hadley the same nervous, uneasy feeling as the Army recruiting posters. One part of his mind told him they had made it that way on purpose and the whole thing was high-pressure salesmanship. And another part quavered and glowed, and down inside his chest his heart turned soft like mushy bacon fat melting in the pan.

It was strange that a man he'd never seen or heard could make him feel that way. But it had happened before. At least, parts of his feeling had come before. That was the strange thing—his feeling was all the previous feelings rolled into one, as if all the men who had attracted him were present now. And for another thing, he was convinced that Beckheim was a Negro. He had never liked Negroes. . . . It didn't make sense. And he was convinced that most of Beckheim's followers were metallic, chattering old women, like the ones who munched salad and tapioca pudding at the counter inside the Health Food Store. He hated women like that.

The clock read four. Right now the Health Food Store was almost empty. The women had all skittered back to their offices and homes. Betty was heavily clearing the dirty counter of dishes and cigarette ashes and half-empty coffee cups crammed with wadded paper napkins. At one of the tables a drab little man in a striped suit, steel-rimmed glasses perched on his nose, a wisp of a mustache above his thin mouth, was quietly spooning up tapioca pudding and reading an article in a magazine.

Hadley entered the Health Food Store and sat down at one of the counter stools, hands clasped before him on the moist oilcloth surface of the counter.

"What is it, Stuart?" Betty asked wearily, with the faint trace of a smile.

"Give me a bottle of fizz water and one of those little jars of celery extract. So I can make a celery phosphate."

At his table the man in the pin-striped suit pushed aside his magazine. "Stuart!" he called in a thin friendly voice. "By golly, how's the boy?"

"Hi, Wakefield," Hadley answered noncommittally.

"Come on over and join me." Wakefield waved his spoon invitingly and grinned a gold-toothed jovial grin. Hadley got to his feet dully and moved listlessly over to the table. "I'm reading an interesting article on vaccination," the little dried-up prune of a man asserted proudly. "By Bernard Shaw, the great English playwright. You might be interested."

"I have to get back to the shop," Hadley said vaguely. "How are things in the flower business?"

"Can't complain." Wakefield nodded, solemn and dignified when his flower shop was mentioned. "Drop in sometime and I'll fix you up with a nice bright purple carnation for your buttonhole." He scanned Hadley's suit critically. "Hmm, with that suit maybe a white gardenia would be better. The purple would clash. Something white, I think . . . yes, a gardenia." He leaned close to Hadley and grated in his ear: "It's like pumping arsenic in a child's bloodstream. Billions of corpses of dead germs. Ground up and pumped into the child. *Diabolical!* Read this article." He pushed the magazine insistently against Hadley's wrist. "They spread disease all over the world. The only real way to health, as any sane person knows, is through proper eating. Remember, *what you put in your stomach comes out of your soul.* Isn't that right?" He raised his voice. "Isn't that right, Betty?"

"Yes, Horace," Betty answered wearily as she lugged the two bottles to the counter and sank down on her stool. "That will be a dollar forty, Stuart."

Wakefield caught Hadley's wrist with his thin, cold fingers. "You know what causes cancer? Eating meat. Pork and beef fat, especially pork. Lamb fat is the most difficult substance known to digest. It lodges in the lower gastrointestinal tract and putrefies. Sometimes a lump of lamb fat lodges for weeks, rotting and stinking." His lips drew back from his gold teeth in a grimace of disgust; behind his steel-rimmed glasses his enlarged eyes danced excitedly. "A man turns himself into a garbage dump. Stinking mounds of filth and rubbish, flies and worms buzzing around. There's those trichinosis worms in pork. They burrow into your muscles, all through your body. Big soft white worms burrowing, burrowing . . ." He shuddered and returned to his tapioca pudding. "Remember, Stuart," he said quietly as he intently spooned up the last of the pudding. "What you put in your stomach comes out of your soul."

Hadley paid for the two bottles and started out of the Health Food Store into the blazing sun. In the back of his mind was a vague idea he had mulled over the last few weeks; he hugged the bottles carefully as he made his way down the sidewalk. He plunged into the cool gloom of the TV shop, his eyes on his feet.

Fergesson was surrounded by customers at the front counter. Olsen, the huge bent-over serviceman, had come up from the basement to help him. He was resentfully finding a needle for a dumpy colored woman and at the same time answering the phone. Fergesson shot Hadley a look of wild fury, but Hadley was intent on his two bottles. He carried them carefully through the store and up the narrow back stairs to the office.

Sitting at the desk making out his pickup tags was young Joe Tampini, the handsome black-haired Italian boy who managed the deliveries. Tampini smiled up shyly as Hadley seated himself by the typewriter table and painstakingly laid down his bottles.

"What you got there, Mister Hadley?" Tampini asked, curious and polite, a sensitive youth lingering hopefully on the periphery of the store's social life.

Hadley began searching in the debris-littered desk. He found a stained tumbler and finally a bottle opener. "Something to drink," he muttered. "What's it look like?"

"Do I get some?" Tampini smiled wistfully, but Hadley promptly turned his back and ignored him.

"You wouldn't like it," Hadley said. Surrounded by filing cabinets, piles of invoices and bills, dusty photos of nude girls, pens and pencils, the old Royal typewriter, Hadley cautiously opened the two bottles and began fixing the celery phosphate.

"Drink it," Hadley urged Fergesson good-naturedly.

"What in the name of God is it?" Fergesson demanded.

"A celery phosphate. It's good for you . . . . Try it. It's got an unusual taste but once you get used to it it's really fine."

Fergesson snorted with disgust. The store was finally empty; rows of TV sets bellowed to themselves below the office. Olsen had escaped back down to his service department. Tampini was out in the truck for the final deliveries of the day. "Where the hell were you?" Fergesson demanded. "You took an hour and a half for your damn lunch—I ought to dock you."

Indignation rose up in Hadley. He angrily withdrew the tempting glass of celery phosphate. "That's not so—I got stopped by a streetlight, that's all. Maybe a couple of minutes." The whole thing had become indistinct to him; he couldn't see any use in talking about it. Hadn't he just bought over a dollar's worth of celery extract for Fergesson? "Sure," he said hotly. "Take it out of my pay."

"What's the use," Fergesson muttered to himself. "I'm going out on a prospect. I'll be back in half an hour. . . . It's probably stone dead by now." He disappeared down the steps to the main floor, and then rapidly out the front door.

Hadley sighed and lit a cigarette. He knew he should go downstairs; there were three new Philco TV combinations to be adjusted and set up. The job was his; he had the patience and dexterity to sit tinkering endlessly, day after day. But instead of going down he remained at the office desk, the cigarette between his fingers, idly touching the side of the celery phosphate glass. He absently sipped a little of it, but the fizz had already begun to go, and what remained was stale and vegetable and not exciting.

An old woman dragged her way into the store and stood puffing and sagging before the front counter, her vast lumpy shopping bag resting on the floor. Hadley gazed down at her mildly as she panted and muttered and darted quick suspicious glances around the deserted store, impatient for the salesman to make his appearance.

A dull, numbing tiredness crept through Hadley's bones. Lazily, the miasma drifted up like gray cigarette smoke, into all parts of his body. First his feet, then his legs and hips, his shoulders, finally his arms and hands drifted off to sleep. His chin wobbled and sank as he continued to gaze blankly at the old woman. She reminded him of his grandmother whom he had visited in Baltimore. Only, her face was too hard and mean. Her eyes darted restlessly. And she was smaller and older. He wondered what this old woman wanted. Maybe there was a broken Atwater Kent radio in the dumpy shopping bag. Maybe there was a paper sack of dusty old radio tubes to be checked, each one wrapped in newspaper. Maybe she had a radio downstairs in the service department, an immense floor model combination it would take three men and a donkey to haul up. Maybe she wanted a package of Kacti needles for her windup phonograph.

He yawned, and the sound attracted the woman's attention. Guiltily, Hadley moved into motion. He stubbed out his cigarette and clumped stiffly down the stairs to the main floor. His legs wobbled under him; he could hardly push behind the counter. The old woman, the store, the booming TV sets, were lost in a drifting haze of sleepiness. He had got up too suddenly this morning. He should have got up slowly, breathed deeply with each motion. Opened the window and done a few of his special chest exercises. Maybe taken an ice-cold shower. At least had a methodical breakfast. The whole day had started off wrong. . . . Now that it was ending, his last energy was dwindling away.

"Can I help you?" he asked the old woman.

Two tired, crafty eyes, ancient and faded, gleamed up at him. "You work here?" the old woman demanded.

"Yes," Hadley said.

"That's funny," the old woman said. There was bright suspicion on her seamed face. "I've never seen you before." Firm conviction entered her voice and hardened there. "You're not the man who waits on me when I come in."

Hadley could find no words of protest.

"No," the old woman said, with a half-plaintive, half-weary shake of her head. "You're not the man who waits on me. The man who waits on me is much older. You're just a boy."

"I've worked here for years," Hadley said, stunned.

"The man who waits on me is darker and shorter. He has a good face. He is a kind, helpful man. He understands my radio. He's waited on me for thirteen years. Ever since I came to California and took my room at the National Hotel."

"I have a wife," Hadley said helplessly. "I'm not a boy."

"This man owns this store. He fixed my radio when nobody else would even look at it. He has a way with radios. There's a wise kindness in his face. There's no kindness in your face. Your face is empty and cruel. It's a bad face. It's pretty and blond, but it's a bad face."

"You want Mr. Fergesson," Hadley managed. "He's not here. He's out somewhere."

"Mr. Fergesson is the man who waits on me," the old woman said emphatically. "You say he's out somewhere? Well, don't you know where? When will he be back? I have my radio here in my bag. I want him to look at it. He can tell me what's wrong. Nobody else can."

"He'll be back in half an hour," Hadley mumbled. "Maybe you want to wait for him. Or maybe you want to leave the radio."

"No," the old woman said with finality. "I can't leave my radio."

"You can wait, then."

"Do you think I could wait half an hour? An old person like me can't stand on her feet that long."

"I'll find you a chair," Hadley suggested.

"No," the old woman said. She moved toward the door, her heavy shopping bag dragging after her. "I'll come back some other time." She searched Hadley's face with her tired, disappointed eyes. "Are you sure you work here, young man? I've never seen you before. Are you sure you're not just waiting?"

"I belong here," Hadley said thickly. "I'm not just waiting."

"You're waiting here for the man to come back. The man who owns the store. No, you don't belong here. I can tell. I don't know where you belong, but it isn't here."

She wandered heavily away.

Hadley stalked numbly over and snapped off the row of blaring TV sets. They sank into sudden silence, and at once the dim emptiness of the store rose up around him and suffocated him. He turned one set back on and then convulsively made his way out of the store, onto the front sidewalk.

The old woman was crossing the street with a knot of drab shoppers. He watched her go until she was lost from sight. What did the old woman mean? Who was she? Inside the dim store the TV muttered to itself; its single eye flickered fitfully in the murky shadows. Shapes came and went, diffuse figures of men and things that hovered temporarily and then passed on.

Hadley turned his back to the store and the television set. He persuaded his ears to fill up with the honk of car horns, the staccato stamp of human feet on the hot late-afternoon sidewalk; he managed to exclude the dead sounds exhausted of color and life, the sullen cry and fuming from inside the store. Standing against the plate-glass window, his hands forced deep in his trouser pockets, he fervently inhaled the warmth of sun and people, the flow of bright activity.

But still the old woman's words whined in his head.

She was right; he didn't belong in the store. He wasn't really a television salesman. Longingly, he watched the people pass. He should be out there with them, a part of them. Hurrying by, not cut off and isolated in the stagnant backwater of a little dried-up store.

Along the sidewalk came a well-dressed young man. He was somewhat plump, but immaculately groomed. A soft-bodied man in an expensive English suit, shoes obviously hand-fashioned. His hair was thin, black, faintly shiny. A rich aliveness glowed in his brown eyes as he glanced briefly at Hadley. His nails, his cuffs, his bearing, everything about him, spoke his breeding, a Continental background.

Avidly, Hadley watched him pass. This might have been Hadley. Under other circumstances, it would be he, Stuart Hadley, carrying a gray topcoat over his arm, tall and dark and dignified. A faint aroma of men's cologne hung about him. Hadley could imagine his apartment: modern prints on the walls, cushions on the floor, Chinese mats, Bartók playing in the background on a custom-built phonograph, French novels in French paperback editions. Gide, Proust, Celine . . .

He watched the man turn into a parking lot and approach a tiny European sports car. The man climbed in, started up the motor, and zoomed from the lot, out onto the street. In a moment the car and its driver were gone, lost behind a bulging GM truck. Hadley turned away. Alas, he didn't even know what kind of car it was. Slowly, unhappily, he left the sidewalk and reentered the store.

For a time he stood in black gloom as his eyes adjusted. The chill of the old woman, the gray smell of age and death, had finally begun to drift away. Hadley picked up the heavy-duty staple gun from the counter and fired staples here and there. The gun had always comforted him; he loved to operate it. Fiercely, staples clicked against the walls, the display racks, onto the floor, behind the television sets; gripping the gun like a serious weapon, Hadley advanced on the muttering, flickering TV set in the center of the row and fired point-blank in its face. The staple bounced back gratifyingly and he wandered away. As often before, he now fired staples at random, but no more satisfaction remained: he had exhausted the gun's possibilities. He tossed it back on the counter and stationed himself in the doorway, gazing moodily out at the passing people and plucking at his coat pocket for his cigarettes.

The old woman was right. He had to leave the store.

He thought about the dog, the puppy he had plucked from the box in Pop Michelson's garage. Death, dropped in a rain barrel, discarded like debris. Useless waste, old papers and tin cans. Rescued by accident . . . passed from hand to hand. And that was *his* life; that was how he lived. Wandering aimlessly, drifting, passed here and there at random. Without purpose. Saved by accident, condemned by other accidents. In a meaningless world.

Across the street glowed a neat attractive neon sign. The Peninsula Travel Agency. Huge letters described a trip to Mexico; a brightly colored poster showed a brown-skinned woman with white teeth and black hair and magnificent half-bare loins. *Welcome to Mexico. Land of warmth and sunshine. Song and laughter. Come to sunny Mexico.* One hundred forty dollars.

He got out his wallet and examined the bills wadded and stuffed inside it. Ten dollars, the remains of his wife's household money. He shook out eighty-four cents in change from his coat pocket, along with match folders, paper clips, slips of dirty paper with customers' names, pencil stubs, and the remains of a paper napkin.

That was all he had in the world. That was the bones, teeth, and dust of Stuart Hadley. That was what would lie in a little pile in his coffin through all the ages. A pocketful of trash and ten dollars and eighty-four cents. He threw the match folders in the waste-box under the counter and stuffed the money away. This was the manifestation of the inexpressible entity *Stuart Hadley* . . . this, and a swollen sleep-drugged wife lying in a messy bed; a drawer of unpaid bills; eight or ten expensive suits; endless shirts and socks and handkerchiefs and hand-painted neckties.

He examined the calendar pasted on the cash register. Ten days before the next paycheck came; and in the middle of the month there were no sales commissions. It was June 6, the fly-soaked middle of summer. An expiring procession of empty afternoons lay stretched out ahead of him, and nothing else. He couldn't go to Mexico on ten dollars; he was stuck fast, glued tight.

But on June 6 Theodore Beckheim arrived from Los Angeles and spoke. Nervous hunger twitched through Hadley. That was something, perhaps. Anything to break the monotony. Any hope, any straw.

He would go listen to Beckheim. Stuart Wilson Hadley would be there.

———————

Dave Gold, the living embodiment of Hadley's ties with the past, lay stretched out on the couch in the Hadley living room, sleeves of his white shirt rolled up, hairy thin arms stuck out, legs crossed, pipe between his fingers. Stuart Hadley sat across from him in the big easy chair by the TV set. In the kitchen Ellen and Laura Gold shrieked and chattered about the dinner that was slowly baking itself to death in and around the stove.

In the years since college, Dave Gold's body had become paler, thinner, and more furry. He had changed his gold-rimmed glasses to horn-rimmed glasses. His trousers were still too big, too unpressed, too dirty. His shoes needed resoling. His teeth were dirty. He needed a shave. He wore no tie; his furry, sunken chest was visible above his sweat-crumpled yesterday's shirt. He earned his living writing articles and editorials for labor and left-wing publications; he had a national reputation of one sort or another.

Across from him the owner of the apartment listened dully to what Gold was saying. Stuart Hadley, clean shaven, delicately perfumed, well dressed, handsome in a boyish, vacant-eyed Nordic way, could not refrain from noticing what a bum his friend Dave Gold looked like. The contrast between them was considerable. It needled Hadley that somebody who wore no tie, who didn't use Arrid, could have a national reputation of any kind. It was absolutely without sense.

"You're looking at me funny," Dave observed. "What's the matter?"

"I was just thinking. Some things haven't changed. You're still the way you were, only more so."

"I wish you were," Dave answered. "I never thought you'd wind up this way, working in a TV store."

In high school he and Dave Gold had been in the chess club together. Dave had inveigled him into going to a meeting of the Young People's Socialist League, whereat Hadley gave up twenty-five cents for the success of the revolution, a concept he had previously been ignorant of. In college, Dave had maneuvered himself onto the staff of the university literary magazine and the monthly humor magazine and the weekly newspaper.

In 1948 Dave Gold persuaded Stuart Hadley into joining the Independent Progressive Party, and into going to listen to Henry Wallace and Glen Taylor, candidates of the party. Ellen Ainsworth typed mimeograph stencils for Students for Wallace. When Wallace ingloriously lost, Stuart Hadley left the IPP. Dave Gold, on the other hand, joined the Civil Rights Congress and began taking Russian at the California Labor School in San Francisco.

In the kitchen, Laura Gold's loud raucous laughter brayed out over the sounds of boiling water. The apartment was warm, cozy with food smells, bright with yellow light, close with the presence of people and untarnished possessions. There was less contrast between the two women. Ellen, tubby and awkward, waddled about the kitchen, her soft brown hair tied back with a rubber band, her blue maternity suit bulging in front of her. The obesity of her abdomen made her legs seem spindly and pale; she wore white bobby socks and laceless moccasins, no makeup or nail polish. Her skin was lightly freckled, soft, almost milky; her lips and eyes were colorless. Laura Gold was a permanently heavyset woman with coarse black hair, thick ankles, grubby hands, and protruding teeth. She wore a gray sweater, rumpled black shirt, and hiking shoes. Her nose was warty and bent.

As Stuart Hadley gazed moodily at her he wondered to himself how he could have got mixed up with Jews. Of course, Dave was different from most of them: he wasn't a pusher. But still, he had a lot of Jewish habits: he had their uncleanness. . . . He chewed his food with his mouth open, left greasy bits of food around his plate, stains on books. . . .

Hadley tried to trace back the connections; how had he begun going around with Dave Gold? He remembered the high school physics teacher with his flowing white cape; he had managed the chess club and discussed Darwin and Einstein with them in the long afternoons when school was out. And, of course, in those days both he and Dave were Democrats; both of them wore Roosevelt-Truman buttons and fought bitterly with Republican youths from the wealthy houses up on the hill.

Both of them had been united in the Democratic Party in those days. Dave Gold, whose father was a wood finisher at a furniture factory, a workman with a lunch pail and overalls; Stuart Hadley, whose father had been a wealthy upper-middle-class doctor in New York before his death in an auto accident. Stuart, in high school, wore a white shirt and jeans; so had Dave. They wore common dress against the rich boys from the hill, who dressed in expensive slacks and sweaters and drove polished cars, who belonged to fraternities and held dances. Later, the common dress and common party had broken down. What had seemed to be a deep sameness between them had dissolved into overt difference. Looking back, he could see that the Young People's Socialist League had been for him only an academic lecture, a presentation of ideas, like physics and chess. Dave Gold's father had been a Wobbly, had been beaten up and jailed. Had served on picket lines, distributed Marxist leaflets. Stuart Hadley's father had been a respectable doctor with a practice and office and reputation, a dignified professional-class man who had driven his wife and children about in a LaSalle, and belonged to the AMA.

"Have you listened to a word?" Dave asked. "A word, maybe, out of all I'm saying?"

"No," Hadley admitted. "Sorry . . . I'm all beat out from working. Friday's the worst day of the week, this damn working late."

"It's over. You can relax."

"I'm too tired to relax. And there's tomorrow—Saturday!"

"I can't understand how they can work you six days a week," Dave Gold said, puffing on his pipe. "Can't you get yourself into the AF of L retail clerks' union? Has anybody ever tried to unionize your store?"

"Fergesson would close down first."

"This Fergesson must be quite a fellow. Is he the one I see, middle-aged man in an old-type blue suit, with a vest and pocket watch? My God, he's out of another century. Virtually a living fossil."

"That's him."

"He doesn't believe in unions? Little businessmen identify themselves with big business; he probably has ambitions to get a chain of stores."

"That's right."

"You think he ever will?"

"He may. He's been saving up. Some kind of deal." Brooding, Hadley dismissed the subject. "You should have been along with me earlier."

"What did you do?"

"We delivered an RCA combination to a minister up on the hill. Huge house. Immense garden. Like a monastery . . . probably brought over from Europe. His wife, one of those tall English ash-blondes. Both of them looked like kings."

"King and queen," Dave corrected.

Hadley gazed darkly down at the floor and went on: "We set up the combination, got the yagi set up on the roof. When we were through, Anderton— the minister—offered us a drink. Whiskey, beer, whatever we wanted."

"Fine," Dave said approvingly.

Hadley stirred with wrath. "A minister! Offering people liquor—you call that fine?" He got up suddenly and crossed the room to pull down the shades. Thinking about it brought back all his feelings with a rush, his amazement and resentment, the sudden disgust he had felt at the great house with its massive gardens and furnishings. "I don't think ministers ought to have liquor around," he said.

"Did you take the drink?"

"Just to be polite. I wanted to get out of there. If ministers serve whiskey who's going to keep people from doing wrong? He didn't even wear a special collar, just a regular business suit. And all that luxury—I thought a minister was supposed to live in a little barren room. And he shouldn't marry."

"You're thinking about medieval monks."

Hadley paced restlessly around the small illuminated living room. "I don't see that there's any spirituality when a minister has a big wealthy house and garden and a wife and liquor like every other successful businessman. That's all it is . . . another business."

"True," Gold admitted.

"There's nothing left of religion! You go to a church and the minister reads out of a best-selling novel. He's nothing but a psychologist. They go out and tell soldiers it's fine with Christ to kill the enemy—that's what God wants."

Gold reflected. "Back when we were in school you hoped all the Japs and Germans would be wiped off the map. It's interesting; now you're not responsive to prowar slogans."

"They hurried the Korean War along too fast," Hadley said.

Gold grinned. "Yes, they should have waited a little longer. They should give time for the depression to come in between, so people are glad to go off and fight. This time they got their stage directions fouled up."

Ellen and Laura came lumbering into the room. "What's this about stage directions?" Laura demanded. The two women lowered themselves into chairs; in the kitchen the dinner continued patiently drying by itself.

"The war," Dave Gold said.

"I wish you wouldn't talk about the war," Ellen said, shivering. "Everybody's always talking about it; every time I turn on the radio or the TV or pick up a magazine or go past the headlines, there it is." To Laura she said: "If the baby wasn't on his way, they'd have taken Stuart. Of course, his liver trouble helps . . . but you never know."

"See," Laura said, in her brash, loud, stupid way, "they're going to need kids growing up for the next war. They're planning ahead." She bellowed with laughter, leaned back, and fumbled in her greasy sweater for cigarettes.

Stuart glared at her with annoyance. His own wife sat placid and undisturbed, as if the source, not the contents of material, was the element to which she objected. It was all right for Laura to babble about war and death because that was woman's talk, done between women, in the kitchen or nearby. When men said it, the sanctity of the home was invaded. The menace of outside war was brought close. Stuart Hadley was not permitted to touch on dire topics, but another woman could rave out her stock of superstitions, her old wives' fears and querulous aches. Laura Gold, Progressive witch of the present, could stand beside Ellen flooding her ears with the raucous garbage of her trade, and meet not outrage but blandness, passivity. Another woman—any other woman—was in many ways closer to Ellen than he was. Even this crude imitation of femininity was on the inside, party to secret revelations and references. There were regions he couldn't claim, areas he couldn't enter, even in his own home. Another dimension existed to women; he had never penetrated it. No man could. Women were the metaphysics of the world.

"How can we not talk about it?" Hadley demanded. "It's all around us!"

"That's why I don't want to hear about it," Ellen said simply. She smiled dreamily around the room, contented with this shoddy collection of guests; her hostess instincts were satisfied by dinner prepared for one unpleasant young couple. "Stuart, get some music on the radio, not that news commentator talking away."

Marriage, pregnancy, had softened and mellowed her. The sharp cautiousness of the old days, when the possibility of having to learn typing and shorthand and earn her own living existed, had rapidly blunted. Deprived of the impetus of economic competition, Ellen had sunk to a fecund vegetable level: she was a generative principle, not a person. She was rooted, planted. A ripe moist melon within panes of glass. As sweetened and fattened as any kept prostitute, made complacent by her blanket of respectability.

And Hadley knew that Dave Gold saw with understanding this transformation from sharp-eyed practical little bride to massive vegetable; Dave's calm alert gaze blinked out critically from behind the thick lenses of his glasses. Puffing on his pipe, Dave nodded, not in agreement, but in comprehension. "There's hysteria in the air," he said. "Cold wind of witches . . . the fear of death. Cunning men prey on this, feed on this. McCarthy, a clever man."

"Don't mention that rat!" Laura protested, making a disgusted, furious spitting motion. "That fascist!"

The women were united in bonds of not wanting to hear things distasteful. A common bond that connected them, the mystical psychology of the separate female race. Hadley, speaking to Dave Gold, harshly continued the conversation where it had been interrupted. "Sure, I approved of fighting the Nazis and Japs. I was glad as hell when we got in the war. Roosevelt said the Axis was the enemy of mankind and I wanted to wipe them off the map. I was so excited December seventh I couldn't eat dinner."

"That was a Sunday," Ellen said nostalgically, deflecting the conversation again. "I remember, my aunt and uncle were over for the afternoon. Relatives, all so stiff and formal. I was just dying to go off to the show. . . . There was some Maria Montez picture showing."

Looking across the room at Dave, Hadley went on: "Roosevelt told us they had to be totally defeated—not a stick or a stone left standing. Now I look back and I can't understand how I could have felt that way. There was a movie, a newsreel. A Jap running out of a bunker on Okinawa. Some GI got him with a flamethrower. There he was running along and burning up." Hadley's voice trembled. "Incinerating, a blazing torch. Everybody in the theater clapped and laughed. I laughed, too." A cold, hard expression settled over his face. "I must have been crazy."

Ellen shrugged irritably. "In wartime—"

"Yes," Hadley said. "In wartime. The time you believe anything. I believed anything and everything they told me. Why not? I was only a kid. How was I supposed to know we were being snowed? I trusted them . . . It never occurred to me to doubt. When they said the Japs were submen, beasts, I believed that; yes, you could see it just by looking at them. Look at their little bandy legs. Look at their buck teeth. Look at their nearsighted eyes . . . half-blind little savages. Treacherous?"

"Yes," Dave corroborated. "They were treacherous."

"What else?"

"They grinned," Dave said. "As they raped women and bayoneted babies they grinned."

"That was it." Hadley nodded. "When I heard how Tokyo was bombed until it was nothing but flames I was so glad I almost leaped out of my skin. It was like the home team winning the big game . . . cheering crowds, bands, pennants waving. Then I saw that newsreel, that man on fire. That thin silent little fellow hurrying along, trying not to burn up. Springing out of the hole, that cave he had got himself into. Popping out, goaded out like an insect or something. Like a beetle some kid sits and pokes at, hour after hour. And those people cheered." His voice sank into bitterness. "Up to then I cheered, too. But not after that."

"Now it's the Russians," Dave said. "Only they don't grin. And they're great hulking fellows, not small and bandy-legged."

"No," Hadley said, "I won't do it. Once is enough. I'm not going through with it again. I'm not going to hate any more godless atheistic Oriental materialists. They can come and take over America. If there's another war I'm going to sit here and wait for the bomb. We invented it . . . We used it on those Japanese women and tired old men and sick soldiers. We used it on them, and someday they'll use it on us." He grinned a little. "I guess I'm a godless atheist, too."

"But look at the lives we saved," Ellen said, frowning at him. "So many of our boys would have been slaughtered . . . The bomb ended the war."

Hadley's smile increased. "Death ends everything, not just wars. Where are we going to stop? After the godless atheists come the just plain starving."

"It's not our fault," Ellen said vaguely. "And look what happens when we try to help them—they hate us. They're envious."

"They're envious," Hadley said, "because they know our wealth doesn't belong to us. They know it's stolen. They know where it came from; they know part of it should be theirs. We're rotten with wealth and opulence. We deserve to get slaughtered. Can't you feel it? Don't you know it? Our sin, our guilt. We deserve the punishment that's coming."

"Don't talk that way," Ellen said peevishly; her husband was interfering with the easy social air on which she had planned. But it was more than that. She recognized the look on his face, the hard emotionless glaze that rose to the surface when the man's deepest wellsprings of discouragement had been touched. The look made her nervous, taut with apprehension. "Sit down and behave yourself," she snapped.

Hadley ignored her; he continued pacing around the room. "This country is evil. We're big and rich and full of pride. We waste and we spend and we don't care about the rest of the world." To Laura he said, "A minister I met today poured me a highball. He had a big luxurious home and a lovely wife and an eight-hundred-dollar television combination and a refrigerator full of liquor."

"What's the matter with that?" Ellen flared up furiously. "We keep liquor around the apartment; you're always sitting down in some cheap bar drinking beer, like the night before last when you were out until two a.m. and I could hardly get you up to go to work." Face flushed, she hurried on: "You have a lot of nerve talking. Wouldn't you just *love* a big beautiful house . . . If we could afford that eight-hundred-dollar TV set we'd sure as heck get it—and whose fault is it we can't afford it? Don't begrudge others their success. You're jealous, that's what's wrong with you. You're envious of this man." Panting, "What'd she look like?"

Hadley blinked. "Who?"

"His *wife*."

Hadley's memory turned back to the scene. As he and Olsen crouched grunting and sweating, adjusting the television set, Mrs. Anderton had appeared at the foot of the stairs. One hand resting on the banister, she gazed coolly at them, a tall slim figure in a floor-length robe, dark blond hair spilled around her shoulders, face calm, noble. "She was beautiful," Hadley said sincerely. "A princess."

Ellen's face worked. Before she could answer, Laura Gold began giggling stupidly. "Stuart, you're so bourgeois you stink! You're bourgeois through and through."

Hadley glared at her. "I have taste; is there something wrong with having taste and wanting to live nicely?"

"I thought you objected to this man's possessions," Dave Gold said, puzzled and disturbed. "I don't get you, Stuart. You talked as if you wanted these things wiped out . . . but now you say—"

"I don't think he should live that way," Hadley said stubbornly. "It's not right."

Ellen rose, frigid with hostility. "I think I smell the roast. Stuart, go wash for dinner." She disappeared into the kitchen, vast and swaying. Laura followed after her; low voices and then shrill laughter floated out to the living room.

Hadley and Dave Gold faced each other across the room.

"What do you know about the Society of the Watchmen of Jesus?" Hadley asked.

Gold puffed on his pipe. "Not much."

"They're having a meeting tonight."

Gold nodded. "That's so. Stuart, it's none of my business, but you ought to quit your job. You're eating your heart out, working at that run-down little TV shop. You shouldn't be working for that man. What do you care about television? Get the hell out of there."

Hadley spread his hands helplessly. "How? Christ, this is no time to quit, with the baby coming."

"Don't you have anything saved?"

"A couple hundred for hospital expenses." It wasn't really that much; he didn't know exactly what it was down to by now.

"Can't you get anything from your mother?"

"I hate like hell to write back east. I want to make this alone. I—don't write to her unless I really need the money."

Dave brooded. "What about your sister?" He searched his memory. "What became of Sally? I haven't seen her since high school."

"She's married. Living up in Berkeley. I'm sure as hell not going to write *them* for money." Hadley was getting angry; he was more disturbed each moment. "You never knew Sally—you never met her in your life."

"She was always around," Dave said mildly. "Christ, I knew your sister and mother; I've known you since we were in the eleventh grade."

"All right," Hadley muttered, wanting to leave the subject. He loathed the thought of dirty, sloppy Dave Gold knowing his sister, even being in the same world as his sister. "I can borrow on my life insurance if I have to." He had already borrowed on it, of course; now he wondered if it had really been hit for all it was worth. "I could even borrow from Fergesson. . . . He lent me a hundred bucks when we got married."

"Crumbs," Dave said, disgusted. "He probably got it back from your salary."

"How else would he get it back?"

Dave knocked his pipe against an ashtray and fished in his sloppy trouser pockets for his tobacco pouch. "I wish to hell we could unionize you petit bourgeois white-collar workers. There must be millions of you. You don't show up. . . . You're a vast undifferentiated mass. I see you driving your damn cars along the highway on Sunday, going out in the country for picnics. I see you lined up at movie theaters, taking the kids to the show. I see your wives in supermarkets pushing baskets. But goddamn it, you never come to union meetings."

Ellen appeared briefly at the kitchen door. "Dinner's ready. Stuart, get the chairs and set up the card table. You know where the tablecloth is, and the silver."

Hadley roused himself. "Sure," he said listlessly. He went to get the chest of silver his parents had given them as a wedding present; used perhaps six times in the long interval of their life together, the marriage of Stuart Hadley and Ellen Ainsworth.

He was laboriously carrying dirty dishes from the table to the kitchen when Ellen barred his way. "I hope you're proud of yourself," she told him bitterly. "Sitting there not eating, scowling like a little boy."

In the living room Dave and Laura were arguing some point. Hadley heard the note of aggravation in their voices; was it true that he had destroyed the evening? It wasn't often that any of his old high school friends came over; he liked to see Dave, in spite of everything, in spite of Laura. "Sorry," he muttered. "I don't feel so hot."

"You never feel so hot," Ellen rasped accusingly; she moved aside so he could put down the plates on the drainboard of the sink. "If you don't stop acting this way—" A clatter of dishes cut off her words, as Hadley got plates from the cupboard for apple pie and ice cream. "You just *have* to stop acting this way! Can't you see how unfair it is to everybody?"

Hadley boiled. "It's unfair to me; what am I supposed to do, turn my feelings on and off the way you work that stove? All right—" He gouged slimy-hot pie from its store pan and laid the dripping sections on saucers. "I'll laugh and tell funny stories; is that what you want?"

Ellen gave him a mixed look, compounded of misery and outrage, then wheeled and lumbered to the refrigerator for the ice cream. She slammed the refrigerator door and smashed the quart carton down beside the pie. When Hadley looked around for a big spoon, she had left the kitchen, returned to the living room with Dave and Laura.

Silently, alone, he spooned the mushy ice cream from its pasteboard carton onto the pie. Ellen hadn't had enough sense to put the ice cream in the freezer; cold sticky rivulets trickled down his wrists, into his cuffs and sleeves. He grabbed up two of the plates and made his way morbidly into the living room.

Cornered again as he went to see how the coffee was doing, Hadley listened to a brief, explosive tirade of despair. "I don't care if you feel well or not. I'm sick of your moaning and complaining: there's always something wrong with you." Ellen trembled as she collected the dirty dessert plates together in the sink. "God, this awful grocery-store ice cream—if we weren't so broke all the time we could have had hand-packed ice cream from the drugstore." Water roared over the dishes. "And you didn't have sense enough to put it in the freezer."

"Oh," he said, remembering now. It was he, after all. He had brought the ice cream home and absently laid it with the apples and oranges at the bottom of the refrigerator. "You know you could have got it this noon when you shopped," he said defensively. "Take it out of the household money."

Ellen followed him as he collected coffee cups. "*What* household money? You swiped every last cent of it—as you know perfectly well. That morning when you came home, when you were drunk and in jail. When you were in that fight and knocked that man down."

"Let's forget it."

"Sure, let's forget it. Let's forget you lost thirty dollars, maybe more. Let's forget you were arrested and locked up and you didn't come home until the next morning. Let's forget I almost went out of my mind with worry."

The after-dinner coffee was drunk in dismal silence. "Well," Dave Gold said finally, fooling with his saucer, "I guess we're going to have to get going."

Laura screeched like a macaw. "Not without doing the dishes! There's such a thing as doing the dishes before you're ready to leave."

Ellen toyed frigidly with her coffee cup. "That's all right." She didn't look up. "Forget it."

"But—," Laura began.

"I'm leaving them until tomorrow. I think I'll watch TV awhile and then go to bed." Ellen smiled mechanically at Laura. "Thanks anyhow."

As Dave and Laura fumbled into their coats, Hadley examined his wristwatch. It was later than he thought—almost eleven. Most of it was over, of course; but there was still a chance of getting the tail end. "Say," he said to Dave, "I'll come along with you. Okay? You have your car, don't you?"

They walked down the dark, deserted sidewalk, heels clicking loudly in the night. "I think you better go back inside," Laura brayed. "Your wife's going to be mad at you."

Hadley said nothing. He stood patiently by the car while Dave searched his pockets for the key. The Gold car was a tired old Cadillac, without paint or color, a rusting heap of iron that jutted up like a World War I Army tank. Dave unlocked the doors and they swung noisily open. The interior smelled of beer and wet upholstery and burned oil. Hadley pushed aside heaps of old magazines, cushions, a few knobby potatoes fallen from a shopping bag. He settled himself in the backseat, against the window, feet resting on the exposed springs of the seat ahead. After a moment Dave climbed in beside him with a grunt.

"Laura's driving," he explained. "My night vision's too lousy." He lit his pipe; in the darkness it wheezed and glowed like a distant factory. "Make yourself comfortable. . . . It takes a little while to get the motor warm."

In the driver's seat Laura fooled with the controls. The motor coughed and spluttered, then came on with a furious roar that echoed up and down the street. Overpowering fumes rose up and choked Hadley; a cloud of blue gas settled around him, pungent and thick and nauseous. Beneath him the frame of the car jiggled and vibrated; the motor backfired, stalled, caught again, and then settled down.

"This is really living," Dave commented.

As the ponderous car lunged jerkily forward, Laura shouted: "Want to stop at a bar and have a couple of drinks? Or you want to go directly to our place?" She roared the car out into the center of the street; backfiring, bucking, the car rumbled through an intersection and stop sign, gaining momentum as it went.

"Let me off downtown," Hadley said. "Thanks."

"Downtown!" Laura yelled above the uproar. "What do you mean, downtown? Downtown isn't a *place*. Downtown's a bourgeois concept!"

"Just let me off," Hadley said acidly. "Anywhere it's convenient." He didn't feel capable of social niceties; as the huge equipage crawled along the dark street his stomach rolled queasily. Probably it was the poisonous vapors from the motor. Probably it was the bucking of the car, and the blinding headlights from the state highway beyond the edge of town. And the tension with Ellen.

All the conflicts of their married life had been accentuated by her pregnancy. Petty trifles magnified until they squatted like obese nightmares in all corners of his married life. But now that he was out of the apartment cool sense told him that it wasn't Ellen; it was himself. It was the thing inside him, the restless dissatisfaction, the blind striving toward something intangible and unknown. He would not, he *could* not, destroy his marriage; it meant too much to him. Ellen, and the baby.

He tried to picture the near future. The three of them; but it might not be a boy. If it was a girl things would be odd, peculiar, mystical. It had to be a boy; it had to be an entity he understood. There were already too many things beyond his comprehension; his marriage had to remain a finite core around which he could collect himself.

"Listen," Dave said gravely, "are you going to that holy-roller conclave?"

Hadley reflected. "I am, yes. You mean the Society of the Watchmen of Jesus?"

"Whatever it's called. Are you getting mixed up in that?" Dave's voice rose sharply. "Why, that's crazy. They talk about Armageddon. That's nut stuff!" He spluttered excitedly. "That's the most ignorant form of—stupidity! Stupidity, you hear me? Don't you get mixed up in that, you hear me?"

Laura yelled: "What is it? What's he mixed up in?"

Hadley slumped down sullenly. "I'm open-minded enough to go by and hear what they have to say."

"I'll tell you what they have to say. I've been to those things. Some madman gets up there and raves and screams and slobbers . . . Everybody moans and sways and shouts, 'Hallelujah! De Lawd am comin' to save!'" Dave waved the stalk of his pipe in Hadley's face. "You're going there to hear them call Communists hell-hordes of Satan, atheistic godless Antichrist— turn the car around and head back," he ordered Laura. "You must be out of your mind." His voice trailed off in baffled disgust. "I didn't think that trash appealed to anybody but schlumps. No, I won't be a party to this. If you want to go, you can walk."

They drove in silence. "I have a right to go," Hadley complained as Laura turned onto a side street. "Christ, it's almost over anyhow."

Laura turned around and snapped something in Yiddish. She and Dave conferred rapidly, tongues flying; Hadley glared out the window and loathed both of them. "All right," Dave said briefly, having decided. "We'll take you there and go in with you. We'll stay a couple of minutes so you can see what it's like."

"When your curiosity's satisfied," Laura hollered, "then we'll give them the old raspberry and take off. We've got some ice-cold beer at our place." She gave a passing car the raspberry.

"We'll show them!" She commenced to scream a Spanish civil war song she had memorized from a phonograph record.

Hadley was still squashed sullenly down against the seat when the Cadillac pulled up before the Watchmen Hall. Cars were parked solidly up and down all the nearby streets, most of them old and dusty, but a few bright, modern, and expensive. All sparkled moistly in the night mist. The hall itself, a square wood building, yellow and dilapidated, a firetrap, a relic, blazed with lights and banners. A handful of people were visible, loitering at the entrances with armloads of throwaways.

"Let's go," Laura shouted enthusiastically. "Might as well get it over with." She double-parked the car in front of a gray Chevrolet and yanked on the emergency brake. The three of them crossed the street to the main entrance, Dave and Laura on each side of Hadley, like a police escort.

Laura became silent as they passed through the entrance and into the building. First came a small lobby, with fiberboard walls on which notices and pictures had been tacked. Two small doors led to the hall itself; they passed through one, and abruptly they were inside.

Foolishly, embarrassed, they stood inside the door, pressed together, conscious suddenly of the rows of quiet, humble, unmoving people. The three of them had invaded a vast chamber of silence and attention. Dipping waves of rapt faces, many of them Negro, most of them plain working-class, ordinary citizens in jeans, overalls, cheap suits, cotton dresses. The meeting was almost at an end. On the platform, the speaker was answering a question apparently put to him by a woman to one side. The speaker was addressing her, and all the room at the same time.

No one noticed the three who had just come in. The people were intent on the speaker's words, hushed with that tense hunger that comes at the end of a protracted suspense. The rapport was incomprehensible to the three people at the door; at first they were outside it; and then, as they became drawn into the flow of speech, the lecture abruptly ended. With a single flowing motion, like a plate of water overturned, the rows of people slid from their chairs and headed up the aisles. Perfectly expressionless, impassive, they came rapidly forward.

"Jesus," Dave said, urging Hadley and Laura out of the doorway. "Let the steamroller get by."

They found shelter at the bottom of narrow stairs leading to a second floor; a moment later the torrent burst into the antechamber and out onto the sidewalk. A low buzz muttered briefly; then the swarm broke up and dissolved in the direction of the cars, down the sidewalks, into the night gloom. Cars started up; there was a furious interval of rumbles and whirrs. The activity died, and the three people found themselves alone.

"It's over," Laura said, disappointed.

"Come on." Dave started for the car. "Let's get out of here."

Despondently, Hadley followed after them, back across the street and into the Cadillac. Laura turned on the motor and a moment later they were thundering down the street away from the hall. The sounds of other cars died behind as they left the downtown section. Night closed in around them, mixed tendrils of darkness and cold, fetid air from the Bay, as they made their way in the direction of the Gold apartment house.

"What's the matter?" Dave asked Hadley. "Say something."

Hadley sat slumped over. He was dazed with disappointment; he only half heard the man beside him. "Like what?" he muttered.

"It's not my fault it's over," Dave pointed out.

"I'm not blaming you."

"Christ," Laura shouted back to them. "That man was talking about Jonah and the whale!" She honked wildly at a milk truck coming out of a driveway. "Like Sunday school, yet!"

At the Gold apartment lights burned. Music and the noises of people filtered under the door. Dave turned the knob; the door wasn't locked. He hesitated, scowled, shrugged, and finally pushed the door open.

A group of people lounged around the living room. They greeted Dave and Laura enthusiastically.

"Hi, Dave!"

A bass voice boomed: "Where the hell have you two been?"

"The door wasn't locked," a tiny young woman tittered. "We came on in."

And a slender young man piped: "It's about time you folks got home!"

Stuart Hadley shut the door and wandered glumly around the living room. He wished he had stayed at home; God knew how long he'd be here, wasting time with these people. Of course, he could go home on foot, or grab a crosstown bus. He moaned with despair. He had missed Beckheim, caught only a fleeting glimpse of the big dark man, heard a few fragments of his words. And now this.

These people were a familiar type; he had run into them in college. Sprawled around on the floor, they were listening to Paul Robeson records, spirituals and work songs. Albums of jazz lay scattered around: Bix Beiderbecke and Mezz Mezzrow. Lute music of the seventeenth century. Girls, in black toreador pants and sandals, turtleneck sweaters, hair plastered down and stringy, gazed limply up and babbled greetings to Dave and Laura. Thin young men, quaintly dressed, slippery hipped, curled their way forward, with languid observations hanging like sugar from their lips.

"What are you doing down from San Francisco?" Dave asked them.

"Oh," said one of these children of paradise, "we came to hear the talk."

"We came to hear Theodore Beckheim."

"And it was *charming*!"

Laura stood in the corner, pulling off her coat. "This is the bunch from *Succubus*," she muttered to Hadley. A resentful, surly expression rose to the surface of her pitted face like a dead fish floating up to seaweed. "I should have known they'd flock down for this thing."

Hadley was astonished. It had never occurred to him that there was a type of person Laura Gold found objectionable. Mute and disgusted, Laura prowled heavily around the apartment, straightening piles of books and magazines, pushing aside a jar of peanut butter, a box of soda crackers, a carton of sour milk.

The Dave Gold apartment smelled dully of ancient dust-heavy carpets and stale cabbage. Torn curtains sagged against the windows, greasy with grime. Unfinished manuscripts were littered around the rusty Underwood type-writer, mixed with yellowed copies of the *Nation* and *People's World*. Dirty clothes were heaped in one corner, by the closet. The uninvited guests had pushed aside the debris and made themselves at home.

Among the guests one figure stood out. A woman, leaning against the wall, hands in the pockets of her jeans. She seemed to be the center of the group of heaven's children; she was older than the others, taller, less extravagant, more dignified.

"That's the old succubus herself," Laura growled in his ear. "She owns it. Dave did an article for her—the whole thing's arty and mystical—reactionary crap." She padded off into the bathroom to express herself in private.

Dave stood facing the tall, thin women, tapping dead ash from his pipe and fumbling for his tobacco sack. "I know," he was saying aloud, nodding intently. The expression on his face showed that he didn't like her any more than Laura did. "We dropped by for a couple of minutes."

The woman continued talking. Her voice was low, controlled. She was per-haps thirty. High-cheeked, reddish hair thin and cut short . . . With her neatly pressed jeans she wore a green-checkered sports shirt, a western-style leather belt, a heavy silver buckle. For a moment her gray eyes moved in Hadley's di-rection; curiosity was turned briefly on him and then back to Dave.

"What did you think?" she asked huskily. Around her the circle of lotus eaters gazed up in benign rapture.

"We didn't hear anything. And you know what I think of that junk."

Expressionless, the woman continued: "I'm trying to find out if Beck-heim is basing his movement on quietism." Her voice trailed off, lost from Hadley in the murmur of sound and music that hung over the room. ". . . A reaction, too, but not the same kind. You're thinking of nonviolence; qui-etism was more like the Friends' concept of individual inspiration . . . the first heresy . . . Protestant sense of individual conscience."

Hadley stumbled over the ankle of a small girl crouched in a heap, listen-ing raptly. A tiny white-haired thing with huge china-blue eyes and the body of a ten-year-old boy. She smiled at him sweetly and turned back to hear.

"These North Beach intellectuals," Laura grated in his ear. "Queer, every one of them. Degenerate dilettantes. No social conscience." She carried an armload of beer cans from the kitchen and dropped them in the center of the moth-eaten carpet with a loud clatter. "Help yourselves," she bellowed sullenly. "Sorry, no glasses."

The can opener was tossed around. In the background Paul Robeson's rich deep voice rolled forth lower and lower; the record seemed to be gradually slowing down.

> *And all your tears of sorrow,*
> *And all your tears of sorrow,*
> *And all your tears of sorrow,*
> *Mamita Mia,*
> *We shall avenge them,*
> *We shall avenge them.*

Standing at the window, Hadley gazed out at the night gloom. Streetlights glowed yellow here and there, without pattern or visible design. A universe of chance . . . random particles swirling and settling without meaning.

Dave came over beside him. "Do you know her?"

"No," Hadley answered.

"She runs this high-type quarterly up in San Francisco. Critical articles on T. S. Eliot and Jung. Short stories by Capote's bunch . . . or worse."

"I know," Hadley said. *"Succubus."*

"You want to go home? I'll drive you home—it'll give me a chance to get out of here."

"I can get home okay," Hadley said. He wondered why Dave and Laura disliked the woman so intensely. "You don't have to—"

"That's what I'm going to do, though." Dave signaled to Laura; she glared back but made no move to stop him. "Maybe Marsha will be gone when I get home." He pushed open the door to the hall.

"You're leaving?" the tall, slim woman asked.

"I'll be back," Dave muttered evasively.

As the door closed behind them, Hadley caught a final glimpse of Marsha Frazier, arms folded, already continuing her talk in the same low, indifferent tone.

"They never stop," Dave said angrily. "Talking, I mean. That's not the worst of it, either. If that was all . . ." Explosively he said: "I should have known this Watchmen stuff would bring them out of their holes. Goddamn fungus—turn over a rock and look what you get."

Searching his memory Hadley asked: "Is she the woman you did that article for? The one you got in that argument with, and she never printed it?"

"Fascists," Gold muttered. His voice was bleak, troubled with the ring of unhappy foreboding. "Friends of Ezra Pound." He and Hadley strode gloomily down the sidewalk to the car. "Anti-Semites." Furiously, he tugged open the car door. "Hop in and let's go. I'll probably wreck us along the way . . . but I want to get you home. The less you see of those people the better."

Jim Fergesson, forty-two, sound of health, owner of Modern TV Sales and Service, lay in his living room and contemplated gain. His shoes were heaped beside the couch. His newspaper was crumpled on the floor. In the corner, his wife, Alice, rocked back and forth in her chair and hooked away at a rug. The radio, quietly to itself, described a new advance in lawn seed that was to revolutionize outdoor patios.

From an abalone-shell ashtray, Fergesson selected the smoking remnant of his cigar and placed it between his lips. Meditatively, he belched. "I'm going to call Bud O'Neill," he shouted. "What's holding me up? I'm going over there and close the deal tonight."

"Go over and look at the place once more before you decide," Alice suggested.

"I've seen it enough to find my way through it in the dark. If I don't close him somebody else'll grab it." Greedily, he reflected on the gross take. The high percentage of net profits. No, *profits* misstated it; he rejected profits and concentrated on the overall picture. Of course, profits were there; a man didn't go into business to see his name on the state tax certificate pasted over the till. Profits were to a business what roaring down the track was to a train. Profits were the quotient, the juice squeezed from the press . . . They announced that the business *worked*.

But profits became meaningful only when put to work, when reinvested. The driveshaft of a motor attached to nothing merely turned around and around, a useless child's toy.

That was why it was essential he buy O'Neill Appliance, the flashy, classy, shiny-bright, new highway–located appliance emporium, with its gleaming neon signs, overhead spots, white refrigerators, stoves, washers, dryers, a vast bathroom of porcelain and chrome, a tiled Elysium of bosom-white baked enamel that was closer to God than cleanliness. Buying O'Neill Appliance was a spiritual act, almost a mystical rapport with the Almighty. If God lurked anywhere on earth He was present when a massive crate was torn open and a gleaming Bendix spin dryer was slid from its packing frame onto the display floor. If ever there was a holy spot, it was the fifty-foot display window of O'Neill Appliance, spread out like a beacon along Bayshore Highway.

In buying O'Neill Appliance, Fergesson demonstrated the essential spirituality of his soul.

He really loved easing the black-metal pry bar between the slats of soft fresh pine, snipping the twisted wires, yanking the alfalfa and brown gummy paper from the towering smooth-white slab of metal. He got fierce satisfaction squatting down on the floor to struggle the castors into a heavy washer. He was ecstatic, involved in the act of ultimate adoration, when he unboxed the trays and chromium shelves of a nine-foot refrigerator and fitted them into place (they always fitted exactly right). And O'Neill's warehouse was bulging with still-crated refrigerators, never touched or pawed or examined.

"Nobody else will grab it," Alice said gently. "It's been up for sale a year and a half." The wife Jim Fergesson had selected was eleven years younger than he. Plump, black-haired, with competent hands and the firm, alert features of a woman who efficiently managed every part of her home. "You're not usually this way," she continued. "Anything happen to make you incautious this way?"

"No," Jim said shortly. "I've waited a year and a half; how cautious can you get?"

"Remember, if you buy O'Neill Appliance you'll have to work twice as hard as you do now." Alice spoke patiently, firmly. "And you've got plenty to do as it is. Why don't you leave the money in the bank? You're getting two and a half percent interest, probably as much as you'll make out of O'Neill's place. There's too much overhead there."

"We've discussed it before," Jim answered. His wife sometimes took the magic out of things. "I want to expand. I want to grow." Conscious that Alice was smiling understandingly, he pulled himself upright and took umbrage. "Stop laughing at me, you old bat. If I just sit still the damn business will shrink. Turn your back and it gets smaller."

Alice laughed. "That's because when you're away from it you build it up in your mind until it's as big as Macy's."

"I have dreams," Jim said.

"You have a big tongue. You were a salesman during the depression; your tongue kept us alive. Remember how long you talked for a nine-dollar sale? Longer than you talk now for a three-hundred-dollar combination."

Jim Fergesson remembered back. "Those nine-dollar Emersons kept us in potatoes." He grinned to himself. "Remember that winter day I turned on the heater in the back of the store—you were up in the office typing out the bills. And a man came in to look at sets. . . . You wondered why I didn't come out." He roared. "I was sound asleep in front of the heater."

"The only time in your life you missed a sale."

Jim cackled nostalgically. "That sure taught me something. That heater never went on again; too much comfort is bad." He reflected for a time. "Maybe that's what's wrong with the young people today: too much luxury. They're soft. All they have to do is push a button, turn a knob."

"You're selling them the machines, aren't you?"

"A machine isn't good or bad; it's how you use it. . . . If a man gets a machine so he can lie in the shade and sleep, that's bad. If he gets a machine so he can do more work, that's fine." His small, well-muscled body stiffened pridefully. "Remember how hard we worked back in the old days? You did the bookkeeping and kept the place clean while I sold people radios and vacuum cleaners. Boy, we really had to sell; people didn't walk in and buy, like they do now. Anybody can sell something to a man that wants to buy; that's not selling." He chuckled and winked at his wife. "It didn't hurt us any, did it? We had fun."

Alice smiled good-naturedly. "Kept my weight down; I'll say that much."

"And we never wasted anything, by God. We never threw anything away; remember the old trash cartons down in the basement? Remember me jumping up and down, flattening those boxes and baling them up with packing wire?" He shook his head. "You can't teach people today not to waste things. I've seen Hadley use a piece of carbon paper and toss it away—use it once and throw it in the basket."

"If you buy O'Neill's place," Alice said carefully, "you won't be able to run it. You can't open up two stores at once; you'll have to get somebody to handle it for you . . . and you know how you fret when you're not there to boss everybody around."

"Everybody does things wrong."

"By your standards. But different people have different standards."

"I hire them! I pay them good money! If they want to work for me they're going to have to meet my standards." Jim twisted resentfully. "The thing that's wrong with these young kids is they don't know how to work. They expect the customer to walk up and hand them the money. They don't know how to go out and really work for it, like we had to. They're soft. Luxury—that's what's done it."

"I know," Alice said gently. "You've mentioned it before, from time to time."

Fergesson got to his feet and padded broodingly toward the kitchen. "There's such a thing as too much of a good thing. A man gets effeminate with all the stuff they're selling these days. Perfume for men—aftershave, they call it, but it's perfume. Hadley uses it; I can smell it." He halted pointedly at the kitchen door, cigar between his fingers. "Alice, I'm a simple man. I have simple tastes. I like a good meal, I like to read the paper after dinner and smoke this." He solemnly waved the stump of his cigar. "I like a little fun, once in a while. A ball game or a drive out in the country. How long's it been since we've seen a movie?"

"God knows."

"I like a little music—not that longhair stuff: something simple and sweet, with a melody I can follow. Some of that classical stuff you can't make head nor tail of; you know, I think the people who listen to that must be crazy. Or maybe they're pretending. . . . Maybe they know darn well it's just a lot of crazy sounds. Of course, I don't go for this hot jazz all the kids like. It's nigger music; that's what it is, pure and simple. I like the old-fashioned stuff we used to have; it was the stuff you could walk home humming to yourself. It was easy to dance to. You know, the tunes Rudy Vallee used to play. And John Charles Thomas." He jabbed his cigar at her, nodding his head with emphasis. "There's a great artist, that John Charles Thomas. I heard him sing, once. You know, when he sings he closes his eyes. He stands there with his eyes shut and his hands clasped; he's a simple man, Alice. He's sincere. You can tell, when you hear him." Fergesson disappeared into the kitchen. "Nelson Eddy was another. Whatever happened to him?"

"He's still around."

Fergesson rooted noisily in the dark kitchen. "What happened to all the beer I brought home last week? You and your canasta ladies drank it all up, did you?"

"Look down in the bottom of the refrigerator, with the vegetables."

Fergesson poured himself a beer and returned to the living room. There was an intense frown of concentration on his round, red-wrinkled face. He pawed fretfully at the fringe of gray-black hair above his left ear and said: "Alice, what the hell am I going to do? I can't turn Modern over to Hadley—he can't tell his ass from a hole in the ground. But they're all that way! He's the least of them, I suppose, when you get down to it. They're all a bunch of WPA leaf rakers . . . Christ, they just stand there with their hands in their pockets." He sipped his beer resentfully. "Watching TV while people swarm by outside."

"Hooks have gone out of style."

"I don't want high pressure! I just want somebody who likes his work, who likes to *sell*. If I turn Modern over to Hadley he'll put it out of business in a week."

"You can still do the buying," Alice said patiently; they had gone over it many times. "If you want, I'll go down and keep the books. You can get some high school kid to dust the television sets. School's almost out for the summer."

"Yeah," Fergesson admitted reluctantly. "You know, I damn near fired Hadley the other day. He showed up with a hangover, again; he could hardly drag one foot after another and he was shaking like a leaf. If I had any sense I'd let him go. But how the hell can I? He's got that wife of his knocked up, and all those unpaid bills . . . Around the end of the month he's into the till for ten or fifteen bucks. It's pathetic. Every time he goes by a clothing shop he buys himself a new bunch of socks and ties, or maybe an imported cashmere sweater. What's he want with all those clothes? I thought only women bought a lot of clothes!"

"He's a good-looking young man," Alice pointed out. "You ought to go along with him." She reached up and critically plucked at her husband's frayed cuff. "You've been wearing that same blue serge suit for years."

"This is a good suit," Fergesson said with stubborn pride. "I got this suit before the last war. They don't make them this way, not anymore."

"You're the only man I know who still wears a vest. And carries a pocket watch."

"My dad gave me this watch." Fergesson flipped it open expertly. "You know how many jewels it has?"

"I know." Her eyes twinkled, gray and kindly. "None. It cost your dad a dollar and a half back in the French and Indian War."

"Not that far back." Fergesson grinned. "You're trying to make a monkey out of me. You, too, kid. Remember when you used to wrap up an apple and a peanut butter sandwich and a pint of milk for me? Every goddamn day I carried that little paper sack down to the store. How the hell long was that? Almost fifteen years."

"You could try Hadley out for a while," Alice suggested. "For that matter, you need a vacation. Go up and stay in Lake Country at your cousin's a week or so. It's summer—business is slow. Hadley can't do much harm . . . Maybe he'll work out all right. Maybe the responsibility will set well on him."

"I won't have anybody running my store who swills celery phosphates."

"Now you're being silly," Alice said sharply. "Are you going to tell your employees what to eat and drink? Give them *some* life of their own."

"It's not that," Fergesson said gloomily, "not the stuff he swills, in itself. It's what it means. . . . A man who drinks that stuff is unbalanced."

"Is a man who drinks beer unbalanced?"

"You know I'm right," Fergesson persisted. "There's something wrong with

Stumblebum. . . . You can see it in the goofy things he does. He gets mad in the wrong way, not like other people. He's mad all the time. It's always down there inside him. . . . Things bring it to the surface. Someday he's going to bust loose. He's going to go out on a wingding and wind up in jail. Or worse."

"Nonsense," Alice snapped.

Fergesson nodded solemnly. "I know what I'm talking about; I know him. He has no self-control. . . . You just think he has, because he's so damn sweet-looking and dresses up like you damn women dress up. No, I'm not turning my store over to a lunatic. Even if he is clever with his hands—even if he can sit all day tinkering with the same TV set." He protested: "I can't! Understand? I just can't turn it over to him—he's not trustworthy."

"Don't shout," Alice said testily. "I'm not deaf."

Jim Fergesson lapsed into silence. He lay back against the couch, sipping unhappily at his beer, listening to the radio mutter out the symphonic syrup of Morton Gould's orchestra. Alice continued hooking away at her rug; occasionally she glanced at her husband, raised an eyebrow questioningly, got no response, shrugged, and returned to hooking.

If he told anybody it would be her. But he wasn't going to tell anybody, not for a while at least. He had phrased it a number of ways, but no matter how he put it, the substance was the same. He had to buy O'Neill Appliance because if he didn't he wouldn't be in business much longer. He was telling the truth when he said it either grows or it shrinks. The Bel-Rex drugstore chain, with branches in Oakland, Berkeley, Sacramento, San Francisco, San Jose, was considering buying O'Neill Appliance. Once the chain got hold of it, Jim Fergesson was finished.

He had never been a big-time operator. Neither was Bud O'Neill: in fact O'Neill was no good at all. O'Neill was so pitiful an operator that he was selling out . . . with one of the best fronts, inventories, and locations in the business. O'Neill was a natural-born bad businessman. He had poured funds into his store; now he was finished.

In Fergesson's mind the life and history of his competitor lay like a stone; he couldn't dislodge it, try as he might. The way of Bud O'Neill was always there, the open road of mediocrity and final failure.

O'Neill was that special type of idiot who opens a little hole-in-the-wall radio repair shop with nothing more than the ability to check tubes, replace filter condensers, and wire in phonograph inputs to old radios. O'Neill had taken enthusiastically to radio in high school; he had put together a rig, a shortwave transmitter. He had got a license and gone on the air: a ham. This was back in the thirties, toward the end of the depression.

In the early forties O'Neill got himself a job in a defense plant in Richmond,

California, wiring bomber turrets. He made plenty of money; everybody in Richmond was wealthy, including the Okies and Negroes. After the war, block after block of property became worthless; Richmond shut down its plants and shipyards and became a town of federally operated multiple-housing-unit slums and flashy supermarkets. One by one the businesses set up to supply the wartime labor force dwindled and failed. About this time O'Neill opened his first store.

It had been a shoe shop; that is, it came without fixtures of any kind, a barren single room with a filthy bathroom in the back and two flyspecked window ledges for display. The walls were water-soaked; aging nude-girl calendars sagged among cobwebs and dust. O'Neill moved in test equipment (built by hand), a pair of secondhand counters, a stool and a rubber floor mat to keep himself from being electrocuted, a fluorescent lamp, got a man to paint him a sign, and became the Richmond One-Day Radio Service. In the front part of the store he piled rusty old radio chassis, dead portable radio batteries; he set up a record player and sold for twenty-five cents stacks of ex–jukebox records. In the window he placed tall bright new cardboard display posters from Sylvania and Tungsol tubes; and later on, a few tiny personal radios, the kind that operate from 67½-volt cells, the kind that can't be plugged in the wall and are eternally damned by Consumers Union.

The old ladies started coming in with their Atwater Kents and decrepit Philcos, the like of which are built no more, the like of which will never be equaled. O'Neill was a fat squashy man in his thirties, with a dirty wad of a mustache above his thick lips; he wore a faded dirt-spotted quasi uniform that made him look like a filling-station mechanic. Over the pocket was stiched the word BUD in red thread, done by his wife. A Coke bottle rested at one end of his workbench. From upturned radio chassis shrieked and howled metallic cowboy music. Pimple-faced youths came in to have paper bags of dusty tubes checked free. Girls came in for phonograph needles; he got a display board of RCA chromium needles and Recoton twenty-five for a quarter. He was really in business.

O'Neill was stupid, slow, and hardworking. The combination got him nowhere; he made nothing. Most of the sets he worked on broke down within the thirty-day guarantee period. He spent hours arguing with some penniless kid over GE variable-reluctance cartridges. He spent weeks smoothing out crumpled old invoices, trying to find out where fifty 35Z5 tubes had come from, and why. He sat hunched at his workbench until four in the morning, trying to use up consignments of parts that bulged around him in quarter-pint bottles. All day he studied Rider's Serviceman's Manual, trying to discover the secret of keeping Webster 56 record changers from turning off in the middle of the last record. After a year and a half he folded.

The expensive, gaudy store south of Cedar Groves along Bayshore Highway was not bought with funds earned wiring bomber turrets in a defense plant . . . and it was not bought with the proceeds from the sale of Richmond One-Day. It was handled by his wife's family, who had money to invest. One thing about O'Neill, he had talked to enough old ladies, checked enough tubes, argued with enough pimple-faced kids, to spout a good line. He sold his wife's family a bill of goods, got himself staked to thirty thousand dollars, and set up O'Neill Appliance. New stores were going up along Bayshore like fruit stands in summer. A hundred yards to his right was a piano shop that lit on and off all night, seven nights a week. Across from him was a gigantic dime store, as large as a movie theater. Even the bar down the road looked like a Spanish mansion. He had a good location, selected by the San Mateo branch of the Bank of America. He had a good front, designed by a San Francisco architect picked out by his father-in-law. His inventory was a housewife's dream, a bulging cavern stuffed to bursting by the enterprising salesmen of the San Francisco supply houses.

In three years O'Neill was up to his neck. In five, he was dead. Drowned.

O'Neill had no sense. He was an ex-ham, with a meager ability to handle a soldering iron and oscillator, no organizational ability, no sense of how to spend money, and when it came down to it, too honest to be a good salesman. He was ready to throw in the towel; all he needed was a buyer to take the place off his hands.

O'Neill Appliance was the only real competitor for Jim Fergesson's shop. And O'Neill was a dud, without sense. Even his ads were duds; he forgot to trim off the instructions, left words like *your store* where his own plate should have appeared. O'Neill Appliance hadn't cut into Fergesson's gross; the highway shop had been rather a come-on for him, drawing cars to a stop, getting people out on their feet, failing to close them, sending them finally into Cedar Groves at ten miles an hour, wanting to be sold, money hanging out, ready to take any obsolete dog pushed on them by somebody with a carnation in his neatly pressed suit, a sales book and fountain pen in his hands.

Fergesson had got the town's sidewalk trade, its old families, and its highway traffic. He had handled it well: bought close to the belt, not got himself stuck with obsolete radio-phonographs and ten-inch TV sets. Everything was fine; he was well ahead of the game. Except, simply, that if Bel-Rex came in, Fergesson was finished. In six months, by Christmas, Bel-Rex would have O'Neill Appliance high-powered, drawing from a statewide inventory, with unlimited funds for investment and advertising.

Sitting in his pleasant living room, listening to the radio mutter Morton

Gould, Jim Fergesson was scared. Inside his plump, muscular body, he was trembling. His soul was weak with sweat. He couldn't compete against Bel-Rex; he was finished. Big deals, advertised by throwaways, radio, newspapers . . . Famous name brands (we can't tell you what it is but you'd recognize it instantly), fifty bucks under fair trade. Free gardenias to the ladies. Free TV lamp with each set sold. We buy in carload lots. Our buyer has gone crazy . . . come in and rob us. Searchlights at night. Twenty-five salesmen, all on commission and draw—sharp as starving ferrets. Delivery anywhere in the state without charge. Immediate repair service.

"I'm no hotshot," Fergesson croaked aloud.

Alice glanced up. "What, dear?"

Fergesson cleared his throat nervously and went on: "I've never done hotshot business. I can't pressure; I can only sell what I believe in."

Gazing at him intently, Alice said: "I know that, dear."

"I can't carry all lines! Christ, I have Emerson and GE and Westinghouse and Philco and Zenith—isn't that enough? What more do they want? A man can stock only so much." Bel-Rex carried everything, he knew bitterly. Right down the line, to Sentinel and Crosley and Trav-Ler. The works. And complete lines, not just leaders.

"Price cutting," Fergesson muttered. "Buy a TV, get a free toaster. Free twin-lead and rabbit ears. Christ, I couldn't give away a ten-amp fuse!"

"I wish you'd tell me what's wrong," Alice said, eyeing him uneasily. "Have you been reading ads of those big San Francisco department stores?"

"They're not so bad; they have class. It's these hotshot chains that get me. These lit-up joints that cater to Okies and coons. Christ, they're wholesalers doing retail! They buy direct from the factory—it's true. They buy more in a day than I buy in a year. When stuff gets obsolete they dump it in the river. . . . I've got some old Hoffmans down in the basement, the first they made. By God, I'll sell them yet."

He got to his feet and paced miserably around. *You either get bigger or get smaller*. He didn't have a choice; if he wanted to stay alive he had to buy O'Neill Appliance. Goddamn O'Neill—why had he built the place? Why hadn't he left it a grassy lot of beer cans and moldy newspapers?

"You know," he said hoarsely, "maybe I shouldn't have gone in the radio business. Look how it's changed—it isn't anything like it used to be. Now it's TV, nothing but big screen and color, black tube, ultrahigh frequency. . . . Back in the old days we had five-tube superhets and that was all. And this hi-fi stuff, these custom-built things. Fifteen thousand cycles— music for the birds. Reluctance cartridges, tape recorders—it's a madhouse. FM tuners—nothing but grief."

"It'll level off," Alice said patiently. "Be glad you're not in the record business; you'd have those different speeds, those long plays and those little RCA forty-five doughnuts with the big hole."

Fergesson made his way into the kitchen and got a second beer from the refrigerator. His hands were shaking, his knobby, stubby, calloused hands, with their grimy burn-scars up and down the wrists, from reaching into backs of radios. . . .

"That fool O'Neill," he said bitterly. "He'll sell out and get his money. Probably open up a big neon-sign tilted-glass-front whorehouse."

"What did you say, dear?" Alice called.

Fergesson grunted a reply and reentered the living room. He hadn't anybody's family to stake him; he had gone up the hard way, hand over hand, on his own power. He had worked every inch of it . . . and overnight Bel-Rex could slaughter him.

"My dad was right," Fergesson said wretchedly. "He said I was making a mistake."

"Your father didn't approve of any kind of business," Alice reminded him.

"Sure, he was a lawyer. A professional man. He was an educated man."

"He was also an oil speculator who lost everything he had, and came to you and died right here in this house without a cent. And your mother and I cared for him eight years before he finally passed on." Alice's voice rose angrily. "And all that time he never got tired of telling you that business was unworthy of a son of his. Lying there flat on his back insulting you day after day—" Her voice broke. "Why do you *always* bring him up? Why can't you forget about him?"

"He was right." In his vest pocket Fergesson's fingers closed around the ancient gold watch, elaborately engraved, with its fine, thin, black hands and spidery numbers. That was all the tall, dignified old man had left, that and a heavy silver ring bought from an Indian in Utah. And an old leather briefcase full of worthless drilling-rights certificates.

"In a way I can understand how Hadley feels," Fergesson said bitterly. "I wandered into the radio business by accident, like he did. I wasn't going to be a businessman—I was going to be a lawyer, like my father. Maybe that's all that's wrong with Hadley; maybe he wants to be something better than a TV salesman. I sure as hell wouldn't want to be a TV salesman; I'd rather wash dishes. If he had any sense he'd wander back out again."

"And do what?"

"Anything. Join the Army. I was in the National Guard and it didn't hurt me. A year of that would make a man out of him, give him a spinal column. If he wasn't so weak and shilly-shallying he'd quit." Fergesson waved his finger at Alice. "If he was any good he'd walk out! I'll tell you something: his father was a doctor. Dead, now. I can tell you what he'd say if he were alive. . . . The same thing my dad said."

"You don't know that."

"Hadley was raised by women. He's like those fellows in the State Department, like that Dean Acheson. A whole generation of them. Sissy-kissers . . . no spine." His voice sank into baffled gloom. "No wonder America's prestige is going down. No wonder the Commies are winning, with mama's boys running the show. It isn't like the old days."

"It never is," Alice said realistically.

Fergesson wandered over to the couch, threw himself down, gazed vacantly at the heap of brightly colored rug his wife was tirelessly hooking. "The trouble with Hadley," he said, "is he doesn't have any moral standards. He doesn't know right from wrong; nobody taught him the things to live by."

"Such as?"

"Such as going to church. Such as faith in God and faith in his country." Fergesson doggedly sipped his beer. "This is a wonderful country, Alice. Don't ever forget that. If a man works hard he can go a long way. Look at me—when I started out I didn't have a thing. I built it all up with my own hands." He indicated the hardwood floor. "I put in that floor—remember?"

"Of course I remember," Alice said tartly. "I helped you."

"The foundation, I hauled out all that dirt and sank the foundation myself. And the tile in the kitchen. The whole damn sink. This house, the store, everything . . . I built it all up from nothing. I never pulled a dumb deal in my life—if I'd owned Richmond One-Day I'd have made a go of it. If I bought out O'Neill right this minute I'd have that place of his humming!"

"Please don't shout at me," Alice said apprehensively. "What on earth is the matter with you?"

"Nothing," Fergesson muttered. He sipped his beer. "Nothing at all."

Later in the evening he did something that he only partly understood. He put on his coat, went out to the garage, and started up the Pontiac. A few moments later he was gliding down the dark night streets, toward the deserted business section and Modern TV.

It was when he was worried; he knew that. When he was bothered and uncertain: that was when he left his home late at night and came alone to the store. The dark, silent, cold store, with its ghostly shapes. All its lights turned off, except the flickering blue night-light over the safe. Down in the damp concrete vault that was the basement, an occasional beetle fluttered and squeaked and flopped across Olsen's deserted bench: that was the only sound.

As he drove he kept thinking about Bud O'Neill. The failure. The incompetent, without talent of any kind. Harmless, good-natured, full of talk and easy plans. Dazed by the collapse of his gaudy store, not really understanding why it had folded.

Probably constructing an elaborate mythology: ruined because of secret conspiracies. Combines of his competitors.

Fergesson examined his hands, clamped around the wheel of the Pontiac. Competent hands; he wasn't anything like Bud O'Neill. Or was he? Modern TV had once been a place like Richmond One-Day; behind the counter he had hunched much like Bud O'Neill. The old ladies had crept in with their Atwater Kents; he had put in new filters, checked tubes, wired the old sets for phono jacks. In the old days, the early days back in the thirties, when he had taken the store over, there were dead batteries stacked in his windows, too. Tubes and tube displays, secondhand counters, test equipment. The yowl of sets upturned on the bench, protesting against investigation.

All the elements were there, in a fashion. To some old lady, to some young punk, to almost anyone who entered the store, there was no fundamental difference. During the war he had been behind the counter, not working in a defense plant. He had taken over the shop when the previous owner hadn't been able to pay his wages, had owed him a salary covering 1930, 1931, and the first part of 1932. He had been smart enough to get in merchandise to sell; repair wasn't enough. A frugal, close-to-the-chest line of vacuums and washers and radios . . . O'Neill had gone on talking and testing tubes free of charge; he'd be testing tubes again, soon. O'Neill would wind up a heavyset perspiring salesman in a cheap suit, standing in front of some potted palm in another man's gaudy store.

Fergesson parked the Pontiac and snapped off the lights and motor. He got out and walked down the dark sidewalk to Modern TV. Old crumpled newspapers were blown up in the entrance; he stooped down to make a handful of them. While he was carrying them to the gutter he saw the light on in the shop, coming from the back television display room.

He got the door opened and entered. Ellen Hadley, immense and grotesquely pregnant in her blue maternity dress and heavy overcoat, sat gazing at an elaborate RCA television combination. Fergesson had closed the front door and come into the display room before she noticed him and turned her head.

"Hello," she said.

The store was chill, dismal in its barrenness. In the pallid blue flicker of the night-light the girl's face seemed not round: a hollow pointed bonelike thing, a rigid frame supporting her features. Her eyes were deep-sunk, far down in her skull. Her hair appeared transparent, a sheet of dry spidery material, a brown cap through which her scalp and ears were visible. She wore no makeup; her lips were pale, thin.

"What are you doing?" Fergesson demanded, in fright. "Don't you have a TV at home?"

After a time Ellen nodded. "I was walking around. I got tired." She indicated the vast tumor of her belly. "So I came in to sit down." She added: "Stuart went off with some friends of his . . . for a beer and talk."

"I'll take you home," Fergesson said.

"What are you doing?"

"I come down here." He pushed from the display room, over to the counter. Leaning on his elbows, hands knotted into a stubby massed-fist, he gazed intently at the girl, outlined as she was by the night-light and the TV screen. "I come down now and then to catch up on stuff nobody gets done during the day. Somebody has to keep the place going."

Ellen nodded.

"You and Stumblebum have a quarrel?" Fergesson asked presently.

"No, not really. I'm cross these days, I guess."

"How long will it be?"

"Oh, they say three weeks. Give or take a few days."

"You startled me. I didn't expect to find anybody here."

Ellen smiled. "I'm sorry."

"Are you warm enough? Want my coat?"

"I'm fine," she said. "Thanks."

Fergesson, gazing across the counter at her, marveled at the miracle of this bloated creature who sat before the television screen, hands folded in her lap, eyes fixed dutifully on the pale-lit shapes. In spite of her vast bulk, in spite of the wan hollows of her eyes, there was a presence about her that awed him deeply. He felt satisfaction in standing gazing at her, like a man contemplating a religious picture, a stained-glass tableau: static, classic, balanced. In the immensity of her body there was a kind of balance, a completeness, an entirety. She was self-contained; she was what he was not. She needed nothing from outside. Everything meaningful was contained in her body, like the wads and layers of fat a hibernating animal stores up to make it self-sufficient.

"You look pretty smart," he said accusingly. How did that sound? Not the way he wanted. . . . The envy in his voice was audible even to him. "I mean, you look like the cat that swallowed the canary. Do you know what I'm trying to say?"

She smiled faintly. "Yes, I think so."

"It looks good on you. You're a lot older, this way."

"Oh, millions of years."

"Do you have any names picked out?"

"Margaret, if it's a girl. Peter, if it's a boy. Stuart always wanted to be called Pete. He never quite made it."

"Now he will." After a moment Fergesson said: "What did you quarrel about?"

"I don't really know. Something to do with war and God. I'll tell you someday. Not now."

"Ellen," he said, "what's wrong with Stuart?"

"Do you care?"

"I know there's something wrong."

Very simply, Ellen said: "He doesn't know anybody he can trust."

"He can trust me. I won't let him down."

"You already have."

"I have? How?"

"Stuart wants to grow up. But what is there to grow up to? What kind of world have you left him?"

"I didn't create the world."

Ellen smiled. "Couldn't you have put up *something*, some kind of show, an attempt?"

"That's been done," Fergesson said. "He's had that, too. He came along when that was going on. That Man—"

"Yes," Ellen agreed. "That Man. And That Man is rotting away underground."

Unhappily, Fergesson said: "Doesn't Stuart like me?"

Ellen considered. "I don't think he even sees you. I'm afraid he's never learned to see anybody. What he wants, what he's looking for, is much too vague, too remote and abstract. It has no name. A hundred years ago it was called *grace*. It's a search for someone he can have faith in. Someone who won't let him down."

"If he could see me, he'd know I want him to trust me."

"If he could do that, I think he'd be well. But he doesn't know how. So he can only keep on searching for something invisible. Something that nobody has ever seen on this earth and nobody ever will."

Fergesson came around the end of the counter and stood there, temporarily. Outside the store, beyond the locked front door, a man and woman walked past, heels echoing mournfully in the total night stillness. "I'll take you home," he said. "I have the car out front."

Presently Ellen got to her feet. "Yes, thanks. That would be fine."

Fergesson entered the display room and snapped off the television set. The sound had been on so low that only when he bent over the set did the faint tinny blare of it reach his ears. "Were you actually looking at that?" he asked.

"Not exactly. Just thinking." She moved toward the door and he followed after her, checking in his automatic way to see if Hadley had turned off all the sets before leaving. He unlocked the front door and stood aside as Ellen pushed through, out onto the frigid sidewalk.

"It's cold," Fergesson said as they got into the car. Ellen didn't answer. "Damn cold for June. I'll turn on the heater."

She nodded, and he did so. The motor came on with an even hum of power, and Fergesson backed carefully out into the deserted street.

"Will he be home?" he asked her as they turned onto Cedar Street.

"I suppose so. I don't really know." Ellen gazed calmly out the window at the dark shapes of houses and trees. "You and Alice have never had any children, have you?"

"No." He didn't elaborate; he had been kidded and sympathized with often enough. "My fault," he finally added. "According to the doctors."

"Would you like to have children?"

"Well," Fergesson said tightly, "I have my store. And my little flock to watch over."

They drove the rest of the way in silence.

Horace Wakefield, the following night, gratefully perceived the exact moment when six o'clock arrived. Released from servitude, Wakefield ran to the door of the flower shop, closed and locked it, turned off the outdoor neon, and hurried back to clear the counters for the night. In this, he had the help of little Jackie Perkins, the child-eyed girl who assisted him in such chores as making up corsages, giving change, wrapping potted plants, selling Ferry seeds, dusting the fixtures.

"Time to go home!" Wakefield began to cry thinly, rushing about the store in a travesty of efficiency. To the closet he hurried, got down his beaver-style coat, halted for a moment before the mirror to hold up his lower gum and examine the white sores on the soft underside, blew his nose in a Kleenex from his special box under the counter, briefly touched his hernia belt to be sure it hadn't crept up, and then clapped his hands together loudly.

"Let's go!" he bleated. "End of the day! End of the week! Time to go home, kiddies!"

The flower shop lay in a thick, heavy, sweetly scented fog steamed up by endless hot moist flowers. Jackie began carrying certain ones to the refrigerator for the night, a weak smile on her immature face, long thin fingers carefully gripped around her burden, yellow-red nails digging in like claws.

"You go ahead, Mister Wakefield," she said faintly. In her black skirt and gray turtleneck sweater, sandals on her feet and copper bracelets on her wrists, Jackie worked rapidly, happily, back and forth, lips pressed tightly together, a damp line of perspiration beading the faint down beneath her nose. "I'll lock up," she called.

"Thank you, Jackie," Horace Wakefield replied, with pleasure. He accepted the tribute to his position with grave dignity. "Yes, I'll go on. You have your key?"

Jackie indicated the tiny square of cloth at the end of the counter that was her purse. "I'll put the money away in the safe; I have to stick around for a while, anyhow. Bill is coming by at half past to drive me up to the City."

"Ah," Wakefield joked, grinning a knowing gold-toothed grin. "Going out tonight? Big doings?"

A lofty, superior look swept Jackie's face into a sneer of derision. "Big doings, but not the way *you* mean." She made it sound as if Wakefield's words had dripped coarse innuendo. "We're going to the symphony."

Ha-haing to himself, Wakefield good-naturedly bustled from the store and out onto the sidewalk. He waved gaily and crossed with the lights to the far side. At the mailbox he halted to drop in a handful of bills and cards, straightened his coat, lost his jolly leer, and continued, with an expression of dignity on his face, toward the Health Food Store.

It was closed, and the shade was pulled down. He rapped twice on the door, then a third quick tap with his knuckles. Lights gleamed under the door and he could hear the sound of people within. After a moment the key was turned and the door moved open just a crack.

"Good evening, Betty," Wakefield said solemnly.

"Come in, Horace," Betty said wearily. She locked the door after him and shuffled over to the counter. "Sit down anywhere. Do you want some tea?"

"Thank you," Wakefield said as he seated himself at the counter. Tea was poured for him from a glittering Chinese pot into a fragile cup so tiny that Wakefield had trouble getting hold of the handle. The tea was dark amber; rich vapors drifted up and tickled his nose. A thick, exotic, Oriental tea.

"Sugar?" Betty groaned. "Lemon?"

Wakefield sipped the tea. "Just right, Betty."

There were others sitting at the counter and at the tables, with their fragile teacups. Mostly women; he was almost the only man. Eight or nine of them, smartly dressed, chatting quietly among themselves. Tension crackled in the air: they were waiting expectantly for eight o'clock, the lecture hour. Posters of Theodore Beckheim hung above the counter. Society books and tracts were on display by the cash register. Free pamphlets, copies of the *People's Watchman* . . . The central poster in the window had been reinforced by small informational displays. Theodore Beckheim seemed to be all around the store, in every corner and alcove.

Wakefield did not specifically object to this invasion of his privacy, but the tension of the women annoyed him. He could tolerate the looming, dark features of Beckheim gazing significantly at him from every part of the store, but he could not bear the unending excited mutter from dry female throats. Normally, the Health Food Store was vacant at this hour; it was after closing and only the employees and a privileged few were supposed to be allowed behind the door. Tonight, a horde perched around him, spoiling his dinner, turning what was customarily a personal ritual into a public spectacle. He resented it. He wished they would leave; hadn't he come here every night for ten years, eaten his dinner in the dark quiet of the locked-up store?

"Good evening," the woman next to him said, in a harsh, dry rasp.

Wakefield winced, and glanced furtively around at her. She was tall, white-haired, a stern woman in her middle fifties. Her feverish eyes snapped; her thin lips twisted. She raised her cup of tea as if in toast. Wakefield was embarrassed; he turned angrily away and concentrated on the marzipan display above his head. "Evening," he muttered apprehensively.

"You manage the flower shop," the woman stated. "You've been there thirteen years."

"Fourteen," Wakefield corrected. The woman made him uncomfortable. She was quite tall; hard-featured like a bird of prey; pebbled yellow skin and tangled brows. Her mane of white hair was coarse and thick; it hung over her ears and neck like an old man's. Her cheeks were sunken; her dark, unpleasant face burned with a fiery inner fever that made Wakefield think of TB patients.

"Mrs. Krafft eats no meat," Betty said. Addressing the white-haired woman she said: "You and Mister Wakefield should get to know each other."

Wakefield's mouth opened slightly; he was suddenly interested. His annoyance vanished and he turned eagerly to face Mrs. Krafft. "Is that right? You don't care for meat?"

The feverish glow of the woman's face increased. "I care for meat," she cried. "But I can't eat the flesh of higher creatures who have as much right to live as any human being. In certain respects I admire higher animals more than man. Their ability to bear suffering without complaint and their natural dignity, their nobility and freedom from carnal vulgarity—"

"Yes," Wakefield agreed. A flush crossed his own small face; he was embarrassed and pleased, and his hands began to twitch. Words came with difficulty; tides of emotion swept up in his throat and made him cough and turn apologetically away. He removed his steel-rimmed glasses and polished them shakily with his pocket handkerchief. "Yes, I know what you mean," he managed. "It's a moral issue." He replaced his glasses on his nose. "Fat's unclean. Unhealthy. Every time I see a meat market I think of the city dump, decaying meat and tin cans and rotting garbage." He broke off. "I can't stand the sight of meat."

"Have you ever looked in their eyes?" Mrs. Krafft said.

"Beg pardon?"

"When I was a child on the farm my father killed cattle. He hit them on the head with an ax and cut their throats. I had to hold the bowl. As they died I saw into their eyes."

"Yes," Wakefield agreed vaguely. "Their eyes. Terrible thing."

"When I see some of the people walking around—worse than any jungle beast." Mrs. Krafft's voice rose shrilly. "*Pigs!* Obscene creatures that ought to be put away. No dumb animal could sink to the depths of viciousness and brutality of man. Man is the cruelest animal, the wickedest animal. The only really disgusting animal. You see them with their big cigars, spitting and laughing and slapping each other on the back. Telling dirty jokes and belching and swilling down their beer and fried oysters." She managed to control herself with difficulty. "When I'm taking dictation at conferences sometimes they start laughing and joking with each other. Coarse, bestial creatures . . ." On her thin, feverish face gleamed a lifetime of resentment. Mrs. Krafft had clearly suffered at the hands of men, degraded to a second-class citizen, forced to creep about in the shadows.

But there was more to it than that. Mrs. Krafft, he realized, was reacting to the vulgarity of the world as was he; both had come to the Watchmen Society to escape cruelty and viciousness, to enter into an environment of spirituality. He thought of it as a venal, corrupt society; but being a woman, Mrs. Krafft identified it with *men*. He wondered which of them was right. If it was men, then Horace Wakefield carried the taint. It was all right for a woman to feel that way, but if *he* listened to that philosophy . . .

Suppose a man did revolt at vulgarity and coarseness, at animal passions . . . and saw those not in society around him, but in his own masculine nature. What then? The revulsion would be for one's self; the struggle would be internal. Where would a man go? What would become of him? Driven across the face of the world, wandering restlessly, tormented, hating his own nature; his lower parts, as it were.

Wakefield considered his own lower parts and saw nothing there but pale pink skin, the same as the rest of him. He had no lower parts: it was all right. He relaxed and sighed. Horace Wakefield had but one nature, and that nature was pure.

He finished his Chinese tea and pushed the fragile cup away. "Very tasty," he said to Betty.

"How long have you been in the Movement?" Mrs. Krafft asked him fiercely.

"I heard Theodore Beckheim speak late last fall, when I was down in Los Angeles," Wakefield answered, examing his carefully manicured nails. "I believe the Movement originated in that area."

Mrs. Krafft caught her breath and was engulfed by emotion. "Los Angeles! You heard the Los Angeles speech? I'd give ten years off my life to have been there." Her voice rose to transcendental levels. "That was when he cured the girl of paralysis. He had her up on the stage. That was when he was just beginning to understand his power of healing."

"Oh," Wakefield agreed, "that was in the early days. We were just beginning. I mean, it was just healing then. We hadn't found God." He added: "We've worked up from there. In those days Mister Beckheim was a practitioner." Mention of Los Angeles recalled to him all the old aspects of the Movement: the magnetic belt which he himself had purchased and worn, the special radioactive waters in which he himself had bathed, Beckheim passing his vast hands over the naked bodies of children to cure them of various catarrhs and hay fevers. "It was just bodies then. Now we know the body is nothing." In Wakefield's mind there was a dim fog when it came to thinking about bodies. "It's the soul that counts."

"Exactly," Mrs. Krafft agreed. "Disease is a manifestation of improper mental attitudes."

Wakefield didn't know about that. "Well now, I suppose in a way you're right," he murmured grudgingly. "But it's always seemed to me that disease is the result of improper diet, although I suppose a person with the wrong mental attitude would eat the wrong food. But it seems to me that it's what you put into your stomach that determines your mental attitude; do you see what I mean? You are what you eat, do you see? Eating meat causes bestial attitudes—eating fruit and clean vegetables purifies the mind. It seems to me, and of course I might be wrong, but it seems to me that states of consciousness are the result of diet."

Mrs. Krafft couldn't go along with that. "I agree with you about meat, of course. But I don't recall having had any coarse thoughts in my childhood, when I still ate meat. It's the killing of animals—nobody with a pure mind could destroy a helpless animal. When we've brought real purity to mankind there won't be any slaughtering of dumb animals. Murder, hate, disease, will be wiped from the earth. They're all the same thing, anyhow."

Wakefield fooled with his empty teacup. "Do you think," he said slowly, "that the Movement will ever reach all mankind?"

Mrs. Krafft was shocked. "The Movement's getting larger every day! Why, we're all over the world; look how we've grown since the days back in Los Angeles. You remember that—just the one building, and only a few thousand followers, and almost no funds. Now look at us . . . every country in the world, branches and offices, publications, followers everywhere, except in the Communist world, of course."

"That's what I mean," Wakefield said thoughtfully. "You've hit it, Mrs. Krafft. The Communist world. It's a big world . . . there're a lot of people who believe in that stuff."

"They deny God!"

"Yes," Wakefield agreed. "They deny the soul—they deny God and everything spiritual. Don't you think it's the same old thing? God against Mammon . . . They're meat eaters, Mrs. Krafft. Every time I see a picture of Stalin I look him square in the eye and I say: You're a meat eater, Joseph. You're big and heavy and you're full of rotting meat. Now, that was one thing I'll say for Adolf Hitler. He was a vegetarian, Mrs. Krafft; did you know that? Adolf Hitler may have done a lot of wrong things in his life—he was too wild and excitable, I think—but he never touched meat or liquor. I have to say that about him; give the devil his dues, I always say."

Mrs. Krafft learned close to Horace Wakefield. "Do you know why they all set on Germany and destroyed her?"

"Well," Wakefield began.

"Because," Mrs. Krafft snapped, "she was going to set up a clean new world. England saw the handwriting on the wall—it was England, you know. Shopkeepers—that's what Napoleon called them. And he was right! Money, trade—" She leaned even closer to Wakefield. "I don't know if you know this, but there's Jewish blood in the royal family."

"Eh?" Wakefield said.

"I'll tell you how it got there. *Disraeli*. He and Queen Victoria." Mrs. Krafft nodded. "And it's been since then—they used to have a soul. Back in the days of William Shakespeare. But not anymore. Now they're shopkeepers, Mister Wakefield. And you know why."

"Well," Wakefield said, unconvinced, "I don't see how I can approve of all that violence. I don't think people should go out and kill other people." Down in the little man's core was a positive horror of violence. "Those

Northern people sometimes do that. I remember a Finn, a janitor living down in the basement of an apartment building I once lived in—although I'm certainly not living there, now. One day he went completely out of his mind. . . . Let me tell you, he took that wife of his and just cut her up terribly. It was the most awful thing in the world. . . . They called the police and ambulance, but"—Wakefield made a gesture—"it was too late. Why, he just cut open that woman like you would butcher a hog. That's the way those Northerners are. Berserkers, they call them." Tautly, he finished: "Underneath their nice blue eyes and blond hair there's something ugly. Something that frightens me. They look so pleasant, but sooner or later it comes out. . . . It boils over and destroys and breaks and tears down."

Mrs. Krafft was not paying much attention. "Germany had spirituality!" she cried indignantly. "Her music—Bach, Beethoven, Schubert—we have nothing like that here. Great painters, artists, poets, scholars. Germany was the soul of Europe, Mister Wakefield. And they killed her, the way they always kill those with souls. They can't stand those with souls—it reminds them of their own bestiality. When Germany died, a light went out. And the darkness has been creeping in since." She brooded. "I'll tell you this, Mister Wakefield. We must reach all mankind. We must bring them warning, so they can save themselves. When the Great Battle begins, we're going to need all the help we can get. It's going to be a terrible ordeal."

For a time neither of them spoke. Then Wakefield asked uncertainly: "Do you think the struggle between the free world and Communism is—the Great Battle? I mean, are we seeing Armageddon already? There's some difference of opinion about this in the Movement. I know some feel we're fighting it now, when we fight Asiatic Communistic atheism. But there're others who feel that we're just as materialistic and guilty as the Russians."

"We're contaminated," Mrs. Krafft said furiously. "America has got to go, too. The purification of the world can't begin until the war levels everything. I tell you, Mister Wakefield, I'm looking forward to this war! When the bombs begin to fall on the cities of men, when the walls begin to fall everywhere, the way they're falling now in Korea—I know that's the *rain*. The same rain that fell on the ancient world. . . . And there will be those who'll be saved, as Noah was saved. And the Lord is speaking to us now, telling us to come and save ourselves, speaking to us through this man—" She jerked savagely at the picture of Theodore Beckheim on the wall above their heads. "It will be through him that we'll be saved. And the world will be scorched clean and pure by the sacred holy fire of God. And all the pestholes of iniquity, all the marketplaces, the slaughterhouses, the cities, the buildings, all the works that vain man has built up, his puny attempts to govern himself—"

"That's so," Wakefield agreed nervously, wishing she wouldn't shout. "The League of Nations failed, and the UN is going to fail the same way."

"Man can't govern himself! Man is too sin-ridden, too corrupt!" Her voice soared excitedly. "Man denied God—man stood up to God and said: I can take care of myself. And now we're paying the price! It's scientists who've got us where we are, tampering with the universe. Scientists with their bombs—science is the devil's way. They and their A-bombs and bacteriological warfare. It's God's judgment!"

Wakefield winced at the shower of saliva and words that poured from Mrs. Krafft's impassioned mouth. "Yes," he muttered, and edged away. It was easy to sense the deep forces rumbling inside the white-haired woman, and they made him uneasy. All the women in the Health Food Store were that way, all except Betty, who never got excited about anything, except the time the toilet drain leaked all over the drums of dried apricots down in the basement. The whole room buzzed with suppressed emotion; to Wakefield it was like twenty radios dinning in his ear at once. He thought of his room, his quiet little combination bedroom and living room. His piano, his books, and his easy chair. His old-fashioned lamp and slippers. In his microscopic kitchen he could fix himself a bowl of soup and some soy fritters. Potatoes and fresh string beans. Perhaps some stewed prunes for dessert. He didn't have to eat at the Health Food Store; all at once he wanted terribly to get away.

"Good evening," he muttered hurriedly, and got to his feet. "Thanks for the tea, Betty."

"You're going?" Mrs. Krafft demanded in astonishment.

"Home," Wakefield muttered. "Things to do. Fix dinner. Company coming later. Glad to have met you."

"You're not going to go hear *him*?" Mrs. Krafft was incredulous. Several other ladies had ceased chattering and sat blinking in amazement at Wakefield as he stood indecisively at the door. "We'll all be going down together—can't you wait?"

He *did* want to hear Theodore Beckheim again. But it would be well over an hour. How could he sit there with Mrs. Krafft, feeling the tension of her body, hearing the roaring undercurrents of her pent-up hates? It was bad enough eating lunch there; at least he had his table in the back where nobody bothered him. Why couldn't Theodore Beckheim visit him in his own little room, all by himself?

"You have to wait," Mrs. Krafft said authoritatively. "You can't go."

"You sit down and wait," Betty wheezed. "We're all going over to the hall together in Mrs. Krafft's car."

"But I'm hungry," Wakefield complained peevishly, feeling caught and helpless. "I still haven't had my dinner."

"We'll fix your dinner right now," Betty said. "Lulu!" she shouted."Come out here and find out what Mister Wakefield wants for his dinner."

Wakefield pawed his coat pocket anxiously. Did he have his knife and fork with him? He pulled the little leather and velvet case out and snapped it open. There they were, the two gleaming-clean shafts of silver. "Could I eat in the back?" he asked nervously. "I hate to eat out here with everybody."

"Fix up the back table for Mister Wakefield," Betty said to the tall brown-eyed colored woman who had emerged dutifully from the back, hands dripping with dishwater. "Clear it off and get him his chair."

"There's rice and cheese sauce with egg and tomato, macaroni salad and sliced bananas with cream," Lulu announced. With a swirl of her heavy skirt she again disappeared into the back through the dusty yellow curtains. Wakefield hesitated, then followed anxiously after her.

He had hardly seated himself at the big wood table and was setting out his knife and fork, when Mrs. Krafft appeared.

"I'll sit with you while you eat," Mrs. Krafft announced, seating herself across from him. As Lulu methodically began getting out the food, Mrs. Krafft sucked in deep lungfuls of baked oven air. "Ah," she said. Her sharp, alert eyes fixed themselves on Wakefield. "This place radiates peace," she stated suddenly.

Wakefield nodded and muttered something, too dazed by misfortune to speak.

"It radiates peace," Mrs. Krafft repeated. She gazed up at a display of pills for diabetes, high blood pressure, bottles of dark liquid for ulcers, varicose veins, special sugar-free cookies and pale dried honey, vitamin capsules, packages of cracked wheat and bran. "There's a fullness about it. A completeness. There is no out-of-balance here. This store is wholly realized."

Wakefield waited miserably for his cheese and rice and wished she'd leave.

He had seen them in there. He had gone past the door, caught the blur of female motion, heard the sharp shrill sounds, and continued on past. Behind the fruit and date display he saw a brief glimpse of Horace Wakefield sitting in the middle of them, teacup in his diffident fingers, dabbing daintily at his lips with a paper napkin.

Now Stuart Hadley sat at the drug counter across the street, arms folded in front of him, a Coke glass of ice water by his elbow, a menu lying on its face. He gazed sightlessly at the moist counter, waiting for the memory and impressions of the Health Food Store to fade. Here and there a few patrons crouched over their hot beef sandwiches, coffee, apple pie à la mode. Behind the counter the pretty little dark-haired waitress, pert and busy in her starched white uniform, hurried to complete his ham and cheese sandwich.

The drugstore was dully noisy with cash register sounds, people's voices, the coming and going of middle-class women buying Alka-Seltzer, Bayer aspirin, mineral oil, chewing gum, magazines. Down the counter from him a heavyset man in a black leather jacket was reading the comic section of the *San Francisco Examiner*.

Stuart Hadley brooded. How could he go there? Into a place like that, among people like that. . . . The word came up in his mouth like sickness from his stomach. *Cranks*. All of them, cranks and crackpots—nuts. He couldn't play games with himself: that was what they were, and if he went in there and sat and listened to the lecture, he would be a crank, too.

A young blond-haired man in a clean-cut blue suit: that was Stuart Hadley. Personable, likable, friendly, social—a good mixer. A good salesman. A good husband. A man who kept his shoes shined, his trousers pressed, his chin shaved, his armpits rubbed with aluminum sulfate. A man who looked good and smelled good, a man who could walk into the Top of the Mark and be speedily served.

Not a wild-eyed madman with a flowing beard, sandals, straw in his hair, and a sign grasped, reading:

JESUS SAVES

He couldn't imagine himself apart from his shirts and cuffs and single-breasted light-colored suits. He couldn't picture himself independent from his closet and dresser drawers, his jar of Arrid, his Wildroot cream oil, his Dyanshine shoe polish. And yet, there had to be something more to Stuart Hadley than *that*; surely there was a core, a center, beyond the bottles and clothes, beyond what was reflected by his shaving mirror perched on top of the dresser.

Could that core, the inner Stuart Hadley, be as crazy as Horace Wakefield? Inside the shell of affability, was there a demented, unstable entity, aching to come creeping out, a furious wailing larva struggling to emerge and crawl around, slimy and odd, not human, not ordinary, not pretty?

There was nothing pretty about the Health Food Store.

There was nothing attractive about Horace Wakefield with his hernia belt, Kleenex, and glasses. In his withered face, in the dead-fish eyes of the little prunelike people, there was a musty, stale, unhealthy fuzz. A stench of illness hung over them, not the usual kind, but a deeper illness. The Wakefields were a public sidewalk, sneezed on, spat on; there was a dried layer of filth over them that was so old it no longer could be identified as filth. It looked more like wax. Like varnish. Wakefield's small face was carefully varnished with offal; behind it he grinned and talked and went about his business. He had polished it until it shone: he was proud.

Conjuring up the image of Wakefield made Hadley feel uncomfortable, as if he had given birth to Wakefield from his own body, out of his own mind. All at once he wished he could crack open the polished, brittle shell that was Horace Wakefield; a quick fantasy momentarily held him, a vision of the little head splitting open like a dried seedpod, and Wakefield's brains scattering in tiny dry fragments, blown here and there by the wind. Perhaps to grow and take root all over again, in some dark, slimy place, where there was moisture and silence for nourishment. A race of Wakefields, growing up from the nocturnal soil, like mushrooms.

His fantasy surprised him; how could he consider hitting a harmless little crank? He imagined Horace Wakefield flying apart at the first touch, glasses going one way, perhaps his whole head, his legs and hernia belt another. Horace Wakefield was the sickly inner portion of his own mind, and he imagined himself stamping and jumping on the withered dried-up body until there was nothing left of it. The way, as a child in Washington, he had trod again and again on puffballs growing in the dirty open fields.

Shame touched him, and collapsed his fantasy. Without meaning to, he had recalled an event of his early childhood; now he sought to return it to the hidden parts of his mind, where he would not have to think of it or entertain its existence.

There he was, a child, a boy of five, scampering through the yellow sludge and ice of an eastern winter. Dressed in red mittens, knickers, rubbers, a stocking wool cap yanked down over his ears. What was he doing? Grimly, intently, he was chasing a little girl, a child's hoe gripped between his hands. As he ran he slashed violently at her; the girl wailed and screamed as the two of them raced across the open field between the grammar-school building and the gym. Halfway there—the memory of it refused to depart— he savagely brought the hoe down on the child's head. The child, with a shriek, fell face-forward on the frozen gravel; at that, Stuart Hadley turned and scampered back the way he had come, drained of hostility.

It seemed doubtful that he could have done such a thing. Something, perhaps, the girl had said; some reference to his stutter. As a child he had stuttered; it had been impossible for him to get out the thoughts and feelings that choked his throat. Laughing, poking fun at him . . . she deserved what she got. Only, he had spent the next six months in a special school operated by the city, for problem children.

"Say, you're asleep."

Hadley grunted and glanced up.

"Here's your sandwich and Coke." The counter girl, laughing and amused, pushed the plate in front of him. "Wake up."

"Thanks," Hadley said. He came gratefully back to the present. "Thanks a lot."

The girl lingered, coy, innocent, cheeks warm with joking intimacy. "What's your wife say about you sitting here? Don't she fix your dinner?"

On Hadley's left hand was the gold band of his wedding ring. He rubbed it self-conciously. "She's sick tonight."

"I bet," the girl said, leaning against the counter. "Don't kid me," she said. "I'll bet you're going out," she said. "This is Saturday night."

Hadley ate his sandwich, Coke, plate of greasy potato chips. He pushed them into his mouth listlessly, eyes blank with thought, seeing only a vague white-cotton shape where the girl stood. Here he was, passing away the time until the lecture started. Wandering around aimlessly by himself, without Ellen, killing two hours until time to head for the Watchmen Hall with the rest of them, the Wakefields and the shrill overdressed women.

Why did the wealthy middle-aged women appear? What interested them? Wherever a movement of this kind arose, there came the fat old women with their money and leisure. Paying for, providing meeting places for, pulling wires for, listening to, whatever was done and said. Didn't they have anything else in their lives? With their big homes, Chryslers, clothes, money, were they still unsatisfied?

It was a mystery.

Yet, it explained something. The wealthy old women were not the same as Horace Wakefield; the withered flower clerk lived in a single rented room with a tiny kitchen, a sterile, neat little cell where no bird sang and no warmth stirred the barren carpets and walls. The Movement drew different types: it drew fretful old women and impotent clerks; and he had seen solemn Negro faces row after row. What did sturdy Negro shapes have in common with the thickly perfumed old women? Laborers and their wives; he had seen them, too. And young people—a handful of skinny devout kids, overflow from Youth for Christ. Fervent teenage fanatics.

And himself.

Gloom descended over him again. For a brief moment he had thought his real self was revealed, trapped as it rose to the surface. Disgusting as it was, shoddy and terrible, it was the real Stuart Hadley: another Wakefield. He had been revolted, thinking of himself as another dour-faced clerk with a hernia belt and a private box of Kleenex . . . but at least he was located. Now that was gone. Again he was lost: Stuart Hadley was going to hear Beckheim speak, but that did not tell him who or what Stuart Hadley was.

He might be a crank. Or he might not.

"Anything more?" the girl asked him as he pushed away his plate. "Dessert? Ice cream? I bet your wife fixes you your dinner every night and darns your socks and tucks you into bed at night. You're so helpless. . . . You spilled your water all over the counter." Wistfully she added: "That's sixty-five cents. You can have more coffee if you want; refills are free."

He paid and left the drugstore.

The evening streets were cool and dim. Lonely. Hands in his pockets, he headed toward the hall, past the bright, modern stores of the downtown business section. He continued on, toward the Southern Pacific tracks that neatly divided the newer, more prosperous town from the older slums that had been Cedar Groves fifty years ago.

A commuter train from San Francisco was spilling out steam and weary trails of hunched-over businessmen in long coats. Their wives greeted them and hurried to drive them home to dinner and bed. Beyond the train tracks hulked warehouses and factories. Traffic slowed down as it felt its way along the twisting, narrow streets. Negro toughs lounged in front of yellow hole-in-the-wall grocery stores. Tiny wooden shops, dirty and ill-kept. Fat Negro women strolled by with bulging sacks of groceries. Then the slum business section: pool halls, cheap hotels, shoeshine parlors, run-down bars, dirty cleaning establishments, and a filthy garage with a field of rusted, ruined auto wrecks beside it.

Here the poor lived, while not more than half a mile back, modern dress shops, barbershops, jewelry and floral shops glittered swankly along El Camino Real. Here there was nothing but ramshackle old yellow-board tenements, ancient rubbish heaps left over from the turn of the century. Relics that had survived the earthquake. Trash and debris were strewn along the sidewalks and gutters; bits of the tottering buildings that had flaked loose and blown away.

Groups of dull-faced men drifted aimlessly around, hands in their pockets, eyes blank and empty. Slick-haired Negro girls swayed and minced past. Workmen in jeans, gripping lunch pails and folded newspapers, tramped wearily home. Dirty crumpled cars let tired-faced Irishmen and Italians and Poles off in front of their crowded yellow tenement buildings, stale with the reek of cabbage and urine, narrow hallways of dusty carpets and deformed potted plants.

Stuart Hadley wandered through the thickening night gloom, dully aware of neon signs flickering on here and there, the push and jostle of tired people. He still had an hour to go. His stomach turned over queasily from the potato chips. His head ached. The thought of going home entered his mind. For a time he worried the thought, chewed at it, turned it around; finally he rejected it.

The feeble glimmer of a red neon attracted him. A bar. He plunged into its somber darkness and felt his way by touch, past the bar, to the phone booth in the back. With the door pulled shut after him, he dialed his home.

"Hello," Ellen said expressionlessly.

Hadley licked his lips. "How—are you?"

"Fine."

"Still mad at me?"

"I wasn't mad at you." She seemed a long way off: remote, detached, tired. "Wait a minute while I go turn down the TV." The phone was mute for a while. Presently a thump, and Ellen continued: "Where are you calling from?"

"A drugstore," Hadley answered.

"Have you had anything to eat?"

He explained what he had eaten. "Ellen—if you want, I'll come home. I won't go to this thing."

"Of course I *want*!" Her voice broke with melancholy. Presently she finished: "Go ahead, go to it. When is it over?"

"I don't know. Around eleven, I guess."

"Are you alone?"

"Sure." He was puzzled. "Who would I be with?"

"I don't know. Anybody, I suppose." She seemed to be drifting farther and farther away from the phone. "You always seem to be able to find somebody."

Hadley was silent. There was little he could say; a continuation of the old argument lay ahead, nothing more. "Well," he said, "I'll see you later."

No answer.

"I mean," he said awkwardly, "I'll be home, soon. After the lecture. Is there anything you want? Something I can pick up?"

Ellen laughed metallically, and hung up the phone.

Face flushed scarlet, Hadley left the booth and headed for the bar. He crawled onto a stool, ears red with outrage and shame. His hands were shaking; he clamped them together furiously, bit his lower lip, waited for his blood pressure to drain back to normal. The little bitch—he choked the thoughts off. The big bulging heap of a bitch, hanging up on him. Hatred, fury, flooded over him in waves. Wildly, he wanted to run home and smash her in the face.

Turn her smart, disrespectful features into a pudding of mashed bone and shredded flesh. He wanted to leap on her, up and down, crush her bones like boxwood. He wanted to kick her skull from wall to wall of the apartment.

"What'll it be, Mac?" the bartender asked.

He roused himself and ordered bourbon and water. There were other men at the bar, most of them dull-eyed workmen. Paying for his drink, he sat sipping it, gripping the glass and gazing straight ahead, aware of the quiver of his mouth and the fog of constriction in his bronchial tubes.

It wasn't until the bartender came back with his dice cup that he realized he had already gulped down his drink.

"Shake you for the next one," the bartender said, tensely waving off a fly that crept in the pool of spilled water on the surface of the bar. Dice bounced out and lay on the wet, corroded wood. "Six," the bartender grated. "Come on, you motherfucker." His face distorted with furious concentration, he rattled the box and hurled the dice again. "Four!" Flushing beet red, his hands shaking, he collected the dice. "I'll be dipped in piss!" His voice rose with hysteria. "Come on, you —— —— —— ——!"

In spite of himself Hadley roared. A couple of workmen laughed, too. Instantly, the bartender froze, body rigid, and glared up at Hadley with demoniac hostility. "What's the matter with you?"

"Sorry," Hadley said. But he was still laughing. "You take it so seriously."

The bartender's lips worked. "I'll get it. No goddamn dice are going to beat me." He slammed the dice down. Seven showed; he was out. Gradually the crimson fury drained away. The man's face sagged, gray and defeated. With numb fingers he gathered up the dice and aimlessly shoved the box and its contents aside. "What do you want? You want another bourbon?"

Around the bar the workmen grinned, nudged each other. "Hey, Harry," one said, "want to roll against me?"

"Go on, Harry," another urged. "We'll all take you on."

The bartender's eyes flashed fire. "Get away from me, you bunch of —— —— ——," he snarled. "I'm not rolling with anybody."

Hadley's bourbon and water came, his free drink. One of the workmen raised his beer, and Hadley tilted his glass toward him.

This time he drank more slowly. Behind the bar, the bartender crouched in a sullen, brooding heap, mulling over his loss, his inability to control the dice. Hadley was still amused; the spectacle of the man taking a trivial thing so seriously was absurd.

It made him wonder about himself. Restlessly, he remembered the lecture. Gradually his thoughts reverted to their usual path. But it was not the same as before: he was sipping a free drink. Something about getting a free drink in a strange bar made him feel comfortable, as if the regular laws of the universe could be suspended. Things weren't completely bad . . . not with such exceptions.

He examined his wristwatch. How much longer did he have to wait? Forty-five minutes. He gulped convulsively at his drink, pawed for his cigarettes, and prepared himself to wait it out.

He arrived at the hall early. The lecture hadn't begun; only a quarter of the seats were filled. Quiet, unmoving shapes sat here and there, murmuring together in low voices.

At the inner entrance a colored woman handed him a square of paper. Like a chunk of dark wood, her rough-cut head turned slightly after him, brown eyes calm and large, liquid curiosity as mild and harmless as a nun's. When he had gone by a step or two she called after him: "Evening, friend Watcher. You early."

He didn't know if she was amused by his distraught, hurried appearance. He didn't especially care. "Evening," he answered briefly. With the scrap of crude paper clutched, he disappeared down the aisle, among the empty seats and echoing spaces. At random, he located himself, slid from his coat, and made himself breathlessly comfortable. Already, his heart was beginning to labor heavily, rapidly.

Excitement shivered up and down him: the taut thrill he had felt as a child going to the kiddies' matinee at the Rivoli Theater, twelve thirty in the afternoon, surrounded by hundreds of reverent replicas of himself. It was too early for the muttering talk to fade to an awed, expectant silence. Around him, vibrant murmurs drifted back and forth; people peered around for friends, some of them half rising to their feet. Every emotion showed; some of the people were solemn, some amused, sheepish, vacant-eyed, aloof, a variety of people and expressions. Tonight, he could see, there was not the same packed crowd. The curious had come and gone. The faithful were numerous but not numerous enough to fill the hall. It was made for the future: it anticipated.

Now he held the square of coarse paper up to the light and studied its black print. A throwaway, the kind handed out on street corners. He assimilated it briefly, then crumpled it and wadded it onto the floor.

ARE YOU READY FOR ARMAGEDDON?

Bible tells end of the world
soon to come. Prophecies to

be fulfilled. Fire and flood
to cleanse world. "For he is
like a refiner's fire." . . . .
"For the first heaven and the
first earth were passed away."
Subscribe to the PEOPLE'S
WATCHMAN two dollars a year
425 Berry Avenue Chicago, Ill.

The cheap, blatant notice filled him with disgust. He looked around; nobody seemed to be reading literature of any kind. The notices had been accepted and then discarded like a commercial announcement. That cheered him, and he lit a cigarette. Gradually people were trickling into the hall. A family, with much noise and scraping of chairs, sat down in front of him. To his right a handful of powerfully built Negroes sat in a stern bunch, eyes fixed directly ahead of them. Old women were scattered here and there, by ones and by twos. Presently a young woman, thin-faced and nervous, plucked for a seat to his left. She set down her purse and quickly shook off her coat.

The hall was becoming stuffy and hot. Fans worked creakily in the depths. Smoke from cigarettes drifted laboriously upward; Hadley loosened his collar and took deep, impatient breaths. It was an ordeal, waiting. It seemed as if he had been waiting all his life. More and more people were appearing, sliding down the aisles and into seats, noiselessly finding themselves places, inexorably filling up the hall.

Hadley sat up straight and glared fitfully in all directions, at the many people, at the doors behind him, at the rafters above, at the platform. American flags fluttered heavily at each end of it. Behind, nailed to the wall, was an emblem he didn't recognize. A sphere, half white and half black: the black curled up into the white at one side and the white groped into the black at the other. The effect was of motion, as if the sphere were a turning wheel. It was dynamic, but complete. There was a certain satisfying quality to it. He gazed at it for a while and some of his tension drained out and vanished.

While he was gazing sleepily at the emblem, Theodore Beckheim came into the hall.

A presence was felt. At first there was no physical sight, only the sudden rush of awareness from the people. Hadley, startled, blinked and looked quickly around. The hall was not yet full; was Beckheim going to begin already? He glanced at his wristwatch and was shocked: it was already eight. A rustle, a murmur, swept from aisle to aisle; he peered everywhere, but still no physical entity was visible. Was Beckheim a bird, a swallow? Was he swooping up in the smoky rafters? Was he a moth, a ghost, a swirl of wind? The hall lights dimmed. An ominous black mist drifted over everything, a chilling cloud from some distant place, beyond the world, beyond the universe itself. The lights turned from yellow to a sickly red and then died entirely.

Hadley fought down a shriek as the vast, gloomy chamber hushed itself around him. He felt lifted by the tongue of a great sea, suspended briefly over an endless, limitless pocket. Alone, floundering by himself, he struggled frantically to touch something in the darkness around him. An electric instant followed, in which nothing happened, in which nothing moved or lived. And then Theodore Beckheim appeared on the platform, and the empty void was broken.

The effect was magical. The terror drained out of Hadley and he was left limp. He trembled from head to foot as the giant figure stepped up to the microphone. All around the hall people were shuddering as Hadley shuddered; a collective gasp, almost a wail, cut through the silence.

Beckheim was huge. He towered over those near him, an immense column of a man who rested his square hands on the edge of the oak podium and leaned forward to examine the rows of people beneath him. His forehead was flat and deeply wrinkled, careworn, a face like ancient metal, deepset brooding eyes sunk deep in his heavy skull. His lips were full and dark. His skin was a weathered gray-brown. His ears were small and set close to his head. His hair was short and black. His chin jutted, blunt and massive. He was definitely a Negro.

Beckheim surveyed the rows of people with a thoughtful, almost unhappy expression. There was wise understanding in his face, and at the same time an unspoken reprimand. Each person, sitting there in the hall, felt small and a little unclean and strangely uncertain of himself and his habits. As the eyes of the huge man touched on them, the rows of people drew back guiltily, ashamed and suddenly conscious of their imperfections. They were glad when the eyes had passed; but their confidence did not wholly return.

"I am glad," Theodore Beckheim said, in a low, tense voice, "of the chance to talk to you people. If you will sit quietly and listen, I have some things to tell you that will be of importance in your lives."

Beckheim had begun without preamble, without any pretense of convention or formality. His voice was low and hard and full of authority. A blunt voice that rumbled through the hall, stern and inflexible; almost monotonous. It jarred Hadley's bones; something of it got in his brain and ears and danced metallically until he could hardly stand the pressure. He put his hands over his ears but the sound came through anyhow, transmitted by the floor and the chair and the bodies of the people around him. The whole hall and everybody in it were a sounding board on which the ponderous vibrations of the man's voice played.

"You are living," he told them, "in a unique time. Often before it was believed this time had come. Again and again perceptive men imagined the time had arrived, but always they were wrong. Finally a sense arose that the time was a myth. It had been predicted, it had failed, it would always fail.

"In the past, the most learned men had ideas which today we recognize as fantastic. To these men, the ideas seemed natural and sound. They believed the world was flat, that it occupied most of the universe, that the sun moved, that hairs left in water became worms, that lead could become gold, that a man could be healed if certain words were said over his injury. One of the wrong things which men believed had to do with time. They were wrong about the size of the world, its shape, its origin, what made it up, and they were wrong about its age. They had no understanding of the immensity of the universe in any direction. These were men of religion and men of rational persuasion. It was part of their way of thinking to believe that there were only a few years behind them and only a few miles around them.

"This failure to understand the vastness of the universe, both spatially and mensurally, caused confusion. They knew the earth would end but they thought it would end in months or years. They knew only two thousand years behind them and they could not conceive that much ahead. To have told them the earth would last another two thousand years would have been to tell them that it would last forever. To them, two thousand years was the largest unity they understood. It was virtually infinity.

"Now we know that two thousand years is nothing, just as two thousand miles is nothing. There are great spaces and great energies in the universe, and therefore great periods of time, because it takes much time for a being the size of the universe to move. Just as we must divide the age of the prophets by twelve, because of a mistaken Hebrew noun, we must multiply the time units of the prophets by several thousand. Just as we know the universe was not made in seven days but in seven vast periods of perhaps billions of years in duration, so we must realize that the days of life anticipated by the prophets are really centuries.

"And the ancients believed in miracles. Among the other nonsense, they believed that when a natural law was suspended, God was revealed. Now we know that suspension of a natural law would be a denial of God, a demonstration that the universe is chaotic, capricious, chance. It would introduce a random element. It would not be a cosmos, and if there is to be a God there must be a cosmos. This confusion between things not explained—and there were many in those days—and things having no explanation led them to imagine that God worked in unnatural ways. That somehow God could create this vast universe and then reach down into it, supersede its laws, ignore its elaborate fabric, push it aside in His impatience.

"Today, we understand that God does not work against His physical manifestation: the universe. He works through the universe, and that means that we will never see a suspension of its laws. We will never see the heavens open and a giant hand burst through. These are images, figures of speech, poetic license. Let us look by all means; but let us understand that the heavens—that is, the sky itself—*are that hand,* and no other hand will appear in this life.

"The ancients did not understand that God was always among them, that it is impossible to imagine God *not* present. They had lived with God all their lives; God is present in every physical object—what they knew as a physical object was a spatial manifestation of Him. In every man, God is present in His actual form: as a moving spirit. The physical object is an expression of God: the mind of man *is* God—a part, a unit, of the total Spirit.

"Therefore, our forefathers failed to realize that the signs they anticipated would not be thrust magically into the framework of everyday life. The momentum of the universe is *itself* the process anticipated by the prophets. Not a sudden cessation of this process, but the direction of the process itself is the hand of God at work. And if we examine this so-called natural process, we will see everything that was predicted working itself to completion.

"We will see, from our present vantage point, unmistakable signs that the final events prophesied by the Bible are entering their last and most significant stages."

Stuart Hadley, listening to the deep, intense voice, realized suddenly that everyone in the hall was as caught up in the tide of sound as he was. Not the words, but the sheer *voice* had taken them over. And yet, Beckheim was not speaking nonsense. He was speaking wisdom. Or did it only seem like wisdom because Beckheim was speaking it?

Confused, bewildered, Hadley listened to what the great black man was telling him. The others in the hall were onlookers to a conversation between Beckheim and himself . . . so it seemed. Yet he knew it was an illusion. From this multitude, Beckheim could not possibly have picked him out, become aware of Stuart Hadley's specific presence. But Beckheim spoke with the low intensity of one man addressing another, an intimate quality that was free of histrionics and dramatic mannerisms. Beckheim was not trying to convince; he was revealing what he knew, what he had been witness to.

"It was their insight," Beckheim continued, "that the earth was not permanent. In this sense, we must understand that Heaven, rather than being a place spatially removed from earth, is actually the universe which will follow when our earth has been destroyed. We know, from the Bible, that after death, all souls wait for the Last Judgment, that their beings are in a state of suspension; that is, no time, during which there is no duration, no change for them.

"Heaven, rather than being *above,* is *ahead.* Heaven will be manifested here, not somewhere else. In essence, Heaven will be manifested everywhere; Hell itself, all regions which are not Heaven, will be swallowed up. It will not be meaningful to speak of Heaven's location, since there will be nothing else.

"The transition from our world to that which is coming will be marked by violent cataclysm. The transition will be a time of torment and vast upheaval. This is one of the signs by which the advent is known. This, more than anything else, was the key by which the ancients anticipated the Second Coming. They knew that before this first earth perished, vast forces of almost limitless dimension would be unleashed. They prepared themselves for that day; but in their lifetime, it did not come.

"In our lifetime the signs point to a more imminent appearance. We have entered the period in which preparation must be made, in which all men are witness to the convulsions of their world, in which every man must make his choice.

"This choice, which once seemed abstract and theoretical, almost philosophical, is now vivid and pressing. It cannot be avoided. Every atom of our world is aligning itself for the great struggle ahead; every inanimate particle of matter, without wit or conscience, is moving to one of the two sides.

"These witless particles, blown here and there by forces which utterly control them, have no choice. Their side is predetermined for them; they are helpless to alter in any respect whatsoever the final disposition that is made of them. A gun, in the gun rack of an armory, is totally helpless to prevent a soldier from grabbing it down and hurrying it out to battle. It is not free to complain, to prefer the other side, to change over, to swear allegiance to the foe. For it, the foe is whatever army faces it; for it, the friend is whoever grips its stock.

"But human beings are not witless particles. The spark of God is in every one of us. Like witless particles, we *can* be hurried willy-nilly from this side to that; we *can* allow ourselves to become instruments in the hands of whoever gives us a shove. *But we can also decide for ourselves;* each one of us has the moral capacity to make an individual decision. And once having made that decision, there is no power in this universe or in any other that can force us to change our stand.

"Consider what this means. It means that ultimately, even God cannot decide for you. The choice is in your hands; therefore, and this is crucial, you must answer for your choice. It will not suffice to plead that you made no choice: that in itself means, like the gun in the hands of the soldier, that you allowed yourself to be carried into battle by whoever grabbed you from the rack. In that case, you have made your choice, whether you will own up to it or not.

"This struggle which forms now on all sides of us will be total. It will involve every atom in the universe, every physical particle and every living being. Looking back into history, it is easy to see the progression toward this point. Total war was a concept unknown at the beginning of our lifetimes. Try to imagine what will be meant by the term a century from now—if there is still an earth a century from now. There will be war of such totality as to be beyond any present imagination. If you doubt this, I ask you to consider with what accuracy an ordinary citizen living in 1852 could have imagined the napalm and A-bombs of the last world war.

"When I say that we may have a century before us, I do not mean that I predict one way or another how much time is left. I don't know; no one knows. The lessons of the past are clear: it is not possible to predict, from our limited position, when future events will take place. Even exceptional insight will not give us exact information, the day, the month, the year. Do you understand what the prophets were? They were men gifted with this exceptional insight, this special sense, an ability to perceive future occurrences, to remember them as we remember events of the past. The impact of great things yet to come impinged on their minds. Everything they saw will come about; but these events were of such foreign and awesome nature that only by rendering them in elaborate poetic imagery could they translate them into the diction of the times, and represent the events to themselves.

"I ask you to picture a prophet of biblical days, a simple agrarian farmer, suddenly witness to the Korean War, with its planes and tanks, its huge guns, its battleships, its elaborate radar screens. How would he render this understandable to his own people? How would he make it understandable to *himself*? Picture yourself, then, suddenly witness to a world two thousand years from this date. You possess only the words, the terms, the concepts of the present; everything that you see must be rendered in those symbols.

"The final stages of the Great Battle may not arise for many centuries. We have still a puny concept of time and space; it may be thousands, even millions of years, before the total transformation has taken place. Perhaps it will be gradual—perhaps abrupt. For us that does not matter. For us only one thing is important: the polarization into sides is, in our time, visible. That is sufficient. Not that the battle is close or far ahead—*but that the sides are being drawn:* that is the thing we must pay attention to. That is what concerns us. The two hosts are drawing themselves up in clear and unmistakable fashion."

Gazing out across his audience, the great black man told them:

"No living man can hide his head and pretend the formations of these legions do not lie spread out on the plain before his eyes. No man can say *I do not see them.* It is a lie—and God cannot be deceived. No man can stand immobile on the sidelines, saying *This battle does not concern me.* He has no choice: it does concern him, because in this battle the fate of his eternal soul will be decided.

"Fifty, a hundred years ago, there was confusion. There were signs—there have been signs for three thousand years—but it was difficult to decipher them. Many sides struggled in the arena. Each side claimed *I am on His side.* Conflicting claims competed for fealty; the conscientious individual was confused. God understood this confusion—a man could be deceived by the Devil's false claims.

"But today no such confusion exists: the Devil can no longer claim to be anything but what he is. From the smoke and fire of this eternal, ceaseless struggle, the real forms of the combatants are emerging. They are unmistakable. They cannot be confused. At this moment, the last pretensions are being dropped. The flimsy protestations of piety and sanctity are being discarded: no one is fooled. The visible marks show, the terrible brands. By their fruits shall ye know them!

"We know the signs by which the Devil can be identified; they have been familiar for millenniums. Are these signs presently visible? Are they in evidence?

"We see hatred, cruelty, violence, on all sides. We see each nation of the earth preparing itself, girding its loins, to destroy whosoever stands to its left or right. Naked, brute force, the power of the armed fist, has emerged within every nation of the earth: the disguise of law is gone. And naked force is the sign by which ye shall know *him*—the Evil One branded by the mark of God, cast out of Heaven, hurled into the lake of fire!

"In this final struggle the signs are clear. Spread out on this world, on the surface of this planet, are the hosts of Satan. Can there be any doubt? Does any man in his sane mind imagine that in the Final Battle, God's standard will be carried forward by A-bombs and napalm, armored tanks and heavy artillery? Does any man believe that He Who made this universe could also manufacture mustard gas and bacteriological warfare?

"By their fruits shall ye know them. The mark is upon them! Pretense is gone—the filthy, hairy shape stands naked for all to see. He calls them in his own name, and to that name they respond. There is no shame, no horror: they have made their choice. They will fight for him, and when he falls for the second death, they will fall beside him. Many will go down with him; it is written already. Many will perish in the lake of fire: 'And the Devil that deceived them was cast into the lake of fire and brimstone, where the beast and the false prophet are, and shall be tormented day and night for ever and ever. . . .' 'And the sea gave up the dead which were in it; and death and hell delivered up the dead which were in them: and they were judged every man according to his works. And death and hell were cast into the lake of fire. This is the second death. And whosoever was not found written in the book of life was cast into the lake of fire. And I saw a new heaven and a new earth: for the first heaven and the first earth were passed away; and there was no more sea. . . .'

"Many will perish: that is the writing that is written. But not all will be destroyed. The cities will be leveled; the plain will become endless ash; radioactive particles will fall like hot rain; the crops will wither and die from poison clouds; deadly bacteria will be carried by hordes of insects; the earth will tremble and split open from vast bombs: the oceans will writhe with the impact; the air itself will become polluted and foul; the sun will disappear behind black clouds of dust; all this has been written: all this will come about.

"But some will live. Some will be saved. God will not allow all mankind to perish: those who forsake the armies of the plains, the cities of the plains, will sit with Him in paradise. He has promised this: and the promise of God is not a promise that can be broken, like the promise of a man. God has seen all this; to God it has already happened.

"Those who will save themselves must act. They must seek to save their lives; if they do not act they will be brought down, destroyed with the others. Those who will sit with God must renounce the Devil, refuse to support him. They must turn upward, toward God's side. They must turn their backs on the Devil's works, his armaments, his guns and ships, his tanks and planes, his mighty infernal legions. On this planet, great hosts seek to grow larger than each other; they strut and boast and arm themselves more and more. The forces of the Devil are mighty; but before God they will wither and be destroyed. And cast into the lake of eternal fire.

"Renounce, refuse—do not allow yourselves to be dragged along. Throw down the gun when it is offered you. Turn your back on the instruments of death when they are pressed on you. Those who kill will lose their eternal souls. Those who will not kill, who stand firm in God, who do not fear physical death, will sit with Him in paradise.

"Those who forsake the accursed cities and machines of men, the factories and buildings, the streets and weapons, the bombs and air-raid shelters, the sirens and tin helmets, who flock out into the high mountains, will be saved.

"And no one else!"

PART TWO
Afternoon

The baby was a boy, and his name was Pete.

Pete lay in his bassinet and gobbled at sunbeams. He covered himself with bits of the sun, sneezed when they got into his nose, dribbled saliva down his chin when he tried to chew on them, and then became irritable and wet his diapers.

The July morning was warm and friendly; all the windows of the apartment were wide open, curtains blowing drowsily as gusts of fresh air billowed inside and swirled from room to room. In the kitchen Ellen Hadley sat at the little chrome table facing Jim Fergesson, a cigarette between her lips, a bowl of strawberries in her lap.

Jim Fergesson leaned against the sink, his arms folded. Because it was Sunday he did not wear his double-breasted blue serge suit. Instead, he wore a colored shirt with short sleeves, an old pair of canvas work trousers, and garden shoes. It was clear that he was getting bald and fat. Between the buttons of his shirt his paunch rolled out, heavy and solid. His round, wrinkled face was red and moist with summer perspiration.

"Do you think," he asked plaintively, "I could have a beer?"

"Certainly," Ellen said, hulling one last strawberry before getting to her feet.

"I'll get it," Fergesson said quickly. Always, in the girl's presence, he was gauche. "Tell me where the damn thing is—in the reefer?"

Ignoring his nervous protests, Ellen placed the bowl of strawberries on the table and crossed the kitchen to the refrigerator. Since she no longer carried the baby, Ellen was again slim and light. Since it was summer she wore one of her husband's white cotton shirts, with the sleeves rolled up, sandals, and a polka-dot dirndl skirt. Her brown hair tumbled freely over her arms and shoulders as she bent to rummage in a drawer for the can opener.

"Let me do it," Fergesson murmured. "I don't want you to go to any trouble."

As she poured beer into a tall glass, Ellen said: "Maybe I'll have some, too. Can I have what doesn't go in the glass?"

"Yeah," Fergesson agreed, gratefully accepting the foaming glass. "But you know, if you pour it against the side, there won't be so much left over."

Ellen wrinkled her nose at him. "I see what Stuart means about you."

"Is that so." Flushing, Fergesson wandered uneasily around the small kitchen. In his embarrassment he floundered deeper and deeper; the presence of the young mother made an uncertain fumbler out of him. "You ought to rip out this linoleum," he said, indicating the sink. "Put in tile; it won't rot away." He indicated the fixtures. "For God's sake, get Stumblebum to put in a mixer faucet! He can fix things if he wants. He could fix up this whole apartment if he didn't have his damn head in the clouds."

Ellen sat down at the table and took up her bowl of strawberries. "Mister Fergesson, you're a hard man."

At that, Fergesson blanched. It was the term *mister* that shook him; he remembered, all at once, where he was and what he was doing. He got out his handkerchief and wiped steamy sweat from his red-puffed face. "By the way," he said in a low voice, "where is he? That's what I came over for."

"Stuart?" Ellen shrugged. "Out buying junk for the baby, I suppose."

"On Sunday?"

"Well . . ." She reached over to collect her cigarette from the ashtray on the table. "Maybe he drove up the peninsula with Dave Gold. Some of the big highway toy shops are open on Sunday; he'll find one if he keeps looking long enough."

There was silence.

Fergesson wasn't certain if he was getting an evasive answer. It sounded evasive; there was an indifference, a bitter obliqueness that closed the subject tight. Not knowing exactly how to proceed, Fergesson commented: "He sure is nuts about that kid. He's always wasting time gassing about him on the job. Hanging over the counter with one of those color photographs he's got. He and some old lady cackling away at it."

"Yes," Ellen agreed tonelessly. "He thinks a lot of Pete."

"Did he really drive up the highway looking—"

"He went up to pick up his sister. He's bringing them down to see the baby."

"His sister!" Fergesson exclaimed. "I didn't know he had a sister."

"He does," Ellen said drily. "He wants her to see the baby. He wants her to pass judgment. . . . We're all waiting on that."

Fergesson strolled restlessly into the living room. The July heat made him irritable; he slapped at his neck, rubbed his hands together, peered out the window at the orderly street with its green lawns and quiet cars parked here and there, some of them getting their weekly washing. "Since the baby was born," he said, "Stumblebum's been different. More calmed down; I think he's finally growing up."

"It's not the baby."

"What, then? Of course it's the baby! He knows he's a father—he has responsibilities. He can't take off anytime he pleases."

Still seated at the kitchen table with her bowl of strawberries, Ellen said: "It happened before Pete came. Do you remember when that man was here, that Theodore Beckheim? There was a picture of him in the window of the Health Food Store. . . . I saw it when I was having lunch with Stuart one day."

"Oh, that religious sect," Fergesson said vaguely.

"Stuart went to hear him speak. I remember because we had a terrible quarrel about it. I wouldn't go and I didn't want him to go. You see, I knew what was going to happen; I know how Stuart is about things like that. In some ways I know him better than he knows himself. He was so excited. . . . He takes things like that so seriously."

"Too seriously," Fergesson put in.

Ellen jerkily stubbed out her cigarette and lit another. In the July sunlight her bare arms were brown and fuzzy, slightly damp with perspiration. "No, not too seriously. Why? Who are you to say he takes things too seriously?"

Abashed, Fergesson answered: "I mean, he should get out more and enjoy himself. Stop worrying—take in a few ball games, go bowling. Take you out, damn it . . . I'll bet you never get out to a nightclub or a show."

"Stuart doesn't enjoy games," Ellen said shortly.

"Why not? What's the matter with games? At the store picnic he was a damn sorehead—he wouldn't play ball and he wouldn't pitch horseshoes. All he did was eat and then flop down under a tree and go to sleep. A man shouldn't be a bad sport; he should think of others once in a while. He's so damn serious and thin-skinned; he's always brooding about something." With a single motion of his hand Fergesson swept in the whole apartment. "I don't get it, Ellen. What's wrong with a man like him? He has a pretty wife, a kid, a lovely apartment like this—he has everything in the world and still he's not satisfied!"

Ellen continued fixing the strawberries. Her fingers flew irritably: her husband had been attacked by somebody outside the family. "He sees something you don't see," she flared. "Something none of us sees."

"What's that?"

"He sees all this gone. He's sensitive. . . . Sometimes I think he's more of a woman than I am. He has premonitions, too. He's very—mystical. He used to devour all those astrology magazines I brought home; I stopped getting them because of him. He took them so seriously . . . He pored over them hour after hour. But he never went to church. He never had any religious training. His family was very modern and scientific; he was raised in the thirties, in one of those progressive schools. I suppose they were all Communists . . . what we'd call Communists today. It was all very natural and expressive. He wove mats and baked little clay bowls; you know how he is, he likes to fool and tinker, he likes to *express* himself with his hands. They taught him to grow seeds and make ink. They taught him how bread is made and how cows give milk . . . trips out in the country to see the animals. Acquaint him with nature. That sort of thing . . . make him healthy. He ate it up."

"Christ," Fergesson cried, "he's the most unhealthy person I know, him and his bellyaches and his celery phosphate. He's always sick—he's a hypochondriac!"

Ellen nodded. "Don't you see? They left him with such a terrible sense of needing to be healthy . . . of needing to be outdoors, out in the country. Out of the city, out where things are natural. They didn't teach him anything useful; they didn't teach him to live in this world. . . . He doesn't know how to take care of himself. And then his father died."

"I know," Fergesson said. "That was bad."

"If his father hadn't died Stuart might not have got this way. He was only eight. His mother and sister brought him up. They always had money; his father left them property and life insurance. Stuart always had it pretty easy."

"I know," Fergesson agreed. "He never had to work for a living."

"When I met him he was going to be an artist. I met him in college, you know. He had great dreams; he always talked about himself and his future. But there was that hunger he didn't understand; he thought he wanted to paint, but really he didn't have the discipline. He didn't understand it meant work and learning a lot of techniques. What he wanted to do was express himself through his hands some way. Because that was what he had been taught to do. It wasn't really art he was interested in, it was *himself*. He was yearning, and he didn't know what for. I knew. It was a religious thing, and I knew sooner or later he'd discover it. Religion was just an empty void in his training. They sent him to Sunday school a few times. . . . He learned a couple of psalms, heard about missionary work in China. You know, one day Stuart was brooding about God, the way he does. He asked me what church my family went to."

"What'd you tell him?"

"I said the First Presbyterian. I was brought up very strictly. He brooded about that then. He wanted to know why the First Presbyterian. I told him."

"Tell me."

Ellen got up from the table and carried the bowl of hulled strawberries to the refrigerator. "Well, I told him the truth. We joined the First Pres because it was the church closest to our house. It was just down the block."

Fergesson said nothing.

"You see, Stuart couldn't make anything out of that; it wasn't the answer he wanted. And it made him sick; he gets that dismal, moaning way, when he's worried or confused. He moped around the apartment for days after that. I was sorry—" She turned unhappily to face Fergesson. "I knew it was my fault; but what else could I say? I don't know what to do about him; I can't be his father confessor."

"He ought to go to a priest or something," Fergesson agreed.

"One day this last June, Stuart delivered a television set to a minister. He didn't know the man was a minister. He saw the big house, all the luxury, he saw the man's wife, he couldn't understand how the man could be a minister. It had a terrible effect on him. I think that was part of what brought this on."

"You mean this Beckheim business?"

She nodded. "I knew before he went to the lecture what was going to happen. I knew he wouldn't come back the same. That was what he was looking for, and he didn't even know it himself. I knew it; I was afraid." Half to herself, half to Fergesson she went on: "Maybe I'm wrong. Maybe he should change. Sometimes I get so fed up with his moping around I think good God, anything would be better than this, even if he went out and shot himself."

But she didn't mean that. Tears came up and stung her eyes; she walked quickly away from Fergesson and stood with her back to him, gazing out the window. What was she doing? She was delivering him over to his enemies, to Fergesson. Talking about him, deriding him. And all she wanted to do was save him.

"No," she said. "I don't mean it. I don't care how sick and worrying he is." Her voice choked. "He's my husband and I love him. I want to keep him; I don't want to give him up. And if he changes maybe I'll lose him. I guess I'm selfish; I don't know. It just seems to me that he's so—sort of fragile. He looks big and strong—a lot bigger than you. A lot bigger than you'll ever be. But he's not like you; he can't do things. Somebody has to take care of him, somebody who loves him."

Fergesson scowled. "He's old enough—"

"No, he isn't." Her words rushed out furiously, agonized. "I want to take care of him . . . but so did Sally. Maybe she felt the same way; maybe she realized there's something lacking in him. But it's not just that. There's something *more;* he has something; he *is* something. He wants to do so much. . . . That's what's the matter with him. That's why he mopes and gets mad and does strange things. When he wakes up, when he sees the world, you and the store—he doesn't understand how he can be there, just a salesman. That's not him. He wants much more. God, I wish I could get it for him. But nobody can. He can't get it for himself. . . . It isn't possible. He had such dreams; he grew up when dreams were popular. Now it's only reality. And he can't face that. And it makes him angry."

Some meager thread of her words was comprehensible to Fergesson. "Yeah," he agreed, or thought he agreed. "That damn temper of his. Stumblebum's going to have to watch that temper; he can't get mad with customers. I don't care if he worries; that's his business. But I care if he's going to fly off the handle the way he does. My God, he has tantrums like a little kid. . . . When some old lady's chewing his ear he stands there red as a beet, getting madder and madder."

"For a little while," Ellen said tightly, "that's gone."

"Gone! What do you mean?"

Ellen tied on a plastic apron and shakily began pouring soap dust and hot water into the sink. "When he came back from the lecture he was as quiet as a child. He was like a scared little boy; he just stood there, his eyes big and round, not saying anything. I knew it had happened . . . even though after a while he sort of snapped out of it. He came over to me—I was in bed, of course—and sat down on the edge without saying anything. I never saw him look like that before, and I asked him what happened. It was a long time before he'd say."

"What did he say?" Fergesson asked, morbidly curious.

"He said he'd learned something. He'd found out something he'd always suspected. Beckheim told him the world was coming to an end."

Fergesson hesitated, then bellowed with laughter. "The world's been coming to an end for five thousand years!"

"Yes, it's funny, isn't it?" Ellen gathered up the pots and pans from the stove. "I wish you could have been there and seen his face. Maybe you would have laughed; maybe not." For a time she was silent. "He was so—awed," she said finally. "Stuart has always seen beyond this. . . ." She nodded at the apartment, herself, and Fergesson. "He's been aware of it and we haven't. You know what I mean. I mean the war."

"Oh," Fergesson said. "What about the war?"

"That's it. That's the end."

"The end of the world?"

"The end of everything. It fell into place for him. All the pieces running around his mind. You say it's old—but to him it was a great discovery. All of a sudden everything made sense, everything he had seen, all that had happened to him, all that he had ever heard of. The whole process added up to something . . . for the first time in his life. You're lucky—you never lived in the world he was living in. He couldn't see any purpose, any pattern to it . . . to his life or all our lives or the whole universe. It was just a big senseless mechanism to him. And then suddenly it wasn't. Suddenly everything was for a purpose."

"All that Armageddon stuff? God against the Devil?" Fergesson paced around restlessly. "Sure, that's what I was brought up on. But a man's a fool if he takes that seriously! I mean, you can't really go around spouting that stuff. I mean—"

"You mean it's for Sunday."

"Yes."

"Stuart believes the war is going to destroy the whole world. He believes man-made civilization will end. He believes all the armies of the world, all the cities, the factories, the roads, will be demolished. He believes a new world will arise."

"I know," Fergesson said testily, "I've read Revelation." His outrage increased. "But they've talked that way for centuries! Every time there's a war somebody says it's Armageddon, the end of the world. Every time a comet comes around some crackpot gets out and bellows and prays and says, 'Prepare for the Day of Judgment.'" He turned suddenly to Ellen. "My God, you don't believe this stuff, too, do you?"

"No."

"Maybe you can talk him out of it. Maybe it's just a phase; maybe it'll wear off."

"I don't think it will . . . not all of it. It's sunk down into him; it's not on the surface anymore: it's down inside him where it doesn't show. He's just sure all this will pass away. He feels calm. He isn't excited or worried about it. He feels easier in his mind not having to have anything to do with it."

"Escapism!" Fergesson raged. "He's got a job to keep, he's got you and Pete to support! He can't turn his back on his responsibilities."

Ellen shut off the water and turned away from the sink. "Do you read the newspaper?"

Fergesson blinked. "Sure."

"Anything but the sports page and the comics?"

"Sure! Everything, all the way through."

Do you read the front page? About the war?"

"The Korean War? Naturally. I've got two cousins fighting over there. And I was in the First World War myself. In the Marines—I volunteered."

"Do you think we'll be alive ten years from now? Do you think we'll live through a hydrogen-bomb war?"

Fergesson's beefy face twisted. "Look, Ellen, once you start worrying about that, there's no hope. You can't *do* anything about it; it either comes or it doesn't. It's like flood or famine . . . it's out of our hands—so why worry about it? We have to go about our living and just hope it never comes."

For a long time Ellen studied him. The tight, grim expression on her face made him uncomfortable. It reminded him of the way his mother had looked at him when he was a child and said something unspeakably filthy, picked up from the farmhands. He tried to think of what to say, but nothing came. He was baffled. The woman's brown eyes blazed; her lips worked furiously, silently. Her body trembled under her white cotton shirt.

"What's the matter?" Fergesson quavered uneasily.

"You don't understand, do you? You're exactly the way Stuart says; you just don't have any understanding. You live in a little dead stale old world of your own."

"Don't talk to me that way," Fergesson said sharply.

While they stood glaring at each other, the sound of footsteps came from the living room. Fergesson turned slowly around. His wife, Alice, had come into the apartment; she stood quietly in the doorway, in slacks and a red-checkered sports shirt, the car keys dangling from her hand.

"I got tired of waiting," she said to her husband. "Hello, Ellen. Where's Stuart? Where's the man of the house?"

"He isn't here," Ellen said briskly.

Alice sensed that something had been going on; a mild, almost placid expression appeared on her face. "Where's Pete? Can I say hello to him? I've only seen him a couple of times, you realize."

"Sure," Ellen said listlessly. She dried her hands, took off her apron, and edged past Fergesson. "He's in the bedroom; I have the shades pulled down so he can sleep."

"I don't want to wake him up," Alice said gently.

"You won't. He's sound asleep. If he wakes up I'll feed him; it's about time." She led Alice through the door and into the dark, heavy-amber bedroom.

Pete was awake. Exhausted by his struggles with the sunbeams drifting past the shade and over his blankets, he lay on his back, slack and inert, gazing blankly up. The two women stood over his bassinet for a long time, both of them deep in thought.

"He has Stuart's eyes," Alice said. "But he has your brown hair. It's going to be soft and long, like yours."

"He's got his grandfather's teeth," Ellen said, smiling. She lifted the baby from his covers and propped his head against her shoulder as she unfastened the buttons of her shirt. "Always hungry, aren't you?" she said to Pete. Supporting him in the crook of her arm she pushed her shirt aside and lifted her breast to the baby's greedy mouth. Cupped in the palm of her hand, her breast was full and firm, its dark nipple raised expectantly. Pete took it eagerly, and the girl shuddered. Laughing, she said to Alice: "I must be sensitive—I think his teeth are beginning to come through. But it couldn't be, so soon."

Alice pushed the door a trifle shut after them and stood watching Ellen as she fed the baby. "What was going on when I came in?" she asked. "Was Jim trying to tell you how to run your life?"

"No," Ellen answered indifferently. "We were just arguing about the war."

"If he tries to lecture you, pour a pan of boiling water over him. That's what I do." The sight of the young mother and her baby made momentary envy stir in Alice. "The little old goat," she said, with surprising vehemence. "Damn him."

Outside the bedroom, Fergesson stood clutching his beer, eyes fixed on the half-closed bedroom door, hearing the indistinct murmur of the two women's voices, an occasional laugh, and finally, the wail of the baby. They were changing him, probably. He moved over a little to see; for an instant he caught sight of Ellen, the baby in her arms, gazing down intently, absorbed. In the amber light of the bedroom the girl's breasts hung large and dark, a vision that was quickly stolen from Fergesson, as Alice pushed the door all the way shut.

Shame touched Fergesson, embarrassment at having watched. And then a terrible sorrow so great that it was almost past bearing. Miserable, lonely, he turned bitterly away from the closed door, an acid pain cutting across his chest and into his lungs. Baffled, he plunged around the warm bright living room in an aimless circle. Outside, men were washing their cars and listening to the ball game. Empty, lost, Fergesson could no longer stand it; suddenly he had to go and wrestle with the shipment of television sets. He couldn't stay in the apartment a second longer. The hell with Hadley.

"I'm going!" he shouted at the closed door. "You can stay here and gab— I've got stuff to do!"

There was no answer from the bedroom.

As he hurried blindly out of the apartment and down the hall, he fumbled in his pocket for his keys. He found them as he came out on the shattering-white sidewalk. Hopping into the car, he gunned the motor and released the parking brake. For a second he hesitated, half hoping, half expecting, Alice to come out after him. But there was no sign of her. He didn't wait. He pulled out onto the street and in a moment he was on his way home, to the basement full of great three-hundred-pound television combinations in their ponderous brown cardboard cartons.

When they got to San Francisco the ancient Cadillac showed signs of giving out. Steam poured from its radiator; the motor hesitated, roared, misfired, spilled torrents of foul black smoke from the exhaust pipe. At Market and Third it stalled. Horns honked and pedestrians surged angrily on all sides of them: they were blocking the crosswalk.

Looking out at the clouds of black smoke coming from the exhaust pipe Dave observed: "She's burning a little oil."

"Jesus," Laura said wretchedly, hands clenched helplessly around the steering wheel. "What'll I do? We can't leave it *here*."

Dave Gold and Hadley got out and pushed. Presently a grocery delivery truck came up behind them, nosed at them and honked. Dave and Hadley scrambled gratefully inside, and the truck bumped up against the Cadillac.

In summer, in the middle of July, the great city was beautiful. Hot sunlight had burned away the fog; buildings rose clear and sharp, separated by narrow streets no wider than footpaths. Cars crept up sides of hills, wavered, shifted to low, barely managed to reach the ledge that was the next intersection. All hills sloped down and down to the vast blue trough of the Bay. Before the streets and buildings disappeared into the frigid surface of water there was a narrow band of warehouses, piers, docks, a ribbon of commerce solidly ringing in the city.

"Down there," Dave said to Laura as the motor roared into spasmodic life. "Coast down to the Embarcadero and we'll park it. We can walk to Fisherman's Wharf."

The huge old car rattled and rumbled down Pine Street, past the stock exchange and out of the business district, among deserted office buildings and into the commercial section. A few seedy bars squatted here and there among the warehouses, an occasional hamburger stand, gas station. As they came out onto the flat Embarcadero, Dave spotted a parking lot.

"Over there. Two bits—a steal! But what the hell; Stuart'll pay for it."

Laura parked the Cadillac, and they got stiffly out one by one. Gravel crunched under their feet as they passed a billboard and came up onto the sidewalk. The dilapidated stores nearby were shut down, deserted flyspecked windows thick with dust. A few cars moved aimlessly along the wide street; now and then a pedestrian tramped past vacant loading platforms. Behind them, the slope of the city rose, a solid cliff of white houses and buildings that kept going up. The city looked as if someday it might slide into the Bay and disappear. It looked as if it were already sliding.

"I'd worry," Laura said, "if I lived up there. I'd want to go out every morning with a long pole and see how far the water level had risen during the night."

They walked down the street toward the wall of ponderous wooden piers. Ships were tied up here and there, Latin American steamers unloading bananas and hardwood. To the right, beyond the piers, the span of the Bay Bridge arched off to Yerba Buena Island, a thin wand of gray-blue metal that pierced the woolly-green wad of trees and earth, appeared on the far side, and then sloped away to the east side of the Bay. Berkeley and Oakland lay like an uneven white paste, smeared on the long ridge of hills spread out as far as the eye could see. The ridge was gone at last into blue haze and distance.

"You know exactly where she'll be?" Dave asked Hadley. Pipe between his teeth, he stepped rapidly along, coat fluttering behind him, baggy tweed trousers flapping in the ocean wind.

"She'll be on the pier," Hadley answered obliquely. "I'll see her."

They strode along a railroad track, scuffing up dust with their shoes. Boxcars were parked in ragged clumps. The air was clean and dry; gusts of hot wind rustled around them as they stepped from rail to rail like three children going for a hike, Dave in his unpressed tweeds, Laura in a sloppy wool skirt, wool jacket, and bobby socks. Stuart Hadley wore dark brown slacks, a T-shirt, and crepe-soled shoes. In the sky above them, tubby gray gulls screamed and wheeled; they were getting near the Wharf.

To their left lay a wide flat plain, black with metallic dust and grit. Abruptly the sweep of the city rose, a mountain where the industrial plain ended, where squat factories became the perpendicular sprawl of the Italian stores and houses and the bars of North Beach. The flapping white laundry creeping up the side of the mountain might have been the washing of a Mediterranean city. Between the tangle of houses and the dark blue water of the Bay the ugly flat black strip of factories glowered like a legion of trolls: the tanks of oil refineries, the rusty steel scaffolds of soap and ink and dye plants.

Presently the hot summer air reeked with the odor of dead fish.

To their right was the Wharf, a row of gaudy neon signs mounted on square wooden buildings: restaurants and fish stalls. Past that was a railing, below which a fleet of inferior boats was pulled up helter-skelter, like drift-wood washed onto a beach. Couples in gay summer clothing strolled here and there, enjoying the expanse of the Bay, the distant baked-brown hills of Marin, and the swath of ocean itself, beyond.

"There she is," Hadley said. Under his T-shirt his heart thudded heavily, painfully. It had been two years since he had seen Sally.

His sister stood with her husband at the edge of the railing, not looking out across the water, but simply standing. She had changed since he'd last seen her; but he recognized her at once. Instantly, he started toward her. Dave and Laura trailed warily after him; he got there well ahead of them.

She wore, of course, an expensively tailored suit, an imported light gray English weave, with plain, severe lines, cut in sharply at the waist. High heels, long expensive legs, an intricate little hat in her swept-back blond hair, gloves, a square leather purse strapped over her arm . . . and from her ears, hooped copper earrings. Perhaps she wore a little too much makeup for a languid July day; even on the sagging pier she was dressed for an exclusive nightclub. As he came close to her the scent of her perfume drifted around him, recalling in a rush all the tastes and textures that made up her world, her body and possessions, all the fabrics and powders and garments and colors of her room.

"Hello," Sally said, in her throaty, husky whisper, smiling directly at Hadley. For an instant she hugged him, kissed him brushingly on the cheek. Her lips left a trace of redness and moisture; he could feel it lingering there, slowly dwindling, evaporating in the hot summer air. The net lace from her hat danced between him and the familiar features that had lured, awed, hyp-notized him all his life. Again, he saw his own self in her pale blue eyes. Her sweep of heavy hair, yellow and thick as corn syrup, was an ultimate exten-sion, a breathless realization, of his own botched mop. It was all there: her mouth and chin, her cheekbones, her rising neck with its taut cords, her flar-ing nostrils that had thickened only a trifle since he had last seen her. She was mature now. Fully ripe. Twenty-nine, firm and at the peak of her physical powers. . . . He tore himself away and shook hands with her husband.

"Hi," Bob said briefly, crushing Hadley's hand in a vicious man-grip. "How've you been, Stu?"

"Fine," Hadley said. He introduced everybody around; Dave and Sally distantly remembered each other from high school. They greeted each other formally, dispassionately. Bob, dour and menacing in his western-style hat, jeans, canvas shirt, riding boots, hair shaved to a stain of coffee-black over the hard convex slope of his skull, mean little eyes flitting from one to the next of his herd as he moved them toward his vast shiny Nash parked at the edge of the sidewalk.

"Where to?" he demanded brusquely, climbing in behind the wheel. Bob eyed Dave and Laura coldly, cynically. "Let's shoot over to the highway and down the peninsula; we have to get back early."

Sally spoke up as she slid in beside her husband. "I'm hungry. . . . Before we go down the coast let's grab something to eat."

Bob's harsh, bony face twisted into a scowl. "When we get down there Ellen'll throw something together for you. Can't you last that long—or is that asking too much?"

"Let's go over to Chinatown," Sally begged insistently. "Please—I want a Chinese meal. After all, we don't get over here every day in the week." She squirmed lithely around and motioned Hadley into the front seat beside her. "Baby, do you know a good Chinese restaurant? Bob's never had a Chinese dinner."

Hadley trembled at the old name; it had been years, but the magic word leaped back full and alive. Again he became *Baby*, his sister's younger brother, gazing up at her, awed and idolizing.

"Yeah," he murmured, getting in clumsily and slamming the door. "I know a place on Washington we can try."

"No Chink dinners for me," Bob stated emphatically as he eased the car forward. "I'll take ham and eggs any day." The car gained velocity and hurtled ahead; in the backseat Dave and Laura barely managed to get their door shut in time. Soundlessly, the Nash slid around the corner of a narrow side street, edged a Ford coupe against the curb, and headed directly up the mountainside toward the cliff of buildings above.

"Tell me where to turn," Bob said to Hadley. "I don't know this town; never come over here if I can help it."

In the back, Dave and Laura sat huddled up and mute, intimidated by the hulking man behind the wheel. Both Bob and Sally were tall, fully developed people beside whom the Golds dwindled to the stature of dwarfs. In the rearview mirror their dark, lumpy, ill-formed faces hung slack and limp, hands in their laps, reduced to dumb obedience. Hadley wondered at their transformation; in the presence of his sister and her husband, these two Jews had become bewitched, turned back into primordial clay.

For the first time in his life Hadley believed he was witness to different races. Dave and Laura accepted without struggle their servant status; mute and stupid, they gazed dully ahead, jogging with the pitch and roll of the car as Bob spun it expertly through narrow intersections, among other cars, pedestrians, delivery trucks, buses. There was no sound, only the whirr of air and the oily purr of the motor. Beside him, his sister smiled happily, dark red lips parted enough to show the hard white teeth he had envied all his life.

"It's nice seeing you again," she said softly. She reached out and closed her gloved fingers over his. Hadley trembled as the pressure of her strong, slim fingers clutched at him and then remained lightly. He did not look at her; he stared at the passing stores and buildings, the painted signs, the first ornate Chinese establishments of Chinatown.

"How's the television business?" Bob demanded sourly, in his usual heavy, clipped voice. "Still raking it in?"

"Sure," Hadley answered. He tried to ask about the real estate business, but his vocal cords refused to form the social formality. What did he care about the real estate business? He didn't like Bob Sorrell; he was impressed, respectful, properly frightened, but he did not enjoy the man's presence.

"We've been doing all right," Bob said, without having been asked. "I guess you know the Woodhaven tract is ours."

"Oh, yeah," Hadley murmured. "That new tract down the highway."

"It'll be a while before we get our investment back. We're settling a lot of GI's in there at five bills down. That doesn't begin to amortize us; five hundred covers our immediate commission and that's all. Those are forty-year loans—" He forced a delivery truck to the side of the street so he could pass. "The interest adds up . . . and a lot of those GI's eventually default and lose their equities. We get the shacks back in six, eight years. Of course, by that time they practically have to be built over again."

Fascinated, Hadley listened to the words roll from the man's tongue. Easy, confident, relaxed, utterly without emotion, Bob Sorrell showed neither shame nor pride. He was merely stating facts.

"Bob's taken over a whole lot of rural real estate," Sally said, a flush of enthusiasm reddening her cheeks. Her blue eyes sparkled excitedly. "Farms, little stores, and a country newspaper. Up in St. Helena—we're going up there next month for a week or so; we're going to stay and get to know the town. Our vacation!"

"Yeah, well," Bob said, in his hard, impassive voice, "most of that stuff was held by Napa County Land and Investments. We took them over last May." He raised his voice. "Where the hell is this joint? I see plenty of chophouses; or you got a particular one in mind?"

The Nash was flowing rapidly down Grant Avenue; there was clearance for parked cars on one side, nothing more. The Chinese shops with their displays of ivory chess sets, silk scrolls, mandarin pajamas, incense burners, letter openers, bamboo stamp trays, artificial birds, jade and silver jewelry, jars of dried herbs, twisted roots, sea kelp, almond cookies, preserved ginger, cages of ducks and rabbits, bins of yams and knobby potatoes, were of no interest to Bob Sorrell. At intersections sudden glimpses of hills and bridge momentarily broke the procession of stores and bars and restaurants, descents so steep that if a pedestrian slipped and fell he could easily roll all the way to the Bay.

"Oh, lookie!" Sally cried. "There goes a cable car!"

Up the steep slope the tiny archaic box of passengers scuttled, tightly gripping its strand of wire. Banging and clattering, it hurried through the intersection and continued on up, a wood and iron package bouncing at the end of an underground string.

"Which way?" Bob demanded curtly, angry at the time wasters on all sides of them.

"Another couple of blocks," Hadley answered. "To the left."

At Washington they turned up the steep hill. Vendors hawked Chinese-language newspapers. Wizened old men with long beards sold melon cakes: wads of sugar and fat with a core of dripping wet fruit. Above the street the grilled balconies of the many-floored buildings almost touched. Up and down the narrow sidewalks Chinese children raced and scampered, screaming shrilly. Cellar entrances, sudden black squares in the sidewalk, opened onto dark flights of steps leading down. Oriental music—wails and sudden crashes—filtered up to the street noise. Narrow rubbish-strewn alleys, the width of a single car, led between the restaurants, filthy paths of garbage cans, dried feathers in pools of blood.

"There it is," Hadley said.

A small old-fashioned neon sign, lost among the tangle of multicolored tubing, jutted out over a cellar entrance. A long flight of steps led down, turned by a below-surface glass window behind which dead, stripped birds hung, feet tied together with cord. Beyond that were black tables, a glimpse of curtained booths, stubby white-coated waiters, an archaic cash register, Chinese merchants reading newspapers while they ate.

"Where the hell am I going to park?" Bob complained. "I can't park along this alley!" The restaurant disappeared behind them as the Nash swiftly climbed the hill, scattering pedestrians from every crosswalk. "Let's shove it and head down the coast. It's already two thirty!"

"You can park on Stockton," Hadley said. "There're always places up there."

Bob said nothing as the Nash turned off Washington onto Stockton. They were out of Chinatown; rows of dingy apartment buildings stretched out for blocks, shabby shoe and clothing stores without displays or signs. "There," Sally said to him, "in front of that drugstore; that woman's pulling out."

The Nash slid up, briefly halted, and then pulled into the parking spot. Its bumpers tapped the car behind, then the car ahead. Bob pulled his key from the ignition and with a single motion threw open the door and stepped out. "Come on," he commanded. "Let's get moving; we don't have all day."

Bob and Sally strode along the sidewalk. Hadley managed to keep up with them; Sally's high heels clicked sharply just ahead of him and involuntarily he found himself watching their thin points strike the cement. Around her trim, nylon-smooth ankle looped a tiny gold identification bracelet. In the sunlight it sparkled and danced as her legs moved. Hadley kept behind his sister, following her smart, expensive figure at a respectful distance, with a veneration that permeated him, that was automatic and total, that represented every part of him. It had never been otherwise.

Behind Hadley straggled Dave and Laura Gold, even more dwarflike than in the car. Two squat dark puddings of quasi-human flesh, in dirty, food-stained garments, shapeless and unwholesome, faces dour, bodies slumped. A certain pride touched Hadley. He was a cut above them; he lagged behind his sister, but he was one of her kind. The physical heritage was there; they were of the same race, the same blood and stock. Somehow, circumstances had kept him from measuring up to the standards of this stock, but the capability was there. Someday, when he was older . . .

Strange, that in the presence of his sister he should shrink back into his old pattern, think of himself as *too young*. But it was so; ambling along behind the high-stepping woman with her chin up and out-jutting, firm-lined face uptilted, he was a stripling, a colt, a boy. Hands in his pockets, he kicked at a tin beer can, ran a few paces, leaped, became a towheaded boy in looks and actions. He caught up with Sally and her husband, breathlessly pointing down Washington.

"That way!" he shouted, and suddenly fell back in confusion. With a brief glance at him the two of them turned silently at the corner and plunged down the steep hill. Abashed, Hadley raced after them, and behind him the two Golds plodded gloomily along, taking up the rear.

In the dim, boxlike booth, they sat around a stone-topped table, examining soup-stained menus. Beyond the curtain, Chinese businessmen hunched over bowls of boiled rice and steamed guppies, carrying the fish and rice to their mouths with chopsticks. In the middle of the table was a decanter of soy sauce, salt and pepper shakers, more menus.

"You order," Sally said to her brother, raising her head and closing her menu. "You know more about Chinese food. Remember when we used to come over here?"

Hadley nodded. He scanned the menu excitedly; a rush of childish expansiveness overcame him, and in a flurry of wild recklessness he ordered everything in sight.

One by one the tiny doll-faced waiter, his lacquered black hair shining under the overhead light, set the steaming bowls in front of them. Egg flower soup. Sticky-hot fried wonton. Chicken with almonds. Beef cooked with asparagus. Chow yoke, slimy green vegetables served in thick sweet syrup. The fat, soft cakes, yellow and stuffed with meat and vegetables, that were egg foo yong. In front of each of them stood a white round handleless cup, into which Hadley poured hot, steaming tea from an old-fashioned baked-enamel teapot.

Bob Sorrell ignored the bowls of smoking food and signaled the waiter as he bustled out through the curtain. "You have any Seven-Up? Bring me a bottle of Seven-Up."

"No Seven-Up," the waiter muttered.

Bob's hard face darkened. Enunciating each word elaborately he demanded: "You savvy Coca-Cola? You bling Coca-Cola chop-chop?"

The waiter disappeared. A moment later he returned with a Coke bottle, a straw stuck into it. He clinked it down on the table and was gone without a word.

"Don't give me any of that Chink food," Bob said to Sally. "I'll grab a sandwich on the highway." He examined his watch. "I can hold out; it won't be long."

Dave and Laura gulped their food anxiously, afraid of not being allowed to finish. The bowls were emptied rapidly; both Hadley and his sister were hungry. They ate eagerly, as always before, when they were teenagers and had come up to the City to visit the beach, the amusement park, the miles of green grass and flowers that were Golden Gate Park. . . .

Across the limitless white strip of beach the two of them had trudged, in jeans and T-shirts, barefoot, paper bag of lunch bouncing at their belts. The sun poured down, hot and small and high above them. Wind stung sheets of flying sand in their faces, embedded points of fire in their bare arms and legs. Jeans rolled up, the two of them waded wearily through the surf, oozing milky froth lapping at his sister's bare calves as she plodded along ahead of him.

The sight of Sally, the slender figure against the long miles of ocean and sand, buttocks pumping under her washed-pale jeans, body tanned and healthy, blond hair streaming out after her, face laughing soundlessly as she turned to wait for him, gasping for breath . . . that was one picture he kept of her, among the many others. And in the evening, the endless rides on the grinding, tortuous old streetcars, all the miles across San Francisco to the Third and Townsend station. Facing each other, exhausted, crowded in with the shoppers and commuters, the old women with their lumpy shopping bags, the tired-faced businessmen, the shrill roar of the wheels, traffic and clanging signs. Hour after hour they rode, both of them sagging and expressionless, swaying with the motion of the streetcar. And then suddenly he would find her smiling at him, a personal, covert quiver of her lips, a flicker of an eyelid. Across the aisle choked with people gripping straps, a brief glimpse of her unique, intimate face, the beautiful reflection of his own. A quick, meaningful twitch of her features intended for him only, and then the overcoated body of a middle-aged workman cut them off, and the passive exhaustion resumed.

"Well," Bob said, facing Hadley coldly, "you can tell the Army to go kiss its ass."

Stunned, Hadley slowly lowered his cup of hot, sweet tea. "What?" he murmured.

"You've got a kid, a dependent! They're not drafting you, are they?"

"I don't know." He was confused. "I don't think so. . . . I have a liver condition; I've already been classified 4-F."

"No," Bob said emphatically, closing the subject. "They won't take you with a kid." His eyes roved restlessly around; his blunt, thick fingers drummed on the surface of the table. "You still working for that same shop?"

"Yes," Hadley admitted.

"What are you, floor manager now?"

"No," Hadley said. "Commission and draw."

"Five percent?"

Hadley nodded.

Bob Sorrell made computations. "What's that bring you, about three fifty a month net?"

"More like two fifty," Hadley answered.

The two mean, narrow eyes half closed. Tiny eyes, as cold and wet as rocks. "Why, for that I'd tell the old fart to go jump in the creek. You can get that anywhere. You can get that breaking rocks with a coon railroad gang!"

Dave Gold's dark face turned a sickly gray and he abruptly stopped eating.

Both he and Laura seemed suddenly like two cross, tired children kept up too late at night. They settled down unhappily at their places and gazed sightlessly at the table, not saying anything, not moving.

Bob glanced briefly at them and appraised them in one short instant. His eyes summed them up. The rigid square of his shoulders weighed them and rejected them. He dismissed them and turned back to Hadley.

"How long is this going to continue? Wake up, man; you can't support a wife and child on that kind of money. With the way this country is bursting wide open, how the hell long are you going to sit around on your can?"

Hadley pawed clumsily at his fork. "I have a chance of taking over the store. If Fergesson buys this other place he's talking about. . . ." His voice trailed off uncertainly. "Maybe he'll turn Modern over to me. He said he would, once."

"He did?" Bob's gravel voice was faintly mocking. "A swell joe, huh? Dangling the old bait in front of your eyes?"

"I think he will," Hadley answered stubbornly, not able to meet the stone-hard face of his brother-in-law. "I think he's really going to buy into O'Neill's place."

"And how much'll you be making?"

Hadley's fingers twisted together as he studied them intently. "One night after hours Fergesson and I sat around talking about it. He said he'd give me three fifty salary plus my five percent on what I sold. And an additional one-half percent on the gross take. That's pretty good."

Sally got enthusiastic. "Say, that sounds like something!" She glanced at her husband. "Doesn't that sound good?"

Bob remained unimpressed. "Is this a promise? You got it in writing?"

"Of course not," Hadley answered. "The deal with O'Neill hasn't gone through."

Bob made a disgusted noise, waved his big hand, and then turned to consult the wristwatch strapped to his hairy arm. "Time to get going," he announced, and got to his feet. "Let's take off, folks." He eyed the Golds hostilely; their time had come. "What's with you two? Coming along or what?"

"We have our own car," Dave answered hoarsely.

"Where is it? Around here?"

After a moment Laura answered: "In a parking lot. Down on the Embarcadero."

Bob was getting rid of the Golds. Hadley knew it, but he was powerless to protest. Like a cosmic engine, Bob went through the routine of the brush-off. "All right," he said. "I'll drive you down there and let you off."

He moved out of the booth, halted with his body holding the curtain aside, and waited.

"Now?" Laura asked weakly.

"Certainly," Bob answered. "Why the hell not? You're done eating—you've had enough of that slop for six people." To Hadley he said: "Wait here with Sally. I'll be back in a couple of minutes; this won't take long."

Dave and Laura pushed blindly out of the booth after him, and Hadley was alone with his sister.

For a time neither of them said anything. Hadley picked listlessly at his cold, soggy food. Sally had pushed her empty plate away; she leaned back, got a silver cigarette case from her purse, and lit up. Clouds of blue smoke drifted around the booth. Presently Sally unbuttoned her coat and slid it off, onto the back of the chair her husband had vacated. She wore a pale blue angora sweater, long-sleeved, high-necked, stretched tight against her sharply outlined bra, her rigid, white, terribly expensive bra.

"It's been a long time," she said, and smiled quickly at him, blue-eyed, mouth rich and red, proud face tilted high. The old flicker of warm amusement had again touched her lips. The familiar flash of affection between them. Breathing blue smoke from her nostrils, leaning lazily back in her chair, elbow against the table, cigarette close to her lips, she gazed at her kid brother with intense affection. "So now you have a son. My Baby has a little new baby boy. . . ."

The waiter appeared with a pot of fresh tea. Grinning his pardon, he exchanged it for the cold pot and retired through the curtains.

"How's it feel?" she asked.

"Fine."

"You know, Bob won't have children yet. He wants to wait until we're settled. Whatever that might be."

"Bob is a big man," Stuart said.

"He's a hard worker. There's always something going on in that bullet-shaped head of his." Her nose wrinkled, teasing. "Why don't *you* get a butch? But you always liked your hair long." She leaned forward to stub out her cigarette on her empty plate; again a cloud of perfume drifted around him, perfume and the warm smell of her body underneath her sweater, her arms and neck and hair. "I remember, you were always fussing in front of the mirror, combing it and rubbing Wildroot Cream Oil into it. You still use that stuff?"

"Yes." He smiled. "I still do."

"My kid brother. What a dandy you always were! Worse than a girl." She lit up slowly, cupping the lighter between her red-nailed fingers, eyes fixed on him, cigarette dangling between her lips. "What does Ellen say to all your primping and"—she inhaled deeply—"and your clothes! I guess you got it from me."

Stuart Hadley agreed. In a kind of ecstasy he drank in the presence of his sister; unbelievably, he had her all to himself, completely in his possession after all the years that had passed. That interval vanished from his mind; it was a barren interlude of separation, a marking time in which nothing vital had taken place. Achingly, he realized that Bob would be back almost at once; any minute, in fact. He tried desperately to drink in all of her at once, to consume and absorb her in the few precious minutes ahead.

"What's wrong, Baby?" she asked him softly, blue eyes gentle, aware that something painful was happening to him.

"Nothing."

She had taken off her gloves. They lay heaped on her purse, beside her silver cigarette lighter. She reached out now, and again took his hand. Her fingers were long, cool, incredibly slim. Her red shiny nails were like polished glass against his skin as she pressed harshly, convulsively. "I wish you'd tell me what it is. Has—everything been going all right? Are you happy?"

"Yes," he pretended.

"Really?" She watched him intently, leaning toward him, elbows against the table. "You know, Baby, I can read you like a book. Tell me the truth."

"I'm fine," Stuart answered.

Sally shook her head. "Baby, I wish to Christ I could help you." Softly, sadly, she stroked his arm with her fingers. "Is it you and Ellen?"

"No . . . we're getting along fine." He amended himself: "The same as always. Quarrels now and then. Nothing new."

"What will the baby mean?" Singsong, she repeated in a husky whisper: "My Baby's baby. My Baaaaby's baby." She reached up her hand to ruffle his carefully combed blond hair. Red lips slack she sang: "My little peter's little Peter."

They both giggled, rocked close together, bumped heads and drew back, laughing aloud.

"All right," Sally said. "All right as rain. You know, I've missed you like hell. You know?" She puffed blue smoke in his face. "Of course, you have a sweet little wife . . . such a sweet little wife you have. You don't need me anymore."

"I do," Hadley said tightly.

"No." She shook her head. "I can't look out for you anymore. Remember how I used to look out for you? Remember that time you lost your shoe in the movie theater and the usher and I found it for you? While you stood out in the lobby bawling your head off."

"I remember," Hadley said.

Sally listened to his voice, as if trying to catch something beyond, far down, deep inside where it didn't show. "You seem so—oh, my God, Baby." Her blue eyes were full of pain for him. "You seem so beaten."

He didn't understand. "What do you mean?"

"You're not trying! It's all gone—there wasn't much to start with, and what there was is gone." She rushed on wildly: "Baby, you've got to stand up. . . . Not the way Bob does, maybe. But even that wouldn't hurt you!" Fiercely, she jabbed her cigarette at him. "Goddamn it, Baby, it kills me to see you like this. Like something washed up by the tide, the sort of thing we used to kick around—jump up and down on. Remember? You remember; I know. We both remember. It's my fault; I knocked all the spirit out of you. You should have looked out for yourself. . . . You wanted to look out for yourself, once. But I wouldn't let you. I had to take care of you . . . I wanted to take care of you. I made you weak; you weren't always weak."

"I'm okay," Hadley said awkwardly. "What are you worried about?"

"You're not okay, Baby," his sister said softly, gently. "You're in bad shape. . . . You make me want to cry. Damn you," she snarled at him; her blue eyes swam with tears. "I wanted you to *be* something!"

"Like Bob?" Hadley asked bitterly.

"No. I don't know—anything. You used to have such a temper. . . . You used to get so damn mad. Remember that? You weren't always soft this way. Milky."

Genuinely surprised, Hadley said: "What do you mean? What sort of temper?"

"You used to go crazy; you used to go into fits. You could only be pushed so far and then you'd fight. You'd get your back up against the wall—all of a sudden you'd start swinging, at everybody, everything. That's what I want . . . understand? And it was my fault; I knocked that out of you, that backbone, that temper. We teased you—we teased it out of you. And I thought it was good. I thought you had to learn, become—disciplined. Self-control, growing up. That sort of thing. I wanted you to mind . . . like a parent. I wanted obedience. And I got it, didn't I? That's all gone now. When's the last time you got mad?"

"I still get mad," Hadley said.

"Do you? Is it still there?" She leaned breathlessly toward him, elbows planted on the table, hands clasped together. "Then why don't you stand up? Where's your backbone?"

"It's there," Hadley repeated.

"Like it used to be? You used to smash your toys: you remember how you lined them up all of a sudden, and you just smashed them, one after another?"

He remembered it, now that she said it. But only now; a moment ago, he would have denied it. "Yeah," he admitted.

"All your things, everything you had. Something you'd been working on, something you were building. You'd work away on it, hour after hour, sometimes for days. And then, when it didn't come out right, when it didn't turn out the way you wanted, you'd just sit there with it on your lap. . . . I got so I knew the signs. You'd sit there, sort of limp, and your face would get red as a beet. Redder and redder, and you wouldn't say a thing. And then all of a sudden you'd leap up and smash it, whatever it was, smash it to bits. Jump up and down on it. And I or Daddy would come in and spank you."

"Yeah," Hadley admitted. It was something that even now, years later, he only vaguely understood, only dimly comprehended. "I wonder why I did that. All of a sudden I just did it. I wanted to bust whatever meant the most to me."

"I think you broke just about everything you had, sooner or later. But that finally went away. . . . Then you got into fights. Then you beat up kids. Remember that girl you hit with the hoe?"

"Sure," Hadley said.

"You were a bastard. And I set out to change that. Now I wish it were back."

"It's back," Hadley said. "It's there somewhere. It's not gone. I can feel it still there." He grinned at her. "A thing like that can be driven underground, but not away."

Sally turned away, lips tight. For a time she sat, rigid and silent, not looking at her brother. Outside the booth shrill voices screamed banalities back and forth in Cantonese. Chairs scraped, the cash register clanged. Somewhere a man coughed, hawked, and spat loudly.

"I'm sorry about your friends," Sally said, turning to him finally. "I forgot to tell Bob they were coming. He hates people to turn up when he doesn't know them." She smiled waveringly. "I wish you'd get a car again; you and Ellen could drive up and visit us. And Pete. Golly—" Eagerness swept across her face, swift and fluid. "I'm so excited about him! Does he look like you?"

"A little. It's too early to tell."

"Like Daddy?"

"Sure."

She was delighted. "I'm so glad." For a time she sat smoking and gazing at him, and at the walls of the booth, the framed picture of a sleeping dog hung above the row of coat hooks. "What's he going to be?" she asked. "When he grows up. Have you thought about it?"

"Yes," Hadley answered. "I've thought a lot about it. He's going to be something. . . . He's going to get somewhere."

"Don't think too much about it, Baby," his sister said anxiously. "Promise me? Promise you'll think about yourself? Do you understand what I mean?"

He pretended he didn't. "I've got a lot to think of. This business at the store—"

"Look at me." She reached up and turned his face toward her. "Baby, are you stopping completely? You *can't* turn it over to your child. . . . You can't drop it all on him. That's not right—you're so damn young; do you know how young you are? You're just a little boy, a little blond-haired baby. You've got so much ahead of you. You could be so much. . . ."

"Sure," Hadley said, without emotion.

"You don't *want* to be." She shuddered. "You used to be so active—even when you were a kid. Remember the little electric motor you built? And all your mats and baskets, all the things you made. Your Erector set . . . You were always building something. And you loved to fix clocks!"

After a moment Hadley said: "Sally, something's happened to me."

She clenched her fists. "Do you know what it is?"

Hadley laughed. "Of course! I don't mean it the way it sounds . . . like an evil spell or some kind of bone disease."

She was watching him uneasily. "What do you mean?"

"I met somebody."

"Don't tell me in bits—who did you meet? Are you and Ellen splitting up? Did you meet another *girl*?" She looked delighted.

Hadley tore apart a napkin and wadded the fragments into a ball in the palms of his hands. "No, nothing like that." He grinned at her shyly. "You and Ellen—that's the first thing you think of. You think maybe I'm playing around with some waitress over at the dime store."

Sally smiled doubtfully. "Baby, I don't care if you're shacking up with the Virgin Mary. You know that—all I care about is you. Let's face it . . . to me, Ellen's a sweet girl and I think a lot of her. But she's just like any other young gal with brown hair and biiiig sorrowful eyes. I've seen a thousand of them. . . . You know, Baby, maybe if you'd got a wife who could help you—" She shrugged. "It's none of my business. But you need something besides—" She gestured and smiled mockingly at him. "Admit it . . . you can get that stuff anywhere—right? You don't have to get married just for that. You're a nice-looking boy, Baby. I remember what some of my girlfriends used to say about you." Lazily, her blue eyes filmed over, cunning and feminine, the lurking cloudiness of sex. "How long ago was that? Eight, nine, ten years . . . You were fifteen years old."

"Sixteen."

"You're a liar. I know how old you were. . . . I was four when you were born. I remember the day." She raised her voice sternly. "So don't try to kid me."

"I never kidded you," Hadley said simply. "I mean, I never got away with it."

"So don't ever accuse me of trying to make you toe the straight and narrow." Her blue eyes danced. "You know how I feel about that."

"I know." He grinned tightly.

As she lit another cigarette Sally went on: "The thing about Ellen is—" She glanced up. "Do you mind?"

"No."

"What can she do for you? What's she got? She's a sweet kid, Baby, but you need more than that. You've got too much on the ball . . . don't you see? Nothing should hold you back. You want a woman who can work with you . . . somebody with your own ability. You've got a lot of ability."

"Christ," Hadley said mildly, "I haven't painted since college."

"I don't mean just that. But that's part of it. I mean, you're a unique person, Baby. There're depths to you. Layers. You go down a long way. . . . You're complicated. Does Ellen really understand you? She wants to; I believe that." Sally laughed lightly, gaily. "You're a damn fool, Baby—you shouldn't let me say that about your wife."

Staring down at the table, Hadley said in a low voice: "You can say anything you want. Or do anything you want. You never did anything wrong in your life."

"According to you." She sighed. "I wish Bob thought that way. According to him everything I do is wrong. He enjoys it—he gets sardonic humor out of mistakes I make. When I break a dish or drop a bottle in the bathroom, anything where I'm at fault. He's got that damn workshop in the back, all those power grinders and tools—" She broke off abruptly. "Who is it, then? Not a girl? That narrows it down." She eyed him doubtfully, apprehensively. "Baby, in college you fooled around with that gang awhile—when you were painting. It was all right, then; I understood that. But if you're mixed up with them now—"

"No," Hadley said, "this is something else. I—heard a man speak."

"You sound like that popular song, that 'Nature Boy.' God, that dreadful thing."

Gazing intently at his sister, Hadley said: "It's something I still don't completely understand. I don't know how it's going to affect me . . . it hasn't gone through me all the way. I feel there's more; it's still working on me."

The amusement left his sister's face. "What kind of a man?" Seriously, she bent back in her chair, convinced by the tension of his voice. "You really mean it."

"I sure do. You know how so many things never made any sense to me. Things people were doing, all this activity . . . like your husband."

Sally colored resentfully. "Baby—" She shrugged. "Well, what's sauce for the gander is sauce for the goose."

"I'm not going to knock him. I have a lot of respect for him. But I don't understand him; I don't understand what it's all for, all the running around. All the struggling. Sometimes I sit there in the Health Food Store, watching people going by on the sidewalk. They're nuts! Where the hell are they rushing to? Swarming like ants. . . . It's senseless."

"You always did like lying around dreaming," Sally said softly. "You were always the big dreamer. Spinning big deals in your head, all the things you were going to do. Schemes . . . You're a natural-born salesman. I'll bet you really charm the old women."

"And now I understand it," Hadley continued. "Now, when I see them, I'm not puzzled."

Troubled, his sister shook her head. "What do you understand, Baby?"

"What they're doing. Where they're going. Why they're out there scrambling around."

"Why are they out there?"

Hands locked together, Hadley said: "There isn't any way I can tell you that you won't laugh. It sounds so damn silly when I say it."

"Say it."

"The end of the world's coming."

There was silence. Sally's hands were shaking as she tapped her cigarette against the ashtray. "What do you mean? You mean the war?"

He nodded. "Yes, in a way. But beyond that. The war is only a part of it."

"But you do mean the war. You're worried about the war." She cursed harshly, furiously. "Goddamn them—are they still after you, trying to induct you? You with your kid—"

"It's not that."

"What, then?" She crumpled her cigarette out furiously. "You mean you're *afraid*? Christ, Baby, you're a little old woman yourself, a little timid old woman. You're scared of being blown to bits. Baby, you haven't any backbone at all. I'm so goddamn ashamed of you. . . ." She pulled herself together, shuddered. "But I can understand. I guess when you have a kid to worry about . . . I'd worry, too. Well, get away from here. Move out into the wide-open country. Get lost—it's a big country. Buy a farm and raise vegetables . . . you always liked to do that. Leave the country; go to Mexico."

"There's no place that's safe."

Sally's blue eyes blazed. "And this is what you've figured out? That everybody's going to get killed, so all you have to do is just sit and wait for it? Is that what you're doing, just waiting for the A-bombs to start dropping? Who the hell is this man?"

Hadley, staring hard at the table, said: "Theodore Beckheim. You probably never heard of him."

"No, I haven't."

"He heads a religious group. The Society of the Watchmen of Jesus. They have a movement all over the world. A big following in Africa."

"Religious fanatics! Holy Rollers!"

"I guess so. Only, it doesn't seem fanatic. It just makes sense. As if I'd always believed it, but I hadn't quite got all the pieces together. When I heard him it just sort of locked into place."

"What are you going to do?" Jerkily, rapidly, she gathered up her coat and purse, stuffed her lighter into a pocket. "Here's Bob; I can hear him yelling around." She raised her voice. "Over here—this booth!"

The curtains burst apart and Bob Sorrell stood there, feet planted apart, face dark and scowling. "Why didn't you leave the damn curtains apart so I could see you?" he demanded.

"We're all ready to go," Sally said in a thin, clipped voice. "Unless you want something."

"Me?" Bob laughed sharply. "Come on—let's hit the highway." He clapped Hadley on the shoulder as he rose from his seat. "Those are sure some screwball friends of yours. Where'd you pick them up? Christ, when I got a load of that old tractor they call a car . . . They won't get two miles with that thing." He bellowed loudly as they moved away from the booth. "The loose screws aren't all down in the motor, either." He snatched the check from Hadley's lifeless hands and started off with it. "I'll pay for it, buddy."

He strode on toward the cash register, digging silver change from his pocket. He grinned starkly back at Sally and Stuart, and gave them a broad wink.

"This one's on me," he shouted across the restaurant, past the silently eating Chinese. "When we get down in Cedar Groves, Ellen can blow us to a *real* meal."

The warm dense wind of night swirled peevishly into the apartment through the open windows. Flies, moths, beetles, buzzed and tapped against lightbulbs, fried themselves and dropped in tiny sizzling bits to the carpet. Around the living room everybody lounged inertly, facing one another with involuntary relentlessness. It was eight thirty. In the kitchen the dinner dishes were piled and heaped on the sink, stove, table, drainboard. A place had been cleared large enough to open gin and tonic bottles, and to assemble drinks. A tray of melting ice cubes lay oozing sluggishly, surrounded by corkscrews, bits of metal foil, puddles of Gilby's Deluxe, lemon rind.

"It's hot," Sally murmured. "I think it's hotter now than it was this afternoon. It's so—sticky."

After a time Ellen said: "I think there's more humidity here than on your side of the Bay."

"You're pretty damn close to the water," Bob observed. "Every once in a while you catch a whiff of the mudflats."

"Cedar Groves has certainly grown since I was down here last," Sally observed. "When was that, at least a year ago, wasn't it? That Christmas we all got together . . . that was two years, I guess. Anyhow, the town was smaller then."

Sally reached over to take her drink from the coffee table. She gazed down into it, at the bits of lemon floating in the gin.

"Wait until you've used it a couple of times," she said eagerly to Ellen. "It makes all the difference in the world. We'll get it into the mail tomorrow morning."

"What are you talking about?" Bob asked her.

"The Waring blender. When we were in the kitchen I told Ellen we'd give her the two-pint one; it's really too small for us. Then when we come down next time she can whip up a daiquiri for us . . . and you won't have to sit around moping over *that*." She pointed at the glass her husband gripped between his two hands.

Bob Sorrell sat moodily holding his glass of ginger ale; unless things were precisely to his liking he didn't drink.

Beside him, Sally had slipped off her high-heeled shoes and nylons. The sweater, hat, and suit she had worn now hung in the closet in the bedroom; she had put on a yellow drawstring blouse of Ellen's and one of her short, light summer skirts. Her honey-colored hair was down and tossed back, and she had scrubbed off most of her makeup. Thoughtful, subdued, she sat curled up on the couch, her bare legs tucked under her, one pale arm resting outstretched behind her. Grasping her glass with the other hand, eyes half closed, she yawned, smiled, sipped her drink, and listened distantly to the low murmur of the TV set.

Leaning against the kitchen door, Ellen Hadley wore what she had worn in the afternoon. Her smooth, very youthful skin was an even tan in the dim light of the room. Without expression she sipped her gin sling, eyes vacant. Once, she reached down and fondly touched her husband on the shoulder; Stuart Hadley sat slouched in the big easy chair, eyes shut, mouth open, ignoring his glass perched on the chair arm with only dead ice cubes sagging in the bottom.

"This is a nice little apartment," Sally said sleepily. "But you know, paying out rent is tossing it down the rat-hole. We made up our minds right away to buy. . . . That was five years ago, too. Of course, with Bob in the real estate business it would be sort of perverted to rent a place. Anyhow, you've seen our place. Haven't you?" She yawned again. "God, this warm air makes me so sleepy . . ." She slapped listlessly at a mosquito buzzing around her ear. "I feel as if I'm about to pass out completely." She examined her glass. "It isn't this—it's as weak as water."

"The way I figure," Bob Sorrell said, "in ten years of rent a person has paid the original gross cost of income property back to the owner. After that, the owner is getting sheer gravy. If you're going to rent, squawk like hell about everything—the paint, the plumbing, the thickness of the walls, the number of electrical input wires—"

"What's that?" Sally asked.

"Well, you should have three-wire input. Two isn't enough. Two means overload, danger of fire. A tenant should bellow like hell about that. Stick up for your rights or you won't get anywhere. In this world you gotta toot your own horn, buster; ain't nobody else going to toot it for you."

Sally nodded obediently.

"And refrigeration—none of this central piping stuff, this sulfur gas. Too dangerous—pipe breaks in the walls someplace, floods the whole building." Bob rapped on the wall. "This cheap fiberboard wouldn't get past the inspectors these days. Boy, they're really toughening up. When we built that big twelve-story job in East Oakland, those bastards went over every inch with a fine-tooth comb. Made us rip out all the wiring—every foot of it. We had to put it in the whole way, not just between the fuse boxes and the apartments. Why, this place wouldn't get by at midnight in a blinding fog."

"How much rent do you pay?" Sally asked Ellen.

Ellen stirred slightly. "Fifty-two fifty."

At this, Bob Sorrell let fly. "How many units in this joint? Eighteen? Twenty? Figure a gross intake of at least nine hundred a month. Of course that's if they're all rented. That's the big risk on income property; if five of your units in a building this size stand idle, you lose your take. These guys try for the short haul; they raise the rent, goose a few more bucks from each tenant, and then find themselves stuck with half a dozen empty units. And they wonder why they're not ahead at the end of the year."

"Tell them about that place down in San Jose," Sally said. "That government housing business we got into."

Bob's face responded with bleak intensity. "Well, the government leased that land from private investors. For a ten-year period, to build low-cost housing for war workers. Now the leases are dead; and the investors want the property back, to build something solid on. They've been squawking like hell."

"Those wartime units are just cardboard," Sally confided. "We went around, and the walls are cracking . . . You can push them over with your foot."

Bob continued inflexibly, his voice harsh and loud in the small living room. "I put a bid in for the furniture—all that stuff was government owned; the tenants, mostly Okies and coons from the South, brought nothing but their shoes—if they had shoes. Christ, every one of those buildings is six units—that means six reefers, six stoves, six couches, six double beds, six dressers, so on down the line. Six complete three-room apartments of furniture. The buildings had been condemned, of course. They gave everybody sixty days to get out—then they roped the works off and started ripping. There was one week to get out the furnishings—we put in a what-the-hell bid of seventy-five dollars."

"For how many buildings?" Sally murmured. "Wasn't it something like fifty or sixty?"

"Fifty-seven." Bob fooled with his ginger ale glass. "Nobody else bid. We got the furnishings of three hundred and forty-two three-room apartments for seventy-five bucks." He grinned and shook his bony head, still overcome by it all. "The stuff we didn't resell on the used-furniture market we used to furnish apartments in our own units. Boy, that was one sweet deal. Why, there was twenty thousand bucks' worth of furniture there."

Breathlessly, cheeks flushed, Sally said: "Bobby, what about that place—you know the one I mean. Wouldn't they just love it? And Baby could commute from there; isn't there a train that runs right through there? Or he could get a car." She turned eagerly to Hadley. "You ought to have a car, anyhow." Back to her husband she continued: "What about it? It's just going to waste; and it's a *beautiful* little place."

"No," Bob contradicted, with finality. "It wouldn't go. Sure, it looks okay, but when you get down into the foundations and see what's holding it up—" He made a disgusted writing-off squirting noise. "No, that's okay for a short-term investment, but what they want is something permanent."

Sally's red lips blossomed into a disappointed, teasing pout. "I think it's perfect. Just the right size—one bedroom for them and one for Pete. And we could come visit them all the time; we could shoot across the San Mateo toll bridge in no time at all." Face glowing, she addressed Ellen and Stuart. "It's a sweet little house in Mount Eden. Bob's company held a first deed on it, and the people defaulted. It actually belongs to Bob now, in a way. I mean, we could put it through the books—you know. Get it for almost nothing. You think you'd like that?"

Bob raised his voice. "I told you it isn't any good. It needs a whole new foundation—shoot, the damn thing's just sitting there on concrete blocks!"

"Well," Sally shouted back, "they could fix it up! Jack it off the blocks and lay a solid frame!"

"There's no point in getting stuck with a dog," Bob said, closing the subject. "Don't get ants in your pants," he said to Hadley, as if Hadley had said anything. "Just hold your water, buster. . . . You'll make out better in the long run." Fixing his cold, baleful eyes on Hadley he continued: "You'd be better off getting yourself a decent car than a cheap house. With a good buggy you could shoot around anywhere you want. Christ, on weekends we buzz up to Sonoma County. . . . On the open highway the Nash makes an easy eighty-five. You're just breeeezing along." He made a flowing motion with his hand. "Like riding on a cloud."

Sally ducked her head, blond curls swirling in a covert shiver of delicious amusement. "Bob's a deputy sheriff of Napa County. You saw the red light in the back of the car—and he's got a siren."

After a moment Ellen said tightly: "What gives you the most trouble, Bob . . . cattle thieves?"

Bob eyed her humorlessly. "Smart kids hijacking cars," he answered. He settled back against the couch and launched into an account. "I caught a couple of pachucs fooling around with my Dodge—remember the blue Dodge we had last Christmas? Sally and I were in the movie theater, up in Napa. We came out—it was about one thirty—here were these pachucs standing around."

"You know the way they do," Sally broke in. She hunched over, imitating an adolescent slouch. "Hands in their pockets. Bob had the Dodge all shined up. . . . Oh, it was really beautiful. White sidewalls, outside spots . . . everything."

"I could spot those pachucs a mile off," Bob went on relentlessly. "Well, I had a roll of dimes in my hand . . . just happened to be carrying them." He grinned sarcastically, crudely. "One of the pachucs walked up to me—he says, 'How about a ride back into town?' They were going along with us whether we liked it or not."

"Bob hit him right between the eyes," Sally burst in. "That kid went down like a load of coal. The others just stood there staring at him. None of them moved, they just stood there. We got in the car and Bob backed her around, and off we went."

Bob laughed, loud, short, like a bark. "Shoot, when we turned the corner they were dragging the son of a bitch off—his heels was dragging in the gravel; they had him under the armpits. Man, he was out cold. For a week!"

The room was silent for a time, except for the whirr of insects and the murmur of the TV.

Stuart Hadley got to his feet slowly, supporting himself against the chair. He looked tired, completely dragged out by the dry heat of the July evening. He moved unsteadily across the room, shuffling with short, uneven stops, his body stiff and unwieldly. Ellen watched him, perturbed.

"Stu," she said, "where are you going?"

Hadley halted at the bedroom door and turned toward her. His face was pale and puffy, his eyes half closed. He blinked, coughed, and turned back to the bedroom door. "See how Pete is," he murmured.

"He's asleep," Ellen said. "I just looked."

Hadley didn't answer. He disappeared into the bedroom and shut the door quietly after him.

The bedroom was dark and fairly cool. On the dresser in the corner the electric fan whistled creakily to itself, sending a ragged flutter of air across the room. Hadley stood for a time, accustoming himself to the gloom.

Peter Hadley was sound asleep in his bassinet. He wheezed and snorted fretfully, his skin sticky with perspiration, spotted red from the heat. He twisted, fretted, turned over on his side and snored on without waking. He was a big healthy baby. He smelled faintly of sour milk as Hadley wandered over and stood gazing down at him.

From the living room came the sharp, brutal sounds of his brother-in-law's voice. Smashing like a metal hammer against an anvil, the voice vibrated through the thin walls—cheap walls—into the bedroom. Bob Sorrell laughed, raised his voice, spoke to Sally, to Ellen. Hadley, standing in the dark shadows by his son's bassinet, by the sleeping baby, heard his own name mouthed by the man. Sorrell was demanding to know where he was and what he was doing. It was necessary to account for himself and his actions; any moment Sorrell would rise to his feet and stride grimly into the bedroom.

He wondered what to do. He thought about telling Sorrell to leave—telling them both to leave. That was it: it was both of them, his sister, too. How had this come about? He tried to trace it back; when had the thought first come, the original realization that it was both of them, not just Bob . . . ? He could find no origin; the thought had come from nowhere at no particular time. Once in his mind it could not be dislodged. He could not evade it; he was responsible for it. He wanted to get rid of both of them; desperately, he wished they'd leave, go home, drive back up the coast in their huge green Nash, never come back as long as they lived.

The door opened. Ellen slid into the gloom, closed the door softly after her, and hurried over beside him. "For heaven's sake," she grated, "what are you doing in here, just *standing*? Isn't Pete all right?"

"Sure," Hadley answered.

"Then what is it?" Vexation, worry, filled her face. "Darling, you have to come back; you can't hide in here."

His voice rose angrily. "I'm not hiding! I have a right to come in here and see how my son is."

"You can't walk out and leave me alone with them." Ellen's face stiffened coldly. "I'm not going to take it; I'm not going to carry the burden alone. She's your sister, not mine. I'll do my share; I'll put up with them—but not alone. You understand?"

"Okay, Hadley said. "All right, let's go back before he breaks the door down." In the living room, Bob's loud voice boomed and echoed. "How could she marry him?" Hadley demanded futilely. "How could she get mixed up with a man like that?"

"She thinks he's wonderful," Ellen said gaily.

"It doesn't make sense." Hadley moved aimlessly through the half dark- ness, back toward the door. "Every time I see him—it's always the same. He's always been this way; even before they were married he was like this: loud and mean."

Ellen caught his arm. "Darling, you have to expect it. She has her own life—we have ours. My God, she's almost thirty. She's a different generation from us; what do we have in common with them? Look at them—they treat us like kids, patronize us, tell us what to do. . . ."

"I told her," Hadley said.

"Told her what?"

"About the Society."

For a moment Ellen was puzzled. "You mean the Watchmen business? That Beckheim person?"

"All she did was laugh."

"No," Ellen said emphatically, "Stuart, I don't believe it. You're all upset and mixed up in here, just like a spoiled sulking child. Come on back into the living room—honestly, I don't know what I'm going to do with you." Lightly, she hurried on: "You're making us all so unhappy. . . . No wonder Sally wasn't sympathetic. You can't expect us to—"

"It's his fault," Hadley broke in. "She wasn't that way before. He's an ape; he's not human. Did you hear him boasting about beating up that Mexican kid? Some teenager half his size. He's a monster—and she thinks he's won-derful. You should have seen the way he treated Dave and Laura—it was horrible. He threw them out, made them leave."

Ellen linked her arm briskly through his. "Well, she's not so dumb. She's got her wagon hitched to a rising star; I'll say that much for her. She's no fool, darling."

Hadley jerked away. "Did you hear what I said? I told her and she just shook her head. I thought she'd understand—I thought there was one per-son I could go to . . . and she was just like everybody else. A lot of stupid words, bright remarks."

Deep hurt blinding her eyes, Ellen said: "So the one person let you down? I'm sorry. It's too bad, isn't it? Times have changed; you can't go lay your head in her lap anymore."

"What do you mean by that?"

"Come on," Ellen said, "they can hear us; let's get outside. We can talk about this later."

"I want to talk about it now!" He barred her way. "What do you mean?" He grabbed her by the shoulders; the dim light of evening dully illuminated her small face, eyes large and dark, bright with tears, lips half parted, chin quivering. "Goddamn it—" His voice rose wildly. "You're glad!"

"Of course I'm glad. Darling, I'm so glad I want to shout it out at the top of my lungs." Ellen made a hopeless effort to smile; tears slid down her cheeks and dripped onto her starched white shirt. "Her and her damn War-ing blender. She's going to give us the old one, the little one, the one they can't use because it's too small for them. And they're going to fix us up with a house, so we can visit them every week—get our weekly instructions, our briefings. So they can run our lives, tell us what to do, the way she's told you what to do all your life. You don't care; you think that's fine—but *I* care! That damn sister of yours isn't going to tell me how to run my house and my life. . . ." She threw her arms around Stuart and hugged him against her, burying her head desperately into his neck, soft brown hair choking him. "Why the hell can't you come running to *me* with your stories? I'll understand—even if I don't understand. If you want this, it's what I want. I'll go with you; I'll pray and roll around on the floor, whatever it is. . . . It's *you* I care about."

In his bassinet, Pete had wakened up, aroused by the loud voices in the room. He began to cry, shrilly, furiously; his wails rose to an earsplitting scream. In the living room, Sally and Bob got up and headed impatiently for the bedroom door; Bob banged on it noisily and bellowed: "For cripe's sake, what's going on in there?"

Hadley clutched his wife. "I can't stand you talking like that. Get out of here if you're going to talk about her."

"I won't!" Ellen sobbed. "This is my house—I'm not going to leave and you can't make me leave. For years I've had to listen to you talk about her—I'm sick of hearing about her. I'm through . . . I've taken all I can stand." She yanked her arms away from him. "Don't you hurt me like that." Tears poured down her cheeks; her shirt was spotted with great rings of moisture. "And don't grab me that way anymore."

Over the baby's screams Hadley shouted: "I'm not going to take that from you or anybody. If you had half the class she has; if you were anywhere like her—" His voice choked with emotion. "You're not fit to say her name. You're nothing but an easy lay! That's all you are; she's right—you're nothing but an easy piece of tail!"

Shocked, terrified, Ellen stood gazing mutely up into his face. "Please don't say things like that to me." She looked around pathetically for help: her voice trailed off to a whisper. "Stuart, please don't do any more. Please!"

He grabbed her tight, pulled her against him until her ribs cracked. "I can't stand it anymore," he gasped. "I'm finished. I'm leaving—I'm getting out."

"No," Ellen said, weak with terror. "Forget what I said; let it go. Please let it go—I'm sorry."

Hadley's face flushed a dark, ugly red. Apprehensively, Ellen shrank away as he released her. It was a look she had seen before; she dreaded it more than anything else in the world. He was going to do something; she knew it. The look always meant something; involuntarily, she put her arm up over her face. Once, only once, he had hit her. But she had hit him first; she had slapped him. Immediately, he had sat down on the couch and cried like a child; she had tried to comfort him. After that, he had got up and socked her in the eye. But he wasn't going to do that now; he was going to leave. She wished frantically that he would hit her; she wanted him to hit her. Anything was better than having him leave, having him walk out on her.

"Don't," she gasped, pushing between him and the door. Now she *prayed* he would hit her. "I'm not going to let you go; you can't go."

Hadley's lips twisted. Convulsively, he raised his arm; she saw his elbow lift, sharp and hard, a triangle of bone inside the soft fabric of his sleeves. Then abruptly he grunted and jerked away, his hand fumbling for the doorknob. "Take care of yourself," he said obliquely. "Have a good time. I'll write to you."

At that moment Sally pushed the door open and entered the gloomy bedroom. "My golly, you two kids can be heard all over the place! Come on out of there—" She herded them briskly into the living room. "Now kiss and make friends." Curtly, she examined her wristwatch. "We're going to have to fly; we've got to be out of here by ten."

Bob had turned and was lumbering into the kitchen. "Can we get some fresh coffee going?" He began rooting around in the cupboards over the sink. "Ellen, where the hell's your Silex? I'm not tackling that freeway without some hot coffee to wake me up."

For a brief instant Stuart Hadley and his wife held on to each other. Then Hadley broke away from her. "I'll see you later," he said.

"Where are you going?" Ellen demanded fearfully; she hurried after him. "Please—take me along with you! I don't care where it is; can't I come along?"

"I'm going over to Dave's," Hadley said, at the front door of the apartment. "Somebody ought to apologize to them."

Tearfully, Ellen caught up with him. "Please, Stuart, let me come along with you. I'm afraid you won't come back!"

"You have to stay with Pete."

"I'll bring him along!"

Hadley laughed sharply. "On foot? We don't have any car, remember."

At the door of the kitchen, Bob Sorrell stood with the Silex in his hands, his heavy face wide with surprise. As Hadley tore open the front door he saw Sorrell's amazement darken to angry resentment. Then the door closed after him; he was out in the dim, stuffy hallway.

He hurried to the stairs and descended two at a time, his hand on the banister. He rushed through the lobby, out past the open front door, onto the wide concrete steps. The night air was fresh, clear. He took a deep breath of it, hesitated momentarily, and then plunged off in the direction of the Golds'.

For an endless time he walked the hot, dark streets, hands thrust in his pockets, brooding and trying to collect his thoughts.

Already, he regretted what he had said to Ellen.

He crossed the street, passed run-down pool halls, bars, shoeshine parlors, cheap cafés and hotels. He was getting near the Golds' place; he quickened his steps.

The Laura Gold who opened the door for him was chastened and quiet. "Hello, Stu," she said, in a voice so faint he could scarcely hear it. "Come inside and have some wine."

Like a dull, dead pudding, she stumped across the room and threw herself down in a chair. Hadley stood uncertainly by the door, adjusting himself. There were people: Dave Gold sitting at his desk, smoking morosely and watching him; two children; and a slim woman in slacks and a checkered shirt.

"How's the painter?" the slim woman asked him.

Hadley was confused. He started to look behind him, then realized she was speaking to him. He identified her: she was Marsha Frazier. In the center of the room a low table supported a half gallon of dark purple wine, glasses, a package of potato chips, a mass of blue cheese with a table knife sticking into it, a box of soda crackers, a jar of peanut butter. The boy lay restless and bored, curled up with a magazine at the end of the Golds' ratty old couch. He was perhaps nine, in faded jeans, tennis shoes, and a T-shirt. Like Marsha, his hair was tinged a faint rusty red. Sound asleep in a chair in the corner was a small girl, perhaps three, in a rumpled playsuit.

"Are these your children?" Hadley asked the woman.

"Haven't you met my progeny?" Marsha nodded toward the boy. "That's Timmy."

The boy glowered up briefly. "Hello," he boomed in a deep voice; and returned to his magazine.

Marsha indicated the sleeping girl. "That's Pat." Lifting her wineglass, she sipped thoughtfully, eyes on Stuart Hadley as he awkwardly found himself a place to sit.

Dave spoke up. "Marsha drove us home."

"The Cadillac broke down," Laura said faintly, in a voice small with shock. "We only got a few blocks. We had to leave it; we took a bus across town to Marsha's place."

Marsha Frazier was tall, gaunt; her face was bony with deep hollows. She wore no makeup. Her eyes were gray. Her skin was faintly freckled. There was an ascetic bleakness about her . . . but Hadley did not find her unattractive. A cleanness of line: her body was as trim as a young boy's, as straight and simple as that of her son's. An unadorned body, with no useless bulges or flesh. Her arms, below her rolled-up sleeves, were bone and muscle, without softness. Her hands were strong and competent. As before, the conversation moved around her: she was the natural pivot. Both Dave and Laura were sunk in silence and apathy, withdrawn into stoic acceptance.

"Is that your coupe out front?" Hadley asked her. "That gray Studebaker?"

Marsha nodded. "It needs a bath."

"It's a nice-looking car."

"It rides well," she admitted. "But it doesn't have any power. It's easy to see out of it . . . the back of the cabin is almost completely glass."

"I know," Hadley said. "I've driven them. They're nice."

"The Cadillac can't be fixed," Laura spoke up dismally. "I guess we're going to junk it. We can get twenty bucks for the parts." She added: "It's parked up on Mission. I guess tomorrow the San Francisco police will tow it away, anyhow."

"That's too bad," Hadley said. He tried to speak with feeling, but his sympathy for the Golds was rapidly dwindling. Their dark, unpleasant faces repelled him. Two trolls, he thought. Hoarse-voiced trolls, with big feet and shovel hands. Warty and gruff, exactly like in the fairy story. He had lost interest in them already; his attention had turned toward the slim, gray-eyed woman.

He poured himself some of the cheap wine. "Why did you call me a painter?" he asked Marsha.

"We told her," Laura said. "About your pictures—you know."

"I haven't done anything for a long time," Hadley said. But it made him feel strange; he could easily think of himself as a painter, he realized. "You run a magazine?" he asked. "You're the editor of *Succubus*?"

"That's right," Marsha said, in her toneless contralto. A rational voice, secure and efficient. A voice certain of itself. "But we're like you. . . . We haven't put out a copy in six months."

"Why not?"

"No money."

There was a pause while all of them considered money. The Golds looked blank, aimless. Timmy, knees up, magazine in his lap, was uninterested. The magazine was a quarterly art review; he was probably used to seeing them around, as Hadley had grown up with the house organ of the AMA.

Outside the apartment, beyond the dark squares of open windows, cars honked and signals changed. The dull odor of the Bay filtered in, corroded rubber and oil. In the next apartment a shrill radio squalled remotely. Thumps, the movement of people overhead. The room itself, cluttered with books and papers, heavy with the smell of dust, decaying food, rubbish and debris.

"What does it cost to put out a magazine?" Hadley asked.

Marsha smiled; her teeth were, like her hair, skin, and eyes, a neutral mixed shade: not shiny, not metallic. As if she were compounded from old wood and bone, rubbed and aged to a dull finish, with the bleached roughness of driftwood. There was a solid earthy quality about her body; in spite of her slimness, her small face, narrow arms, she looked strong. "It depends," she answered, "on what sort of magazine you intend to put out. The *SEP* for example costs in the hundreds of thousands."

"What's that?" Hadley asked.

"*Saturday Evening Post*. We don't have much income, a little trickle from university fellowships, a few thousand now and then from the Ford Foundation." She grimaced wryly. "But we've lost that. . . . No more from them."

Hadley wondered if he should say he had never seen a magazine called *Succubus*. He tried to imagine what it looked like. He recalled the college literary quarterly; it probably looked like that: square, hygienic pages of prose and poems, no capitals on the cover, modernesque title page. Heavy book-bond paper, white and porous. Fifty cents. Consisting mainly of critical essays on Capote, Proust, Gide, Willa Cather. No advertising, except, perhaps, an occasional textbook shop.

The room was peaceful, too peaceful for conversation or thought. Hadley relaxed into contentedness, lay back and sipped his wine. Nobody spoke. The tension was gone, here; like Sunday afternoon on a park bench, there was no pressure of time, no struggle or ambition. Even Laura, usually full of brash talk, had nothing to say; their experience of the day had deprived her of will. The Golds had come up against a brick wall, in the form of Bob Sorrell. His huge, brutal cruelty had shocked them into impotency. They had not protested or fought back. They had collapsed in the face of it, wilted by the sheer massed weight of his heedlessness. Bob Sorrell could ride roughshod over such people as the Golds; they were incapable of giving back the treatment they had received. Under their veneer of loud talk, quick gestures, was a gentleness easily exposed. Like Hansel and Gretel, they had been lured out into the world and then systematically mashed flat. The dazed blankness in their eyes was clouded with bewilderment; they still did not comprehend how they had been hustled about, shoved aside, sent off and disposed of. They had been handled like inorganic objects; their basic humanity had been ignored. In them was no response, no adjustment. In the face of brutality they simply died.

But Hadley relaxed and enjoyed this void. The absence of braying talk lulled him; he was grateful for Laura's silence. And the quietude that lay about Marsha Frazier was not the crushed stupor of the Golds'. The woman's equanimity came from confidence, not fear. She was totally in control; it was her way of life.

"As a painter," she said, "you should be interested in materials. Inks and papers . . . We experiment with various processes. We're especially interested in new methods of reproducing cuts."

Hadley nodded. His agreement was part of the fiction he knew was being maintained: she understood he was not a painter, but she chose to speak of him as a painter. It was her pleasure, and it was his to hold up the other end. It was agreeable to him; astonished, he noticed how different it made him feel. And that, perhaps, was the reason for the fiction. Shrewd, watchful, she was creating him. What she said affected and altered him; in a few simple words she had distinctly remolded Stuart Hadley.

"We want," she said, "to do more work with woodcuts—with blocks. That slows printing speed, and the number of impressions. But"—again she smiled her thin colorless humorless smile—"we never even began to sell what we printed. We never had that problem."

In the corner at his desk, Dave Gold puffed on his pipe, stared down at the floor, listened to what was being said. His soft, flabby body, shapeless in baggy tweeds, unpressed heavy fabric, invited attack. A helpless slug to be stepped on. Dave Gold completed the unit of which Sorrell was one part. The hitter and the hit. There was a maddening quality about the Golds; silent or vocal, they culled hostility.

Hadley had come over to apologize. He had thought he was sorry for them, shameful for what had happened to them. Now he was angered. Instead of being apologetic he was outraged; he believed, suddenly, that he had come to complete what Bob Sorrell had begun. Dave and Laura sat mutely waiting for him to begin on them. The former loud talk had been spurs to goad him on; apprehensively, the two of them sat in their own apartment, prepared to receive whatever was in store for them.

But he said nothing. He merely ignored them and talked to Marsha Frazier. He recalled what they had said about her; he was amused. They didn't like her. His amusement increased. For a time he no longer felt sick and unhappy; he was perking up. In the presence of the slim, competent woman, he regained his manhood, preened his feathers. She was interested in him. . . . Then it occurred to him to wonder about the two children.

"Are you solely responsible for them?" he asked her. "The two children, Timmy and Pat."

She laughed. "Parthenogenesis? No—I'm divorced. I was married to an Army major." After a time she added: "During World War II."

Stuart Hadley studied the two children and realized that what she said was not true. The girl Pat was three at the most; and the war had been over seven years. But it seemed all right. It fit in with the leisure of the room: truth had been dissolved by contentedness. The artist in him, the dreamer, the salesman, all responded equally. The little-boy liar spinning his big plans for the future crept to the surface and lay over him, again, like a familiar warm hide. Everything in Stuart Hadley answered to this genial flexibility, where small became large, large became incredible. Gratefully, he was drifting back to a happier age, a primeval core of his life. If Marsha Frazier cared to utter a statement, the statement rang with the higher veracity of pleasantness. It was true, in the old sense, the ancient sense that he remembered so well: it pleased the teller and the hearer.

"I've seen your magazine," Hadley said, Prometheus unbound. "Nice-looking . . . I didn't get a chance to go too deeply into it, but what I saw seemed fine."

This was weighed carefully, and accepted. A rapport existed between the two of them, from which the Golds were excluded. "I wish you could see our projected fall issue," Marsha said, nodding. "We have some of the dummy set up, but we've had to mark time until we know where we stand financially."

Stuart Hadley listened, contemplated the thought of a layout for a magazine. What kind of magazine? What did he really know about it? But it didn't matter. He was content to express knowledge, and she was content to hear.

It was a strange relationship that was building up between them. Neither knew a thing about the other; both had substituted a higher intuitive awareness. To her, he was a painter. . . . What was she to him? He questioned himself, trying to put together the fabric of his own hopes, desires, the stuff of his own world.

"I used to be active in literary circles," his usual voice announced, a casual reference that shocked him into almost wakefulness. There was no truth in the statement whatsoever. "I helped put out a college publication, nothing of any importance. I was art editor."

From the lean pickings of his past he had assembled this masterpiece of misinformation. In high school he had contributed a cartoon to the semester yearbook: the *Green and Crimson*. He had dated a girl who proofread manuscripts. He had been interested in photography: when pictures of the graduates were taken he had fixed the lighting. He had done well in mechanical drawing; he had been interested temporarily in layouts and designs. And he *had* been on the art staff of his college newspaper; Dave Gold had got him the job. All these were now combined to form a new object. Handled by his mind, the object arose and announced itself.

"We tried various lithographic techniques," it uttered, through his vocal organs and mouth. "Of course, for the kind of material we were presenting, there was no general public market. We failed to find a mass response . . . but that's not surprising."

Slumped over at his desk, Dave Gold gave no sign that he had heard this fantastic invention. Probably he had. Probably he felt helpless to do anything about it. Probably it seemed useless, trivial, to point out that Hadley had done nothing but paste mats to layout sheets. It was beside the point.

Drowsy with the summer-evening warmth, the glass of wine in his hands, Hadley lay back and conversed with Marsha Frazier. Her son, Timmy, fell asleep; at his desk Dave Gold drooped lower and lower, his pipe out, his body limp. Laura sat like a lump of stale dough. Outside, along the sidewalk, people strolled back and forth, walking off their night restlessness.

When Marsha and her children left, Hadley left with them. He carried the little girl downstairs and placed her in the backseat of the Studebaker. Pat stirred and settled against the upholstery. Behind him, down the apartment-house stairs, came Marsha, holding on to Timmy's hand. The boy peevishly made his way to the car and crawled into the back, where he curled up beside his sister in a sleepy, cross ball.

Hadley stood uncertainly on the sidewalk as Marsha strolled around to the other side of the car, long-legged, very straight and thin in the evening darkness. "Hop in," she said briefly. "I'll take you home."

"You're sure—," he began. As he protested, he climbed in and closed the door. "It's not far; I can walk it."

Marsha, unlit cigarette between her lips, started up the motor. "Takes a minute to warm." She leaned over to light her cigarette. "It killed those two to come running to me. Dave and Laura. They were completely demoralized."

"I know," Hadley said.

"Their ability to function crumbles under the first hard knock. It's all a sham." Gazing straight ahead of her, she watched the distant movement of cars and people, the brightly lit cluster of neon signs that was the downtown business section. "Sham, sham, sham." She started up the car, snapped on the lights, and glided out into the street.

She parked in front of his apartment building, and they sat for a time, the only two awake anywhere in sight. Both children were sound asleep in the back. No shapes were visible on the dark sidewalks. Up and down the silent streets lights were beginning to snap off one by one. It was almost one o'clock.

"You're married?" Marsha asked.

He told her about Ellen and Pete.

"How old is the baby? A month?" She dusted her cigarette against the open car window. "You're lucky. You've got a lot ahead of you . . . I remember when Timmy was a baby. It's a different world. Every change in him is a change in yourself."

"Do you come down the peninsula much?" Hadley asked.

"Sometimes. When I feel like it. I was down the days Beckheim spoke here. . . . That's when I met you. You went with Dave and Laura. You heard him . . . but only the last part, you said."

"I went back the next night and heard it all."

"You did?" Marsha reflected. "What did you think of him?"

"I thought—it seemed to me he was very impressive." Hadley let out his breath with a rush. "I thought he spoke well."

"He's an unusual man. I've been interested in him. Do you know anything about him? I'll tell you what I know, for what it's worth. Theodore Beckheim is fifty-five years old, although he isn't sure that's exact. He was born in Vinegar Bend, Alabama."

"He's a Negro, isn't he?" Hadley asked.

"That's right. When he was thirteen he ran away to New Orleans. He got a job with a coffee-roasting factory. Every day he rowed out into the bay and climbed aboard coffee ships coming in from Brazil. He sampled the different coffees. . . . He got twenty-five cents an hour for that. When he was eighteen he got married. He had children, three sons. His wife died in 1916. In 1918 he joined the Army; they sent him overseas. He didn't come directly back. . . . He traveled down into Africa, to the Gold Coast. In South Africa he worked in the mines. He came back to the United States just before the big bust. He had a little money—he invested it in land. He was going to farm, he and his three sons. When the bust came they lost the land; they couldn't meet the mortgage payments. They left the country—it was in Virginia—and drifted back into town. To Chicago. The Black Belt."

"Did—he start the Society?"

"No," Marsha said. "There was a lot of religious activity in Chicago in the early thirties. There was even a cult of Mohammedan Negroes. . . . There was a Middle Eastern heresy, called Baha'i. A lot of sects, mystical movements. The Watchmen Society was founded back in 1887. A splinter fundamentalist group, split off from the Baptists. A little old man, a Negro, was running it: John Middleton Frisbey. They had a soup kitchen . . . gave out food as a come-on. To get the food you had to listen to their story, read the *People's Watchman*. Beckheim and his sons wandered into the mission, got the food and the pitch along with it. Those were tough times. . . . You don't remember that."

"Do you?" Hadley asked her.

Marsha smiled, started to answer, then smiled again. "What do you think? How old do I look? An old woman with two kids . . ."

Hadley made a guess. "About—thirty."

"I'm twenty-six. Timmy was born when I was sixteen. I'll tell you about that sometime. No, I don't remember those days. But I've heard Beckheim speak about them."

"In private? In conversation?"

She nodded. "Oh, yes."

"Where is he?"

"In San Francisco. He had a heart attack early this month." She spoke dispassionately. "He's resting up . . . then he's going north, to Sacramento, up to Oregon and Washington."

"Will he be all right?"

"I think so. But he's got to take it easier. He does too much. . . . He doesn't realize he's getting old."

"How do you fit in with the Society?" Hadley asked her.

Presently she said: "I can't give you an answer. I don't know, myself. I've done a lot of thinking about the Society. In the next issue—if it ever comes out—we want to run an account of it. We have good photos, and drawings, I think." She glanced at him. "Tell me what you think of this idea. Sketches of the types of people who make up the Society. Listening to Beckheim . . . drawn at the meetings. Of course, we can take all the photographs we want. But I want to capture more."

"Yes," Hadley agreed.

"Part of the dummy is made up, part isn't. We still have blanks here and there. Since there's no rush . . . no deadline to meet." Abruptly she tossed her cigarette out the window. "Well, another day." She reached over and pushed open the door on his side. "Maybe I'll see you again. Good night."

Without warning, Hadley found himself standing on the sidewalk. The car started up, Marsha waved briefly, and the car roared off into the darkness.

For a time he stood. Then he turned and walked slowly toward the apartment building. All the things that had happened, all that had been said and seen, flowed through his mind out of control. He gave up battling; there had been too much for him to assimilate just yet. Maybe later. Or maybe not. He found his key, unlocked the heavy front door, and entered the lobby.

Under his door there was only the dim glow of the night-light. Sally and Bob had gone back up the coast in their magnificant green Nash. He let himself in, grateful for the silence. The bedroom door was open; Pete lay in his bassinet. Ellen was a vague heap in the center of the double bed. Sound asleep . . . He locked the door and began untying his shoes.

He was out at lunch, the next day, when Marsha brought the copy of *Succubus*.

At the counter, Olsen stood with the telephone pressed to his head, conversing angrily with a customer. Fergesson was in the TV display room, showing a big Westinghouse combination. Hadley hurried downstairs to the crapper. He urinated rapidly, washed his hands, smoothed down his hair and examined his face, teeth, and appearance in the mirror. He picked at his teeth, spat into the bowl, unbuttoned his shirt and rubbed a trifle more Arrid into his steaming armpits, and then raced back upstairs.

Olsen was off the phone and on his way down to the service department. "Where the hell have you been?" he demanded gruffly. "Some twat was in here looking for you—not your wife." He jerked his thumb at the counter. "Left something for you—waited around and finally took her can out of here."

"Who was she?" Hadley asked, his heart thudding.

"Never saw her before." Olsen disappeared down the stairs three at a time. "Anyhow, turn them upside down and they're all alike."

Hadley rummaged around behind the counter until he found a flat manila package. Trembling, he laid it on the counter and, opening it, slid out the contents. At first he was disappointed. Advertising? A free sample? It was a periodical, a magazine. And then he identified it. The back of his neck twitched and shuddered as he read the black hard lines of type.

SUCCUBUS
a magazine for
people who want to know

He turned it over. A slip of paper fluttered from it to the floor; he grabbed it up. In neat, precise woman's pencil it read:

". . . couldn't wait. See you tomorrow at noon. You owe me one dollar for the copy . . . m.f."

He pocketed the note deep in the cavity of his wallet. Sitting down on the bottom drawer of the tube cabinet, he began leafing nervously, tautly, through the copy of *Succubus:* the magazine for people who couldn't stand not knowing.

It was not what he had expected. For the rest of the day he took his free minutes to pore over it.

This was not a college publication. There was no musty academic timbre, no critical articles on Henry James. He began to breathe slowly, shallowly, as he turned the pages.

Succubus was a political sheet.

For a long time he stood holding it in his hands, wondering what came next. When customers entered, he dropped it behind the counter, reassembled himself, and headed out to wait on them. As soon as they were gone he was back poring over it.

Not political in the ordinary sense: not a newsmagazine, or a party organ. Not a "journal of interpretation," with contributions by Elmer Davis, Clifton Fadiman, John Flynn, Frieda Utley, or any names he knew. It was slick—that much fitted his expectation. The cover was glossy, multicolored, a work of art. It showed a medieval alchemistic flask of some kind as a backdrop; superimposed on the flask in bold thick strokes of ink was a symbolistic Communist figure.

It took him a long time to unscramble the cover, and even then he wasn't sure he had it all. Apparently, it was to show the infiltration of Communists into colleges: the Communist was posing as a savant. Within the alchemist's trappings (symbols of knowledge) were the beard and bloody hand, the dripping hammer and sickle.

Inside was a lead editorial. The paper was glossy, heavy; the type was black and clean. The format was routine, but satisfactory. It was not arty: it was firm and solid. At random, he found a whole section of photographs of Frank Lloyd Wright's buildings. And after that, schematics of what Berlin would have been like had the Nazis won the war.

One section contained a section of a mural; or rather, a projected mural. Stiff, heavy figures. Workers, soldiers, holding flags and standing together. Mothers with children. Big-faced peasants. All very sturdy and healthy. Terribly healthy. Men tilling the soil, sorting grain.

He skimmed an article on Hollywood: a photo of Sam Goldwyn stared fleshily up at him. A cut of Barney Balaban. A cut of Bernard Baruch. A cut of Henry Morgenthau.

JEWISH CONTROL OF THE FILM INDUSTRY:
FIVE BILLIONS IN POISON

Another article couldn't be ignored:

INSIDE WALL STREET: THE INTERNATIONAL
PLUTOCRATIC CONSPIRACY

And another:

KARL MARX—PROPHET OF ZIONISM

Weakly, Hadley slid *Succubus* back into its manila folder. He could understand why Dave and Laura disliked Marsha, why they had been completely demoralized by having to ask help from her. He could understand now the depth of the conflict between them, why Dave did no work for *Succubus*.

Succubus was a racist, neofascist tract.

But it didn't look like a racist, neofascist tract: it wasn't crude and bombastic. He would have expected a racist tract to be printed on cheap newsprint: a disreputable, ugly four-page throwaway with glaring headlines, insulting to intelligence and taste. He would have expected fantastic filth: wild charges, half-crazed assertions and denouncements. Something that reeked of the crackpot, slimy with violence. A militant, fanatic sheet, pornographic and disgusting, words misspelled, faulty grammar: the work of ignorant, vitriolic men, wizened little men bitter and acid with hate. A sour, ranting sheet. A vulgarity.

Succubus was expensive, tasteful, beautifully printed. It was not avant; there were no experiments with format or type. It was heavy, conservative—like the men and women shown in the murals. It was not daring, artistically; it was a solidly built object, well bound and well organized. The articles were written lucidly, with erudition and poise. No ranting. No fantastic charges; the overall impression was one of moderation. Could a fascist, racist sheet be moderate?

There was nothing lunatic-fringe about *Succubus*. He realized with growing wonder that this was designed to go into the best homes. In its own way, this was *respectable*. On an imported Philippine mahogany coffee table, beside an inlaid ashtray, a handsome lamp, *Succubus* would look lovely. It would grace the most tasteful living room.

After the first shock, Hadley did a lot of thinking. Again and again he opened the folder and peeked in at the thick white packet of book-bond paper. A dollar. It looked like *Fortune:* a kind of political, artistic version. But it had no circulation. Probably it was distributed one copy at a time. This issue bore no date: undoubtedly, most of them were mailed out directly, not put on stands. He couldn't imagine *Succubus* appearing on a newsstand.

About two in the afternoon he began to wonder about Beckheim. What did this tell him about the Society? Not much. He couldn't connect the *People's Watchman,* the rows of kindly faces at the lecture, with this elegant publication. This had class, prestige. It wasn't directed at the kind of people who had flocked to hear Beckheim.

He understood, suddenly, what kind of world Dave and Laura lived in. With organized enemies ready to destroy them; and the Golds had been forced to go to one of these enemies for help. Delivered over to them: they had been helpless to resist. It was wrong; he knew how wrong it had been, that there was no other place they could go.

The Golds hadn't asked for this world, any more than he had. They had been born involuntarily. And now that they were here their presence was resented, as if they had somehow conspired to exist, as if their birth were part of some occult scheme. As if, by being born and trying to live like everybody else, they were getting away with something. Managing to put over a dishonest enterprise.

And the great exposers were only calling attention to the enterprise. By pointing at the Golds they proved the reality of the conspiracy. By being born, the Golds validated the theory. The Golds had only to occupy space and breathe air to offend the theorists. They had already demanded too much. The theorists had to reveal nothing more than that the Jews existed; that was sufficient. By showing that Jews could be found standing on street corners, or sitting in movie theaters, or driving buses, or telling jokes on the radio—wherever a Jew existed he proved the dogma of the theorist. Only by ceasing to exist was the Jew safe. Only by quickly dying could he erase the taint, the guilt of trying to survive.

Thinking of this, Hadley saw how much the Golds were like himself. He had no place, either. But still he had no sympathy for them. Because he had no sympathy for himself. In a terrible deep-down way, all the way to the bottom of his soul, he despised them for being victims, as he despised himself for being a victim. He didn't want to be like them. He didn't want to be taken for one of them, one of the victimized group. He wanted to get out, climb above that.

He was not content, as the Golds were. All they sought was to keep what little they had; they didn't demand anything more. But he demanded more. And he loathed them for letting Sorrell walk over them. He loathed them for letting *him* walk over them.

The Golds were the weak mute victimized image of himself, and in his rage, he was bursting out of that image. He couldn't stand that image any longer—Stuart Hadley: victim. And Marsha Frazier, her image was becoming clear, too. She was another side of him, strong, calculating, ruthless, efficient. Knowing what she wanted, doing what she wanted. Letting nothing stop her. In him something responded. In him, something admired those things about her, her assurance, her unequivocal sense of self. He admired her—and he was frightened. He was rising to that specter-presence; he was moving that way.

"What's that you have there?" Fergesson demanded good-naturedly, appearing in front of him, hand extended. "Let's see it."

Hadley blinked. Embarrassed, he stammered and stalled; he hadn't seen Fergesson come up. "You wouldn't be interested."

Fergesson stopped being amused. "I'm interested in anything you're reading on my time." He sensed guilty resistance. "What is it, a dirty magazine? Pictures of girls?"

Hadley reluctantly handed *Succubus* over. Laying it out on the counter, Fergesson flipped the pages rapidly. "See?" Hadley said belligerently, his ears beginning to burn apprehensively. "I told you it wasn't something you'd care about."

"Christ," Fergesson said softly.

"What's the matter?"

Fergesson's face twisted with disgust. He dropped the magazine as if it were alive with vermin. "Where'd you get this garbage?"

"Somebody gave it to me," Hadley muttered evasively.

An outraged, baleful expression on his face, Fergesson glared at him. "What is it about you? How do you do it?"

Nettled, humiliated, Hadley muttered, "Do what?"

"Good God . . . you always manage to get mixed up in something cracked. You have a knack. If there's anything crazy, you're in on it. You head straight for this nut stuff, don't you? How do you manage it?"

Trembling, Hadley retrieved his magazine. "What I read is my own business." In a blind haze he shoved it back in its folder. "This is a free country; I can read what I want. You can't stop me. You can't keep me from reading this. Understand?"

Shaking his head, his face stony, Fergesson strode off.

Hadley did not take *Succubus* home. He stuck it away in the back closet, behind some old Atwater Kent display signs, where no one would find it.

At home that night, he brooded about it. What was he getting himself into? Maybe Fergesson was right. It was easy to imagine Horace Wakefield carrying around a copy of *Succubus,* slipping it out of his coat to show to friends. Secretly confiding the articles to the select few he could trust. Having it ready as he sat in the Health Food Store eating his tapioca pudding and carrot salad. Like the article by G. B. Shaw on vaccination . . . more ammunition to be fired at the corrupt world.

He could picture Wakefield delighting in the mystical knowledge of Jewish world power. The Protocols of the Elders of Zion: if Wakefield knew about them, how pleased, how excited he would be!

Ellen brought in a plate of melting vanilla ice cream she had churned up in the freezer of the refrigerator. "Stu," she said, "what are you thinking about?"

"Nothing," he answered, accepting the ice cream.

"Has—Fergesson said anything to you about buying that store? I think he's really going through with it. From what Alice told me . . ."

"No," Hadley said shortly. "He hasn't said anything."

The matter dropped, and he continued brooding. He was moving down a long corridor, the end of which was obscured from sight. And yet, this was why he had been attracted. *It was new*. It was not a warmed-over rehash of old things, stale routines repeated from his past. He had never before experienced a man like Theodore Beckheim. He had never met a woman like Marsha Frazier, or thumbed through *Succubus*. He didn't even know what *succubus* meant.

Getting a dictionary from the bookcase, he quickly looked it up. What he expected he didn't know; in any case, he was surprised. *Succubus:* a male demon who assumes female form to tempt men from the virtuous path by having sexual intercourse with them during the night. The word came from the Latin *succubare:* to lie under. And from the Latin *succuba:* a whore. It was quite a title for a magazine. He closed the dictionary and put it away.

The next day, Tuesday, he prepared his arrangements well in advance. "I'm meeting somebody for lunch," he told Fergesson. "At noon—okay? I want to get out promptly."

Fergesson, checking over invoices, grunted and nodded without answering. As Hadley descended the stairs to the main floor he realized what a narrow rope he was walking: there were a dozen ways Ellen could find out. Fergesson might tell her. She might walk in the store looking for him while he was out with Marsha. Dave Gold might mention it to her. And so on.

He was going to have to bring it out in the open—or forget the whole thing.

While he was meditating about forgetting the whole thing, Marsha Frazier strolled into the store.

As before, she wore slacks, tight-fitting and pocketless, a wide leather belt, a heavy checkered shirt. Her reddish, sandy hair was brushed back. She carried a gigantic leather briefcase under her arm. At the front counter she paused, glanced slowly around, and saw him.

He hurried over. "Hello," he said to her. "I got the magazine."

Thoughtfully, she nodded. "Are you able to leave the store?"

Hadley rushed upstairs, told Fergesson he was leaving, got his coat, and rushed down the steps to the front of the store. Marsha had strolled back out again; she stood in the entrance, expressionless, clearly not wishing to waste time. He joined her breathlessly.

"Where do you want to go?" he asked. It was just noon; people were starting to appear in quantity. "How about in here?" He indicated the Health Food Store. "Okay?"

Marsha preceded him into the Health Food Store, a stately figure moving slowly toward the tables in the back. She glanced momentarily at the dried root and yam display, then plucked back the chair and seated herself. She was getting a package of cigarettes as Hadley awkwardly sat down across from her.

Betty came wheezing over, her gray-dough face twisted into a grimacing smile. "Morning, Stuart." She nodded to Marsha. "Good day, miss. Nice hot weather, don't you think?"

Hadley agreed. "Very nice." Marsha said nothing.

"There's creamed chipped beef on toast," Betty recited laboriously, "macaroni salad, green peas, and banana cream pudding."

"Just coffee," Marsha said firmly.

Hadley ordered the meal for himself, and off went Betty to give the order to the colored cook in back. Women were beginning to pour in, well dressed, heavyset, middle-aged. The cackle and bustle had begun.

"What do you think of this place?" Hadley asked Marsha.

"It's interesting." The expression on her face showed she was totally uninterested. "Did you have a chance to examine the magazine?"

He answered: "Yes." Without elaborating; he didn't know what to say because he didn't know how he felt. At this point he didn't understand his own mind at all.

"What did you think of it?" Calm, dispassionate. But a question that he was going to have to answer.

Hadley fooled with the strap of his wristwatch. He studied the sugarless canned fruit displays that were stacked up to the ceiling behind Marsha, shelf after shelf of tasteless peaches, pears, plums, packed in water for diabetics. "I was surprised," he said finally. "It wasn't what I expected."

"What did you expect?"

"I don't know . . . a literary journal, maybe. Like our college quarterly."

Marsha smiled her thin, bloodless smile. Her face was skull-like, bony. Eyes set in deep hollows, dark shadow beneath the cold gray pupils. "No," she agreed, "we're not printing poems about Venice and short stories about abortions in North Carolina. It's nice-looking, don't you think? Good paper, good printing. The cover is five-color."

"I knew the cover looked unusual."

"The food came, and Hadley began devouring it. Across from him Marsha sipped her coffee and stonily watched. "Did you have a chance to read any of the articles?" she asked.

"No," he answered, "I didn't take it home. I left it at the store."

"Why?"

He hesitated. He couldn't answer her truthfully. "I forgot it," he said instead. "I'll take it home tonight." He couldn't help asking: "Is there any particular—reason? I mean, is there any rush?"

It sounded wrong to him. But he was uncomfortably aware that he was being subjected to an inquisition; he didn't like it. He felt that he had been tricked in some way; *Succubus* wasn't what he had expected, and magazines should never contain surprises. In this simple, elemental manner, he was able to feel resentment; it neatly overbalanced his guilt. He tried to pretend that this concerned the business process of buying and selling; he told himself that he was facing a seller who had misrepresented her product. He felt an American indignation. And yet, at the same time, he knew that the situation was infinitely more complex; it wasn't really a business transaction at all. Marsha wasn't trying to sell him a copy of *Succubus* or even a subscription. . . . She wasn't trying to solicit funds from him. She was after something more greater.

"This coffee is terrible," Marsha said.

"It's not real. It's bran meal, health-food stuff. No caffeine."

"Why not?"

Hadley waved his hand. "You know—nothing stimulating. Nothing unnatural."

Marsha got to her feet and crossed the room to the counter. She returned a moment later with a glass of orange juice. Hadley watched with interest as she seated herself. She had carried the glass with grave intensity, as if it were a thing of importance.

"You're worse than I am," Hadley said jokingly. "You take things too seriously."

"Do people tell you that?"

"They tell me I should go to ball games. Have a good time. Stop worrying and thinking."

"Do you go to ball games?"

"No."

Marsha nodded. "You're not frivolous."

He hadn't thought of it that way. "What do you mean?"

"They're out to enjoy themselves. . . . That's all they're interested in. The whole mass thinks in terms of pleasure. They want excitement, artificial thrills. Amusement parks, fast auto races, baseball games, liquor . . . cheap sensations. They're jaded, restless, bored."

"Yes," Hadley said.

"But these are symptoms. Only indications . . . not the cause. On Saturday night the kids wander the streets in packs, looking for something to fill their empty lives. Standing around drugstores, just waiting. Waiting for what? Five, six hours. What for? Girls go by . . . they just stare."

"They get in fights," Hadley suggested. "I was reading an article in the *Chronicle* about the rise in juvenile delinquency."

"The fighting is a symptom, too. It's a spontaneous return to a natural primitive combat. Going out in bands, like the ancient tribes. Fused together, loyal to each other, by blood oaths. Doing battle, the medieval concept of valor . . . virtue in the old Roman sense: manliness. The trial, the purification, metal against metal. You know Wagner? The forging of the sword Notung, from the pieces of the old, down in the smoky forges of the dwarf Mime." She smiled at him over her glass of orange juice. "Down in the deep, dark caves under the surface of the ground, where Siegfried grew up . . . not knowing who he was, not knowing his father, his mother."

Fascinated, Hadley asked: "Who were his father and mother?"

"His father was Siegmund, a survivor of the ancient warrior race . . . the Wälsungs. His mother was Sieglinde . . . Siegmund's sister."

"Brother and sister?" Hadley asked huskily, his body suddenly taut, frozen in its motions of eating. "They—were married?"

The cold gray eyes were fixed on him. "It's an old myth. The *Nibelungenlied*. The Rheingold . . . the accursed symbol of all earthly power."

"Earthly power," Hadley echoed slowly. He was spellbound. "It was cursed? Why?"

"Because it was stolen. The lecherous dwarf Alberich stole it from the Rheinmaidens. . . . He had hidden himself to watch them bathe. He stole the gold. . . . They put a curse on it. Whoever owned the gold would be destroyed."

"Did it work out?" He was like a little boy at the lap of his mother, hanging on every word of her tales.

"The dwarfs quarreled over the gold. . . . The gods stole it from them, finally. Because of the gold the gods grew old and withered. . . . They lost their virility." Marsha sipped her orange juice and added matter-of-factly: "Of course, it's been said that the dwarfs represent the Jews. Their greed for wealth and power. You know, in Goethe's *Faust*, Mephistopheles represents the Jew. Tempting Faust from his destiny. Tempting him with the worldly kingdoms: the fleshly joys and pleasures we were just discussing."

There it was. His flesh turned cold as he heard her words. Because it was as if he were speaking, as if a portion of him were saying it. A terrible image of him had sprung out; there it sat, across from him, slim and smiling. Succubus—a male demon in female form. Yes, it was she. And it was himself, too.

His dread grew . . . but he could not end the fascination. She said it aloud; but that portion of him that believed those things was afraid. It couldn't speak out: it was too weak. It didn't dare. In spite of himself, he still admired her.

"You know," he said hoarsely, "you're vicious. Like a hawk, a bird of prey. I sit here listening because I can't help it . . . because something in me responds."

"I know," Marsha said evenly. "You do respond."

"And I know it's wrong. I know it's the vicious part of me, the part that wants to be strong and cruel. Like you—without feeling. Indifferent to others. To suffering and weakness. Contemptuous of weakness."

"You just don't want to hear," Marsha disagreed. "You're afraid. It's fear that makes you resist."

"No," Hadley answered. "No, it's conscience."

For a time Marsha reflected. "Once," she said finally, "there was a little boy who stood in a parade and watched the king pass. The king had no clothes on. Everybody knew it, everybody saw it, everybody experienced it, but nobody could bring himself to say it aloud, because they had been taught it was a terrible thing to say. But the little boy went ahead and said it. And finally everybody had to say it, because they always knew it was true. They always said it privately. All those people standing there watching the king go by naked, and nobody said anything. Do you think it was better to say nothing? Do you think if a truth is unpleasant it shouldn't be said?"

"*Is* it a truth?"

"Tell me what you say. Not just you . . . everybody, in the privacy of their homes and offices. What do you say about the Jews?"

"We're depraved, too. All of us, a little."

"There's a thing called folklore. You know what that is? A body of knowledge evolved by the collective mind of the people. The wisdom of the race. Their highest wisdom . . ."

Hadley sat silent and horrified. But this personification of his shadow-self hypnotized him; the words she said cut all the way down inside him. The shameful depths were out in the open; she made no secret of what she was, how she felt. No guilt. No sense of sin.

"You're a strange person," he said, troubled. "You're like one of those—what do you call them? Telepathics."

She didn't laugh. "Yes, we have a rapport. The racial unconscious links the two of us. You think of yourself as a unique entity; you think you're cut off, alone. Separate and terribly isolated."

"Yes."

"You're not. Only the external shell is unique. . . . Deep inside you're part of a collective entity. Haven't you ever felt that? Haven't you felt that this separation is artificial? That you shouldn't be cut off?"

He nodded.

"There's so much ignorance," Marsha said. "Jung had to go out of the West, all the way to China, to get what he wanted. I'll lend you some of his works sometime. *Modern Man in Search of a Soul.* Have you read that? He worked with classical Chinese verse; he studied Buddhism. The Tao. Brahminism . . . He's a great scholar, one of the really great men of our times. He went back into the Middle Ages . . . the alchemists."

Hadley didn't know what to say. "What you're telling me sounds so—" He didn't know that, either. "What the hell does it mean?"

"Don't you feel you understand it? Not verbally, maybe. Don't you feel it makes sense?"

"I don't know." He was completely confused. "I've had a lot on my mind the last few weeks. Pete being born, this business with Beckheim. And I haven't felt good. I think there's something wrong with me. Fergesson wants me to go see his family doctor, but what the hell—I've seen so damn many doctors in my life. And none of them ever did me any good."

"There's nothing wrong with your body," Marsha said. "You're physically sound. You're very well made, in fact."

"What is it, then?"

"Your soul."

Nobody had ever told him he had a soul. He felt like bursting out laughing. What was that? Where was it? Maybe he had lost it; maybe it was already gone. Maybe somebody had stolen his soul. Maybe he had sold it or lent it and forgotten about it. Maybe people weren't born with souls anymore. But the word wasn't empty; he responded to it. It flattered him, as if in some way he were responsible for having one. Or having a soul was unique: an achievement. He felt as if she saw something in him nobody else saw. Something they had overlooked.

He grinned. "Words like *soul, heaven, devil*. They don't mean anything anymore."

"Beckheim uses them."

"I know." He twisted. "But there it seemed all right. Like in church— everybody listening, the auditorium, a big man like that. But here, in broad daylight." He indicated the shelves of fruits, dried tubers, jars of vegetable juices. "It's—unreal. It's like trying to watch a movie in broad daylight. . . . You can still see the images on the screen, but they're not convincing."

"You mean, the illusion is gone."

"I guess so."

"Perhaps *soul* isn't an exact word. It's hard to find exact words for spiritual things. All right, Stuart Hadley. We will use any word you want." Her cold gray eyes danced. "What would you prefer?"

"I wouldn't prefer anything. I don't feel well. My head hurts and my stomach's upset." He examined his wristwatch. "And I'm going to have to get back to the shop."

"I've done all this?"

"No . . . I always feel sick. There's always something wrong with me." He tried to express himself. "I've been sick all my life."

Marsha nodded. "I know."

"What do you mean? How do you know?" He was infuriated; his core of rage boiled out. "You don't know anything about me! You just met me!"

"Everybody is sick. You can't live here without being sick. Don't you see—Beckheim's right. We've got to have a rebirth. It can't go on this way, dirty and corrupt and venal. There has to be a spiritual return. . . . We've dropped down on all fours like animals. We wallow and chase after thrills . . . We're beasts! We've just got to go back; it was clean and simple, before. It's all gotten complicated and mechanical and bright—" She pointed through the window of the Health Food Store, at the big neon sign of the Bank of America Building. "Like that. Money and gaudy signs. Commercialism, filthy factories . . . We have to get back to the soil. We need roots—we have to find the land again. Rediscover the simple old ways."

Hadley responded. But he was frightened. "But all this hate—you hate the Jews."

"We hate venality and greed. We hate corruption. Is that bad?" Her voice remained calm, thin. "We hate rich plutocrats who grind down the people and make them robots. Slaves in factories. The machine is destroying man. The Communist ideal: every man the same . . . ground down to a common denominator. The brutal, bestial factory worker, covered with soot and grime. Like an ape in the forest."

Hadley asked: "Does Beckheim feel this way? All these things—*Succubus*. Is this what Beckheim stands for?"

"Beckheim," she said quietly, "is a Negro. But the forces of resurgence are working through him. We've watched for some kind of spiritual upsurge . . . Beckheim is an involuntary prophet. He isn't aware. He thinks like a primitive. . . . He *is* a primitive. He has naive categories of thought, like a child. Heaven, Hell, Armageddon, salvation. But he has integrity." She raised her voice. "He speaks for all of us. The pure child, the guileless fool come to save us. Parsifal . . . you see?"

Hadley didn't answer. He finished his plate and pushed it aside. As he began on the banana cream pudding he said: "What does Beckheim think of your magazine?"

Marsha frowned. "He's interested." She sounded vague. "He may finance it."

"Is that why—"

"We've been discussing it from time to time. The matter comes up. . . .

There's a great deal we don't agree on." She smiled. "He's a powerful man, Stuart Hadley. He's a great man . . . more than a man. He's a force."

Hadley said: "It must be an experience to meet him."

"It is." She sounded as if she meant it. "It's like sitting down in the same room with God." She finished her orange juice. "I'll wait until you have a chance to read over the magazine. You may want to ask me about different parts of it."

"Maybe." He was noncommittal. Suddenly he demanded: "What do you care if I read it? What's it matter to you?"

Marsha met his furious gaze calmly. "I think you have the potentialities to comprehend it. We've all been living under a fog. Like the gods . . . withered and old, because of a curse. The gold has tainted us. . . . We can't stand up straight and be ourselves. Be young and strong. We can't see things as they really are." With a rush of excitement, hollow cheeks bright red, she exclaimed: "Stuart Hadley, you have so much to learn! There's so much ahead of you, so many things to throw off! Like a cicada coming out of its old shell. Like a grub coming out of its cocoon and turning into a butterfly. Don't you see—all these years have been marking time for you, suspended time . . . in the cocoon. You've been waiting—don't you feel that?"

"Yes," he said slowly. "But I didn't think anything would come." He continued: "I didn't have much hope."

"You should have! There's so much to the world—it's big and full of things. There's a fundamental core of vitality; the world's full of energy and excitement. Once you cut through and get down all the way, strike the bedrock that's down there, under all the lies . . ." She pushed back her chair and abruptly got to her feet. Matter-of-factly she said: "What night will you be free? I'll pick you up and we'll drive up the coast, along the ocean highway to San Francisco."

"Why?" he demanded, astonished.

"So you can meet Theodore Beckheim."

Hadley could say nothing.

"He's staying with me," Marsha continued, "while he recuperates from his heart attack. I want you to meet him before he leaves."

She walked rapidly out of the store without looking back. A trim, boyish shape, sharp chin up, rusty hair a corona around her bleak skull. In a moment she was gone.

Dazed, Hadley continued eating his banana pudding, an empty reflex of raising and lowering his spoon. Marsha had disappeared. An empty orange-juice glass was all that remained; she had gone as suddenly as she had come.

He wondered, fearfully, what night he would be free. To meet Theodore

Beckheim . . . He was overwhelmed. For that, he would do almost anything. Put up with anything. The avid hunger grew . . . *to meet Theodore Beckheim*. To speak to him, be with him. Touch him. Talk to him face-to-face.

Thursday? Ellen was taking Pete over to her family's house. But how was he supposed to get in touch with her?

Obviously, he didn't have to. At the realization he felt a shudder of dread. The ominous specter, the fascinating but dangerous presence against which his physical system was already moving to protect itself, would see to that. Marsha Frazier would get in touch with *him*.

Wednesday morning when Stuart Hadley came out of the TV demonstration room with the polish rag and bottle in his hands he discovered the telephone lying off its hook. He watched it intently as he carried the polish rag and bottle past the front counter, to the combinations in the window. Nobody was using the phone; nobody was in sight. An uneasy, foreboding sensation moved through him; he sensed an invisible presence waiting silently, patiently, at the other end of the line. Waiting for him.

"What's this?" he said to Jack White when White came up from downstairs. "You on the phone?"

"Oh," White said, blithely remembering. "It's for you. I forgot; some dame calling."

Chilled, Hadley lifted the receiver to his ear. The hum of the wire was the only sound: the dame had hung up.

"How long ago was that?" Hadley asked as he hung it up. "Was it Ellen?"

"It was maybe fifteen minutes ago," White said, "and it wasn't your wife. I'm sorry, Stumblebum. I went downstairs looking for you and I got to talking to Olsen." He straightened his hand-painted silk necktie, a tall, slim man in a gray double-breasted suit, small mustache, shoes neatly shined. "My fault."

An hour later she phoned back. This time Hadley got it. With a quake of dismay he recognized the calm, dispassionate voice as soon as she asked: "May I speak to Mister Hadley, please?"

"It's me," he answered, with reluctance. His distaste surprised him; did he dislike her that much? Deep in him the aversion to the woman was growing. More and more he sensed the unwholesomeness in her, the frigid malgrowth, as if she were reptilian, snakelike. But she was his only link with Beckheim; and he had to reach the big black man. "Where are you calling from?" he demanded.

"San Francisco. I called before, but the man—whoever he was—never came back. I debated for a while. . . . It occurred to me you were trying to pull out of this. But then I decided it was probably an accident. . . . You couldn't be certain it was me."

"It was an accident," Hadley said huskily.

"What night are you free?"

"Thursday. Ellen's taking Pete over to her family's. Like I said, I'm not expected to go along. Her family never liked me very well." His voice was monotonous; if he expected to meet Beckheim he would have to put some life into it. "So we can get together—right?"

Silence for a moment. He could imagine her: hollow-eyed bony face, gazing straight ahead, pale lips slightly parted, analyzing his words, the tone of his voice. Reading into them first this and then that; trying to decide how he felt. It would be quite an accomplishment. . . . His emotions were a tangled mess. And Marsha probably sensed that; she seemed to know what was going on inside him.

"All right," she agreed. "You get off at six?"

"A little after. I have to count the money and reset the register tape. Turn things off, close up the store. Say, about six fifteen."

"I'll come by with the car. Stuart?"

"What?"

"Bring some of your work."

For a moment he couldn't imagine what she meant. Then he realized that she was talking about his paintings. "Okay," he said; he couldn't help responding. Then he sensed how difficult it would be to get them out of the house. "I mean—"

"I'll see you at six fifteen," Marsha interrupted coolly. "Good-bye, darling . . . I have to scoot." She hung up.

Sweating and apprehensive, he turned to wait on two elderly women who stood grimly at the counter, a cloth-mesh shopping bag between them. Obviously, Marsha had something built up. Elaborate plans made without his knowledge or consent. "Can I help you?" he asked automatically, reaching for the shopping bag. He could see the square outlines of a little old Scottie radio wedged in the bag. "Troubles?" he asked absently. There was no telling what she was up to; she might do anything. But he did want to meet Beckheim. It would be worth it, for that. Anything would be worth doing, to meet Theodore Beckheim. "What sort of troubles?" he asked the old ladies. "What does your radio do?"

In many ways it was a mistake—and he knew it. But in spite of his foreboding, his sense of squandering his life and intimate world and personality, he got the pictures from the closet on Thursday morning. It was eight ten; Ellen was still in bed asleep. He let her sleep. Making his own breakfast, washing and shaving rapidly, very quietly, he finished dressing, grabbed on his coat and hat, and tiptoed to the bedroom door.

Ellen lay sprawled out in the middle of the bed, brown hair tumbled over the pillow and sheets, one arm extended limply. He could hear her breathing: the low, harsh panting of deep sleep. From the closet he got the dusty package that was his collection of pictures, the brown bundle tied up with heavy wrapping twine. He carried it out of the apartment, set it down in the hall while he locked the door after him, and then hurried off with it to the store.

The pictures stayed downstairs in the service department, stuck upright among the overstock television combinations and spin dryers, until Thursday night.

At four o'clock business began to die. Blazing hot July sunlight shimmered off the sidewalk and into the store; the television screens shrank to gray squares of unconvincing shadow. Cars muttered along in unbroken rows. Fergesson took off in his Pontiac to deliver a radio-phonograph he had sold to a lifelong friend. At five thirty Olsen drove up in the store truck and came struggling in, loaded down with radio chassis.

While Hadley was showing a Zenith table-model seventeen-inch TV to a young couple, Marsha entered the store. He was aware of her without turning around; the unique flow of her slim shape through the doorway told him she had arrived. He glanced at his wristwatch. It was a quarter to six: she was going to be hanging around for half an hour.

At the end of the counter, Marsha took up a silent, watchful station. Like a permanent fixture, she stood with her arms folded, purse resting beside the tube checker, leaning slightly against the cash register. Her lean body bent on an angle, she contemplated the back of Hadley's neck and the young couple buying the Zenith TV: all three of them could feel her eyes.

"We'll have to think it over," the young man said, grinning nervously. "A lot of money for these days." His wife tugged urgently at his arm. "We'll be back—we just have to give this some thought. . . . You know."

Hadley gave them his card and followed them out onto the glaring sidewalk. He lingered a moment before returning. It would have been nice to stay there, watching the people going past, smelling the hot July air. But he had to go back: he knew it. There was no choice. When he reentered the store she was still watching him. She hadn't taken her eyes from him.

"Hi," he said gruffly.

"Is that the kind of people you make most of your sales to?" she asked him, without preamble.

He shrugged peevishly. "It varies." From the cash register he got the day's tags and began sorting them. "You're early; I won't be off for half an hour."

"I have to pick up some things at the drugstore; I thought I'd drop by and make sure you hadn't forgotten. You have your pictures?"

"In the basement."

"Got a cigarette?"

Resigned, he offered her his pack. She accepted one, and he lit it for her. At the far end of the store stood Jack V. White, hands behind his back, feet apart, like a soldier at ease. Watching Hadley and Marsha with frank interest, with a salesman's morbid, boundless curiosity.

"Who's that man?" Marsha asked, her eyes narrowing.

"Jack White. A salesman—like me."

"Is he the one who answered the phone the first time I called?"

"That's him."

Marsha eyed White coldly as she gathered up her purse and moved toward the door. Today, instead of slacks and shirt, she wore a severe English summer suit, masculine and expensive, low-heeled leather shoes, a large square purse that hung from her shoulder by a strap. "I'll wait for you in the car," she said. "It's parked up the street a block, in front of the liquor store."

"Fine," Hadley said, with relief. She wouldn't be hanging around after all. "I'll close up as fast as I can. Don't get worried if I'm not there by six fifteen. . . . Sometimes it drags on to six thirty."

Marsha nodded and headed briskly out of the store.

Half expecting her to come back, he kept a watchful eye on the door until the last customer was out and the lock had been thrown. There was no sign of her. Down came the shade; the night-light was plugged in; Jack White checked all the sets downstairs and pulled the main switches; at the cash register Hadley began counting the money into gray cloth bags.

"Another day, another dollar," Jack White announced as he passed the counter on his way out. "Can you finish up alone, old man?"

"Sure," Hadley said, glad to see him go. "You run along."

White lingered. "Who's the dame?"

"What dame?" Hadley was instantly on his guard.

"The one that was in earlier. The one who's waiting for you up the block."

Hadley evaded; this was exactly what he had dreaded—and known he couldn't possibly avoid. "How do you know some dame is waiting for me up the block?"

"Christ, I heard her say it." White beamed and thumped Hadley cynically on the arm. "While the cat's away, eh? Have a good time and remember to keep your pants buttoned." He unlocked the front door, waved cheerfully, and slammed it after him. His hard, efficient heels echoed away down the busy sidewalk, and Hadley was alone.

Hurriedly, Hadley carried the money to the safe, tossed the sacks in, and locked it. He spun the new tape into position and closed up the register. A brief check showed that everything was turned off and in its place; he got his coat from the back closet and followed in the steps of Jack White, out the door and onto the sidewalk.

The air was hot, stuffy, and unpleasant. The glare gave him a headache. Wishing the woman hadn't appeared, wishing he were too sick to make it all the way to her car, he tried the door handle to be certain it was locked and then walked slowly up the sidewalk toward the liquor store.

The first thing Marsha said to him was: "You forgot your pictures."

For a moment he considered the hell with the whole thing. Common sense told him to get out now, while it was still possible. With the car windows rolled down, Marsha sat listening to the radio: a Dixieland jazz band, harsh and blaring. They faced each other a moment, and then Hadley shrugged, defeated. "I'll get them," he agreed.

"Want me to drive you back?"

"No, I can walk."

He slowly returned to the store. His feet dragged; only with great effort was he able to turn the key in the lock and get the door open. Fatigue from eight hours of work lay over him, and his hungry, queasy stomach growled fretfully. As he was passing the counter on his way out, the package of pictures under his arm, the phone began to ring.

Three rings passed before he answered it. The chances were that it was only a customer wanting to know why Olsen hadn't returned her set. It might be Fergesson calling in about something. Or it might be Ellen.

It was Ellen.

"I'm glad I caught you." Her voice came, soft and sad, from a vast distance. "How are you?"

"Great," he answered. He pulled the phone cord out as long as he could, to where he was able to reach out and lock the front door. He didn't want Marsha showing up while he was talking to Ellen. "What do you want?"

"I wondered—" She hesitated wistfully. "Stuart, why don't you come over? Mother says you know you're welcome. And Pete's yelling his head off."

"Why?"

"Because he misses you." She added plaintively: "I miss you, too. Please, won't you come on over? You don't have to stay; just come by and be with us for a little while."

The cloying, childish tone of her voice, the pleading female sound that he hated so much, decided him. Staring fixedly up at the calendar over the tube chart, Hadley answered: "Honey, I can't. I told some people I'd be over for dinner. I'm late as it is. If you'd called me sooner—"

"What people?" There was no suspicion in her voice, only unhappy interest. "Dave and Laura?"

"Customers I know," Hadley explained, his eyes still on the calendar. He might as well do a good job of it. "I don't think you ever met them. I was up at their place a couple of times, showing them an RCA combination. They're nice people, about ten years older than us. He's a stockbroker."

"What—time will you be home?"

"I'm not sure. He'll probably try to sell me some stock. . . . It might be late." He added: "Maybe I'll stop off for a drink on the way back. I'm beat; I can use a drink."

Worry clouded his wife's voice. "How much money do you have? It's getting near the end of the month . . . I'm all out of the money you gave me."

"I've got plenty," Hadley said impatiently; his ears had picked up the sound of a car motor outside. A car was coming into the yellow freight zone. "Look, honey, I've got to run. If I have a chance I'll call you later, from their place."

"Have a good time," Ellen said faintly, miserably. "And don't eat any onions; you know how sick you are if you eat onions. Promise me?"

"So long," Hadley said brusquely, and broke the connection. He hurried to the door with his pictures, unlocked it, and stepped outside.

Marsha's gray Studebaker was parked in the freight zone. He locked the door of Modern TV and strode over. "What kept you?" she asked, opening the door for him.

He slid in beside her. "Phone call. Some customer wanting to know about his set."

The car backed out expertly; a moment later they were moving down Cedar Street toward Bayshore Highway. A solid wall of traffic lay ahead of them: grim commute traffic on its way home from San Francisco.

"We won't have to tangle with that," Marsha said; "it's all coming this way." She made a rapid, efficient left-hand turn onto the highway. "Hardly anybody going up the coast but us. This is the best time to travel."

As they drove along the highway, Marsha asked: "Why did you come? You don't like me—you find me unpleasant."

"It was a struggle," he admitted.

"I'm right, aren't I? You don't enjoy being with me."

"It's not pleasant, no. That doesn't mean I don't like you." He laughed tautly. "My God, how could it be pleasant? Look at what I'm doing—I may be giving up my wife and son, my family. What am I getting out of it?"

Marsha considered. "Well? What do *you* think you're getting out of it? You must think you're getting something."

It was a good question. He watched the brown fields go by on both sides of the car, flat and bleak and deserted. Now and then a faded, drab sign flashed past: WHEN YOU'RE IN SAN FRANCISCO STOP AT THE MARK HOPKINS . . . NEXT TIME TAKE THE TRAIN . . . MOBILGAS AND MOBILOIL ARE YEARS AHEAD. "Well," he said, "I get to meet Beckheim."

"Is that all?" Marsha asked brightly. "That's the only reason you're here?"

"If I wasn't here, where would I be? Sitting around in my two-room apartment, watching TV or reading *Time*." That seemed to express his feelings as well as he knew how. "Or maybe a show. If we can get somebody to stay with the baby. Dinner, and an hour of dancing. Some two-bit band like we had at high school dances. Guys in green tuxedos with bow ties, playing saxophones. Middle-aged couples pushing back and forth."

"Surely you have more imagination than that! Can't you think up something better to do with your time?" She indicated the bundle of pictures. "What about those?"

"That's all in the past. Let's face it—I'm not an artist: I'm a television salesman. Look at this suit and tell me if it's the kind of suit an artist would wear."

After a moment Marsha said: "Deep down inside of you, you know you're not a television salesman. Do you think a man is nothing more than the job he holds? Herman Melville was a customs inspector. Borodin was a doctor. Kafka worked in a bank. James Joyce was a Berlitz School translator."

"All right," Hadley said irritably. "I get the idea."

"Do you? I wonder. The whole Communist doctrine is to get people to identify themselves with their economic function . . . in this country as anywhere else. But you know your inner life isn't at all touched. . . . Your real personality doesn't come into play when you're selling a television set. Don't you feel the difference between the man who goes through the motions of selling a TV set and the man who you really are?"

"Well," Hadley admitted bitterly, "sometimes I feel as if I'm carrying out a deception. Sure, I hate my job. Sure, I don't get any satisfaction out of it . . . but what choice have I got? I'm not there because I like it."

"Quit."

"And do what? Starve?"

"You won't starve—nobody starves in a modern industrial society. Start painting again. . . . You have the ability."

Hadley flushed angrily. "You've never seen anything of mine; you don't know what I can do." He was flattered and disgusted at the same time. He wanted to hear words like that . . . but he couldn't kid himself that much: it was absurd. It was a parody of praise. A woman he had met only two or three times, who knew nothing about his life, his work, telling him that he had artistic ability. "For all you know," he said, "these canvases may be blank."

"I can tell they're good," Marsha said calmly, "because I know *you*. They would be an expression of yourself, of your inner being. And I know what that's like."

Nettled, he gave up and didn't comment. He retired into himself and brooded. She was serious, almost fervent—but there was no telling what went on inside her. What she did and said was separated from what she really was; there was a lapse of time, an open gap: there was no spontaneity. Everything was measured, studied out in advance. Marsha was a spectator to her own actions: she was above, remote and detached, putting a life-sized puppet through its paces. Here was real deception. Marsha was tangent to the outside world at no point: she was capable of breaking off totally, a sphere that revolved smoothly, silently, without touching the universe. Suspended in an invisible medium: an eighth of an inch from the world of matter.

"Have you ever read Sartre?" Marsha asked.

"No."

"I have a book of his I'll lend you—it's very small. The fundamentals of existentialism. It's a philosophy that's worth looking into . . . especially for a person like yourself."

"Why do you say that?" He was curious, since it had to do with him. "Why me in particular?"

"I'd have to go into what I think are the basic causes of your dilemma."

"Go ahead."

Marsha sighed. "Do I have to? Well, You're a renegade intellectual. That's the main thing. You're in hiding . . . going around in a powder blue suit and French cuffs, disguised as a bright eager young salesman, going up in business. And in reality, you're not interested in business at all. Sham, all a sham, isn't it? But you can't go back to the world you escaped from. . . . You don't want that either. You don't want to be a Dave Gold: impotent and full of words. Making extravagant gestures, mouthing intricate doctrines. You know, Louis Fischer asked an old Russian peasant woman how things had changed for her since the Revolution—am I boring you?"

Hadley shook his head. "No."

"The old woman answered: 'Well, people talk more.' I think that sums up Marxism. You don't want to go back to hollow words, talk for its own sake. . . . You've seen the little avant-garde groups sitting around holding forth, and the little splinter socialist groups. Empty, hollow words. Talk, and no action. Words that lead only to more words. Dogmas. Vast tomes. Treatises. Books, discussion and argument, proposals, resolutions." She made a disgusted sound. "Sartre shows that a man exists only through his actions. You understand? It's not what you think but what you do. What you think has no meaning. . . . You could sit and think forever—and what different would it make? It's action that counts: the deed."

At dusk, they drove up the coast highway to San Francisco. Few cars were on the road; empty stretches of dim gray pavement writhed in front of and behind the little Studebaker. Tumbled bleak cliffs of scrubby green matting dropped down to the ocean. A cold wind whipped through the shrubbery, carrying bits of old newspaper, sticks and weeds, bouncing rusty beer cans and debris down the steep gullies into the leaden surf. Here and there NO DUMPING signs broke the monotony. On the right, sagging telegraph lines swayed dismally. Uniform scorched-brown hills stretched off and were lost in the thickening darkness. No living human was visible anywhere.

"It's dreary along here," Hadley remarked.

Marsha agreed as she expertly twisted the wheel. "Except for that," she said, pointing ahead.

Lonely and forlorn, a truck was parked on a dirt shoulder at the edge of the highway. A big hand-painted sign reading FRESH EGGS 59 CENTS DOZ whipped mournfully in the evening wind. A man and a boy were loading crates of eggs back into the truck; the day was over for them. Their shapes were barely visible in the gloom. Around the truck, debris, blown by the wind, was heaped and littered ankle deep. White urban filth that had been excreted by passing cars, then collected by the ocean wind.

Watching the truck fall behind, Hadley was overcome with depression. The dismal, abandoned coastline unnerved him; the man and the boy toiling silently to collect their unsold eggs made him conscious of the futility of endeavor. Undoubtedly, the two of them had stood there all day while luxurious cars raced past.

"I wonder if they sold any at all," he said aloud. To him, the isolated man and his son represented all those he cared about, the halt and feeble and helpless about whom he was concerned. The defenseless people Marsha had dismissed with a wave of her hand.

"Same price as the downtown supermarkets," Marsha said. "Strictly sucker stuff." She shifted into second gear to climb a long grade. "Motorists are always looking for roadside buys; the country people stick them good."

"I don't like it here," Hadley said. "It's so damn deserted. What if the car broke down?"

"It won't," Marsha said easily.

"But it might. We might get stuck out here; who the hell would come along for us? Nobody. Maybe we'd stay here forever. It's like sliding through a crack in the ground."

"Someday," Marsha said, "all this will be built up. Little ranch-type California suburban homes, with Chryslers parked out front, or maybe Fords. Neat little one-story houses, all alike."

The car was entering San Francisco. A long park lay on their right; to the left was a ridge of trees, and beyond that the ocean.

"This is a country club," Marsha said. "Run for the rich colonels from the Presidio. So the plutocracy can have a place to play golf."

The trees were black pools of shadow. Overhead, stars had begun appearing in the dull violet night sky. Far off, beyond the country club, the massed yellow lights of the city winked and glowed, row after row, disappearing into black chunks of mountains. In the twilight gloom the city might have been some cosmic mining operation, working soundlessly, effortlessly, infinite machinery rising up from the ground, disappearing into the layer of drifting fog that hung over the Bay.

Hadley gazed out yearningly at the lights; he drank in the vision of purposeful activity. "Beautiful," he said softly. Cars swished past them, headlights flashing. The sounds of human life clanged against his ears: the sweet din of motors and traffic signals, radios, blaring metallic voices. He was relieved to be out of the desolate spaces between cities. That was what the country meant to him: empty wastes where nobody lived or came. The country was the arid land outside the cities, nothing more.

"We're here," Marsha said grimly; her reaction was virtually the opposite of his.

They turned off the coast highway and moved rapidly into the city itself. Modern white concrete apartment buildings whisked past on both sides; the street was broad and smooth, lit with yellow sodium vapor lamps. Hadley rolled down the window and hung out. Inhaling the presence of the city, he gratefully allowed the cold night wind to slap him across the face. He enjoyed the harsh sting; half shutting his eyes, he gazed around appreciatively.

"You get security from it," Marsha observed sourly. "You want to lose yourself in the mass. Make yourself indistinguishable. Safety in imitation."

"Damn it," Hadley said resentfully, "I like people. I like to be with them. What's so unnatural about that?"

"They're grinding you down! They're pulling you down to their level. Look at you—" She gestured. "You and your suit and tie and cuffs; you look like a million bright young salesmen, or vice presidents, or stock managers, or any kind of executive. But you're not. Underneath, you're not!"

"What am I?" Hadley asked, eternally curious.

"You're an artist, of course. And you know it. So don't try to pretend! Don't try to creep off and hide in that salesman disguise; damn it, you're going to have to stand up on your own two feet like a man and face your destiny."

Hadley scowled darkly; he knew it wasn't true . . . but was it untrue? She believed it, evidently. Maybe she was right and he was wrong. Maybe it took somebody outside to know; maybe a man could never know who or what he was; he had to be *told*.

"We'll stop at my place for a drink," Marsha said. She studied her wristwatch. "Then we'll go over and see Ted."

Hadley felt nervous cold sweat stand out on his palms. The reality of Theodore Beckheim swam closer; it was beginning to become convincing. Licking his dry lips, he said: "I don't want to butt in, if he's busy. He's probably got a lot to do."

"Of course. But it's important that you meet him. I've told him about you; he wants to meet you."

Hadley snorted. "That's a laugh! What kind of a pitch are you trying to hand me? What's in this for you? Christ, I'm not some hayseed mark to be led by the nose up to the knackers, so somebody can fleece me. I'm not walking into the slaughterhouse of my own free will—you must think I'm really in love with myself."

"I'm leading you away from the slaughterhouse," Marsha said mildly.

The street had narrowed. Up the side of a long hill the Studebaker crawled; modern apartments gave way to tall old-fashioned wooden houses, joined by a common wall. There was no grass or plants in sight, only the gray cement sidewalks. The pavement was rough and uneven. Here and there men and women shuffled along. Small stores, slatternly and dirty, winked in the evening darkness. Liquor stores, shoeshine parlors, cheap hotels, dingy grocery stores, pawnshops, bars.

"This is the Hayes District," Marsha said as the Studebaker reached the top of the hill, wavered, and then began creeping down the far side. "This big dip is called Hayes Hole. I live three-fourths of the way down."

Cars were parked on the sidewalks and in driveways. Beyond the dip, the far ascent was alive with lights and the movement of traffic. Buses nosed rapidly upward; at intersections swarms of people packed tightly together pushed across to the other side. Presently Marsha slowed the Studebaker, stuck out her thin arm, and then swerved across the line, through the left-hand lane, and into a narrow concrete passage between two towering wooden houses. The car emerged in a circular parking area, in front of a row of tumbledown garages. Marsha drove the car from the concrete into the tangle of moist grass and dirt that made up the yard of one of the houses. She yanked on the parking brake and snapped off the motor.

"Well," she said briskly, "we're here."

Hadley got stiffly from the car. Cold wet fog lay over everything; the sky was overcast. To his right stood a dripping wood fence, enclosing a backyard littered with rusty beer cans and huge weeds. Boxes of soggy newspapers were stacked against the line of garages. An overturned bathtub lay half buried. Around a burned-out shell of an incinerator was strewn charred, burned garbage and refuse. The building itself ended in a jumble of sagging steps, water pipes, cracked slabs of concrete walk, rotting gray porch and railing.

"Not very pretty, is it?" Marsha observed.

Hadley remembered the desolate hills between towns; this was the same abandoned ruin. He shivered and moved toward the apartment building. "How do we get in?" he demanded impatiently.

Marsha led him up a rickety flight of steps, past lines of flapping, mildewed washing, to a screen door. She pushed the door open and led him into a kitchen that smelled of bacon grease and rancid vegetables moldering in dark bins. A light came on overhead, naked and glaring. One side of the kitchen was a massive sink and drainboard; dirty dishes were heaped in great piles all along it. Empty beer and wine bottles filled paper sacks on the linoleum floor. The kitchen table was littered with empty glasses and stuffed ashtrays, crumpled cigarette packages, corks and bottle stoppers.

"In here," Marsha said, leading him firmly from the kitchen. Hadley followed glumly into a carpeted hall. The odor of an ancient bathroom drifted through the hall, caught and stagnating in its corners. Into a living room the woman strode, reaching up for a light cord. She found it, and the living room struggled fitfully into being.

Hadley faced a huge high-ceilinged room that had been repainted by hand. The walls were dark blue; the ceiling was green. Asphalt tile had been laid over the flooring. Instead of chairs there was a wide Hollywood-style bed; on the far side were heaped cushions and pillows tossed about the floor. In the center of the room was a low table made of Arizona sheet slate. On it was strewn a chessboard. In one corner dangled a mobile. Half of the room was a bookcase made of bricks and boards, stuffed with paperbound and hardcover volumes. The walls were obscured by thumbtacked prints. In every corner were stacked bound piles of magazines and newspapers. At the end of the Hollywood bed, Hadley made out a bulging cardboard box of unassembled *Succubus*es.

"Sit down," Marsha commanded. "I'll pour you a drink. What do you want, scotch or bourbon?"

"Bourbon," Hadley murmured as he gingerly seated himself on the Hollywood bed.

From the floor beneath he could hear the tinny shrill of a radio. Outside, cars honked and swished past noisily. A dull throbbing rattled the lamp and slate table—probably the refrigeration system of the building. The room was cold and damp; he shivered and fumbled in his pocket for his cigarettes. In the kitchen Marsha rooted about for clean glasses.

While he was sitting and smoking and waiting, an immense white wolfhound padded in and eyed him. The dog sniffed, and then padded back out.

"Good Tertullian," Marsha shouted commandingly at the dog.

The dog halted and turned toward her.

"Go back to your pallet and lie down," Marsha ordered it.

The dog padded past Hadley and into the kitchen. It disappeared under the stove; with a sigh it folded itself up on a hair-filthy mattress and gazed out sightlessly over its pale shaggy paws.

After an interval Marsha came quickly into the living room carrying two tall whiskey glasses. "Okay," she said, seating herself on the bed and setting down the drinks in the center of the slate table. "Help yourself."

Hadley accepted his drink morbidly. "This place gets me down," he said abruptly. Restlessly, he twirled the cold glass between his palms. "Look, is this on the level—or are you stringing me?"

Marsha's cold gray eyes met his. "What do you mean? Is what on the level?"

"This business about Beckheim. How do I know you're not stringing me along?" His eyes strayed sullenly around the room. "I don't see any sign of him; where the hell is he?"

"He's not *here*," Marsha said sharply. Her voice rose. "Why should he be here? Do you have some reason to expect to find him here?"

"Calm down," Hadley said uneasily.

Marsha sipped her drink. "I don't understand why you should suspect me," she said thinly.

"Suspect you! Of what?"

"Let it go." She was trembling violently. "I can't have you suspecting me. Is that the way you feel about me? Don't you have any trust or confidence in me?" Eyes bright and swimming, she rushed on: "Have I ever done anything to make you feel this way? No, it's in you. It's your fault, not mine."

"What the hell's the matter?" he demanded irritably.

"Nothing. I just can't have you feeling this way. Please—" Abruptly she broke off and turned her head away. "I don't want to talk about it."

Neither of them spoke for a moment. Hadley was shocked; it was the first time he had really seen inside the brittle shell she had erected. Now, briefly, the underlying clinging uncertainty of the woman had emerged.

"You're terrified," Hadley said, astonished. "You babble on, tough and ruthless. But you're terrified of my disapproval."

"*Forget it.*" Blindly, she groped around. "Give me a cigarette, will you?"

He gave her a cigarette from his pack; she leaned forward convulsively, fingers shaking. For a moment their faces were close together: she smelled faintly of soap and a dull woodsy scent. And of ragged, unstable fear. Then, rapidly, she leaned back, settled her thin shoulder blades against the wall, pulled up her legs and tucked them under her, folded her arms, inhaled from her cigarette, lifted her breasts a trifle, and smiled thinly at Hadley.

"You're going to have to learn," she said, in a weak, hard voice. "You can't treat people this way."

"Take it easy," he told her. "You're upset; there's nothing going on. Nobody's treating you any way." Eyes bright, she continued to gaze at him until he got to his feet and paced fretfully around. "I don't like this waiting, either," he protested.

Marsha leaned over to knock ash from her cigarette; the frantic, rigidly controlled grimace remained.

"How long's it going to be?" Hadley demanded. "How long do we have to sit facing each other? If I'm going to meet him then let's get it over with."

Carefully, Marsha said: "It won't be long. Try to stand my company a little longer."

"Why not now?"

She continued to gaze fixedly at him; there was no answer. Was he supposed to infer a cosmic process? An inexorable ritual beyond the control of man? His tension increased; her instability affected him until he was almost overwhelmed. Suddenly he cried: "Let's call the whole thing off! I'm going back!"

"Sit down and drink your drink."

"No." He faced her defiantly; they glared at each other with a kind of mute, rising hysteria until finally Marsha shuddered and looked away. "Stuart," she said wearily, "you look so foolish standing there. Please sit down and act like an adult."

Flushing, he threw himself down, back against the wall, and grabbed up his drink.

"That's better," Marsha said, pleased at having regained the initiative. "What do you want to hear?"

"Hear!" he bellowed. "What do you mean?"

Marsha indicated a section of the wall. Controls, and the outlines of recessed doors, were visible. "Custom-built high-fidelity system." Matter-of-factly, she slid to her feet. "I'll show it to you; we mounted it in the wall."

"I'm not interested," Hadley muttered angrily; but he watched from where he sat. A section of the wall was shoved back; albums of records were visible. Another section revealed a vast speaker and heaps of tangled wiring. The drawer came out, a complicated record changer and pickup cartridge.

"Diamond needles," Marsha explained. "One head for long-playing records, another for the old shellacs."

"Fine," Hadley growled.

"You have no preference?"

"Play whatever you want. If you have to play something."

"Most modern music is degenerate," Marsha stated as she lifted out a handful of LPs. "The Schönberg circle . . . atonality. All of the Viennese Jewish stuff." She slid a record from its stiff jacket; carrying it by its edges, she placed it on the changer and started the mechanism. "See what you think of this."

Violently, high-pitched and metallic, the phonograph screeched out the ponderous sounds of a massed symphony orchestra.

"A transcription of a Schubert piano work," Marsha explained as she reseated herself. "Schubert never lived to score it. . . . Isn't it lovely?"

"Beautiful."

For a while the two of them were silent. Facing each other, they listened to the blare of the high-fidelity sound system. In the kitchen, glasses and cups rattled in response to the din. At first the crashing concussions of sound beat furiously against Hadley's brain; his head hurt and his eyes smarted. He winced and tried to tense himself against them. But gradually the sound deadened his brain; the sound receded and became a muffled noise in the distance, without form or meaning. It blotted out thought and concern; for that he was grateful. Everything in the room was taken up and absorbed into the music; the room and its contents jiggled and vibrated excitedly. In time,

Stuart Hadley surrendered and gave himself over to the music. Tired and resigned, he ceased resisting. After that it was almost pleasant.

The room dulled. Objects lost their shapes and fused together indiscriminately. Probably it was optical fatigue; he sat staring blankly straight ahead, partially hypnotized, his cigarette dying away in the ashtray on the table. The frenzy of the phonograph became partly visible, manifest in the colors of the walls, the pattern of the asphalt tile. A kind of darkly metallic blur effused itself around him, and he accepted it. In the kitchen, on his pallet under the stove, Tertullian dozed.

At the end of the record side, Marsha got to her feet and crossed the room to the amplifier. With an abrupt twist of her fingers she turned off the intricate equipment. The noise withdrew back into the speaker, and the room was freed. Nervously, Marsha paced back to the bed; she was as taut as Hadley.

Hadley felt that he had undergone some kind of vague and cruel ordeal, the purpose of which was unknown to him. Perhaps it was unknown to Marsha, too. In any case, it was over. He took a deep breath and reached to take up his drink. He blinked, resettled himself, drank a few swallows.

"Where are your children?" he asked. "I don't see them around."

"They're away." Jerkily, Marsha dusted the ash from her cigarette. "Up in Sonoma County, at summer camp."

"Do you live here alone?"

"No."

"You just rent this place, don't you?"

Marsha nodded rigidly. Suddenly she leaped up and crossed to the phonograph. She turned it back on, flipped the record over, and left it to play quietly, withdrawn into the background. Again she seated herself, stiff and tense. Hadley felt purged of his tension; the music had done it. Having endured, he had now passed into a stage of feeling the inevitability of things. It was obvious that things were proceeding by their own laws; concealed dynamics were at work. He could not expect to hasten or postpone: he could sit and wait. Gracefully, he waited.

While Stuart Hadley lay listening, the door of the apartment opened and a man entered. It did not seem surprising or strange that the man was Theodore Beckheim. In a dark blue suit, a hat on his head, a heavy coat over his arm, the huge Negro latched the door after him, laid his coat and hat down on a table in the hallway, and then entered the living room.

Hadley arose to his feet. The two men came toward each other, and Marsha hastily put aside her drink to introduce them.

———

Theodore Beckheim held out his hand and the two men shook. He was old, round-shouldered, and immense in his antiquity; his suit was rumpled and threadbare, a hard suit, very ancient, stiff and formal, too tight around the wrists, too short at the cuffs. His old-fashioned black shoes were shiny, scuffed, dignified. He wore a vest, buttoned, in the middle of summer.

"How do you do, Mister Hadley." Beckheim regarded the blond-haired young man without expression; his dark eyes were large and vaguely discolored. Yellow fluid swam around the intense pupils. He glanced briefly at Marsha, then back at Hadley. The old man's skin was as rough and pebbled as leather, dried and horny, a thick hide stretched tight against the knobby bones of his skull and cheeks. His black lips were thin and chapped, drawn back from his gold-filled teeth. His hair was dark gray, short and woolen. He gave off a faint musty scent, the odor of old garments; and behind that the stale sweat of his body. He was a heavy, tired old man. It seemed to Hadley that he was at least seventy. It was hard to tell. There was very little of the vitality visible now, the fire that had streamed out of him that night in the auditorium.

But Hadley was not disappointed. He was awed. That night, Beckheim had been an impersonal instrument speaking to an auditorium of people. This night, Beckheim was a human individual; and the transition moved Hadley more than any repetition of the dynamic oratory. It seemed to him that this was more than he could have hoped for; Beckheim was a man who could be talked to, spoken with. The gap between Hadley and Beckheim could be bridged—at least at this moment. Beckheim, tired and rumpled, had stepped down. Here was no public posture, no declamation or prophetic oratory. This was only a hulking black man in an old-fashioned suit and vest, holding on to Hadley's hand and gazing at him curiously.

"I heard you speak," Hadley said.

Beckheim's thin lips moved, twitched faintly; a nervous spasm that was almost a smile, almost a grimace. "Where?" he asked.

"Down in Cedar Groves. Last month."

Beckheim nodded wryly. "Oh, yes." Vaguely, he moved away from Hadley, letting go of his hand. "You came up with Miss Frazier?" Beckheim and Marsha drew off together in the corner of the room; Beckheim began talking to her in low, rapid tones. At first Hadley thought he was being discussed; he thought Beckheim was asking her about him and his presence. Then he realized that Beckheim had not seen her for a while; he was giving her information on general topics and asking questions that had nothing to do with Hadley. For an interval the impersonal, public figure reemerged.

Then Beckheim and Marsha moved out of the room entirely, into the hallway and then the kitchen. Hadley was alone.

Embarrassed, tense, he moved aimlessly around the room, hands in his pockets, doing nothing, waiting and not looking or listening. Finally he threw himself shakily down on the Hollywood bed and got out his cigarettes. He was jerkily lighting up when Marsha reentered the room, smiling her bloodless, imperative smile down at him and reaching for the two whiskey glasses.

"Back they go," she said briskly. "Ted says so."

She was gone, and the drinks with her. From the kitchen came sounds of activity. The huge, looming dark shape of Beckheim crossed back and forth before the doorway of the kitchen; as it momentarily cut off the light, Hadley involuntarily glanced up. Beckheim had taken off his dark jacket and tossed it over his arm. He wore a light blue shirt and black tie. His cuffs were visibly frayed. Under his arms were vast dark moons of perspiration. Without his jacket he was even more hunched than before. He plucked at his chin, murmuring, strode here and there, glanced once at Hadley, smiled slightly, and then again looked away.

The two of them came from the kitchen together, walking as a pair, without touching each other, faces rapt with reflection. "I'm sorry," Beckheim said to Hadley, turning his attention away from whatever it was he had been discussing. "Society business . . . of no interest. There was no intention of excluding you." The preoccupied look returned. Beckheim's words were clearly not a spontaneous statement; they were a carefully measured, almost formal utterance that Beckheim had decided upon.

"That's okay," Hadley murmured huskily, rising to his feet awkwardly and facing the two of them. He was trembling; it seemed to him that now Beckheim had really come toward him. Now Beckheim was really seeing him; he had caught the man's attention.

"Sit down." In a kindly way, Beckheim indicated the bed, and the three of them seated themselves. Some of the room's tension slipped away, and Hadley smiled nervously.

"Coffee's heating on the stove," Marsha said faintly, in a withdrawn, diffident voice. She sat stiff and prim; not nervous now, but silent, obedient, attentive, like a carefully trained child. "We're going to have shortbread cookies with it. In a couple of minutes."

Beckheim sat with his huge black hands resting on his knees. His nails, like his hair, were gray and luminous, and partly transparent. The black flesh was visible beneath, as if seen through water. "Do you live in Cedar Groves?" Beckheim asked. His voice was low, hoarse, without racial or regional accent.

There was no special quality to it; except for its depth, its unusual lower timbre, it was an ordinary man's voice. He spoke informally; Hadley felt very near to him, for this finite interval, this thin section of time cut out of the limitless flow.

"Yes," Hadley said. "My wife and I live down there." He sensed and gratefully appreciated the friendliness of the man. But he knew, at the same time, that Beckheim's attention was forced; that any moment it might be broken off. That any moment it was going to end, and never resume.

"You have children?" Beckheim asked.

"Yes. A boy. Pete." Hadley fumbled automatically in his coat pocket, his fingers eager and rushed. Then he changed his mind, conscious of the time slipping away. "He's only a month or so old."

"How long have you been married?" Beckheim asked.

"Several years." At this moment, he wasn't sure how long.

"What line of work are you in?"

"I'm a salesman." Reluctantly, with much trepidation, he admitted: "Television sets."

Beckheim pondered, glanced over at Marsha with an expression Hadley could not read, and then asked: "Are you a churchgoer?"

With difficulty Hadley admitted: "No. I'm not."

"What faith is your family?"

"Protestant."

Beckheim smiled gently, understandingly. "We're all Protestants, Mister Hadley. I meant, what portion of the Protestant faith does your family belong to?"

"I don't know. Some kind of Congregationalists."

"Modernists?"

"Yes."

After a moment Beckheim asked: "Did you come up here to see me?"

"Yes," Hadley answered. He tried to put his feelings into the word; he tried to put across how much it meant to him.

"Why?"

Hadley's mouth opened, but he could not think of what to say. He felt too strongly; all he could do was mutely shake his head.

Eyes still on Hadley, the great Negro softly asked: "Are you ill, Mister Hadley?"

Gratefully, Hadley rushed to answer. "Yes. Very ill." He gazed down at the floor, shaking and terrified.

"Are you ill enough to die?"

"Yes," he managed to answer, nodding vigorously.

Beckheim's thin lips pulled back. "Well, we are all ill enough to die, Mister Hadley. That is a great sickness, and we are all down with it badly."

"Yes," Hadley agreed, fervent and overwhelmed with emotion. He felt as if he might cry. He was unable to take his eyes from the floor; he sat silent and unmoving, hands clenched together, perspiration rolling down his neck. Around him and Beckheim the room was dark; nothing stirred, nothing happened.

"Do you want to be well?" Beckheim asked presently.

"Yes."

"Very much?"

"Yes, very much." Hadley's breath rasped in his throat, quick and fluttering with abject fright. In a way, he felt as if he were playing out a macabre and formal ritual, form without content. But in another way the words being said had great meaning, and he felt with overpowering emotion everything he said. His words, his responses, came from deep inside him; and at the same time there was a timeless impersonal quality to them.

He wanted the words to have meaning. He willed himself to accept them; and presently the feeling of ritual dimmed. But it did not go away. As he sat across from Beckheim a part of his brain remained aloof, a spectator, cold and detached, amused and grimly cynical. He loathed that part of him. But he could not excise it. To that part of his brain Stuart Hadley and the great black man across from him were absurd puppets, grotesque, dancing and gesturing foolishly. That portion of his brain began quietly to laugh; and still he sat listening and answering.

"Who do you think can make you well?" Beckheim asked, in his toneless, measured voice. "Do you think I can make you well?"

Hadley hesitated, shuddered in a spasm of emotion. "I—don't know."

"No," Beckheim said. "I can't make you well."

Hadley agreed, nodding his head.

"But you can," Beckheim continued. "It's up to you."

Hadley agreed to that, too. For a time the two of them sat facing each other, silent and waiting, as if in the immediate interval there might be some change manifest. As if Hadley were expected to heal himself now, become well on the spot, without further delay. The tension rose until, for Hadley, it passed bearing. All eyes, and there seemed to be millions of them, were fixed intently on him, unwavering, without mercy, without any kind of emotion. As if he were being scrutinized from beyond the world, beyond the universe.

Then suddenly Beckheim turned to Marsha. "The coffee's boiling."

"Oh," Marsha said guiltily, and got hurriedly to her feet. "Cream and sugar?" she asked Hadley.

"Yeah," he answered, dazed and blinking, coming up to the surface, blinded by the sudden glare of the room. He grabbed his cigarette and stubbed it out violently; the spell was broken, and Beckheim had taken out a newspaper from his jacket pocket; he was unfolding it and beginning to scan it. The moment was over; Hadley had been dismissed. He hadn't realized how far down he had gone . . . if *down* was the proper term. In any case, he had gone a long way. He wondered where.

In the kitchen, Marsha bustled and prepared. The clink of dishes awakened Tertullian on his pallet under the stove; the dog glanced up, alert and avid, then lowered his muzzle as the woman swept past him, carrying a tray into the living room.

Hadley took his cup and automatically began stirring the contents. In the center of the tray was a glass plate of pale cookies. They remained after the three cups had been taken, a circle of pasty store-bought dough taken from some cardboard and cellophane package, each cookie exactly like the next. Presently Beckheim selected one of them and began gnawing on it.

Fascinated, Hadley watched the man eat. Beckheim took a second cookie, and then a third. He inserted each into his mouth, chewed and swallowed, took another, as mechanically as a machine. Visibly, Beckheim did not taste the food. He ate without pleasure or interest; it was a functional process of no special importance to him. Again and again his hand moved between the plate and his mouth; his attention was focused totally on the crumpled newspaper, and nothing else.

"I see," Beckheim said, reading from the newspaper, "that American fliers complain there are no targets of importance left in North Korea. They complain it is useless to try to bomb one Chinese carrying an armload of ammunition over a mountain." He closed the newspaper and added: "Napalm has taken care of the villages and crops."

Hadley said nothing. He sipped mutely at his coffee, all of him a spectator now, withdrawn and detached from the two people in the room with him. Like a quiet domestic couple, Beckheim and Marsha sat drinking coffee and reading the newspaper, a closed circle from which he was excluded. He did not protest, however; he accepted his place without agitation.

Abruptly, Beckheim folded the newspaper away and got stiffly to his feet. "If you'll pardon me," he said to Hadley. Moving away from the Arizona sheet slate table, he got out a case from his pocket and fitted a pair of black horn-rimmed glasses onto his nose. Rolling up his sleeves he slowly left the room, an expression of deep meditation on his face. Hadley saw into a small study, littered with papers and books; an ancient rolltop desk occupied one corner, with a goosenecked lamp and wooden swivel chair. Beckheim seated himself at the desk and began rummaging around in the stacks of papers.

Marsha arose and hurried after him. "You want the letters?" she asked. She burrowed among great cardboard boxes of printed pamphlets; Hadley recognized the cheap throwaways that the Society distributed on every street corner.

"You went through them?" Beckheim asked in his low rumble.

The conversation became a blur, and Hadley turned his back. But there was nothing else to look at or think about; the big black man hunched over at the desk was the only center of activity in the apartment. Marsha, standing behind Beckheim and leaning over his shoulder, was pointing out various papers as they came from the cardboard boxes. Beckheim was sorting mail. Black elbows resting on the surface of the desk, he studied a letter intently, then pushed it aside and selected another. After a time Marsha turned around and reentered the living room.

"More coffee?" she asked Hadley.

"No thanks."

Marsha seated herself and began mechanically tearing to shreds a bit of paper envelope. "There's a lot of work to do," she explained. "A thing like this is a full-time job, keeping accounts straight, that sort of paperwork."

In the study, Beckheim labored over the heap of letters. From some he extracted inserts—checks or money—and carefully put them into a square metal box. Each letter was slowly read and studied, then marked with a dark scratch from his heavy gold fountain pen. Above the desk was a framed reproduction of the ubiquitous bearded youth with his fatuous half-parted lips, eyes upturned; the imaginary, romantic re-creation of the young Christ. At one side of the desk stood a small brass electric heater. Behind that three wicker chairs were crowded together. On the arm of one lay a tattered red sweater.

Without raising his massive head or looking around, Beckheim said: "Mister Hadley, what is your wife's name?"

"Ellen," Hadley answered, coming quickly to life.

After a time, when the heavy gold pen had scratched off half a dozen letters, Beckheim continued: "How old is she?"

"Twenty-two."

Beckheim presently asked: "How old are you?"

"Twenty-five."

For a while Beckheim continued working in silence; the only sound was the scratching of his pen and the rustle of paper. "Had you thought," he asked presently, "of joining the Society?"

Hadley became critically tense. His mouth dry, his vision swimming, he gazed down at the floor and answered: "I hadn't thought much about it. Not that way. It was more that I wanted to meet you . . . as a person."

Nothing more was said for a time, and Hadley's tenseness burgeoned. He climbed to his feet and paced from the living room into the study. Beckheim continued working as Hadley came up behind him and stood awkwardly, hands in his pockets, licking his dry lips and wondering what to say. Beckheim seemed to be waiting; at least, he had nothing more to ask or add.

"I never paid much attention to religion," Hadley said clumsily. "I really don't know anything about it."

Beckheim nodded slightly and went on with his work. In the other room, Marsha sat alone on the Hollywood bed, her cup of coffee between her fingers, face blank and expressionless. Outside the apartment building the noises of a big city at night clanged and jarred dully. Cold fog, rolling in from the Bay, drifted around the warped frames of the windows.

"What is your little boy's name?" Beckheim inquired.

"Peter."

"Do you have a picture of him?"

This time Hadley got out his wallet; he stood holding it uncertainly while Beckheim continued working. All at once Beckheim pushed his letters aside and reached for the wallet. He laid it on the desk and glanced at it critically.

"He's healthy-looking," Beckheim observed as he resumed his work.

"Yes, he's always been healthy and full of pep." After an uncertain moment Hadley restored the wallet to his pocket. "We're keeping our fingers crossed, of course . . . but so far he seems to be fine."

"Do you have a picture of your wife?"

Again Hadley got out his wallet and opened it. He laid it dutifully down; after a time Beckheim peered over at it, pen held above a long letter in a woman's shaky handwriting. Behind the stained, almost opaque celluloid folder, the snapshot of Ellen Hadley lay exposed for the old man to see.

"She's attractive," Beckheim said. "Ellen Hadley . . . Stuart Hadley. I've seen many young couples like you." He put down his pen and spun around on his chair to face Hadley. "But not alike; everybody is different. You're unique. . . . Every man is a new combination, in some way or other. Haven't you felt that about yourself?"

"I guess so," Hadley said.

"What would happen if Stuart Hadley died? What would come along to take Stuart Hadley's place? Could there be another Stuart Hadley?" Behind the horn-rimmed glasses the dark, large eyes bored upward at Hadley. "I think there could not be. What do you think?"

"No," Hadley admitted.

"Do you mean that?"

"Yes." Hadley nodded. "I've felt that."

"But you will die. How do you explain that? What's the answer to that paradox?"

"I don't know."

"Of course you know! You know the answer as well as I do; use your head. . . . You just don't want to think. Your brain is rusty; it's painful to think. Open the gates inside your mind. . . . There isn't much time left."

"No," Hadley agreed, "there isn't much time."

Beckheim picked up Hadley's wallet. "This is Stuart Hadley," he said, holding the corroded package of leather and paper and celluloid in his hands. "Money," he said, examining the paper bills stuffed into the money pouch. "Change." He emptied out some dimes and quarters from the little compartment. "This is a woman's wallet; do you know that?"

"No," Hadley said, astonished.

"Only women's wallets have change compartments." Beckheim laid out a little heap of bent white cards. "These are to give to customers? 'Stuart Hadley: television salesman, Modern TV Sales and Service. 851 Bancroft Avenue, Cedar Groves, California.'" Beckheim examined a stained, rumpled card on which was printed a crude drawing of a braying donkey. At the bottom of the card was lettered the legend *Come to the donkey roast. Get yourself a piece of ass*. "What is this?" Beckheim asked.

Mortified, Hadley muttered: "Just a joke. A trick thing; doesn't mean anything."

Beckheim put the card away and burrowed deeper. He brought out a crushed pack of slips of folded paper, on which were written, in lead pencil, names and addresses and phone numbers. "Customers," Beckheim guessed. "Prospects for sales."

"Yes," Hadley agreed. "And personal friends."

"Keys." Beckheim laid out a car key and two door keys. "One to your apartment. The other to your store?"

"That's right," Hadley said. "And the car key's for the store truck; sometimes I have to pick it up at the garage."

"What's this?" Beckheim laid out a dingy flat disk of uncertain metal. Punched in the center was a square hole.

"My good-luck charm," Hadley answered, embarrassed. "A Chinese coin; I found it on the beach when I was a kid."

Beckheim deliberately turned the glassine flaps. One by one he examined Hadley's identification papers. "Your Social Security card. Driver's license. Your draft card . . . You're 4-F?"

"Liver trouble," Hadley explained.

"Membership in the Elks." Beckheim turned to the next set of sweat-stained cards stuffed in the corroded, yellowed squares. "Photostat of your birth certificate. You were born in New York?"

"That's right. I grew up in Washington, D.C."

"Library card." Beckheim plucked some cards stuffed behind others. "Blue Cross hospitalization card. Stubs for Regal Gasoline Lucky Prize drawings . . ." He passed by the photographs of Peter and Ellen. From the last glassine envelope he plucked a snapshot jammed out of sight. "Who is this woman? Not your wife, is she?"

"No," Hadley admitted begrudgingly. "That's a girl I used to go around with, a long time ago."

Beckheim solemnly studied the photograph; it showed a shy, smiling Italian girl with heavy dark hair and large lips, wearing a tight cotton summer dress that accentuated her inordinately prominent breasts. "And you still carry this picture around with you?" Beckheim inquired.

"I never threw it away," Hadley said defensively. "Anyhow, the girl's living someplace up in Oregon now."

Beckheim had come to the end of the wallet. He put back the contents, closed it, and handed it back to Hadley. "And all this," he said, "can be wiped out, destroyed in an instant. And after that—what?"

"I don't know," Hadley said.

Beckheim's face darkened angrily. "You do know! Why do you keep saying you don't know? What don't you know? Do you think you can be wiped out like those papers? Do you think fire can destroy everything that makes you up? Isn't there something that won't burn, that fire can't consume?"

"I guess so. I don't know." Confused, Hadley shook his head. "I don't know what to think."

Harshly, Beckheim demanded: "Then you're just going to stand there and wait? Doing nothing?"

"I—suppose so."

The old man smiled wryly and spread his big gray hands. "Well, my friend, then there's nothing anyone can do for you. Do you really want help?"

"Yes," Hadley said quickly.

Beckheim sighed and again picked up his heavy gold fountain pen. He turned his chair back to the desk; moving a stack of letters forward he proceeded to examine the top one. "I wish," he said, "that there was more time. So many people, and so little time . . . time running out, getting shorter every day. I see by the newspapers that we may be at war with China one of these days. Four hundred and fifty million people . . . Of course, atomic bombs will cut down that number. But so many people . . . and after that, the rest of Asia. Country after country, endless millions. And finally the rest of the world. The torch, the sword."

Hadley said nothing.

"Open the drawer by you," Beckheim said without looking up. "The top drawer."

Clumsily, Hadley pulled the heavy wooden drawer open. It was crammed with bottles of ink, paper clips and pencils, heaps of cards tied with rubber bands, booklets and pamphlets and scratch pads. "What did you want?" he asked uncertainly.

As he wrote, Beckheim said: "You have interesting hands. . . . Do you know that?"

"I guess so," Hadley answered.

"Get me one of those blue cards, there. In the front of the drawer, by the glue bottle."

Hadley plucked at a stack; one card came loose and he lifted it awkwardly out. "This?"

Beckheim pushed the drawer shut and reached up for the card. With his heavy gold fountain pen he wrote the name *Stuart Wilson Hadley* in the blank space in the center of the card, a firm flow of black ink in the middle of the ornate printing. Carefully, with measured dignity, he selected a blotter and blotted the writing. He handed the card back to Hadley.

Turning it over in his hands, Hadley discovered that it was a membership card in the Society of the Watchmen of Jesus.

"Put it in your wallet," Beckheim said. "With your other cards. With the rest of Stuart Hadley."

He did so, with numb fingers. For a moment he stood by the desk, but Beckheim continued working. Presently Hadley gave up and started aimlessly from the study, toward the door.

"A dollar fifty," Beckheim said over his shoulder.

Hadley came back. "What did you say?"

"A dollar fifty. For your membership."

Crimson, Hadley dug out a paper dollar and two quarters. He clutched them, then convulsively dropped them on the desk. Beckheim put down his pen and accepted the money; he spread it out, got a large ledger from the center drawer of the desk, and entered a notation under "misc. received." The dollar bill and the two silver quarters were placed in the square metal box with the other money and checks; and Beckheim resumed his work.

When Hadley reentered the living room, Marsha was collecting the cups and saucers. She smiled at him fleetingly, apprehensively. "More coffee? Do you want something to eat?"

"No," Hadley said curtly.

Hurriedly, Marsha carried the dishes to the kitchen. When she reappeared she was fastening on a short suede leather jacket; while he was talking to Beckheim she had changed her clothes. "It's time to go," she explained. "I'll drive you back down. . . ." She indicated the massive, hunched back of Theodore Beckheim. "He has to work."

"I see that," Hadley agreed, his voice thick and stricken.

Marsha opened the door to the front hall; the grim odor of stopped-up drains filtered into the living room, along with the tinny blare of radios and human voices.

As the door closed after them, Hadley caught a last glimpse of Beckheim. The black man did not look up; he continued working, silent and intent, elbows resting on the desk, solemnly going through the heaps of letters.

Before they left San Francisco, Marsha pulled the Studebaker into the parking lot of a vast neon-lit supermarket and locked the parking brake.

"Wait here," she instructed Hadley, sliding from the car. "I'll be right back."

She skipped into the rear entrance of the supermarket, slim and boyish in her slacks and leather jacket. Hadley sat glumly waiting for her, watching the other shoppers coming out and going in, getting into their cars, driving off down the dark streets.

It was hard to believe. He had met Beckheim, talked to him, and then been ushered out. The moment was over; already it had begun to sink into the past, like an object slowly settling into gray, leaden water.

He felt cheated. Resentfully, he lit up a cigarette and then stubbed it furiously out. What had he expected? A miracle, perhaps. Something more than his brief interview and dismissal. But he had not been disappointed . . . he had been awed. Awed, and very much cheated at the same time. The power was there in the hunched, blackened old man with his horny skin, the heavy figure that smelled of stale sweat and musty closets, who looked as if he had already passed through the fire of Armageddon and come out again. Beckheim had power . . . but he had withheld it. That had been the cheating: Beckheim could have saved him, helped him, but he had not.

Brooding over this, Hadley watched Marsha's knife-sharp silhouette hurry from the supermarket and across the dark parking lot. He pushed open the car door and she slipped in breathlessly behind the wheel. A bulging paper bag was deposited in his lap; it clinked moistly as he took charge of it.

"What's this?" he demanded, opening it. In the paper bag was a fifth of John Jameson blended scotch whiskey.

"That's for us," Marsha explained as she started up the car. "You never got your drink; God, I can use a drink now myself."

She drove across the streaming band of light that was Market Street and plunged into the Tenderloin beyond. Tiny shops pushed together in uneven rows, spread out on both sides of the narrow streets; crowds of men milled aimlessly between the cheap bars and cafés. Marsha turned off, past deserted factories and industrial warehouses; a few moments later the car entered the broad strips that made up the freeway.

"We'll make better time this way," she explained as the little Studebaker gained velocity. Sodium vapor lamps flashed past them; beyond the dividing strip endless headlights glowed and slithered. "I'll turn off at San Mateo."

They drove for a time without speaking. Finally Hadley asked: "Where did he come from?"

"Beckheim? He was born in Alabama; I told you that."

"I didn't realize he was that old."

"He's not so old. He's tired. . . . He's done so much." She turned curiously to him. "What did you think of him?"

"It's hard to say." He felt that she was worried about his reaction, unsure of herself until she knew how she felt; as if her own opinion hung in the balance, too.

"Were—you disappointed?" she asked.

"No. Of course not—" Hadley broke off moodily. "I resented all those questions. What business is it of his, all those things he asked me? About Ellen and Pete. Looking through my wallet that way."

He glowered out the window at the dark countryside beyond the freeway. Neon signs beamed here and there. The night sky was vaguely purple. A few stars sputtered fitfully; the fog lay behind them now. Hadley rolled down the window, and warm night wind promptly whipped in around him. Fresh wind that smelled of baked fields and sagging wooden fences.

He wondered if he would ever see Beckheim again. The Negro's words faded and blurred together when he tried to remember them. What had

Beckheim actually said? What had he meant? Hadley touched his wallet; the membership card was there, but what did it signify?

The card lay against him, a seed slipped in close to his flesh. Warmed by his body, perhaps it would take root and grow. Perhaps the card was alive. Beckheim had buried the card in Hadley's body; Hadley had received it for better or worse, whatever it meant. And that was all that had come out of the moment between the two of them: a thin blue pasteboard card. A dollar and fifty cents' worth of membership in the Society, the same for him as for thousands of others: workmen and Negroes, the lowest elements of the cities and towns. Aimless, unsatisfied riffraff and cranks. Wakefield carried an identical card, no doubt. And Marsha, sitting beside him at the wheel; probably there was a stiff little pasteboard card somewhere in her purse. Only it wasn't stiff any longer; it had been taken in long ago. It was limp and soiled by now.

Beside him the woman sat gripping the wheel with one hand, her left arm resting on the sill of the open window. She leaned back against the seat, chin up, reddish hair tousled by the wind. The suede leather jacket flapped back and forth; Marsha turned suddenly and smiled at him, teeth white and even in the faint light of the sodium vapor lamps.

"Nice," she observed. "The wind, the motion of the car. This little car is so smooth. . . . It's like flying." She pressed down on the accelerator; the car seemed to float forward over the dips and rises of the road. There was no sound or presence of the motor, only the roar of the wind as it entered the cabin and rushed around the man and woman. Presently the sodium vapor lights ceased and the highway became dark. There were fewer cars now. Marsha leaned forward and clicked off the dashboard lights. The luminous numbers, letters, dials, faded away; the cabin was totally dark. Ahead of them the bright swath of headlights was a circle of orange in the summer night.

Conscious of the gradually increasing velocity of the car, Hadley closed his eyes and lay back against the seat. He sensed the dangerous murmur of motion under him; he knew without seeing that the car was going too fast. But there were no other cars; there was nothing else in the world but the little Studebaker and the slim figure beside him. He was tired. The interview with Beckheim had exhausted him. Now that he could look back at it he was conscious of the tension that had held the two of them; in the few words they had exchanged there was a tight ordeal of discovery and investigation.

He wondered vaguely if Beckheim was as curious about everyone as he had been about him. He wondered if Beckheim probed and needled everybody who came into his sphere. Hadley's thoughts wandered off groggily. Perhaps Beckheim had taken a special interest. . . . The giving of the card might signify something momentous. A sign. He could ask Marsha if it was common. Beckheim had singled him out. . . . He yawned and relaxed. He had been selected. In the nebulous confusion of his thoughts the image of Beckheim arose briefly, large and heavyset, black horn-rimmed glasses, sleeves rolled up. In the warm night air Hadley smelled the presence of the black man, as if the summer mists settling over the fields and roads were perspiration collecting on the ancient black body.

Opening his eyes he watched a long, extended ridge to the right of the highway. The car was moving toward it. In the corrugations of the hill he imagined Beckheim's features: his nose and forehead, his thin lips. A portion of the ridge was Beckheim's thick jaw and chin. Beckheim lay all around; it was a pleasant, comforting thought. Hadley could reach out his hand, through the open window, into the night, to touch Beckheim. Reach up and touch the dark, horny cheek. Run his fingers over the knobby cheekbones, the intense ridges of the old man's brows.

With a bucking jerk the car halted. Hadley sat up wildly; the car had stopped and Marsha was turning off the ignition. He had fallen asleep; the long ridge was gone, and they were no longer on the highway. The night was utterly still. The wind had ceased. There was no movement or sound, only the faint cheep of crickets a long way off. And now and then the occasional soft rustle of nearby shrubbery.

"Where are we?" he murmured, pulling himself together and collecting his thoughts. "What time is it?"

"About midnight." Marsha struck a match in the gloom; it flared up briefly, and then glowed down to the dull red of a cigarette.

"Where are we?" he repeated. He could see nothing outside the car, only the outline of bushes and the rock-strewn surface of the road. To the right was a vague opaque presence that might have been a building. Apparently they were between towns, out in the open country. He didn't enjoy the feel of it one bit.

"We're almost there," Marsha assured him. "A mile or so more. You fell asleep."

From his pocket Hadley got out his crumpled package of cigarettes. He leaned over to get a light from Marsha. "I know. That business with Beckheim wore me out."

In the darkness the woman's cigarette glowed against his own; he inhaled deeply, his hand on the seat behind her shoulder, accepting light and warmth from her. The pungent smell of smoke mixed with the presence of her hair and skin; he could see her close to him, invisible and alive, leaning forward until their foreheads met.

"Thanks," he said, drawing away. A certain kind of tight stricture hardened around his chest; he breathed carefully and slowly, forcing himself to take things easy.

After a moment Marsha said: "Get a glass out; there's one in the glove compartment." From her purse she got the key and handed it to Hadley. As he opened the glove compartment and fished around inside, she began on the bottle.

"See it?" she asked.

He found the glass and brought it out. Marsha filled it, and the two of them sat passing it back and forth, the car doors open, letting the night air swirl around them. Now Hadley could make out the woman's figure. In the faint starlight Marsha's features were sharp and small, transluscent as old parchment. Her warm bodily processes had calcified; she was hard as polished stone, her face faintly luminous, eyes and lips without color. Half smiling, lips apart, chin tilted up, she sat gazing off into the distance, a demure, thoughtful figure in leather jacket and slacks. Presently she kicked off her shoes; in the dim light her feet were bare and pale, ghostlike.

Somewhere, a long time ago, he had sat in the darkness and quiet of a car, beside a woman. His mind focused, and he remembered. It was not a woman; it was a girl. Ellen and he had sat this way, in his little old Ford coupe, up in the hills at night. Dreaming and murmuring, exchanging plans and extravagant hopes. It seemed like a long time ago, but it was only a few years. Very much like this; the same crickets creaked in the shrubbery, the violet summer sky, the baked woolly smell of the car's upholstery. But then there had been beer and potato chips, and the Andrews sisters on the radio. The jeans and T-shirt of adolescence . . . the plump, ripe body of his fiancée, flesh instead of polished bone. The woman beside him now was cold and hard and mature. The tempered skeleton, chipped and refined by experience.

It seemed impossible that Marsha could ever have been a girl, young like his wife, foolish and silly and full of expansive nonsense. Giggling and murmuring and playing elaborate erotic games of chase and capture, teasing and fooling until dawn. The elaborate ritual of love . . . Marsha was bleak and austere, with an unchanging finality. Outside of time, perhaps. Not subject to the laws of development and decay.

"Mulling away," Marsha said softly. "Aren't you, Stuart Hadley? Mulling and brooding and worrying your life away." She reached out and touched his arm. "You worry so . . . all the time. You know, you have wrinkles; your forehead's like an old man's."

He grinned. "It's you prophets of doom that make me worry. When I come to work on Saturday, there's an old lady with a bunch of those 'Prepare for the Day of Judgment!' pamphlets."

Marsha reflected. "No . . . it's the other way around. The worried old lady is you, Stuart Hadley. All the worried old ladies go out, sooner or later, with their pamphlets. They're standing out there because people are already afraid."

"I was just kidding," Hadley said. With the close, personal intimacy of a woman's body nearby him, he did not particularly feel like discussing abstract topics. He wanted to think about what lay close at hand, the immediate reality of the car.

"You don't like being called an old lady, do you?"

"Of course not." He shrugged. "It doesn't matter."

"I don't mean to hurt your feelings. Did Ted hurt your feelings?"

"No." Hadley dismissed the subject. He sipped more of the whiskey; it was thick and alive as it felt its way down his throat. A furry, fluid shape without distinct form . . . the water of life. He choked a trifle; he wasn't used to straight whiskey. And it was lukewarm.

He yawned sleepily. "I'm tired. But not in the same way I was. I'm relaxed. . . . This stuff unfastens."

"Remember, you have to go to work tomorrow." Her voice sounded a long way off. Remote and small. "It's late."

"Maybe I won't go to work." Hadley said boldly.

"What instead?"

He hadn't worked that out. So many things . . . The world faded off into infinite being. But nothing specific, only the vague sense of futility that tomorrow at work brought him. "Anything," he said lazily. "Picking apples down in the valley. Shoveling gravel on a road gang. Sailor. Truck driver. Forest fire-fighter."

"You're a romantic little boy," Marsha said gently.

"Maybe." He peered stupidly forward, out into the darkness, his mind fuzzy with fatigue and the fumes of the John Jameson. The unbinding warmth made him sink easily down; it was no longer easy to place himself in time and space. He wondered dully where he was . . . when he was. Which Stuart Hadley was it, along the chain of Stuart Hadleys? Child, boy, adolescent, salesman, middle-aged father . . . Dreams rustled drowsily in his mind. Stirred from corners and compartments, blends of ambitions and fears drifted here and there, eddying currents that had always been a part of him.

"Go away," he muttered. "Not you," he explained to Marsha. "The inside bees."

She smiled. "Inside bees? You're a strange one, Stuart Hadley."

Annoyed, he scowled. "Why do you always call me Stuart Hadley? Either Stuart or Hadley, not both."

"Why not?"

He concentrated, but nothing came. Irritably, he swept the question away. "For God's sake, what kind of a person are you? I don't understand any of you . . . a bunch of toadstools popping up. Preying on us—what are you after?" He pulled angrily away from her. "What am I supposed to do, get down on my hands and knees and *pray*?" His resentment surprised him; it boiled up in and around him, carrying away his tongue. "I came all the way up here—what's he want me to do? He tells me it's up to me; you think if I *knew* what to do I'd be here?"

Listening intently, soberly, Marsha said: "I didn't realize you were so angry."

"Of course I'm angry! I came all the way up here for nothing. . . ." His voice blurred off in baffled confusion. "I don't think it's fair. He didn't do anything; he just sat there working."

"What did you want him to do?"

"I don't know."

"Miracle healing?" Gently, she continued: "He's not a saint; he can't raise the dead and multiply bread."

"At least he could have listened to me!"

Queerly, she asked: "What did you have to say?"

Hadley shook his head dumbly. "He should have known. I thought he would know. I wanted his help—I didn't get a damn thing except a blue card. And it cost me a dollar and fifty cents."

"Maybe," Marsha said, "it's too late to help you. I don't know, either. Probably he understands you better than I do. . . . I'll ask him."

"How could he? He only glanced my way a couple of times!"

Marsha's even white teeth flashed in laughter. "He sized you up, Stuart Hadley."

Shocked fear swept over Hadley. "Oh, you mean I didn't measure up?" His voice shook. "I'm not worth saving? I'm not part of the select group, is that it?"

"Stuart Hadley—"

"Stop calling me that!"

The woman's nostrils flared. "Nobody decides who can be saved. Nobody selects, like a draft board picking eligible men. You're saved for the same reason a ball rolls downhill—because of natural laws."

Hadley grunted sullenly and subsided. "It doesn't make sense.

Predestination—I remember that stuff. The saved and the damned." His voice rose bleakly. "Damn it, I'm not going to sit around. It isn't fair. I have to do something; I thought he'd tell me what to do—" He broke off.

"You'll have to decide for yourself," Marsha said. "He told you that; remember? You're the only one who can decide."

"Forget it." Hadley gulped down more of the John Jameson. He was beginning to feel sick; his stomach turned over queasily, and a raw, metallic deposit rose thickly in the back of his throat and gagged him. Lumberingly, he turned around and poured out the contents of the glass onto the dark pavement.

"What are you doing?" Marsha asked sharply.

"Urinating."

She laughed. "You've had enough; give me the bottle." She took the fifth and jammed the lid over it. A sudden metallic click; she had stuffed it and the glass into the glove compartment and locked it.

"Maybe I will do something," Hadley asserted after a while.

"What sort of thing?"

"I don't know yet. Let's not talk about it." The night wind was beginning to turn chill; he reached out and pulled the door shut.

"Do you want to leave?" Marsha held up her thin wrist and examined the dial of her watch. "It's getting late; I'll take you home."

"Wait." Convulsively, he grabbed her hand as she reached to push the ignition key into the lock. "Not yet."

For a moment she held her hand there; then she smiled and put the key away. "The man of action asserts himself."

"I don't want to go back yet. And I don't like to be driven around by a woman." He added: "I'll drive the rest of the way."

"Can you?"

"Of course. I drive the store truck all the damn time."

Marsha shrugged indifferently. "Whatever you want. But we can't stay here much longer. . . . It's getting cold and I have to go all the way back to S.F."

Abruptly, Hadley pushed the car door open and stepped unsteadily out. He slammed the door after him and moved a few uncertain, wavering steps into the darkness.

"Where are you going?" Marsha called shrilly.

"Home. You go on back—I'll walk." He stumbled over the rising shoulder of the road, managed to regain his balance, and began systematically tracing his way along the edge of the gravel.

"For God's sake," Marsha snapped excitedly. She leaped out of the car and raced after him. "You don't know which way it is; you don't know what you're doing!" Exasperated, she caught hold of him and shook him furiously. "Get back in the car and behave like an adult!"

"Let go of me." Muddled and embittered, Hadley tore her small cold hands loose from his coat and shoved her away. "I know where I live; I'll find my way back. I've walked longer walks than this."

"You damn fool." Half laughing, her voice trembling with cold and rising hysteria, Marsha hurried along beside him. "You'll pass out and some car'll run over you."

"Not me," Hadley said. Brooding as he stumbled along he mumbled: "Why not? Get it over with. After all, it won't be long. Beckheim says so; listen to the Master." He stepped from the road into the dry shrubbery at the edge of the shoulder. "All right, I'll walk along here. Off the goddamn road."

Running around in front of him, Marsha furiously blocked his way. "Stop it!" she gasped. Hands digging into his shoulders, she pushed him back toward the car. "Get in and I'll drive you home. For God's sake there're houses around here—somebody'll hear you."

Hadley caught hold of her arms and held on to her. Under his fingers ran the taut cords and ligaments and muscles of her body; there was no excess flesh, only the mechanisms that made her a functioning machine. The suede leather of her jacket was moist with night mist; in her hair, particles of light glittered and sparkled. He pried her fingers loose by lifting her arms; gripping her by the elbows, he raised up until she winced with pain.

"Stop it," she whispered, turning her head away. Suddenly she was terrified of him; she sensed the deep violence and hatred in him. He no longer was a human being. He was a force, impersonal and beyond reason. "Please," she whispered.

He stepped down onto the highway beside her. In the night stillness her breathing was audible: harsh and rapid, very close to him. Awareness that he still had hold of her came to him. There wasn't anything she could do. Silent, biting her lip, she stood waiting, hoping he would relent and let her go.

It was not a sexual thing he was doing. He felt no desire or passion, only a cold ache, a growing bitterness. Her body repelled him; the nearness of it made his flesh crawl. Dry, faintly warm, her body was snakelike. . . . It was loathing and disgust that rose up in him, and a gathering drive for revenge.

"Goddamn it," he snarled, "it isn't fair." All his disappointment was coming to the surface, his deep-rooted frustration. He had been cheated again, and it was her fault. "It isn't right!" he shouted, and in his pain he clutched her tighter and tighter.

"Stop it," Marsha quavered. In panic, she struggled to get away from him. "I'll yell—for Christ's sake!" One small hand tore loose and flashed up at him, sharp nails gleaming in the cold starlight. He knocked it down from his face and yanked her around in a half circle. Half carrying, half dragging her, he plodded back to the car and dumped her onto the seat.

"No weeds," he said thickly. "Not in the rubbish and weeds."

Marsha stopped fighting. "I give up," she grated. "Will you let me go? All right, I'll do it. Come on, *let go of me!*"

Abruptly, he released her, and she sat up, brushing her hair back and fumbling around on the seat. Now, at least he had brought it to a level she understood; his drive had finally channelized in a recognizable form. Or so she imagined. She thought it was sexual desire he felt, physical longing generated by her presence, the dark night, and the liquor; but she was wrong. "I think I dropped my purse out there," she said shakily, beginning to recover a trifle.

"Here it is." He found her purse on the floor of the car and brusquely handed it to her.

"Thanks." Trembling, she groped in it. "The keys are in here, thank God." For a moment she sat leaning back against the steering wheel, getting her breath. "Look, do you know what you're doing? Or are you drunk?" She was stalling for time.

"I know." And he did know; it was true. She was the one who was mistaken. . . . He could sense the easy misevaluation in every line of her thin, proud body. And his ruthless hostility grew.

"You really want to? You're crazy." Her voice softened wearily. Fear was going; she sensed him as a person again, not possessed any longer. It, whatever it was, had left. For the time being, he was an ordinary man again. "It's late and I'm exhausted," she said. "Not here—oh, you're so completely off base on everything. You would think this is just the place. And all this big pushing-around." Her voice broke miserably. "It's my fault. This is a hell of a place, Stuart Hadley. It just won't do. . . . It's all wrong."

"It's okay," he said stubbornly; a grim kind of determination had overcome him. He meant to finish what he had started. "Come on, let's get going."

"You damn fool. Please—oh, what the hell. I give up." She pushed his grasping hands away. "Let me do it, at least." Quivering with cold and unhappiness, she slid out of her leather jacket and tossed it into the backseat. "Is that what you want?"

"Fine."

Struggling up, she rapidly unbuttoned her shirt and snatched it off. She threw it violently away and unhooked the catch of her bra. Bending forward, she pawed the straps from her shoulders and dropped the bra onto the floor.

"Now what?" she demanded. "The rest? All right!" Half sobbing, she savagely kicked her shoes off and unbuttoned the snaps of her slacks. "I have to stand up. Please, get out of the way so I can get up!"

Hadley backed awkwardly out of the car and Marsha flowed after him. The night mist swirled around her as she stood leaning against the damp side of the car, struggling out of her slacks. Her body was as he had expected: pale and firm, without excess flesh or lines. A slender, competent body, tall and graceful, almost totally hairless, breasts small and sharply pointed. Shivering, she turned to stuff her discarded clothing into the car.

"What now?" she demanded breathlessly, teeth chattering with cold. "Come on—for God's sake, let's get going if we're going to!"

He eagerly followed her into the car. As his hands closed over her he felt her breasts leap and quiver; attracted by the heat of his body, her nipples rose and hardened against his throat. Under him she shuddered and squirmed, her fingernails digging into his back. Gasping and panting, she fought to pull herself up. . . . Her nipples grazed his face and then she was gone, away from him. The hot, pulsing presence of her body ceased.

"Aren't you going to take off your clothes?" she shrieked. "Aren't you even going to take off your shoes?" In a split, tortured second she visibly changed her mind; her nipples died and the resigned openness of her body vanished. Frigidly, she closed against him; she fought him away and managed to kick herself back against the car door. She knocked the door open and tumbled backward, scrambling animal-like to her feet.

"Come back here." Futilely, he grabbed her by the wrist and dragged her into the car. She collapsed over the edge of the seat, bent knees stark and bony in the faint starlight.

"It won't work," she snarled, eyes wild and darting, body slippery with mist. "No, I'm not going to." She swept up her clothes and blindly began untangling them. Tears spilled down her hollow cheeks and dripped wetly onto her thighs. In her lap the bundle of clothes twisted and flapped between her plucking fingers. "We're both crazy. It's that goddamn booze, and it's late and I'm dead tired." Her voice trailed off wretchedly; for a moment she sat unmoving, resting against the seat, head down, her dark tumble of hair spilled forward, chin sunk down against her collarbone. Finally she shuddered alive and slowly resumed separating her clothes.

"I'm sorry." Nervous and pleading, Hadley touched her bare shoulder.

"Let's go somewhere else; a motel or something. Where we can talk and—"
He broke off impotently. "Where it'll be all right, not like this. Not out here
in this godforsaken hole."

She shook her head. "I'm sorry, Stuart Hadley. It's not your fault." Again
she stepped shakily from the car. "Excuse me for a minute." As he watched
apprehensively, she pulled on her long slacks and then hooked her bra into
place. Presently she slid back in beside him. "While I'm dressing," she managed to say, "will you light me a cigarette?"

He did so, and put it between her slack lips.

"Thanks." She smiled jerkily up at him as she placed it in the dashboard
ashtray and pulled her shirt around her. "It's freezing. . . . I'll turn on the car
heater."

"The heater won't work, will it?" he mumbled. "Without the motor running?"

"No," she said, laughing thinly. "Of course it won't. Well, what the hell,
we'll be going soon." For a moment she halted her swift motions. After a
pause she leaned forward and reached up to him. Her small cold hand traced
itself across his face; briefly, she ran her fingers into his hair, turning her face
up to him and peering unhappily at him, lips quivering, mouth close to his
own. Her breath was warm and rapid against his cheek.

"I don't understand," he said dismally. "Why not? Because of Ellen?"

Marsha finished buttoning her shirt; she grabbed her cigarette from the
ashtray and sucked on it until it glowed bright and orange. "Stuart, I should
never have got mixed up with you. It's got to stop—I'll take you home and
leave you off, and that's that. I don't want to see you again. . . . I *can't* see
you again. Go back to your television shop and your family."

"What are you talking about?" he shouted, stricken. "What is this?"

"Maybe later," she continued, rapidly and breathlessly. "If you had got
going quicker—or if you had waited awhile. But not now." She glanced
up, eyes wide, mouth twisting defiantly, agonized. "If you weren't such a
woolly-headed little boy you'd have figured it out. Anybody else would.
I'm living with Ted. To be more exact, he's living with me. It's my apartment; all the things are mine, except for the desk. He brought that along.
Maybe we'll get married; maybe not. I don't know, in some states you
can't."

Hoarsely, Hadley demanded: "You mean you're—sleeping with him?"
His body, his lungs and vocal cords and throat and tongue and palate,
formed the words: "You're living with that big black nigger?"

After she slapped him he sat back against the door and stared out at the night darkness. Marsha finished dressing, tossed her cigarette into the weeds, and started up the car motor. She drove rapidly back to the highway, turned in a wide, shrieking squeal of tires toward Cedar Groves, and brutally drove the car up to seventy miles an hour.

Neither of them said anything. Finally the bleak countryside of hills and shrubbery and fields gave way; the lights of houses flickered here and there. Presently a glowing Standard gasoline station appeared beside the highway, and after that a roadhouse and a Shell station.

At a traffic light Marsha slowed. They were in Cedar Groves. A few cars came out on the highway beside them. Soon they were passing dark houses and closed-up stores.

"Here we are," Marsha said curtly. She parked the Studebaker across the street from Hadley's apartment house. The motor running, she shoved the door open for him. "Good night."

He hesitated, unwilling to get out. "I'm sorry," he began.

"Good night." Her voice was clipped, empty of emotion. She gazed straight ahead, one hand on the shift, her toe on the accelerator, breathing rapidly, in dry, short gasps.

"Listen," Hadley said to her. "Stop acting this way; try to understand how I feel. If you had any sense you'd know—"

"It doesn't matter. Go back to your wife and your television store." The car edged forward; the open door swung back and forth.

Slowly, Hadley stepped onto the sidewalk. "You really mean it. You're really that crazy. As far as you're concerned, it's over."

For an instant the calcified mask that was the woman's face remained intact. Then, as if split from inside, it suddenly caved in and dissolved. A thin, high-pitched wail rose up out of her, a pain so sharp that it paralyzed him. "That's right!" she screamed in his startled face. "It's over!" She reached to slam the door after him, tears welling up in her eyes and spurting down her cheeks. "I'm sorry; it's nobody's fault. I made a mistake—you made a mistake. Everybody was wrong."

"Everybody?" Hadley demanded. He shoved quickly forward, trying to get at her, trying to force his way into her crumbling personality. "Was *he* wrong? Don't sit there and lie to me; are you trying to make me believe—"

The car roared up and was gone into the darkness. The words hung on his lips, baffled and unspoken. There was nobody to ask; he was alone. He could shout the question out at the top of his lungs: it made no difference. For a time he stood on the sidewalk, looking helplessly after the car. Then he turned and crossed the street to his apartment, fumbling automatically for his key.

As he got his wallet out, the stiff blue edge of the Society card grazed his hand. He pulled it out, stood holding it, and then tore it furiously apart. The bits fluttered down onto the pavement; a gust of night wind picked them up and whisked them away.

By the time he had the front door of the apartment house open, the bits were scattered across the gutter, along with the other night debris, the littered newspapers and rubbish, the empty beer cans and cigarette packages. Trash to be swept up and collected by the city.

He stiffly mounted the bleak carpeted steps to his own floor, his body heaving with cold. It wasn't until he was actually opening the door and entering the dark, lifeless apartment that he remembered his pictures. He had left them in Marsha's car.

It was too late to get them back now.

PART THREE
Evening

Alice Fergesson, her face flushed and hectic from the heat, hurried back and forth, satisfying herself that the big house was ready for guests, that dinner was progressing through its intricate stages of preparation, that it was not yet eight o'clock.

In the living room stood her husband, his hands stuffed in his pockets, gazing moodily out the window. Alice paused a moment and called sharply to him. "What are you doing? Just standing there? You could help me, you know."

The small, heavyset figure stirred grumpily; Jim Fergesson turned toward her and impatiently waved her away. He was meditating again; for the past week he had been meditating constantly. His red, wrinkled, prunelike face was twisted into a worried scowl; he stuck his stump of a cigar between his teeth and abruptly turned his back to her.

A pang of pity caught up the woman as she resumed her cooking. There was something forlorn and pathetic in the sight of the little round worried man, chewing on his cigar and trying to keep all his plans and problems straight in his mind. She concentrated on the sizzling swordfish steaks broiling in the oven, and forced herself not to pay any attention to him.

"What time is it?" Jim Fergesson demanded behind her, suddenly close and insistent.

Alice straightened up quickly. "You scared me."

"What time is it?" he asked again, blunt and noisy, with the almost childlike directness that dominated when he was worried. As if it were urgent, as if something vital hung on knowing at once, he repeated: "Damn it, where'd you put that electric clock? It used to be over the sink; where is it now?"

"I won't tell you," Alice said firmly, "if you're going to shout in that tone of voice."

Fergesson howled: "I have a right to know what time it is!" He flushed angrily. "You women, you're never satisfied. Didn't I spend a whole afternoon running BX cable around there for that clock?"

"Take these." She pushed plates into his hands and steered him out of the kitchen, into the dining room. "Then get out the good silver; it's in that old green-felt box—you know, your mother's."

"Why? For Stumblebum?"

"Because it's company."

"He can use the regular silver we always use." Fergesson resentfully began setting dishes around the long oak table. "Don't make such an occasion out of this—what are you women up to, anyhow?" He glared fearfully at his wife. "Have you and Ellen Hadley got your damn heads together again? This whole thing is rigged!"

Ignoring him, Alice turned her attention to the salad. The tray of white poppy-seed rolls was ready to be slipped into the oven, as soon as the swordfish steaks were done. The béarnaise was made. The frozen peas lay in their damp carton, melting and oozing. What had she forgotten? The wine gelatin and shortbread cookies had been accomplished the night before. . . . All that remained was the baked potatoes: they reposed like inert lumps in the top of the oven, refusing to cook rapidly or evenly.

In the dining room the sounds of motion ponderously rolled forth: Fergesson was dragging open the drawers of the big chest in his search for the silver. For a moment she considered getting it herself; the sullen stirrings made her uncomfortable. What was there to upset him? It was spreading to her . . . Fergesson was infecting the house with tension and gravity. Sighing, Alice knelt down and again examined the swordfish steaks.

Under the dull blue flame of the oven the steaks oozed white fat, steamed languidly; drops of bacon fat burned and sparkled across the hard gray surface. Well, fish fillets were nice on a warm summer evening. Nice for the cook, at least; the oven didn't have to stay on all afternoon. She tried to remember if Stuart ate fish; according to Ellen there were so many things he wouldn't eat.

But fresh saltwater fish never hurt anybody. Impatiently, she closed the oven and stood up. Stuart was a big strong boy; it was time somebody sat him down at the table and made him eat. On the outside, at least, he was healthy and well fed as a pig; in fact, he was beginning to bulge a trifle at the middle.

For a moment she halted to get her bearings. So many things to keep in mind: an evening of trying to keep Fergesson and Hadley from arguing; trying to keep Ellen from curling up on the couch like a sick cat, demanding that everybody wait on her; trying to keep the conversation from degenerating into redundant shoptalk and commonplaces about the weather and the state of the Union. Trying to mix four people no two of whom mixed, let alone the whole group. She grabbed the pan of rolls and jerkily pushed it into the oven.

Apprehensively, Alice bent to slap dust from her skirt; kneeling to peer into the oven was ruining her clothes. Briefly she searched the closet for a longer apron. There was none, and she slammed the little plywood door irritably. Probably Ellen had borrowed her long blue plastic apron. . . . She could understand Fergesson's impatience at Hadley; youth seemed to stand with its hands out, a silly, weak smile on its face, the aimless, hopeful, trusting smile of a child. Stuart and Ellen. Borrowing, asking, depending on . . . but then, her mother had said the same thing about *her,* and so on back.

In the dining room, Fergesson prowled testily, with nothing to do; he had found the silver and dumped it onto the table. She could sense him pacing restlessly, mulling over his two stores, his burgeoning responsibilities. *Why the hell did you buy it?* she wanted to yell at him in exasperation. If all you're going to do is worry about it, then for heaven's sake sell it back!

A long way off came the sound of voices and the shuffle of shoes. A split second later the doorbell clanged; her heart gave a wild jump and she rushed to take one last look into the oven. They had come. The evening had begun.

"Would you go?" she called anxiously to Fergesson. "I have to watch the fish."

Grunting resentfully, Fergesson padded down the hall to the front door. She caught a glimpse of him halting briefly in front of the hall mirror to peer at himself; he tipped his head and critically scrutinized his bald spot, vaguely visible under his ill-combed hair. Her poor vain disheveled worrying husband. . . . He yanked open the front door, and Stuart and Ellen entered the house.

How much taller he was than Fergesson; she saw that in an instant and then totally dismissed it. Slim, blond, straight, he came quietly in, his arm partway around Ellen, guiding her past the step. For the occasion he had put on a brown sports coat and neatly pressed dark gabardine slacks . . . cord-soled shoes and a spotted bow tie. Well groomed, natty, his chin smooth and pale with talcum, his ears faintly pink, his hair cut short and carefully in place, Stuart Hadley waved cheerfully at Alice.

"Hi," he called.

She smiled back. "You're early."

Ellen smiled, too. She stood holding the blue bundle of blankets and apparatus in which Pete slept. Her face glowed round and radiant, suffused with sleek pride in her bulging armload. As long as possible she paraded her child; it seemed as if she were never going to put him down. Then Stuart led her into the downstairs bedroom; their voices faded as Fergesson moved glumly after them.

". . . not too drafty, is it?" Ellen's voice drifted.

"This is August!" Fergesson protested angrily, as if she had insulted the construction of his house. The sound of objects being moved, a window shut . . . The three of them emerged, Fergesson glowering, his hands still in his pockets, cigar between his teeth, as always.

In the cool yellow light of the living room, the rich colors of Ellen's skin and hair came out and glistened. Youth and blooming health . . . Alice couldn't repress a whirr of envy. Ellen, standing in the center of the room as the two men seated themselves, turned this way and that, displaying her returned slim figure, her pretty summer dress. Tumbling brown hair, and the graceful flow of her green silk skirt, the flash of her smooth legs . . . On high heels she glided into the kitchen and greeted Alice.

"What can I do to help?" she queried, eyes sparkling.

"Nothing," Alice said. "You go back and entertain the boys; it's almost ready."

Eyes bright, lips half parted, Ellen moved around the kitchen. Her high, trim bust quivered excitedly. . . . It was amazing what an expensive bra could do. "This is so wonderful. . . ." She ran her hands over the chrome and tile sink Fergesson had personally installed. "I wish we had this. And these nice faucets." She gazed up at the ventilation pipes overhead. "Jim put those in?"

"He put everything in," Alice said practically as she popped the frozen peas into the pan of boiling water. "How's Pete?"

"Fine," Ellen said joyously. "Alice, you have such a lovely house. . . . I'm so jealous! All the wonderful hardwood floors . . . and they're all *polished*."

"Waxed," Alice corrected.

"How do you ever find time to keep up a big house like this? And the garden . . . it's practically a mansion!"

"It's all routine," Alice said vaguely, her mind on the dinner. "You get it down to a discipline."

In the living room the two men were consulting in loud, assertive voices. Facing each other, legs crossed, settled back in their chairs, they were going over the items of the previous day.

"That Leo J. Meyberg shipment come in?" Fergesson was asking.

"It came by Trans-bay. Most of it's away."

"Much back order? I'm going to cancel our back orders; we're building up too much. That's a racket—they know that stuff gets duplicated. We got fifty 5u4's, twice what we can use. I'm sending half of them back."

"We finally moved the big Zenith combo," Hadley said.

"I noticed the tag. Your sale?"

"White and I split it . . . I talked to them first, but he closed it. They came back."

"You should have closed it the first time," Fergesson said sourly.

"Nobody puts out four hundred dollars the first time."

"Let them out the door," Fergesson said angrily, "and you've lost them. You got their names?"

The conversation died down into a hostile mumble.

"They get right at it," Ellen observed fatuously. "They're so—serious."

"It's going to be that way all through dinner," Alice said, resigned.

Awed, her brown eyes wide, Ellen said: "I'm so glad when he wakes up and takes an interest in things . . . He's usually so sort of—" She shrugged and smiled. "You know. Always dreaming around." Quickly, she added: "He has a lot of ideas, of course. I hope he gets a chance to tell him about his idea on new counters; he sketched out some designs and they're really swell. Alice, you know he has ability. He should have been an architect or something." Anxiously, she followed Alice around the kitchen. "Can't I do anything?"

"You're doing fine," Alice said drily.

Ellen opened the refrigerator and poked at things. "Can I put Pete's bottles in here?" she asked hopefully.

"Certainly," Alice said.

"Thank you." Ellen left the kitchen to get the bottles. "They're in the bedroom with all his things."

Alice continued preparing dinner. Ellen had halted momentarily in the living room to smile at the two men . . . but as the girl returned to the kitchen, Alice saw the wrinkled tension of her forehead.

"Relax," Alice said to her.

The sweet, aimless smile spread like honey over the girl's face. "Oh, Alice—you're so used to these social things. I wish I had your savoir faire."

From the oven came the smoking hot swordfish. It was placed on the heavy platter, surrounded by lemon slices, and then carried from the kitchen to the dining room. Everybody watched respectfully as Alice bustled breathlessly back to the kitchen after the bowls of peas, the béarnaise sauce, the baked potatoes, the salad, the Silex of coffee, the rolls.

"Looks great," Hadley said, approaching the massive oak table with its solemn display of old silver and china and linen napkins in horn rings. He grinned appreciatively. "A real feast."

Without formality, Fergesson seated himself and began pouring steaming black coffee into his cup. "Come on," he said, "let's get started." He helped himself to cream and sugar as Hadley seated his wife, and Alice hurried back to the kitchen for the butter.

The meal began silently, tensely. Alice ate in quick, businesslike snatches, her eyes on the two men and the young woman seated around the table. Fergesson plowed into his dinner without comment, his flushed face expressionless, stowing food away like a dockworker. Beside him Ellen picked daintily at her plate, a mouthful now and then, her red lips twisting into nervous grimaces. Several times she excused herself to trip into the bedroom to see about Pete; watching the girl's skirts swish around her trim legs, Alice wondered if she was acting, or nervous, or both. Both, probably; when Ellen emerged from the bedroom, Alice again caught the momentary flash of genuine panic in the girl's brown eyes.

While his wife struggled to make things come out all right, Stuart Hadley happily gulped down fish and baked potato and rolls and green peas, his handsome blond face devoid of guile.

For a time nobody spoke. At last, when the silence was becoming difficult, Fergesson spoke up. "Well," he said, to no one in particular, "I see they raised the draft quota again."

"It's always going up," Hadley responded, his mouth full. He swallowed some coffee. "They'll never get me, not with my liver trouble."

Fergesson eyed him. "You're sure proud of being sick. You don't look sick to me; there's nothing wrong with you."

"For the Army, there is," Hadley answered haughtily.

"I volunteered in World War I," Fergesson growled. "Marine Corps—Second Battle of the Marne, Belleau Wood. It never hurt me any."

"You weren't married," Alice reminded him. "It's different when you're married."

"When you're married," Fergesson pontificated, "you've got more to fight for. You've got a stake in this country. A man ought to be glad of the chance to pay back his country some of what he owes it, for what it's done for him." He wiped his mouth with his napkin. "You're 4-F?" he demanded. "They're not going to change it?"

"No," Ellen said quickly. "He's got a certificate that says he's permanently ineligible."

Fergesson grunted and returned to his food.

"With the peace talks," Alice said, "the war should be over soon."

"Never," Fergesson said flatly. "Those Reds are stalling; they'll never sign. You can't talk to them; the only kind of language they understand is military strength. The Democrats are going to hand Korea over to them—what we need is a clear-cut military victory. Any child knows that!"

Hadley said: "You want to fight Red China?"

"When the time comes," Fergesson said, "that Uncle Sam can't stand up to a bunch of Orientals—" He fiercely gulped down his coffee. "That's what's wrong with people today; they're soft! One atomic bomb and those Chinamen would run clear out of China. We've got to show some force; we've got to show them the kind of steel we're made of. Words, words, words—all they do is talk. That's all—sit around a table gabbing. And while we're sitting there in Panmunjom, those Reds are taking over the world." He pointed his finger at Hadley. "It wouldn't hurt you to do a little less talking and a little more work; according to what I hear you spent most of yesterday standing around chewing the fat with the Basford salesman."

Hadley flushed. "I was trying to save you a couple of bucks; I was turning down that package deal they've got rigged up for the Christmas market."

"You let me worry about that," Fergesson said. "I already told H. R. Basford we're not taking any package deal; we'll get the regular discount and return, none of that lump stuff. Where's that order book they sent around? I'm cutting it up for scratch pads."

"All right," Alice reproved. "Wait until after dinner."

Fergesson stormily pushed away his plate. "I'm done."

"There's dessert," Alice reminded him.

"Well, trot it on."

Around the table everyone had stopped eating. Ellen, her plate half full, glanced anxiously at Fergesson and then at her husband. Alice felt momentary compassion for her; it was enough to discourage anybody. Getting to her feet, she began collecting the dishes. "Don't get up," she said to Ellen as the girl started convulsively to her feet. "I can do it."

"It's that overhead skylight," Fergesson was saying when she returned with the wine gelatin. "Get that damn thing covered and you won't get too much glare. Or turn the sets around the other way."

"They've got to be visible from the street," Hadley answered. "People come along and see the TV going; they stop and watch; they drift in without knowing it."

"Put one in the window," Fergesson grunted.

"That's bad! Makes it too much like a free show; you know, something you pay admission for, like a movie. We want the sets where people can come in and handle them—get the idea they're for sale, something for the home."

"I suppose so," Fergesson admitted. "Personally, I wouldn't have one around the house." With suspicion, he accepted his wine gelatin. "What's this?"

Alice explained. "Eat it with the cookies." She served herself last, and took her seat. "Before it gets warm."

Gingerly, Fergesson poked at the shimmering dark yellow mound. "It's got *wine* in it?"

Ellen tasted the dessert and turned rapturously to Alice. "It's just wonderful," she gasped. "It's so sort of "—she hunted for the word—"so continental."

Earnestly, Hadley continued his conversation with his boss. "I don't think you've got the right idea about TV. You can't merchandise it like fifteen-dollar radios. Take our ads; they're nothing, just a couple of boxes in the throwaway *Shopping News*. What we want is one of those full-page mats every week—from Emerson and Zenith and RCA, all the big companies. In the *S.F. Chronicle* or the *Oakland Trib,* not the *San Mateo Times;* that hasn't got any circulation. Our best customers ought to be those big estates out of town, the people with plenty of money to spend. We ought to get in some of the custom-built TV combinations, something better than Admiral and Philco. At least DuMont."

"I'm not going to tie up my inventory in a bunch of those thousand-dollar combinations," Fergesson answered sourly.

His face eager, Hadley rushed on: "Damn it, you're missing the gravy! Once we tap people of that group, we can really rake it in. You work all day selling one measly Admiral table model; how much do you net on that? Markup is about thirty percent; you net maybe twenty bucks, by the time you figure overhead and commission—right? You work just as hard selling some laborer, some factory worker and his wife, a table-model plastic Admiral as you would selling some rich guy a deluxe custom-built job for a thousand bucks—harder! These rich people want to buy; they have the money to spend. You know where they go to get their TV? Up to S.F. To the big downtown department stores . . . the swank outfits in Stonestown, for example."

"I'm no big-time operator," Fergesson said grumpily. "I just want my share."

The meal was finished in uncomfortable silence. Ellen excused herself as soon as her dish was empty; she hurried into the bedroom and did not reemerge. Finally Hadley finished and disappeared after her. Fergesson and Alice were left alone.

"You old bear," Alice said. "Muttering away."

Fergesson lit a cigar and belched. "I'm going to bed early," he announced bluntly. "I have to get up at five thirty."

"Why?"

"I'm driving up to the city; I have to see some of the wholesalers. I want to straighten up some old consignment bills of Bud O'Neill's. . . . They claim I've got a lot of stock that doesn't belong to me." His lower jaw came out and stayed. "I paid for that stuff; it's mine."

In the bedroom Ellen and Hadley were talking together in low tones. The conversation abruptly ended; Ellen appeared at the door, glanced at Alice, and then rushed up to her. "I'll wash," she pronounced breathlessly. "Where's an apron?" She rushed into the kitchen and came back tying a dainty white apron around her waist. Rapidly, she began collecting the dessert dishes and coffee cups from the table. Hadley came slowly after her and stood.

Fergesson arose. "Let's get out of this," he said to Hadley. "All this activity."

"Good idea," Hadley agreed.

The older man waddled grouchily toward the long couch in the living room, and Hadley came along behind. They sat down facing each other across the room. The room was cool; Fergesson had installed an elaborate air-conditioning system down in the basement. A faint breeze licked around them. Outside the house the August night was hot and close; a few people moved listlessly along the sidewalks, men in their undershirts, women in sweat-stained shorts and drooping halters.

"What do you think of my air-conditioning system?" Fergesson asked.

"Seems to work."

"I dug out the whole damn basement myself. I really worked on this place. I put in new foundations—I must have carted out ten tons of dirt. I built up a patio in the backyard with it."

"I remember when you took time off from the store."

"I put in this air-conditioning thing just in time. God, the heat used to blister the wallpaper in here. We get the glare off the Bay. It hits us full blast from nine in the morning until noon. And I put in radiant heating." Proudly, Fergesson indicated the tile floor. "The hardwood in here was pitted, anyhow. I like this tile. I laid the pipes and then the tile over it. Works pretty good."

"You've done a lot," Hadley said thoughtfully. After a moment he asked: "What does it give you? A sense of permanence?"

Fergesson shrugged. "Any job worth doing is worth doing well. You ought to know that—instead of piddling around, you should finish what you start. You're always leaving half-finished jobs around the store. Everybody cleans up after you."

Ignoring him, Hadley made a gesture that took in the room, the floor, the whole house. "You feel more rooted? Fixing this up gives you a sense of being anchored? Having a center?"

Fergesson frowned. "I don't know what you're talking about."

"Let it go," Hadley said.

"It gives me a feeling of pride. When you can look around and know you did things yourself . . . you know you're not dependent on somebody else."

Hadley licked his lips and said: "When you're on your own you have a chance to work out ideas . . . you can get something accomplished."

"What sort of things?" Fergesson demanded doubtfully.

A glow crossed Hadley's face, an expression of feverish need. "You can set things into motion." He raised his hands in a compulsive gesture. "Now you take Modern; there's a lot of improvements that have to be made. Modern—that's a laugh. Modern has one of the oldest fronts on the street."

"It's good enough," Fergesson answered shortly.

"Twenty years ago, maybe. But things have changed! Things have to expand! You can't sit still—"

"I'm not sitting still," Fergesson interrupted. "I just took over O'Neill's place; you call that sitting still?"

Hadley's hand gestures increased spasmodically. "You don't see Modern the way some guy barreling through town in a big yellow Cad sees it. Here's this narrow old store, and all these modern places; naturally he's not going to stop and park and go into a dingy, dirty store; he wants a tilt-front window; he wants good modern lighting. . . ." Hadley was beginning to warm to a fever pitch. "You've seen those places that have brick up to around your knees, or maybe some kinds of stone? And then a level of flowers; a bunch of plants, sort of a long windowsill? And then the tilt-front glass . . . and recessed lighting that shoots up from among the flowers; not a glaring spot but a sort of radiance. And inside the shop everything rises, so somebody coming past sees the merchandise sweep up. No stairs—a sort of gradual rise."

"Spending my money! You know what that sort of stuff costs? Thousands of dollars—and you know I don't own the premises! Mason & McDuffy owns that; I'm just throwing it away. All I've got is a five-year lease; if they don't renew—"

"In two years you'll make it all back," Hadley interrupted impatiently. "Look, a front like I'm describing is the coming thing; you've got to have it.

You haven't improved the front since I've been there; only that coat of white paint."

In the kitchen, as the two women washed and dried the dishes, Ellen said rapidly: "I couldn't get him to bring the sketches he made; if Jim could see them he'd understand what Stuart means. It's so hard to explain. . . . People just look at you blankly when you're trying to create an ideal—and that's what Stuart has: an ideal he wants to put over. He's really creative, Alice. Most people are so—well, so sort of ordinary. . . . They don't have that spark; you know. They're just sort of clods . . . they don't see things; they don't see how things can be improved and made lovely. Stuart has really such a wonderful sense of beauty; he could work with materials, like stones and building woods, and with flowers—he could work with plastics and fabrics. He has a real eye for color." Blissfully, desperately, she finished in a rush: "Stuart's a real artist, Alice. He's got such wonderful sensitive hands. . . ."

"I know," Alice said sympathetically. "But if you get a chance, *tell him to go easy.* You know how suspicious Jim is when anybody does a lot of talking. He thinks they're trying to sell him something."

"But he has to understand!" Ellen cried, agonized. "I mean, Stuart could do so many things for that store—he really could, Alice. He could just transform it. It wouldn't be the same store."

"That's what I'm afraid of," Alice said tartly. "Tell him to pipe down."

She laid the last dish on the drainboard and went to get the pots and pans from the stove. Ellen, with the dish towel in her hands, stood helplessly waiting, glancing now and then into the living room, trying to hear and gauge what was being said.

"Sometimes it's better not to try too hard," Alice said to her mildly. "Just relax and take it easy. We'll sit around for a while . . . try to keep them from turning this into a debate on store policies." She added: "Especially a debate on how to deal with the Meyberg salesman."

They finished the pots and pans, cleaned up the sideboard and sink, removed their aprons, and strolled tautly into the living room.

"Penny for your thoughts," Ellen said nervously to her husband. She sank down on the arm of his chair and put her soft arms around his neck.

Alice seated herself on the couch and said: "Have you two finished yelling at each other? Or is there more?"

"We weren't yelling," Fergesson explained. "We were discussing business problems."

"Have you finished?" Alice repeated.

Fergesson stirred fitfully. "What do you mean by that? Of course we haven't finished. How could we be finished? What do you want me to do, lie down and go to sleep, and let the stores fall apart? What kind of a business-man would I be? How long do you think we'd be able to pay our bills, and you could afford those damn frilly dresses and shoes and hats and things. . . ." His voice trailed off dully. "I'm tired. I've got to get to bed early tonight."

Ellen blanched; her arms tightened convulsively around her husband's neck. Hadley gently disengaged them. "Sure," Hadley said aloud. "And I've got those Philcos coming through the door. I've got to clear room for them downstairs."

"Make sure the cartons are up off the ground," Fergesson warned gloomily. "It's okay now, but in a couple of months that whole damn back cellar will be dripping wet. Make sure there's nothing touching the cement."

"We could make the city reroute that slough," Hadley said. "It's seepage into the soil; that's why it starts so early. It's not rainwater; it's flow off the hills."

"Nonsense," Fergesson contradicted. "Those pipes are sealed; my God, they go under fifty stores and a thousand houses—the whole town! If there was any leakage—"

"Now look here," Alice broke in, exasperated. "We're not going to sit here yelling back and forth about city sewer mains."

For a time nobody said anything. Finally Fergesson spoke up. "Can I ask Hadley if he called West Coast Supply about that damaged cabinet?"

"I called them," Hadley said. "They told me their inspector has to come out and examine it."

Fergesson nodded. "That's fine."

"I think they'll come through," Hadley said. "We saved the carton, of course. They can see it was dropped."

"Gee," Ellen said plaintively, "this is a lot like Christmas. Remember when we all got together that Christmas?"

A flood of recollections swept over Alice. On Christmas Day it had been cold and wet; rain lashed against the windows; icy wind whipped through the tall cedars along the path. The big house had been full of people: Jack V. White, his wife, Peggy, and their two children; Stuart and Ellen; Joe Tampini and his girlfriend; Olsen and his wife; a handful of neighbors; rela-tives; and old friends. They had had a big turkey dinner at two tables, and then they had all sat around the living room listening to the rain and sipping little mugs of foamy eggnog. The FM had played Christmas music softly, a Bach Christmas cantata. Everybody and everything had been quiet and peaceful.

"I remember that," Fergesson said. He smiled at Alice. "Who were all those people? Friends of yours, I suppose."

"This is a lot like Christmas," Ellen repeated. "Only it's hot instead of wet, and there aren't so many people here."

"It's nicer this way," Hadley said. He got to his feet and wandered over to the heavy radio-phonograph in the corner. After a moment he turned it on and stood dialing the knobs. There was only popular jazz, so he shut it off again.

"The radio's just terrible," Ellen spoke up. "I have to hear it all day— nothing but soap operas and commercials. I hate those singing commercials; they drive me crazy."

"They're supposed to," Fergesson said.

"That's awful, if they're supposed to," Ellen answered. "What kind of a person thinks up things like that? There ought to be good music. . . . Radio is so tasteless and cheap. Of course, I suppose the average man likes that sort of thing. . . . They have to aim their programs at the greatest possible number."

"Which means morons," Hadley added.

Fergesson chewed his lip and asked: "Have you ever met anybody who liked singing commercials? If you took a poll of this country you wouldn't find a damn person who likes singing commercials."

"Then why do they have them?" Ellen asked.

"Because they sell products," Fergesson answered. "They irritate—they're repetitious. People hate them, but they remember the sponsor's name. They work; that's why they keep turning them out."

"Look," Hadley said. "What about this? You ought to have a TV program or a radio program; you can't reach enough people through newspapers. I mean," he hurried on, "you don't have to sponsor a program; all you have to do is pay for spot announcements. In the evening, maybe; around six or seven o'clock. Over one of the big S.F. stations, like KNBC. You could bring down people from the Bay Area, and people from the whole penin-sula." Enthusiastically, he finished: "KNBC is clear channel—people get it all the way down in Bakersfield."

Alice eyed him and wished he would stop having ideas for once in his life. It was easy to read the distrust on Jim's face; he was suspicious of innova-tions, especially those which cost him money.

Getting quickly to her feet she started for the kitchen. "I'll be right back," she said over her shoulder. From the refrigerator she got a bottle of chilled French apricot brandy and rapidly found small wineglasses. She poured four glasses full, set them on a tray, and briskly returned to the living room.

Fergesson greeted the brandy with appreciation. "Fine," he murmured gratefully, sitting up and reaching for a glass. Pleased and joking, he inquired: "How many for me? Two? Three?"

"Just one," Alice answered sternly, swooping the tray away from him and over to Stuart Hadley.

"Thanks," Hadley said; he accepted the brandy but did not drink it. Setting it down on the arm of the chair he sat gazing intently forward, his blue eyes cloudy with thought. He opened his mouth to speak, but Alice was instantly ahead of him.

"Maybe you shouldn't have any," she said to Ellen. "Or is it all right now?"

"It's all right," Ellen said shyly, reaching for a glass. "Thanks a lot, Alice. It looks wonderful. . . ." She sipped. "It tastes glorious."

Inwardly, Alice sighed. She took the last brandy glass and reseated herself.

"I understand Joe Tampini's going to get married," Fergesson said. "That same girl?"

"The same one," Hadley said. "The cute redhead."

"I guess he's going to want a raise," Fergesson complained drearily. "Like you, when you got married."

"She's a lovely girl," Ellen said. "I always envy women with red hair like that."

"Redheads are either awfully pretty or ugly as hell," Fergesson agreed. Turning to Hadley he said: "Remember that kid who used to come into the store when we had that pile of jukebox records? Green eyes, red hair . . . She liked those trumpet records."

"I remember her," Hadley agreed. "Her name was—Joan something. I managed to get her name on an order card for a Bix Beiderbecke record once."

"She wasn't over eighteen."

"Eighteen, hell. She was a high school kid."

Fergesson pondered. "I've been thinking we need a girl in at Modern . . . to make it more attractive to the family trade. It was okay during the war— all we did was repair radios. We had those big-tit calendars up on the walls and nobody kicked; it was mostly men we did business with. But now we're getting more couples. If we had some girl in, maybe as a bookkeeper, or to wait on people. . . . She could check tubes, make out service tags, answer the phone."

"A receptionist," Hadley said.

"Would there be enough work to keep her busy? I'm not paying any girl to stand around wiggling her ass at customers; she's got to sweep and keep the place clean. I think a woman's better at that; polishing and dusting is women's stuff."

"Oh, sure," Hadley agreed readily. "There'd be plenty of work she could do. Making out the bills, like you say. The filing, all the paperwork—"

"But we don't want her stuck up in the office," Fergesson pointed out. "We want her down front, where people can see her."

"That's a point," Hadley said, "and it's interesting, because I was thinking along those lines myself. The other day I had a thought on that; I'll give it to you for what it's worth. Maybe you won't see anything in it, but I think we ought to put in an expanded record department. I'll tell you why—it'll bring a lot of people in, and we can turn them into TV and radio-phono sales. The two tie in together; we could knock out the back wall and use the storeroom for listening booths—maybe even partition it into a lot of booths."

Fergesson shook his head. "That's out," he said emphatically. "Modern will never do a real record business." He peered up intently at the ceiling. "O'Neill is better. And there's more display space. Records take too many counters and racks." Sourly, he concluded: "Records break all the time."

"Not the new LPs," Hadley reminded him.

"Those scratch." Fergesson studied his two hands, which were pressed tightly together. "Of course, I wouldn't put you in O'Neill's place . . . that's for me. I'm keeping you at Modern."

"I know that," Hadley said.

"If I put in a full-sized record department I'll get down some queer from Berkeley to run it . . . like you see in the Berkeley record shops. They know all those classics, those Lily Pons and Toscanini. I'm not messing with that."

"Right," Hadley agreed. "That's a specialty."

"So forget about the records. But we'll think about getting some girl in. You think a high school girl could handle it?"

"Better get one from the business college," Hadley said. "That place upstairs across the street from Modern. They're older, more experienced. You know the ones I mean? Heels and sweaters—the ones you see in Woolworth at lunchtime."

"I thought they were secretaries."

"No, they're going to that business school. They're looking like hell for jobs."

"Fine," Fergesson agreed. "I'll go over there one of these days and see what we can scare up."

"I don't know if I like this idea," Alice said tartly. "You two are too darn interested."

"I don't know either," Ellen piped up, caught between joking and genuine concern. "I think Modern looks all right."

Ignoring the two women, Fergesson continued: "On second thought, maybe I'll let you handle that. Do what you think best. We'd have to pay her two hundred a month—in a year that's two thousand four hundred dollars . . . and that's for a five-day week."

"True," Hadley admitted. "There's the state law."

"Would you rather have a couple of thousand to modernize the front? Maybe you could brighten it up more that way . . . new lighting fixtures, that glass you were talking about." He waved his hand. "All that fancy stuff."

The room was abruptly silent. Everybody sat frozen, watching Hadley.

"I'd have to check into construction costs," Hadley said finally. Gripping the arms of the chair he said thickly: "Labor is the big item; all that stuff's union."

"Well, it's something to think about. There's no rush on it." Fergesson lifted his head and peered crookedly across the room at the blond young man. "But if you're going to run that place you've got to learn to make decisions."

"Sure," Hadley said huskily.

Fergesson sat chewing on his cigar. The room was tense and strained; nobody dared move or breathe. Outside, some people walked along the dark sidewalk laughing and talking. The sounds died into silence and there remained only the whirr of the air-conditioning system Fergesson had installed with his own two hands.

"Hadley," Fergesson said, "I think you've calmed down now that you have a son. Maybe I'm wrong, but it seems to me you're beginning to grow up."

Hadley's face showed that he was trying to find something to say; but no words came.

"You've got a wife and child now," Fergesson continued. "You've got responsibilities you didn't have before. You've got a great future ahead of you, if you really bear down and stick with it."

"Sure," Hadley agreed, in an almost inaudible voice.

"Of course," Fergesson continued inexorably, "you've got more expenses now. It costs a lot to raise a kid these days. Medicine, clothes, food—everything special."

Alice smiled a little. "The authority," she said softly, not loudly enough for her husband to hear. There was no point in hurting his feelings.

"I realize that," Hadley said. He tapped his wallet. "It's already begun to cut in."

"You're making two fifty a month," Fergesson said, "plus five percent. Running Modern means you won't be on the floor as much; you'll be upstairs a lot, running out to people's homes. . . . It'll probably cut down your actual sales."

"I suppose so," Hadley managed.

Fergesson studied his hands and mulled. "I can't go above three hundred. On the commissions, I'll take away the five on what you sell and give you a flat one percent on the gross take of the store. That means on all commissionable items . . . not tubes and phonograph needles and repairs."

"I get it," Hadley said swiftly.

"That means you won't have to compete with White and Tampini; you can let them close the stuff, while you keep the ceiling from falling. It's going to be a big job. . . . In the long run you'll make more, but you'll really have to work. And if you get in a girl, or maybe a high school kid . . . You'll have to get in somebody to sweep and clean; you can't fool around with that."

"Sure," Hadley agreed. "I know."

"How does it sound?" Fergesson demanded belligerently. "I know three hundred doesn't sound like much, but around Christmas a one percent on the gross ought to really roll it in for you."

"It sounds fine," Hadley said.

"Thank God," Alice breathed, getting to her feet with a sigh of relief. "I'm certainly glad that's over."

"What are you talking about?" Fergesson roared, outraged. "You goddamn women, sitting around like a bunch of witches—you had this all arranged!"

Stuart Hadley and his wife walked slowly home along the dark, warm streets. Overhead, scattered clouds of stars winked. A faint night wind stirred the Oriental plums along High Street. The rows of houses were dark and still; front doors stood wide open to admit fresh air. In her arms Ellen clutched the bundle that was Pete wrapped in his robes and feeding apparatus.

"Well?" Ellen said. "What do you have to say?"

"I guess I got the job."

"How—do you feel about it?" Anxiously, she pushed against him and squeezed his arm. "Tell me how you feel, Stuart; are you glad? It *is* what you want, isn't it?"

Searching his mind, Stuart Hadley groped for an answer. He pictured himself as manager of Modern TV Sales and Service; it was no fantasy: it was genuine. Tomorrow morning he would open up the store as its manager. Jack White, Joe Tampini, Olsen, and if they got a girl, her, too—he was in charge of them all. Responsibility, position, power over others . . . The store was an object which he could mold and shape as he saw fit, a plastic object to be formed and re-formed.

He thought of the world outside the store. An infinite chaos of shifting shapes . . . Outside, there was nothing to stand on, only chill shadows and the dim light of stars too remote to be touched. The store was a neat little cosmos, an orderly square of firmness around which a meaningless nether-universe drifted and swirled.

Suddenly he was terrified; he couldn't stand it outside the store. Even now, walking the dark quiet streets with his son and wife—it was too dangerous, too much of a risk. The world was out of control. Nothing could be depended on . . . the ground under him tilted away wherever he walked, spilling him into the shadows.

In his mind came the vivid image of opening the store on a bright summer morning. The crisp, moist air, smelling of night dew, sparkling off the cars and sidewalks. The hurrying secretaries; the businessmen unrolling their awnings; the Negro sweeping trash into the gutter; the sound of people and motion, a city coming to life and starting its busy routine. Coffee from the Health Food Store . . . the telephone ringing . . . Olsen climbing crossly into the truck with the day's repairs.

"Sure," Hadley said desperately. He increased his pace; the darkness terrified him. It reminded him of that night with Marsha, the deserted road, the parked car, the crickets. The utter bleak loneliness and desolation. "Let's get home and hit the sack—I have to get up early tomorrow."

"It's cold," Ellen said. She shivered against him and hurried to keep up. "Here, you take Pete awhile."

Hadley grabbed his son from her; the baby stirred fitfully but did not waken. Overhead the cold stars seemed more remote each moment; it was a huge universe, too large for one man to cope with. He wondered how he could ever have wanted to venture out into it; arid and hostile, it stretched out to infinity, utterly indifferent to human affairs. Even now he yearned for the familiar store; it was human-constructed, under control. And it was the only world open to him. He was eager and grateful to enter fully into it, to pull it around him.

"I'm glad," Ellen was saying breathlessly. "Everything worked out all right. . . . It's so wonderful."

Hadley wasn't listening. His fear grew; and it was fear of himself, fear of what he might do. He might destroy himself; he might suddenly, blindly, burst out and destroy the safety of his microcosmos. In his archaic fury he might smash, demolish, pull down the only world in which he could exist.

In his mind were forces that could destroy it; in him was the possibility, the energy to annihilate himself and his tiny universe. As before; as in all his life. It was not new; it had always been there. In one moment he could collapse every fragment of himself. That was the terror; that was what made the universe awful and foreboding.

Again, he might struggle out into the infinite hostile regions, striving to find something, catch hold of something vague and dim, something he could never really find. Something beyond the reach of his groping hands.

"You're walking too fast," Ellen protested breathlessly, hurrying behind him, trying to keep up. She listened; she fervently examined his voice, trying to hear how he felt. "I'm so glad," she told him. Desperately, she ran to keep up. "I want you to be happy; I want you to have what you need. It's wonderful, isn't it? All this . . . It finally came through."

Hadley didn't answer.

"You know," his wife gasped, her voice thin and pleading, "I think I'm happier now than I've ever been in my life. What do you think about that? Isn't it wonderful?"

There was no response. Hadley strode on, gripping his sleeping son. Tugging his wife after him, along the dark, deserted streets.

Every Thursday, by a fantastic union ruling in direct opposition to the laws of God and commerce, all nurseries were required to close. As the flower shop in which he worked was subsumed by the Cedar Groves Nursery, Horace Wakefield had a day off. He therefore got up at eight o'clock instead of seven, on this particular morning, a hot day late in August. And he had stewed prunes and cream instead of cornflakes for his breakfast.

His little room was clean and neat. All his anti-vivisectionist magazines were stacked carefully in the corners and along the walls. He opened the windows wide and allowed fresh air to circulate. He enjoyed August; he liked the days long and dry and hot. Along the street sunlight danced and glittered from the pavement. The mailman moved slowly along, weighed down by his pack, his face glistening with perspiration. Down at the corner a laundry truck was parked and the driver was lugging a heavy white bundle up a flight of concrete stairs into an apartment house.

Wakefield filled a bucket with water from the bathtub tap and carried it out to the sundeck. In pots and in flats, huge roses and chrysanthemums grew everywhere. He watered them carefully, then stood for a moment enjoying the steamy smell that drifted up from the black soil and manure. The world spread out below him on all sides made him feel immense: practically a giant. Miles high, he gazed up at the sun and sheer blue sky and sucked in vast lungfuls of air.

He had the whole day to himself. In his mind he ran over the things that needed to be done. First, there were three letters to newspapers that needed to be written and sent off. The laundry truck reminded him that his shirts were waiting down at the Pioneer Laundry. He had to take his watch over to the jeweler for cleaning. He had to change the sheets on his bed; the landlady was willing, but Wakefield preferred to do it himself.

And then there was the real work.

Wakefield returned to his room. He put on his hat and coat and marched down the long dim stairs, with its elaborate oak banister and railing, to the little foyer where the ancient mirror and hat rack greeted him every morning of his life. He patted his thinning black hair in place, adjusted his glasses, blew his nose, and then pushed the massive front door open and stepped out in the dazzling sun.

Because it was such a nice day, Wakefield walked all the way across town to the Society of the Watchmen of Jesus hall. He hated the stuffy buses; especially he hated the clouds of poisonous vapors that poured out of them, and the grinding and bucking of their motors. As he walked he continued to breathe in deep drafts of air and rejoice that he was alive on such a beautiful day in such a beautiful world.

The nearer he got to the hall the more he could feel the *stirring*. The air vibrated with activity. The hall radiated a vast sense of urgency; things were happening, events were in the making. Wakefield found himself almost running. When he arrived he was out of breath and panting excitedly. The desire not to miss out made him race up the two flights of steep stairs to the rooms above the main hall, which the Society was using for its business offices. The main hall had been turned into an organizational and recruiting center; dues were collected and processed; activities were assigned.

Again he realized that a religious movement was much more than a band of people united by belief; it was a functioning machine. Simply to believe was not enough, in this world. . . . Those who believed made arrangements to have others believe. The apparatus of the Society lay spread out in this hall and in similar halls scattered throughout the world. Earnest middle-aged women baked pies and collected old clothing and held raffles . . . but that was not all; indeed that was not at all all. Leaflets were printed, phonograph records were pressed, radio scripts were constructed, money was collected. Beneath the level of well-meaning ladies was the hard core of astute directors for which religion was a full-time job, a way of life. A world, not merely an activity.

Awed by the sight of these tireless functionaries, Horace Wakefield stood planted at the entrance. He admired them, and he was afraid of them. The sight carried him back to the days of his childhood, to the revival meetings his father had driven the family to, in their little upright Ford, down the long dirt roads between endless peach and apricot orchards. In the meetings, under the vast canopy of dirty brown canvas, men and women packed in tight listened attentively, dispassionately, to a screaming man who leaped and waved his arms and foamed at the mouth. It was not the revivalist who had terrified Wakefield; it was the sudden inexplicable sight of an ordinary drab-haired woman, or a thin country youth, or perhaps a pimple-faced girl— ordinary people, the kind that shopped in the country towns on Saturday, the kind that sat around farmhouses in the evening pulling long strips of greasy taffy—anybody, in fact, suddenly leaping up and rushing wild-eyed to the platform to testify.

Testimonials terrified him like nothing on earth because it seemed a kind of madness, like the bite of the tarantula which makes people dance themselves to death (or so he had heard). As a child he had sat huddled against his father, biting his lips and clenching his fists, petrified for fear the craziness might strike him: that he might leap up, hobble, leap, and roll his way down the aisle to the platform and, in sight of his friends and neighbors, begin to scream shrilly, to tear off his clothes and whatnot, to yell and slobber and finally dunk himself in the tub of water through which the old souls were made new.

An acute awareness turned his thoughts back to the present. Mary Krafft was standing by a huge wall chart, gesturing and talking to a group of heavy-set women. With dismay, Wakefield realized that she had seen him; she nodded and jerkily waved him over. With slow steps he reluctantly made his way into the room. . . . Of all people, Mary Krafft irritated him the most. By the time he reached the group of women his good spirits were gone; he was listless and out of sorts.

"Morning," he muttered.

Breathing hoarsely, Mrs. Krafft caught hold of his arm and spun him around to face the wall chart. "Well," she cried, "what do you think?"

Wakefield could make nothing of the wall chart; it showed a map of the United States with little colored pins stuck here and there. Disengaging his arm he answered with dignity: "It looks very nice, of course. Very neat and orderly."

"Everywhere!" Mrs. Krafft spluttered in his ear. "Do you see? Contributions from every state in the Union. We're getting our message all over the country—we're catching fire!"

Wakefield winced and tried to edge away. "Very nice," he mumbled. "Very impressive." The ring of ladies gave way, and he made his escape back into the center of the booming hall. There he stood, wondering what to do, wanting to pitch in and help but not wanting to involve himself with the grim-jawed women feverishly working on every side.

"Here," an authoritative voice said; a large colored matron was approaching him. "There's too much to do for standing around; come over here and I'll put you to work."

"Oh, yes," Wakefield said guiltily, starting into life. He hurried toward the colored woman. "I mean, I just came, of course. What do you want done?"

The colored woman strode among tables to a corner of the hall. Wakefield trotted after her, hoping it was something important, hoping that he had been singled out for some unique assignment. The woman halted in front of a long table on which were stacked folded papers and boxes of stamped envelopes. "You can stuff these. Or you can operate the mimeograph. Take your choice."

Abashed and disappointed, Wakefield stammered: "Well, I guess I'd rather stuff the envelopes." He lingered plaintively. "Isn't there anything else?"

"What do you want to do?" the woman demanded haughtily. "Let Mister Beckheim stuff the envelopes while you preach?" She strode off, leaving Wakefield standing mutely by the table.

He sat miserably down and began pushing the mimeographed inserts into the envelopes. One of them fell open; he gazed at it dully. Beckheim had left San Francisco and was retracing his long journey down the coast to Los Angeles. In huge amateurish letters the sheet proclaimed another lecture in Cedar Groves as Beckheim passed through. Wakefield refolded the paper and pushed it sullenly into an envelope.

Standing in the entrance of Modern TV Sales and Service, Stuart Hadley surveyed the August street. It was a blazing afternoon; the sun beat down on the passersby creeping miserably along the baking sidewalks. Two young women passed in shorts and halters; Hadley watched their sweat-glistening legs until they disappeared around a corner.

Behind him, the store was cool and dark.

From the depths the sound of Olsen's repair bench filtered up tinnily. In the back display room, Jack White was showing a big RCA combination to a family of four. Impatiently Hadley gazed off down the haze-dulled street: Joe Tampini was supposed to be back from his lunch any moment. Whereupon it was time for Hadley to go out for his early-afternoon coffee.

Old man Berg from Berg's Jewelry Store came ambling along, wizened and shrewd, tiny eyes glittering. He clapped his clawlike hand over Hadley's shoulder and wheezed in his ear: "Say, boy, I hear you're top dog now."

"That's right," Hadley answered, grinning absently.

The old man's strong fingers dug into Hadley's flesh. Rancid, oniony breath billowed in his face as the old man rasped: "Say now, you're doing all right for a boy, aren't you? You're right up there, Stuart, right up there on top. How's the TV business these days? How's the summer treating you? Business a little off?"

"Can't complain," Hadley said good-naturedly.

The old man laughed and spattered saliva on Hadley's coat. "You're a good boy, Stuart. I've seen you in there working. You have what it takes; I knew you'd get up there." He poked his bony finger against Hadley's chest; he squeezed his arm; he leaned over and gasped noisily in his ear: "Remember this and you won't go wrong: Don't give credit to coons. Never trust them; make them pay cash—you hear?"

"Sure," Hadley agreed.

The old man slapped him on the shoulder. "All right, boy. Take care of yourself. You've got what it takes; I always said so." He scurried off down the sidewalk; in front of the big men's clothing store he cornered two elderly women and began an intimate, wheezing conversation with them.

Inside the store the telephone began to ring. Hadley turned and regretfully stepped back through the doorway, into the darkness. The broom stood upright in the corner against the tube cabinet; he hadn't finished sweeping. Strewn across the counter were bits of brightly colored cardboard; he was in the process of assembling an elaborate window display from Zenith. Already he had emptied the dusty, flyspecked radios and TV sets from the windows; a squat Zenith TV combination had been dragged up from downstairs to go in their place. It stood blocking one entrance behind the counter, a solid square of imitation hardwood and electronic apparatus.

"Modern TV," he said into the telephone. Leaning back against the battery display, Hadley made himself comfortable, one hand on the thick yellow service-call book. From where he stood the bulging trash box under the counter was visible; he made a mental note to empty it. Dead batteries, wrapping paper crumpled in brown wads, bits of string, broken radio tubes, lay strewn on the floor around it. Polish rags, old tags, the moldy remains of someone's lunch, endless empty coffee cups . . .

"Hello," the telephone said, a gruff man's voice. "I brought my radio in last week; I wonder if it's ready."

"Can you give me the number on your receipt?" Hadley said. "And what kind of radio was it?"

He wandered downstairs to the service department. The basement was chill and cold; Olsen sat huddled on his tall stool, legs wrapped around the rungs, face screwed up in an intent scowl as he poked into the works of a little Philco upturned on his bench.

"Goddamn it!" Olsen screamed, throwing the radio against the oscilloscope and leaping from the stool. "I'm through with the whole fucked-up mess! I'm getting out of here! The fuck with it!" He grabbed his coat from a hook over the bench and headed for the stairs: it was his way of going out to lunch. "What do you want, Hadley? What's up your ass?"

"I'm looking for a radio," Hadley said, knee deep in a pool of repaired sets lumped across the cement floor. He gave Olsen the number and description. "Is it done?"

Olsen's rage knew no bounds. "Christ, the old fart just brought it in!" Purple with wrath, Olsen swept up the radio in question and savagely examined the tag. "Tell him to go stick it up his ass! Tell him next year. Shit, I'll talk to him myself." Olsen raced furiously for the stairs. "Where is he? Upstairs?"

"On the phone," Hadley said, grinning. "You go on and eat; I'll take care of him. You think it'll be ready tomorrow?"

Dancing with fury, Olsen screeched: "Fix it your goddamn self! You're such a goddamn big shot around here—you get all the credit, you might as well do some work." As he disappeared up the stairs three at a time he shouted back: "Tell him late tomorrow. The hell with it—I'm never coming back. I'm going in the Army!"

Hadley climbed the stairs and crossed the store to the phone. He informed the man that his radio was on the bench being worked on; the serviceman wanted to be sure it was all right and would like to keep it playing until tomorrow.

"All right," the man said. "I'll come by tomorrow."

As Hadley hung up the phone, Joe Tampini entered the store. "Sorry I took so long," Tampini said. Dressed in a neat single-breasted suit, brown shoes, and silk tie, his curly black hair carefully oiled and combed, Tampini was an impressive sight. "Anything happen? Anybody buy anything?"

"Those people you were showing the Admiral table model to came back," Hadley said. He pushed the tag from the register onto the counter. "I closed it for you—it's going out sometime this afternoon."

Tampini flushed happily. "No kidding?" Visibly, he added up his commission. "Gosh, that's twelve bucks!"

"You better check the set over," Hadley said. "I think the vertical lock is off; I had it on for a couple minutes and the picture was foreshortened."

"Right," Tampini agreed, searching behind the counter for the screwdriver. "Where's the mirror? Probably in the truck. Will you be around, or were you going out? You're pretty good at setting up this stuff."

Hadley remained long enough to help Tampini set up the Admiral. He pushed the uncompleted Zenith display to one side of the counter, carried the broom to the back closet, and then wandered out onto the hot, bright sidewalk.

The familiar routine of the day had settled gradually into place. It was as it had always been; after the first hour, it seemed as if he had always been manager. There was really no difference. It was the same store; the same counter and displays, the same television sets, the cold basement, the filthy bathroom, the littered upstairs office, the ringing phone . . . everything was the same. The permanent reality of a small retail store.

Lighting a cigarette, he stood by the gutter, his hands cupped around the match. Sleepily, he watched the people stroll past. Brightly dressed women. Hurrying businessmen in white shirts, crisp sleeves rolled up. Children on bicycles. Cars. He waved the match out, dropped it in the gutter, and crossed the sidewalk to the Health Food Store.

The heavy odor of dried prunes and sacks of graham flour lay over the low stools and glass display cases, the scrubbed linoleum, the endless shelves of cans and jars and packages. He seated himself at the counter, by the marzipan display; only two other people were eating, a plump woman consuming a pear-and-cottage-cheese salad, and a small man with steel-rimmed glasses, sipping a tall glass of milk.

"Stuart!" Horace Wakefield cried, pleased. He waved down the counter at Hadley, past the woman and her salad. Getting to his feet, he carried his glass of milk over and sat down on the empty stool beside Hadley. "How have you been?"

"Fine," Hadley said noncommittally.

From the back, Betty pushed her way through the curtains and came wearily over. "Afternoon, Stuart," she gasped. Her thick, pulpy face was wet with perspiration. She batted at a fly. "Well, it'll be winter soon enough." Resting her doughy hands on the counter, she asked: "What can I do for you? Some nice iced tea? Some brown Betty and hard sauce?"

"Just coffee," Hadley said, rolling a dime from his trouser pocket and up onto the counter.

Carefully, Betty got down a white cup and saucer from the shelf behind the counter. As she poured the steaming coffee into it she said: "You know,

Stuart, you have practically all of our cups over there. I wish you'd bring them back."

"I sure will," Hadley answered. "You bet your life."

Putting the Silex back on the warmer, Betty said to Wakefield: "Things are going to be different. Stuart's manager of Modern now. Did you know?"

It was amusing to see Wakefield's excitement. His small face alive with astonishment, he half rose from his stool, eyes wide, mouth open. "Stuart!" he shouted. "Is that so? you're *manager*?"

Hadley laughed. "Sure, why not?"

"But—" Wakefield spluttered in confusion. "Why, that's marvelous! Where's Mister Fergesson? Did he retire?"

"Jim bought another store," Betty explained as she took Hadley's dime and rang it up. "I don't know the name of it, but it's on the highway somewhere."

"O'Neill's place," Hadley said.

Wakefield was still dazed. "I can't get over it. My goodness, that's just wonderful."

"And he has a sweet little baby boy named Pete," Betty continued, beaming wearily and showing her false teeth. "Isn't that nice?"

Wakefield could only open and shut his mouth.

"His wife looks so cute now, with her figure back," Betty said. "She's a lovely girl, Stuart. Look what you've got to be thankful for; yes, really have . . . You've got such a pretty little wife, and a fine healthy baby, and now you're manager of a store." She shook her head resignedly. "How's Jim doing over at the new place?"

"All right," Hadley answered. "The place needs a lot of work; he's putting in thirteen hours a day. But he likes it."

After Betty had gone, Wakefield continued: "I can't get over it. Mister Fergesson must have a lot of faith in you, Stuart. That store's been his whole life as long as I can remember. Twenty years, at least . . . a long time before you came. Why, you've just been working there a few years. I never thought Mister Fergesson would turn that store over to anybody else as long as he was alive."

"Well, he's got the new place," Hadley said absently. He was listening intently for the phone; it was dimly audible from where he sat. He wondered if he should forget his coffee break and go back. . . . It was hard to know how his privileges stood, now that nobody was looking over his shoulder.

"Say," Wakefield said awkwardly, "maybe you'll let me pay for your coffee, as a sort of celebration."

Hadley laughed. "It's already paid for."

"Then I'll buy you a soyburger sandwich," Wakefield offered eagerly. "You know, it certainly makes me feel good to see a young man get someplace so early in life. You take care of yourself, Stuart; like Betty says, you've got a lot to be thankful for. I certainly envy you . . . especially your family. I have my work, of course. . . ." His voice wandered off, baffled and momentarily unhappy. "That's something, at least. Not at the flower shop; I mean the real work down at the hall."

Hadley tensed as he sipped his coffee. "How are things coming?" he asked tersely. Pulling his cup toward him he half rose to his feet; he didn't want to hear about the hall.

"Things are fine," Wakefield said. "You know, don't you, that Mister Beckheim will be coming back down this way in a few days?"

"No," Hadley said rigidly. He braced himself. "I didn't."

"We're getting prepared for another lecture. You were at the last one, weren't you?"

"Yes, I was," Hadley said. A cold, fearful numbness crept over him and he settled down again on the stool. "I was there, as you know perfectly well."

Wakefield blinked at the sharpness in his voice. "What do you mean, Stuart? You weren't disappointed, were you? My, I thought he was terribly impressive that time."

"I've got to get back to the store," Hadley said bluntly; he was fighting up through the numbness. "The damn phone's ringing." This time he got all the way to his feet. "I'll see you later. Take care of yourself."

But Wakefield refused to let him go. "Stuart, I guess with all your new responsibilities you won't want to come. I was hoping maybe you'd like to come. As a matter of fact, it's young people like you that ought to come. We old people won't be around much longer, you know."

"None of us will be," Hadley said harshly. "Isn't the world going to come to an end?"

"Of course," Wakefield said, with dignity. "But not right away—not for a while. You know, Stuart, I think you've been a lot healthier since you went to hear Mister Beckheim. I was thinking that maybe there's a relationship between your going and hearing him, and all the health you've been enjoying. It seems to me that you used to have a weak stomach. Didn't you used to have a weak stomach?"

"You bet," Hadley agreed, "and I still do."

Wakefield was disappointed. "I thought it was gone. You know, Stuart, good health isn't something we create; it comes directly from God. He gives it to us and He can take it away. I know the Christian Science people are always talking about having pure thoughts, but it seems to me—" He broke off. "I wish you'd come, Stuart," he said plaintively. "There're all those old women there, and I hate old women. I wish there were more men mixed up in this thing."

"I came," Hadley said curtly. "I joined. I got a blue card."

Wakefield was doubtful. "Oh, no," he disagreed. "You can't join and get a blue card. Only Mister Beckheim gives out blue cards." He brought out his wallet and showed Hadley his own membership card; it was perfectly white. "This is what you get when you join. Maybe later on, when you've been in the Society for years and years, then perhaps Mister Beckheim takes special notice of you and gives you a blue card. That's something he does personally, for outstanding service." He added wistfully: "I think he's given out only a few dozen of them."

Hadley sat down slowly on the stool. "I didn't know that," he said. A terrible burning panic lodged in his windpipe and stayed there. "I thought it was just the regular card."

"Do you have it?" Wakefield leaned toward him curiously. "Can I see it? Let me look at it."

"I tore it up."

Wakefield giggled. "You're pulling my leg."

"Listen," Hadley said sharply, "is that on the level, about the blue cards?"

"Of course. But Beckheim himself would have had to give it to you; if somebody else gave it to you then it's not really the genuine—"

"He gave it to me. He wrote it out and handed it to me. For a dollar fifty."

For a moment Wakefield didn't understand. His lack of comprehension infuriated Hadley; he was too busy with his own whirling thoughts to spell it out letter by letter for the little man. "I met Beckheim up in San Francisco," he stated briefly. "What's so great about that? Is he a deity or something? I just walked in and met him; that's all. We talked and he wrote out a card. Later on I tore it up."

Wakefield licked his lips and said hoarsely: "I can't imagine why you tore it up, Stuart." He was visibly moved. "Why didn't you tell me? I've never met him face-to-face; I've never talked to him. This is such a terrible thing . . ." His voice broke. "For heaven's sake," he quavered furiously, "will you have the decency to tell me why you tore it up?"

Hadley had never seen little Horace Wakefield angry. Behind his glasses the man's eyes swam; abruptly he jerked out his pocket handkerchief and blew his nose violently. He stuffed the handkerchief away and glared indignantly at Hadley, waiting for him to explain.

Awkwardly, Hadley said: "I'm sorry, Horace; I don't want to get mixed up in this thing. Don't you understand?" Patiently, he traced a line of moisture on the surface of the counter. "I want to live a normal life—not a nutty life. Sorry if this offends you, but you asked me."

"Go on," Wakefield whispered.

Not wanting to hurt the little man's feelings, Hadley stumbled over his words. "I want an ordinary existence, a wife and a family, a place to live. This job—it's perfect." But as he said it the words sounded hollow; he wondered if he really meant them after all. No, he didn't mean them: the job wasn't perfect. "Look," he said fiercely, "I wanted to be a lot of things: I was going a long way. This isn't much; running a television shop is damn small potatoes compared to what I was going to do. Compared to what I still want to do—I've still got a lot of plans and ideas. I'm going to make this store into something; Fergesson has held it back all these years and I'm going to cut it loose. This damn store is really going to travel; I've got big ideas and I know they'll work. Anyhow, I'm going to give them a try."

"But that doesn't mean—," Wakefield began.

"That means I'm staying clear of your damn Society!" Hadley snapped. "There're a lot of things in this world I want to do; there're a lot of wonderful people and places—before I'm ready to write them all off I want to look around. I want to stay here longer; I'm not ready to give up, not quite yet. I'm not ready for the end of the world." Meaning it with all his soul, he finished: "I want to live a sane, meaningful life; I want my life to add up to something. Maybe I can find that here; maybe not. Meanwhile, I'm staying away from you nuts."

Wakefield winced. Fingers trembling, he straightened his tie, smoothed down his coat; he pulled himself upright and faced Hadley. "You can't," he said hoarsely. "You're living in a crazy world, Stuart. It isn't possible to cut out a neat little pattern; this is a world of war and lunatics, and you're in it whether you like it or not." Leaning toward Hadley, he grated: "In a crazy world, it's the nuts who know what's going on. You know we're right; you know this store of yours, this job, everything is a joke! Selling television sets when they're getting ready to drop A-bombs on us!"

"It's my job," Hadley said defiantly. "I want it; I'm staying at it."

"You'll be dead," Wakefield whispered.

Hadley got to his feet; he was shaking violently. "I told you I'm through with nut cults. End of the world—" Savagely he grabbed up his coffee cup and started toward the door. "A bunch of religious fanatics. You're crazy—you're crackpots!"

The screen door slammed after him. He could see the small figure sitting frozen at the counter; Horace Wakefield was reaching automatically for his glass of milk, trying to resume his routine. The heavyset woman, who had been listening to everything, gazed with frank curiosity after Hadley.

Hadley entered Modern, the coffee cup teetering and sloshing coffee onto his hand and wrist. It was lukewarm. Furiously, he shoved the cup under the counter with the others and turned to face the small knot of customers standing by the cash register, waiting to be waited on.

Alice Fergesson was sitting quietly in the upstairs office, a cigarette between her fingers, her purse resting on the littered desk. At first he didn't notice her; the customers had been taken care of and he was fumbling in the back closet for a fresh roll of register tape when he realized she was there. She didn't speak until he had climbed the stairs and stood facing her.

"Hi," he said, nettled. "How long have you been here?"

"An hour or so," Alice answered. Grave and thoughtful, she gazed up at him, a cloud of gray smoke drifting around her. Legs crossed, dressed in a light print skirt and white shirt, she had been calmly watching him come and go, overseeing the happenings, unnoticed by everyone.

Sitting down on the railing where he could see the floor below, Hadley said: "I'm sorry; I'm pretty upset. That little man gets on my nerves." Nervously, he ran his hands through his short-cropped blond hair. "Horace Wakefield; you know him?"

"I've seen him over at the flower shop," Alice answered. She seemed a little tired. . . . She had been shopping.

"He's mixed up in that cult, that Watchmen Society. He got me to go to the first lecture; now he wants me to go again." Hadley shut his mouth tight and abruptly stopped talking.

After a moment Alice asked: "You went before?"

"I went. I listened." Angrily, Hadley said: "I'm not going to get mixed up with it again; once is enough. I wanted to know what it was about; is there anything wrong with that?"

Alice studied him intently. "Is it important?"

"Yes," Hadley said simply. "I went a long way into it. I went all the way down." In a sense he was exaggerating; he had not really gone so far . . . one lecture and a brief meeting with Beckheim. But he would have gone further, if he could; if it had been possible he would have gladly plunged the whole way down. Helplessly, he appealed to her: "Was that so stupid? My God, I used to get so damn tired standing around this store, day after day—" He broke off futilely. "I guess I shouldn't rave."

"I wish you would—talk. If you want."

For a moment he weighed the practical considerations; Alice was, after all, the boss's wife.

"I talk too much," he said morbidly.

"Why are you so disturbed?" Smiling, she said: "It's a little late for that."

"I'm disturbed about what I did. I was taken in; there was something in it that attracted me . . . there still is. It gives me a strange feeling to hear about it. When Beckheim was talking I felt a sort of peace. I could sit back and close my eyes; I didn't have to worry. I didn't expect to wake up and find"—he groped for words—"find the world had collapsed one more notch. It felt as if he held things together around him. A sort of region that was firm."

"Then," Alice said, "you feel—you usually feel that things are coming apart?"

He nodded.

"You feel that now?"

"In a way, yes. Not here; not the store. Outside the store—everything else. The whole world . . . and eventually the store, too. The store seems firm enough to me. But—" He struggled. "I don't know. There's something wrong with the store. It's firm enough, it's solid enough . . . but it's not a world. Is it? It's not big enough to be a world. You can't live in a store. Am I going to have to eat my meals up in the office here? Bathe down in the john? Shave and dress here—*sleep* here? I can't live here; I can't raise a family here. I have to go outside." He raised his voice, baffled. "I don't want to spend my life here! It's too damn small!"

"Yes," Alice said. "You always had such big plans. . . . You had something much bigger in mind."

"Sure, I always wanted to do a lot of things. It used to seem to me the world was large; there was so damn much a person could do. Opportunity . . . I don't feel that anymore. That's all over. The world's a bleak place. Instead of opportunity it's deserted hills and rusty beer cans."

Alice listened uncertainly. "What do you mean?"

"I mean it's all shifting. You reach out for something and it vanishes. Opportunity—it's a fraud. A bunch of lies they bring you up on, like popular songs. Meaningless words."

"But you have to live in this world."

"Live in spite of it, maybe. That's all I hope for anymore. I'd be satisfied with that."

"When you and Ellen were over, when Jim turned the store over to you . . . that night you were excited. Your face was lit up the way it used to be." Alice smiled wanly. "In fact, it was too lit up. You were back to all your old schemes and ideas."

"There wasn't anything else I could do," Hadley answered candidly. "What else was there? Where else could I go?"

"Then," Alice said, "you don't really care about this. You didn't really want the job. You took it because you had nothing else."

"I didn't make up the things I said," Hadley answered. "I forced myself to get excited; I wanted to be excited. I *had* to be excited. But I can't keep it up."

"Do you think you might go back to this—Society?"

Hadley searched his mind. "No," he said finally.

"Really? Are you sure?"

"I can't go back to the Society. I can't believe that stuff either." Thoughtfully, unhappily, he said: "It makes less sense than this does. At least I *understand* this . . . I've been in the store so long I know everything there is to know about it. It's part of my life; it is my life."

"And the Society—"

"It's alien to me. I wanted it; I was drawn to it; a lot of people believe it. If I had been taught it from the ground up maybe I could believe it, too. Wakefield believes it; he was taught the Bible and God his whole life. Not me; I was taught there isn't any God. It's too late now; I can't believe that, even when I want to. And I did want to! I tried like hell."

"I see," Alice said.

"The word doesn't even make sense—it's worn out. Meaningless, empty. When Beckheim stood up there talking I felt it meant something; it meant something to him, and everybody else. But they're different from me. I can't grasp any of the old words; none of them make sense. God, country, the flag, all the old things that people believed in—it's all just vague sounds, as hard as I try. Is that wrong?"

"There's nothing you can do," Alice said.

"I guess I heard about it too late. Now I try to think what the hell I heard instead, and I can't. Nothing—there never was anything in my life. Ideas, maybe. I grew up with grand ideas instead of real things."

"Yes," Alice agreed, "you always were attracted by ideas."

"I put too much faith in ideas. Now I know they're not real. Words, talk . . . That's what my life's been. And it's futile."

"Not completely."

Hadley grinned starkly. "No? Remember how you felt that night, when I was talking to your husband. Didn't you sense it was a lot of meaningless hot air?"

"I guess so. You could have toned it down. . . ."

"I was trying to believe in it again, giving it one last chance."

"And it didn't work?"

"Well," Hadley said, "it got me the job. I'm here; I'm manager."

"How—long do you think you can stand it here?"

"I don't know. We'll have to see."

"Very long, do you think?" Alice went on: "Stuart, maybe you'll find more in it than you expect. There can be a lot of satisfaction in a family; you have a son now; that means plenty. Maybe it'll make all this meaningful; you're not working for yourself, the way you were in college, earning some money for dates and beer and cars. You're working for Pete and Ellen."

"You can't have a family in a world like this."

Alice said bitterly: "Jim and I would give anything in the world to have a son. A little boy like Pete."

"No," Hadley said. "There's no use bringing children into this world. The world's falling apart. I'll be selling a TV set the day the A-bomb falls on us . . . acting out a meaningless routine, like a dumb animal." Brooding, he murmured: "I won't get out from under it. . . . Maybe Pete will. I don't know. Maybe somebody will survive."

"Yes," Alice said quickly. "Somebody will; somebody always survives."

The man's fists clenched. "But maybe it's a good thing. Maybe it's what we deserve . . . We brought it on ourselves. It's our own fault; we're being paid back for what we've done. The whole thing ought to be yanked down; it's rotten and sick. It's vicious. It ought to be wiped out . . . an ocean of water before, a lake of fire this time." His voice trailed off, heavy with hatred and revulsion, the voice of a man weary with disgust. "Cleansing fire that wipes out everything. Until there's only slag and ash. And maybe after that something better will come."

The two of them were silent.

"I wish I could help," Alice said. "I feel it's my fault."

"Why?"

"It's all our faults. Mine and Jim's—especially his." Bitterly she said: "He's been working with you all this time and he never understood how you felt. He never did anything."

"He's all wrapped up in his stores," Hadley said. "Getting another store, making the business a success."

Furiously, Alice stabbed out her cigarette. "Damn him. He's so little and blind. He's so small."

"Don't blame him. He can't help what he is, any more than I can help what I am. Trace my problems back to you; trace your problems back another step. Where does it go? Back forever." Hadley slid from the rail; a customer had come into the store and was standing restlessly at the front counter. "I wish we had talked before. . . . It's so damn late in the game now."

"Is it too late?" Alice asked helplessly.

"I don't know. I think so. Most of the things have already happened; there isn't much left. I'm here; I'm manager. I've got Pete and Ellen; I'm not going back to the Society."

He started toward the stairs; Alice suddenly called: "Stuart, maybe you ought to quit! Maybe you ought to leave here!"

"No," he said.

"It's wrong—this is too small for you. You don't want to be this; you want more than this. It's all right for Jim, but not for you. It's as far as he can see . . . You don't want to take over his little world!"

"Where else can I go?" Hadley asked.

"Out!"

"Out where? There's nothing out there. If I leave here it's the end of me. This is the only world I know. . . . This is the only place I can go. I left here and I came back. I know I can't reach the Society, it's closed to me. Other people can go there . . . Beckheim can save a lot of them. But not me. If I leave this store, I'll die."

"You *want* to leave here!"

"Yes," Hadley said. "Of course I do." He started down the stairs from the office.

"Wait," Alice said breathlessly, coming after him. "Don't go down; stay and talk."

For a moment Hadley stood leaning against the stairwell. "What about the old man down there?" he said. "He has to be waited on."

"Why?" she demanded wildly. "Is he so important?"

"He's got a radio under his arm. He wants it fixed."

"Forget his radio."

"I can't," Hadley said, with irony in his voice. "He's standing down there, waiting for me to come and take care of him. He's sure it's only a tube. Actually, it isn't a tube; it's a power transformer and it'll cost him twelve dollars and fifty cents."

Alice was silent.

"The set," Hadley continued, "isn't worth over ten. He and I will argue half an hour and then I'll take it downstairs to the service department. Two weeks from now he'll be back with it because it still won't work."

"Why not?" Alice demanded miserably as he moved another step down.

"Because Olsen wired the power transformer upside down."

"Why—did he do that?"

"Because he threw away the service schematics Philco sent out for that model."

Rigidly, Alice asked: "Why did he throw them away?"

"Because no fat-assed corporation is going to tell him how to fix sets."

Alice clutched at her purse. "Is there any more?" she asked, when Hadley didn't go on.

"No," Hadley said. "No more."

"What are you going to do?"

"Stay here as long as I can. As long as I can stand it."

"Can—I help?"

"No," Hadley said. "Nobody can help. I thought Beckheim could, but now I know he can't. It isn't his fault; he did what he could. But I'm not going back to him. That's one thing I'm sure of. . . . Seeing Wakefield and listening to him showed me that, once and for all." He stepped another step down the stairwell.

"Listen to me," Alice said desperately. "I want to talk to you more; can't we talk now? The old man can wait."

"He's got a lot of errands to do. He's in a terrible hurry."

"He can do his errands tomorrow."

"His legs are tired from standing."

"He can sit down on one of the television sets." She moved after him. "You don't want to talk to me! You've made up your mind—while you were standing here talking you made up your mind."

"No," Hadley said, "I didn't make up my mind. I'm not going to do anything."

"But you're certain. You're not undecided."

"I know I can't be like Wakefield. I can't live like that. If that's the only way to survive, it's out for me. The cross and the flag. Health foods, revival meetings, prayers and potted plants. And he knows it, too. It scares him . . . but he's little. He's tiny. He's trivial. He'll go on. I can't. I'm finished. Out. Done. *Wakefield,* that's what they mean by the meek. I'm not meek—I want a lot of things. Too many things, for myself and my family. For everybody. I wanted millions of things for millions of people. Big dreams. Big ideas. Bullshit."

"Don't you believe in anything anymore?"

"Nothing that exists. What I believe in is bullshit."

"Then what exists?"

"Terrible things. Things I don't want to have anything to do with. I'm fed up. Maybe I'm not getting enough sleep; maybe that's it." Wryly, he grinned up at Alice. "I could almost believe that. A good rest, plenty of fresh air, a good sermon at church on Sunday morning . . ."

Alice shivered. "I'm sorry . . . I wish I could do something. Please, isn't there anything?"

"No, not now."

"Ever?"

"Maybe never. Thanks." He waved up at her. "It's okay—don't worry about it. You didn't set up the universe. Maybe nobody did. It's all random chance, without meaning. So don't worry about it."

He stepped from the stairwell and walked slowly under the office, toward the front of the store. The old man was still there waiting at the front counter; he had set down his radio and stood leaning heavily against the cash register, weary and resentful.

"Yes sir," Hadley said to him gaily. "What can I do for you?"

It was still light as Hadley walked home that night. His jacket over his arm, he trudged along the evening streets, accepting the fresh, warm air into his lungs, gazing yearningly at the people and houses, the men watering their lawns, the boys scrambling and playing, the old people sitting quietly on their front porches.

He dragged his feet. He walked as slowly as possible, savoring what he saw and smelled as long as he could, all the way to the door of his apartment house. For a time he stood looking back down the slight hill, toward the business section. It was a little past seven; the sounds of radios dinned from houses, mixed with the odor of cooking. Across the street an old woman was laboriously watering her flower garden with a bent sprinkling can. A tattered gray tomcat followed after her, smelling the damp leaves and stalks, standing up to sniff at the dripping petals.

To Hadley, the ordinary sights of evening seemed vital and beautiful. He wanted to stand and look as long as he could; he was achingly aware that even as he watched, it was changing, fading, altering. The old woman finished watering and put the sprinkling can away. The gray tomcat lingered, urinated on some ferns, and then strolled off. One by one the children gave up playing and straggled into the house.

It was getting dark. The summer air sank into coldness. Night was coming on, and with it came tiny dancing bits of opaqueness: the fluttering bodies of dark nocturnal insects. Here and there lights came on. The sounds of people dimmed and faded as windows were closed against the rising coolness.

Hadley turned and entered the apartment building. He made his way silently down the carpeted, deserted corridor to his own door. A crack of light lay spread out; a heavy odor of frying lamb chops filtered out. When he entered he found the living room a blaze of light. Pete lay on the couch, wrapped in his blankets, sleeping fretfully. The fan whirred in the corner, on the bookcase; the evening had turned cool but Ellen had not yet remembered to turn the fan off. Hadley tossed down his coat and moved toward the kitchen. He could see Ellen moving around, fixing dinner. The splutter and hiss of frying, the mumble of boiling water, greeted him as he reached the door and stopped to stand for a moment, taking in the sight and holding on to it as long as possible.

Presently Ellen turned. "Oh," she said. "Hello!"

"Hello," Hadley said. The sight, the vision, slipped away through his fingers and was gone. "I'm home."

"Tired?"

He nodded. "I really am."

Ellen came over and peered up at him intently. She stood up on tiptoe, then quickly kissed him on the mouth. "Dinner's almost ready."

"I see it is." Gratefully, he seated himself at the table. "It looks good. Anything I can do?"

"Just sit." Ellen put the creamed corn on the stove. "Everything's almost ready." She brushed a lock of brown hair from her eyes and halted briefly to slip her bra strap over her shoulder. "It's been hot today. Real Indian summer."

The kitchen was still hot from the fumes of cooking. The girl's face was streaked and flushed with perspiration; shiny drops of moisture had slid down her bare arms, down her neck and into her blouse. She smiled fleetingly at Hadley and began getting plates from the drainboard. He smiled back at her.

"How'd it go today?" she asked.

"All right."

Ellen disappeared into the living room; she was setting the table in there. When she came back there was a large square package in her arms, wrapped in brown paper, tied with heavy packing twine. "Look," she said. "This came back."

Hadley's heart stopped beating. "Back?"

"Your pictures. Some woman dropped them off, some friend of the Golds'." Ellen placed the package in his lap and went on with her cooking. "You left them over there, remember?"

"Yes," Hadley said slowly. That was what he had told her. "I did." He stared at the package uncomprehendingly. "When did she come?"

"About an hour ago. She just dropped them off—I didn't recognize her. Tall, thin, an older woman—about thirty. She had a huge dog with her."

"Did—she come alone?"

"I guess so. There was a car outside; I heard it drive off. Look inside the package; I think there's a note for you."

His hands clumsy, Hadley reached into the open side of the package. His fingers closed over an envelope, and he slid it out. The envelope was crumpled and stained; when he turned it over he saw that it wasn't sealed: the flap had been jammed inside, and the envelope folded. He tore it open and got out a wad of lined notepaper. A short note in pencil, a neat, precise hand, a woman's efficient script.

> *Stuart—Ted and I have broken completely. I'm through with the Society; it's not for me. I'll tell you all about it when I see you. Maybe tomorrow? I'll come by the store; I'm staying in San Mateo with friends. Sorry I kept your pictures so long—I want to talk with you about them—they're pretty good.*
>
> *Marsha*

He sat for a long time holding the penciled note. It wasn't until Ellen roused him that he put it away and got to his feet.

"Time to eat," she was saying. "What's the matter with you? Don't go to sleep until later—get yourself a chair and let's get started."

Blindly, dazed with growing fury, he searched for a chair.

"Are you hungry?" Ellen asked hopefully.

"I'm starved," he muttered savagely.

"I hope you can stand lamb chops again."

Hadley didn't answer. He seated himself and stiffly began unfolding his napkin.

Polkas and ballads, and a Spanish guitar. She closed her eyes, and the people danced wildly to the accordions and violins. Clapping their hands, guzzling beer, long skirts whirling, laughter, warmth . . . the tinny blur of simple people enjoying themselves . . . Marsha Frazier listened as long as she could stand it, and then she snapped off the radio and opened her eyes.

Across the dark street Modern TV Sales and Service was glowing. Her wristwatch told her it was almost nine; he could be coming out any minute. Impatiently, she reached down and clicked on the car's ignition. The motor came on with a muffled roar and she backed away from the curb, out into the slow-moving evening traffic. Sitting and watching drove her crazy; she stabbed down on the accelerator, and the little Studebaker coupe leaped forward.

Twice she drove around the block, slowed to a crawl by the leisurely creeping cars, the drifting clots of pedestrians stalling traffic at each intersection. Store signs, red and green and flashing white, blazed up and down the avenue; on Friday night everything was open wide for business. The sleepy sprawl of August haze lay over the town, dust and moisture blown in from the nearby Bay. At drive-ins and cafés teenagers collected in bright swarms, devouring ice cream, Cokes, greasy hamburgers. Young, healthy, they wandered around town laughing and wiping their chins, sprawling in their stripped-down cars, lounging around drugstores, killing time smoking and punching each other.

As again she came even with the television store she slowed almost to a stop. She peered out and shaded her eyes against the glare of the big overhead neon signs. The glare bothered her; frowning, she drove on a short way, trying to see into the blaring store entrance. Shapes moved, men and women. The dim outlines of big TV sets stationed here and there. The counter, to the left. For a moment the form of a man emerged from the confusion of lights and objects; it was Stuart Hadley. Talking to a young couple, showing them a television combination, he stood outlined in the doorway, a tall, youthful shape in white shirt, tie, neatly pressed slacks. Hadley gestured, bent to adjust the knobs of the TV set; then he faded back into the depths of the store.

Once more Marsha drove the car slowly around the block. This time when she came around and passed by Modern, the front door had been closed. The lights still blazed, but the shade had been pulled down. Up and down the avenue the neon signs were winking off one by one. Merchants closed and locked their doors; aimlessly drifting groups of people appeared, stood listlessly, wandered toward their parked cars and home. Marsha pulled the Studebaker into a parking space and turned off the motor. It couldn't be much longer; the dark face of the Bank of America clock read nine ten. As she watched she saw a man and woman approach the door of Modern TV and try the handle. The door was locked; the man and woman stood for a moment and then gave up. Marsha exulted as they walked off. . . . No more people would be getting in. As soon as those already inside were taken care of, that was it.

One by one the people left the store. Each time, Hadley stood a moment holding the door wide, saying good night to them, smiling and waving out into the evening darkness. Laughter, the easy banter of summer-evening business. Marsha gritted her teeth and suffered through the interminable. It was nine thirty before the last person was out, and the door finally locked.

Laboriously, Hadley began turning off television sets and lights. She watched him go from set to set, trying the knobs, inspecting the plugs. The door shade had been rolled back up; now the overhead fluorescents dimmed off and the interior of the store became a pool of darkness. Vaguely, the tall shape moved here and there, emptying the cash register, setting the tape, plugging in the night-light over the safe, disappearing into the back— probably for his jacket. The minutes passed like hours. . . . She could have screamed aloud when Hadley stopped at the telephone to make a call. For an endless interval he stood leaning against the tube checker, the phone to his face, staring blankly out into the night darkness, his jaw slack, jacket over his arm, kicking intermittently at an unopened stack of brown packages on the floor in front of him.

Somehow she lived through it. At last Hadley laughed, put down the phone, groped in his pocket for his key, and approached the door. He stopped briefly to tick off the outside lights; then he straightened, pulled the door shut after him, and locked it. For a moment he tried the knob; satisfied that it was locked, he swung his jacket over his shoulder and headed away from the store.

Lips pressed tight, Marsha started the motor of the car and hurriedly backed out into traffic. Ignoring a honking bus, she swung over to the center lane; at the next intersection she made a screeching left turn onto the side street. Jamming on the brakes, she halted just beyond the lights of the intersection, the rear of the Studebaker blocking the white-painted crosswalk.

Hadley came down the sidewalk, swinging his jacket and whistling soundlessly. She waited until he had stepped off the pavement and into the crosswalk before she pushed open the car door. Apparently he was a trifle nearsighted; he didn't recognize her until she spoke to him.

"Hop in." She gunned the motor. "Hurry up."

For an instant he stood in the crosswalk facing her and the car. A dark, ugly curtain settled over his face, a closed hardness that made her suddenly uneasy. His eyes dimmed and faded; an impersonal film gathered, a blind innerness from below the level of individual consciousness. It was as if Hadley had gone away and something awful had come and looked out through his eyes, peered at her from behind his face. Chilled, she pulled away.

Another car had made the turn after her; it slowed to a resentful halt and shifted into second.

"Come on," she repeated nervously, her composure shattered. "I have to get the hell out of here."

Hadley came slowly around the side of the Studebaker and climbed into the seat beside her. She reached past him, slammed the door, and bucked the car urgently forward. Rapidly, shifting, not looking at the man beside her, she gunned the motor and swiftly shot away from the intersection. Satisfied, the car behind her followed and went on its way. That car, that unknown random object, had decided things.

Marsha settled back against the seat and tried to concentrate on the cars and lights.

For quite a long time, as long as possible, Hadley said nothing. The familiar interior of the dapper little Studebaker coupe annoyed him; he hated the sight of the clean, simple dashboard, the grille of the radio, the low-swept hood beyond the windshield, the bulging pulled-out ashtray. He knew every inch of it; he had stared at it long enough to memorize every screw and bit of chrome. In a way he hated the car more than he hated Marsha.

"You're acting childish," Marsha said finally.

Hadley grunted and slumped down. He didn't want to talk to her; he didn't even want to look at her. Instead, he followed the outlines of a bread factory to the right, a towering redbrick building with trucks lined up in rows, waiting for their loads. Through the open windows of the car rushed the smell of warm baking bread. Concentrating on the simple, fresh odor, he managed to ignore the woman beside him until she said sharply:

"Damn it, look at me! You're not going to sit there like a sullen child; sit up and behave like an adult!"

"What the hell do *you* want?" Hadley said brutally. "I thought I'd seen the last of you."

The hard, smooth flesh of the woman's face drained perfectly white. Like polished bone her cheeks glistened, cold and stark in the reflected streetlight. "Don't talk to me like that," she said in a thin, icy voice. Without warning she jammed on the brakes; the car screeched to a bucking, jerking halt. "Get out of here. Go on—*get out!*"

He made no move to go. He sat with his arms on his knees, hands dangling loosely in his lap, still not looking at her. There was no incentive to go; he had made up his mind to get in the car and that was that. The decision had been made; he had no intention of unmaking it.

"Look," Marsha said in a choked, uneven voice. "There's no point in going on acting like this. Is there? You don't have to treat me like an enemy. . . . I'm not your enemy." Pleadingly, she muttered: "Did you get my note?"

"Sure." Hadley stirred a trifle to rest his arm on the windowsill. "You walked right into the apartment and handed it to my wife; how could I miss it?"

They were parked in the middle of the street, in a black, deserted block of the factory district. A few blocks ahead was the railroad track, the loading platform and opaque shape of the station building. Inert cars were parked here and there. Nothing moved.

"Let's get out of here," Hadley said morbidly. "I hate this kind of neighborhood."

Marsha shifted into low and started up the car. As the car crawled forward her hands were visibly shaking; she bit her lip and gazed convulsively straight ahead. Swallowing, she asked: "Were you surprised?"

"About what?"

"That—I'd left Ted."

He thought about it. "No," he answered finally. "It seems natural. He probably wasn't the first."

"Not at all," Marsha admitted in a stricken whisper. "One of a long line. But he was the first—" She couldn't get out the word. "What you said. Ted was the only Negro. There never was any other; I wanted to tell you that."

"It's not important."

"You brought it up. About him—that night. I know what you said; so do you."

"I'm sorry about that," Hadley said distantly. "Anyhow, it doesn't matter. Let's forget it." He pointed out the window at the red glow of the Farmers' Commercial Trust Building. "If you turn on that way you'll pass my place. You can let me off practically anywhere."

Presently, as they drove along, Marsha said faintly: "I liked your pictures."

"So you said in the note."

"I mean it." She appealed to him, agitated, eyes wild. "You don't believe me? Isn't that what you wanted? Isn't it important to you anymore?"

"In a way," Hadley said noncommittally. "I'm glad to know what you think."

Gripping the wheel rigidly, Marsha said: "When we get hold of some money we're going to try some lithographs. Have you worked with lithography?"

"No."

"Are—you interested?"

Hadley sighed. "No." He really wasn't. He felt tired; it had been a long, arduous day. His legs, his arms, ached with fatigue. The bones of his feet hurt; he had been standing up for thirteen hours. It had been some time since he had had a decent bowel movement. The dozen cups of coffee he had taken in during the day had coated his stomach with a gritty, metallic deposit. He wished idly for a glass of fruit juice. Orange juice, plenty of it. Cold and thin and clear. And also, perhaps, a lettuce and cheese sandwich.

The car was moving reluctantly toward Bancroft, in the direction of his apartment house. Actually he had no desire to go home; he didn't expect to go home. He was here; he had come of his own free will. He had made up his mind and he did not mean to back out of it. Everything had been thought over, examined and considered, in the silent hours of the previous night. But he enjoyed hurting her; he could see the pain in the harsh, taut lines of her face. Settling back against the upholstery of the car, he grimly enjoyed the ride.

"There it is," he said, indicating the building. "You want to come in awhile? You can meet my family. . . . You met Ellen already. I'll show you Pete." Sadistically he continued: "How about having dinner with us? We haven't eaten . . . I eat when I get home."

The woman had more courage than he had realized. Or he had misjudged her feelings about him. "No thanks," she said icily. "Maybe some other time. I don't feel very well tonight; I don't want anything to eat and I don't want to meet anybody."

Apparently she had accepted the fact that he was going to get out and leave her. She had rallied; he had to admire the stoic jutting of her chin and the bleakness of her eyes. Beyond doubt, she would be able to weather it. It was tearing her apart, but she could endure it; she, too, had made up her mind.

"Well," she said thinly, "it was nice talking to you again." She glanced at him briefly. "You're looking well."

"I should be. I'm manager of the store now."

"Oh?" She nodded, "Fine. More money?"

"Lots more. Power, too . . . I get to boss people around." He added, "All my responsibility, the whole place. Ordering, buying, making decisions. My little kingdom."

Marsha parked the car across from his apartment house; it was, he noticed, almost the same place where she had let him off that night. Turning off the motor and lights, Marsha swung around to face him. Defiant and pale, she said: "I can see you're going to make me pay for that night. All right, I'm paying. But *why*? What was I supposed to do?"

"Forget it," Hadley said, his hand on the door handle.

Her gray eyes moved, flickered; gasping, she hurried on: "I knew I should have told you . . . but damn it, that's not something you can tell people. Is it? I put it off; I waited too long. I got interested in you and then I was *afraid* to tell you. So I got myself boxed in. . . . I *couldn't* go to bed with you, could I? Not when I was living with Ted; it isn't fair, I can't do that sort of thing. You wouldn't want me to do that, would you?"

"No," he said idly.

"All this last month I wanted to get in touch with you. I wanted to come down here; I wanted to see you and talk to you. I started to write; God, I started letters, put them into envelopes—tore them up. I've been thinking about you all this time. Everything's gone to pieces. . . ." She turned away, clenched her fist and shuddered. A choking, grating sob shoved open her mouth and forced its way between her rigid jaws; she buried her face against the upholstery of the car, and for a time neither of them said anything.

"Stop acting," Hadley said cruelly.

"I'm—" She cleared her throat; her voice was weak, almost inaudible. "I'm not acting. I'm in love with you."

Hadley was shocked. A slow, painful burning sensation crept up into his cheeks. Angered and embarrassed, he wrenched away from her, as if something disgusting had happened. As if she had done a bestial thing, admitted to an unspeakable depravity. He wished violently that he hadn't made her say it; that he hadn't pushed her so far. It was something he hadn't anticipated. Revolted, shaken, he yanked open the car door and half stepped to the pavement.

"Are you going?" Marsha said, the ragged edge of hysteria creeping into her voice. "Good night, Stuart Hadley. Maybe I'll see you again sometime."

"Calm down," he told her.

"I'm calm."

"Then lower your voice." He pulled the door shut and reseated himself. "I'm too tired to stand any shouting. I've been working in that store thirteen hours; I've had my share of noise for the day."

With a tremendous effort Marsha managed to get control of herself. "Can I expect you to stay?" she asked haltingly. "For a couple of minutes, at least?"

"A couple of minutes, yes," Hadley answered.

With great care Marsha said: "It offends you to have me say how I feel? But that doesn't change it; I still mean it. I still feel it."

"Don't say it again," Hadley said fiercely. Restlessly, he shifted around, trying unsuccessfully to make himself comfortable. "It doesn't mean anything. It's empty, worthless."

"Not to me," Marsha managed.

"Then keep it to yourself!" Darkly, he went on: "It's like your standing up and reciting the Pledge of Allegiance. Who takes that seriously? Who believes in that? *Somebody* must believe in it, they make you say it, they make you stand there with your hand over your heart every morning, all the time you're growing up in school. But you never expect to *meet* anybody who believes it. . . . Like the lyrics of popular songs. You never expect anybody in real life to talk like that."

"That's what I sound like?" Marsha asked briskly.

"To me, yes. It would sound different to somebody else. Maybe there're a whole lot of people who take stuff like that seriously. Maybe I'm the only person who can't stand to hear about it." He rubbed his forehead moodily. "I don't know. Hearing you say it makes me ashamed of you. . . . I want to look away and pretend it didn't happen. The way I feel when somebody makes a disgusting noise. Something that reveals a different layer, an animal layer."

Marsha laughed, a dry brittle humorless breaking sound. "You're bourgeois—it reminds you of sex. You're afraid it'll lead to something physical."

"Don't kid yourself." Hadley turned to gaze intently at her. He continued to study her until, self-conscious and uncertain, Marsha shrank away and involuntarily glanced over her blouse and skirt. "No," Hadley said, "that's not it. I'm not worried about realities; I'm not avoiding things that exist. Are you?"

Marsha started to speak, then changed her mind.

"You're the one," Hadley said. "You're afraid; that's why you talk like that. . . . That's why you pour out phony talk of that kind. You don't really feel love—you feel what I feel. But you can't say it; you can't talk about it. You're like everybody else; they talk that way because they're afraid to talk about real things."

"What real things? What do you mean?" Two spots of high, bright color glowed in her cheeks. "Don't you believe I meant what I said?"

With an impatient wave of his hand Hadley dismissed her words. "You know what really exists between us; it's the same thing that exists between any man and woman sitting like we're sitting. This is the only relationship; everything else is a lot of hot air. Between us—" He turned toward her. "What is it? What's really there?"

Apprehensively, she waited to hear.

"You can spiritualize it all you want, but what it really boils down to is simple biological reality." He reached down and closed his hand around a fistful of the woman's tweed skirt. "What I want is some of that stuff you have under there. I want to get in there; that's what I'm here for and that's what you're here for. That's why we're on this earth. . . . So I can pull up your skirt and climb in, right up there inside you."

"I see," Marsha said levelly. "Is—that the way you've always felt?"

After a moment Hadley admitted: "No. I had a lot of hot-air ideas, a lot of pink-cloud illusions, like everybody else. But I've come around to viewing things more realistically."

Marsha found a cigarette and got it between her lips. She lit up and sat scratching mechanically at the button on her sleeve. Finally she asked: "Do you want me to tell you why I left Ted?"

"If you want to gabble about it."

Marsha flinched. "I—don't know if I can stand this."

"You want me to get out now?"

She considered. "No." Brightly she said: "Well, I'll go back to the beginning; I feel better when I can talk about it. I don't believe that look on your face means anything; I think you're listening to me. Aren't you?"

"Yes."

It was a terrible effort for her, but she continued: "I left Ted right away . . . I only went back for a couple of days. It was awful—worse than anything before. He didn't say anything; he just went on with his work." Blowing gray smoke through her pinched nostrils Marsha said: "I think he's the finest man who ever lived. He's completely good. It's not like other people, when they're good; it isn't the same thing at all. He just doesn't have the capacity to do harm . . . Goodness is part of his physical body. It's all through him."

"Is that why you started living with him?"

For a time she was silent. "I was attracted by him. When I first saw him and heard him speak . . . I knew he was unique. He has power; it's a magnetic thing, like gravity. He draws people to him. He drew you . . . didn't he? He just reaches out and takes everybody into him. And I came, like everybody else. I wanted to be close to him. I wanted to touch him and be a part of him. What happened came about naturally . . . it wasn't planned out. It wasn't some kind of conspiracy; it was spontaneous." She gazed past Hadley, troubled and somber. "But you know, even living with him, sleeping with him, I never got close to him. He's a long way away; he's always listening to things I can't hear, seeing things I can't see. His mind is—" She shrugged. "You know; you tried to reach him. You can't. He's not for any one of us."

"I know," Hadley said. "I'm out, too."

"We lived together only a month or so. Hardly anybody knows; the Golds don't know, of course. I never followed him very far . . . I stayed in my apartment. He came there; it was a place for him to stay. I opened it to him and he came there naturally . . . the same way he came to me when I opened myself to him. He simply came in and took . . . He took the way he gives. Like a child. With his hand out, trustingly. And then off he goes, when he's received. But—" She laughed. "Well, you saw him eat, didn't you? Eating is nothing for him; he just pushes food between his teeth, back and forth, like a machine. It's the same way with any physical thing for him . . . he does it, he goes through it, has it, gets it over with. But it never really involves *him*; it never really touches him or gets down inside him."

"He's not against sexual relations?" Hadley inquired.

"There was very little sexual intercourse between us." She was willing to talk openly about it, almost matter-of-factly. He had hurt her all the way to the bottom; apparently she didn't have any further to go, any more to lose. Or so she seemed to think. "The first time," she said. "We did it then, and after that a few more, now and then. I forget how many times. He came to the apartment, bathed, changed his clothes, spread out his work on the desk, and worked. Then he came to me, in bed, and that was that. And he went to sleep. It's dim in my mind. . . ." She shook her head unhappily. "I suppose he took it for granted that I felt the same way, that it was as unimportant to me as it was to him. But I wanted it to mean more."

"Women always make a big thing out of it," Hadley said.

"He was right, I suppose," Marsha continued, tautly ignoring him. "I tried to feel the same way; I knew I was wrong. I elevate it so much, like everybody else. Like you, I can't escape from it, either. It's part of me; I was born here; this is the world that trained me. I wanted to go along with him and see things the way he did, but I can't." Earnestly, she said: "He's too good, Stuart. I stood it as long as I could and then I broke off. It was hell because he was so kind. He just let me go. He made no claim on me. Damn him." She glanced up. "And damn you. It was your fault, too."

"Don't blame it on me."

"Oh, yes. That night, when you said that. You called him a nigger. I couldn't stand it, because it was true. He *is* a Negro; I can't forget that; neither can you."

"I told you I'm sorry!" Hadley said angrily.

"It's too late for that. That's what I mean . . . neither of us is good enough. Neither of us measures up to him; we're not worthy. Isn't that so? When you said that word, and when I responded, I knew we weren't fit to be around him."

Hadley nodded begrudgingly. "All right."

"Is it true?" she persisted.

"Yes."

Marsha went on: "So we're in it together, Stuart Hadley. I drove back up to San Francisco knowing Ted and I were finished. He makes me ashamed of myself, and at the same time I'm restless and unsatisfied. The kind of life I want is something ugly. . . . I'll never have it with him. Not ugly, exactly. I don't know what to call it. When I saw you I knew you were my kind; I knew I could understand you and your way of life. And—you're very good-looking. I always did go in for the sweet Nordic blond type. I was physically attracted to you from the start." She laughed shakily. "So you see, it's your fault we split up. You're responsible . . . the same way I'm responsible for messing up your life."

"You would have left him anyhow," Hadley said.

"Of course. But not for a while, not so soon."

"How many men have you lived with before?"

"I'm thirty-two years old," Marsha said. "You saw two of my children; I have a daughter up in Oregon, in a private school. She's fourteen years old. Does that shock you? I was just out of high school; I was eighteen, living in Denver. A midwestern country girl. I was going to be a feature writer on a newspaper. Charlotte—my first daughter—was born in 1936."

"Christ," Hadley said. "I was only ten years old."

"Her father was a very wonderful man, a young engineer. Don Frazier was killed in the Second World War. It'll interest you to know we married, later. In 1940, just before the war. During the war there were a number of them; I've lost track. I lived in England for a while; I was with the Women's Army Auxiliary Corps—attached to the Office of War Information. While I was there I met Sir Oswald Mosley. Most of my political opinions were formed then. I was disillusioned about the war . . . I saw too much of it."

Curious, Hadley asked: "Right now are you legally anybody's wife? Did you remarry?"

"You know that part. I married an Army major while I was stationed in England. Timmy and Pat are his children."

"You're still married to him?"

"Yes."

Hadley brooded. "I don't know whether to believe you or not."

"It's the truth." She coolly blew a cloud of smoke at him. "It doesn't matter; I don't know where he is, probably in New York with somebody. Last time I saw him he was living with a wealthy society woman—he'll get along. Of that I'm positive."

She didn't continue, and Hadley had nothing to contribute. After a time he reached behind him and again opened the car door.

"Where are you going?" Marsha demanded quickly.

"Home, of course. I'm hungry. I want to eat dinner."

Her gray eyes fixed on him, Marsha said: "You really aren't going to forgive me, are you? You're going to make me suffer for not going to bed with you that night."

He didn't have to answer; it was obvious. But that was not the whole story. "I believe you," he said aloud, "when you say you couldn't have. I believe you wanted to, but you couldn't go through with it."

"Then why make me suffer?"

"Because," Hadley said simply, "I'm suffering. And I want to share it."

"Don't go," Marsha said tensely, reaching out and touching his arm. "Stay with me. I'll do whatever you want; there aren't any strings to it, nothing. I'm free; I'm completely cut loose. I saw Ted for the last time yesterday. It isn't the same as it was; now it's different."

"I see," Hadley said thoughtfully. "In other words, you've decided you *would* like to go to bed."

The woman's face withered. She huddled back in a stricken heap, gray eyes swimming.

"Well?" Hadley demanded. "Yes or no?"

She nodded mutely without speaking.

"Answer me!" he demanded.

"Yes."

Hadley reflected. "I'm hungry. I want something to eat first."

After a struggle she managed to find words. "We can stop at a drive-in." Groping feebly for the ignition key, she got the motor going, and then the headlights. "Please, will you close the door? I can't drive with it open."

"Sure," Hadley said easily, pulling it shut.

Tears running down her cheeks, Marsha released the parking brake and edged the car out onto the dark, silent street.

At a drive-in they bought themselves milk shakes and sandwiches. Hadley had the girl wrap them up; he paid her and she carried off the little metal tray, leaving them alone. There were other cars parked here and there in the circular lot around the building itself, mostly high school kids and young couples. The metallic sounds of dance music drifted across the darkness to Hadley and for a time he sat listening, his milk shake and sandwich in a paper bag on his lap.

"It takes me back," he said to Marsha.

After a moment she murmured, "In what way?"

"I haven't had a car since college. Sitting here like this reminds me of the old days, when I was dating Ellen. And before that; when I was a high school kid, like that fellow over there."

A high school youth in a white shirt, sleeves rolled up, arms brown and fuzzy, wearing dark jeans, his heels scraping noisily, hair long and plastered down, sideburns all the way to his jaw, walked in front of the Studebaker to his own hot rod.

"Were you like that?" Marsha asked feebly. She had begun to regain some of her poise. "I can't believe it. . . . You're so blond."

"I dressed that way. Dave Gold and I both dressed that way, except that Dave wore a coat, a dirty brown tweed coat."

"Do you still see the Golds?" Marsha asked.

Hadley sobered. "No. Not since that day up in San Francisco when my brother-in-law dumped them off. That day they came to you for a ride."

"They were certainly—chastened," Marsha said. "I never found out what happened; they just mumbled."

"I dumped them," Hadley said moodily. "I sat there and let him walk over them. The big bastard . . . And I didn't do a thing; I joined in, actually." He stepped from the car and came around behind it to the other side. Opening the door he said: "Move over."

Marsha edged uncertainly away from the wheel. "Why?"

"I'm going to drive. I want to see how this thing runs." Hadley slid in behind the wheel and slammed the door. "Are you ready to go?"

"Yes," Marsha said nervously, "I guess so."

Hadley started the car and backed it from the lot, onto the road. Beside him, the woman watched anxiously as he shifted into high and gained velocity.

"You do well," she said.

"Why not? I've been driving since I was a kid." Slowing for a light he said: "This isn't a bad little car. Cold-blooded . . . It's sluggish as hell—but it's smooth."

"It doesn't use much gas," Marsha said. "It's cheap to run." She clutched the two bags of food, hers and Hadley's. "Where—are we going?"

With a shriek of tires Hadley turned from the town out onto the approach to the freeway. Bits of blinding light flashed along: cars moving at high speed from San Francisco to San Jose. Without stopping he passed through a yellow light, into the first lane and then the second. In a moment he had reached the center lane; with his foot grimly on the gas pedal he began to inch the little coupe up to seventy.

"Take it easy," Marsha said faintly. To their left, beyond the dividing strip, searing headlights shot past in a bewildering trajectory. She squinted and sank down against the door. "I don't like this lane . . . it's too close to the other side. And they go so darn fast."

Ignoring her, Hadley reached down and threw in the overdrive handle. Beneath them the motor sound instantly ceased; the car seemed to fly above the surface of the highway. There was no sound but the roar of wind, nothing visible except the whirr of headlights to their left. "You keep this out?" Hadley asked her.

"For town driving . . . I forget to put it back in." Lamely she murmured, "I'm not on the highway much; I'm usually driving around San Francisco."

They were between towns. On each side of the highway lay black fields, and occasional power lines. The sky was overcast; the wind that rushed about the cabin was chill and acrid with the odor of the Bay.

"Aren't you afraid you'll get a ticket?" Marsha asked apprehensively.

"Not in suicide lane. It's almost impossible to stop a car driving in this lane." A moment later he added: "Anyhow, we're not going far."

He eased the car over to the right and allowed it to drop down to sixty. When he was going fifty he cut into the extreme right-hand lane. To their left, cars swept past them and disappeared into the darkness beyond.

Marsha shivered. "It makes me a little sick, driving that fast. I always wonder what would happen if a tire blew."

"We'd be Swiss steak." Hadley slowed to forty, then to thirty-five. Ahead was a cutoff of sorts, a minor paved road leading to a cluster of neon-lit buildings: a gas station, a few roadside bars, some houses, a factory. At a little over thirty he made the turn and left the freeway.

"Where are we?" Marsha asked.

"Almost there. We'll be drinking our milk shakes soon." He made a wide turn and brought the car around the far side of the cluster of buildings. Turning up a side road he shifted into second and began to climb the side of a gloomy hill. Trees and buildings wavered past on both sides; they were slowly rising into a small roadside town.

"I've never been here before," Marsha said, with visible distaste.

"This is San Sebastian Heights—a tract." The car had reached the top of the hill; Hadley brought it to a halt and pointed. Ahead of them the ground dropped breathtakingly; a wide valley lay spread out, a solid expanse of neatly arranged lights. They were looking down at an immense housing development, a subdivision so large that its edges were lost in the night haze.

"Every house is exactly alike," Hadley said as he let the car begin its descent. "California ranch style, it's called."

At the foot of the hill he made a right-hand turn and passed an illuminated building: the subdivision administration building. Beyond that the road widened into a shopping center. Most of the stores were closed; only the drugstore and bar remained open. The vast supermarket was shut down; the clothing store, the dime store, the shoe store, all were dark and deserted. Hadley drove past a dimly lit Shell gas station and then a launderette.

"Here we are," he said.

Ahead of them rose the luminous red sign of a motel. He shifted into second and crawled up the driveway, past the first ring of cottages, past the black square of lawn, and up to the cabin marked OFFICE. A Vacancy sign was out; Hadley came to a halt and pulled on the parking brake.

"There's always an empty," he explained leisurely. "It's too far off the high-way; they built it when most of these houses were for sale and people came down from San Francisco to look at them. Now this outfit can't pee a drop."

From the motel office came a waddling figure in a heavy overcoat. Mut-tering and peering, the man approached the car and flashed his light into the cabin. "Evening," he said suspiciously, examining the faces of the two people. "One left; you're lucky."

Hadley grinned starkly and reached for his wallet. "Good for *us*. How much is that?"

"Four fifty," the man grunted; in his heavy red face his eyes glittered and shifted. "In-state, are you?"

"That's right," Hadley agreed, a five-dollar bill held out. "Which cottage is it?"

"What the hell," the man said, resigned. "No kids, I suppose." He fum-bled in the pocket of his overcoat for his receipt book. "Yeah, I have to have the money in advance," he said, accepting the bill. "Some people get up be-fore I do."

With the stub of a lead pencil he wrote out the receipt, copying the names from the identification papers in Hadley's wallet.

"Okay, Mr. and Mrs. Hadley," he said, tearing off the receipt and handing it to them. "Third cottage to the right." He handed them the keys and wad-dled sullenly back to his office. "Sweet dreams," he said, and disappeared inside.

Hadley promptly started the car. "These places are more private," he ex-plained, "once they let you in."

In a moment they were parked in front of the dark little cottage. Hadley pocketed the car keys, shut off the lights, and slid out onto the gravel walk. As he mounted the steps to the cottage Marsha came slowly behind with the sacks of food. The door fell open, and the two of them entered, Hadley a step ahead as he felt for the light switch.

A tiny room like a monk's cell flashed into being. Barren, austere, without ornaments of any kind, the room sparkled starkly in the white electric light. Hadley stalked about; he inspected the bathroom, and the cul-de-sac that served as a shower. The place was spotlessly clean, ascetic in its simplicity. It pleased him. This was how he remembered it; years ago he had brought girls to this motel . . . one of them had been Ellen. He tossed his jacket over a chair and went back to close the door.

"It would be hard to sin here," he said as he pulled down the shades.

"Yes, they certainly keep it nice," Marsha admitted. Shivering, she began wandering fretfully around. "It's cold; light the heater, won't you?"

Hadley touched a match to the dwarf gas heater, and in a moment the room sweated with warmth. He lit a floor lamp and turned off the glaring overhead bulb. In the softer light the colors of the woman's clothes attracted his attention; he noticed for the first time that instead of slacks she was wearing a brightly colored print blouse and a tweed skirt.

Amused, he observed: "I'd hardly know it was you."

Self-consciously, Marsha lifted her hands to her breasts. "Why do you say that?"

"You look almost feminine. It does you good—that outfit works out nice." He threw himself down on a stiff straight-backed chair and accepted the two paper sacks of food. As he laid out the packages and white pasteboard cartons he said: "I'd be willing to bet we're the only people here. I didn't see any other cars; it's possible *all* the other cabins are empty."

"Don't say that," Marsha said apprehensively. "It's so morbid; I saw lights in some of them, I think."

"Ghosts," Hadley pronounced.

"Stop it!" Marsha paced tautly around the room, long-legged, lithe. "Do you have your cigarettes? I left mine in the car."

Hadley tossed her his pack. Carefully, he pulled the lid from a pasteboard carton. It contained ice-cold grapefruit juice; it was the only kind of juice he had been able to find. Gratefully, he gulped it down. Presently Marsha seated herself and daintily unwrapped a chicken-salad sandwich.

"I wish we had something hot," she murmured. "To cheer me up." Eyes large and dark she said: "I'm lonely. All you do is just sit—drinking that damn juice." Plaintively, she went on: "I wish you'd pay some attention to me."

"I will," Hadley said soberly.

He finished his juice and opened his milk shake. Sipping it, he began gnawing placidly on his ham and cheese sandwich. Marsha nibbled unhappily on the potato chips the girl had scooped into the bottom of the sacks.

"There's a pay phone up at the office," Hadley said.

"Who do you want to call?"

"My wife."

"Oh," Marsha said, her cheeks coloring. "Well, maybe you ought to . . ." She glanced up bravely. "What are you going to tell her?"

"It's Friday night; I usually disappear Friday nights. For my regular weekly binge."

"Doesn't she mind?"

"She minds," Hadley said, "but she's not surprised." He got up and went over to the window. Rolling up the shade he sat staring out at the empty darkness. The idea of going back seemed vague and unreal; already the image of his wife had begun to recede. It always did when he wasn't actually with her. Sometimes he had trouble remembering what she looked like. . . . In the first months of their marriage he had been terrified that someday he would meet her on the street and not recognize her.

"I would have gone to bed with you," he said aloud to Marsha, "even though I'm married—even though I've got a son. But you wouldn't go to bed with me."

"No," Marsha said tightly. "I couldn't."

"You almost did." He grinned ironically. "If I had taken off my shoes, you would have."

Marsha's thin fingers tore apart her chicken-salad sandwich. "Maybe. I don't know now. I wanted to."

"Let's face it," Hadley said. "We're both the same . . . neither of us has a trace of loyalty in us. You'd betray Beckheim; I'd betray my wife. We're doing it now."

"I don't consider that I'm betraying Ted. I left him; he knows we're finished."

"You betrayed him when you first showed up at the store that day. And I betrayed Ellen a long time ago. Maybe that's what's wrong with us. . . . Maybe that's why we can't find roots anywhere. We've cut our roots by our lack of loyalty. Who are you loyal to? Anybody?"

Marsha didn't answer.

"I'm not loyal to anybody," Hadley said. "It never occurred to me to be loyal to a person—only to an abstract ideal. I never had any loyalty to my boss, or my wife. I betrayed my friends—that was the worst of all. Everybody . . . my country, the society into which I was born. And then I wonder why I can't find something to believe in. I wonder why I can't trust anybody. I search for somebody I can put my faith in . . . but I'm without loyalty. I don't even know what it *means* to be loyal. Yes, something's wrong . . . and the fault is in me."

Marsha said: "But we're rebels, Stuart. We're trying to bring in a different world."

"We're not rebels—*we're traitors*."

There was silence.

"And," Hadley finished, pulling down the window shade, "we're not even loyal to each other. Do you trust me? I sure as hell don't trust you; I know you'll run out on me the same way you ran out on Beckheim when it suited your whim. We're both worthless to the core."

"Don't say that," Marsha protested. Jerkily, she reached toward him. "Here, have some of my chicken-salad sandwich; I can't finish it."

Hadley bellowed with laughter. "All right," he said. "Maybe that'll change things. I'll celebrate my understanding of myself. If we had something to drink we could make it a real occasion."

Giving him the sandwich, Marsha said: "I'm going out to the car; I'll be right back." She opened the door and quickly disappeared outside into the darkness. He could hear her crunching rapidly across the gravel, opening up the car, and rummaging inside it.

A moment later she returned with a fifth of Haig and Haig. Closing the door after her she held the bottle up breathlessly, her cheeks flushed, out of breath and panting. "Okay?" she gasped.

"Okay," Hadley said, taking the bottle from her. The woman's hands were icy; the bottle itself was moist with night mists. "You better go over and stand in front of the heater," he told her. "I'll pour."

He emptied the remains of the milk shakes into the bowl in the bathroom, washed out the pasteboard cartons, and tilted the whiskey into them. Marsha was sitting in a little heap on the couch when he returned, her eyes wide, hands pressed together, face drooping and sad.

"What's the matter?" Hadley asked.

"I—didn't think it would be this way." She smiled forlornly up at him, her lips twisting. "I was coming back to you; everything was going to be wonderful. The two of us . . . you know." She accepted her cup. "Thank you."

"Haven't you felt that way each time?" Hadley asked relentlessly. "Whenever you pick up a new one, don't you hope it'll be *the* one?"

Marsha huddled together and gazed miserably down at the floor. Mutely, she shook her head.

"I know I always do," Hadley continued inexorably. He sipped the whiskey and stood watching her. In him there was almost no feeling for the woman; in a kind of detached way he enjoyed what he was doing. "I guess I'll keep on," he said, "until I get too old to hope."

The woman didn't move.

"Drink your whiskey," Hadley said.

Dutifully, like an abandoned child, she lifted her cup and drank.

"Fine," Hadley said, satisfied. He drank more himself; the whiskey went right to the bottom of his stomach and settled there, a hard ball that made him ill. It was going to be that kind of drinking: nausea and irritability. No escape for him; as he drank, his brain became even more clean, his thoughts cold and hard-etched. The room took on a metallic, brilliant cast; the slight numbness in his arms and forehead only made him feel more remote and detached, as if neither himself nor the woman sitting on the couch were real. As if the room itself were imitation and artificial.

"Drink," he said again, harshly.

For an instant the woman sat gripping the bulky pasteboard cup. Then wretchedly, convulsively, her fingers clenched around it; the cardboard crumpled and gave; dark rivulets of whiskey oozed through her fingers and onto the carpet. A pool of liquid, like animal urine, formed at her feet. Her head fell forward; she slid limply down, in a loose heap.

Hadley set down his cup and knelt beside her. "I'm sorry," he said. But still he felt nothing at all; the inside of him was frigid as iron. Putting his hand out he brushed her dark auburn hair back from her eyes. "I don't mean it. I'm tired."

She nodded.

"And it's this damn stuff." He stood up, grabbed the cup of whiskey, carried it to the door, and tossed it outside. The cup splattered against the steps; he slammed the door and turned back to Marsha.

"I'm okay," she said. "Will you get me my purse? I put it on the dresser."

He found her purse and handed it to her. Marsha wiped her eyes, blew her nose, and sat clutching her handkerchief.

"Do you want to go back?" Hadley asked her.

"Do you?"

It was a good question. But he had already thought out his answer; he had known how he felt before he left the store. "No," he said. "I'm not going back. I'm going through with this."

"Me, too," she whispered. She got unsteadily to her feet and turned toward the bathroom. "Excuse me. I'll be right out. Please."

He let her go, and she closed the door after her.

When she came out she was smiling. She had washed her face and put on a little makeup. But her eyes were swollen and red; her lips trembled as she approached him. "I guess I don't look very appealing," she said pathetically.

"You look good enough," Hadley answered noncommittally. She had brushed her hair and put on some kind of scent; cologne, probably. Or perfumed deodorant. He didn't especially care; to him, the woman was an empty, depersonalized shape without particular attraction. He was conscious of the core of resentment he had carried as long as he could recall; beyond that there was not much else. And the resentment itself was not something he completely understood, or controlled. . . . It did not seem really to be his sole property.

Wistfully, Marsha said: "Would you do something for me? As a sort of present?"

"What is it?"

"I wish you'd kiss me first."

Hadley smiled. "You'll do. Bring your lunch pail."

"What does that mean?"

"An Army phrase. It means—" He put his hands on her thin shoulders. "That's difficult to say. In this case it means that you make me feel a little ashamed."

Marsha uptilted her face, and he kissed her briefly on the mouth. Her lips were cold and moist, and faintly sticky. In a moment her arms closed around his neck; she pulled him down against her hungrily. Without her pose of cynicism, without the haughty, erudite manner she had first met him with, the woman was frail and slight; he no longer felt any of the awe he had once felt. For an interval he allowed her eager hands to dig into his hair and scalp; then he broke away and turned his back.

"Not the couch," he decided. "There's a little sort of bed that slides out; it's more comfortable."

"All right," she said hopelessly.

They slid the bed out from the inner workings of the couch. In the dresser Marsha found sheets and blankets. Carefully, intently, she made the bed; the sheets were crisp and starched and perfectly white.

As she straightened up, Hadley snapped off the lamp. The room dropped into darkness, except for the gleam from the bathroom light filtering past the half-opened door. "Is the front door locked?" he asked her.

"You—think it would be a good idea?"

"I think so," he said, going over to turn the bolt. "This time, at least."

When he turned back, Marsha was sitting on the edge of the bed, her eyes on him, hands gripped together. Waiting and watching, she half rose as he came back.

Hadley removed his tie clasp and loosened his necktie. "Let's go," he said. "Take your clothes off."

Her fingers plucked helplessly at the zipper of her skirt. "I—," she began, and broke off.

Ignoring her, Hadley removed his tie and then his shirt. He laid them over the arm of a chair and sat down to untie his shoes. Standing by the bed, Marsha slowly pulled her blouse up over her head. Shaking herself out of it she dropped it on the dresser and started with her skirt. Piece by piece, the two of them removed their clothing. Neither of them said anything. Neither of them looked at the other; when Hadley finished undressing he found the woman standing naked and pitiful by the bed, her thin body gleaming pale white in the half darkness of the room.

"Could—I have a cigarette first?" she begged.

"No." He took hold of her and moved her toward the bed; she stumbled and sank down, groping for something to hold on to. "Come on; let's not stall around."

Marsha pushed the blankets aside with her body; she slid to the far side, against the wall, and he got in beside her. For a moment he gazed impassively down at her; under his cold scrutiny the woman fearfully drew away, legs tight together, shoulders hunched, arms folded rigidly. Finally, when he didn't say anything, she blurted: "Stuart, for God's sake, please stop it. Please leave me alone!"

Methodically, he reached down and caressed her. Under his hand her flesh rippled and stirred; goose pimples flashed across her belly and loins. She gave a little moan and shrank away, jamming herself against the wall until he took hold of her and firmly pulled her back.

"It's too late to back out," he said. "You made the bed; now get ready to lay."

She shrieked shrilly as he pushed her legs apart and entered her; against his back her nails trembled and dug. With a brutal shove of his knee he pushed her hips back, arched her body down and her thighs high up, buttocks compressed until she panted with terror. Directly below him, her face twisted and lashed; eyes shut tight, lips drawn back until her white gums were visible, she choked and gasped, turned this way and that; perspiration rolled down her neck in large, icy drops. Hadley raised his chest as high above her as possible; gazing calmly down from a great distance he exactly carried out the intricate muscular spasms of sex, on and on, until finally the girl's clutching fingers against his back forced him to pull away from her.

He waited awhile, smoking and watching. Marsha lay breathing deeply, eyes still shut, the sheet pulled over her. Exhausted, frightened, she turned on her side and pulled her knees up against her stomach, a strange, impressive fetal posture that gave him something to think about while he sat. After a while he lit up a second cigarette and handed it to her. She took it with numb fingers and managed to get it between her lips. Presently she sat up a little, weak and drained, gazing at him mutely and pitifully holding the sheet up around her small, pointed breasts.

Without comprehension, she watched him stub out his cigarette, take hers from her, and stub that out, too. It wasn't until he again pushed her down and tossed the sheet aside that she realized it had only begun. Bitterly, furiously, she fought; she struck him on the chest, scratched his face, bit him, screamed and cursed and wailed, tried futilely to kick him away. Without emotion, his mind aloof and remote, Hadley separated her legs and once more forced his vast self into her protesting, despairing body. Into the fluttering cavity he poured all his hatred, all the misery, the resentment, that lay like a dank, stagnant pool deep inside him.

When he had finished with her he got up from the bed and covered her with the sheet and blankets. The night was bitterly cold; it was almost one thirty. Marsha lay in a shivering stupor, breathing harshly through her mouth, her body wet and slack, arms dangling limply at her sides. She stirred a little as he brushed her hair away from her face; a quiver moved through her and a trickle of saliva appeared at the corner of her mouth.

Silently, without turning on the light, Hadley put on his clothes. He was standing by the dresser, fixing his necktie and buttoning his cuffs, when the woman spoke.

"Stuart?" she whispered.

He came momentarily over. "What do you want?"

"I guess you're leaving."

"That's right."

"In the car?"

Hadley sat down to put on his shoes. "I'll leave you enough money to get back to town; it's on the dresser."

After an interval she managed to say: "Thanks."

Hadley put on his coat and examined himself in the bathroom mirror. His face was stark, expressionless. A harsh, cruel face, older than he remembered it. The soft, puffy flesh around his neck seemed gone; the cloudy blue of his eyes had faded to a bleak stonelike color, without trace of emotion.

Turning away from the mirror, he reentered the living room and stopped to bend over the prone form of the woman. Marsha dragged herself up a little on the bed and tried to make him out; she reached up hesitantly, started to speak, wanted to touch him.

"Stuart?" she said.

"What?"

For a moment she rested silently, leaning against the wall, watching him, trying to speak, struggling to find something to say. He could see it all in her face; he stood waiting dispassionately, prepared to hear anything she had to offer.

"Take—care of yourself," she said feebly.

"I will," he said. And very deliberately raised his arm. Instantly, animal-like, she rolled back down; with a faint moan she crawled to one side and scrabbled from the bed, covers clutching and dragging at her. As she crossed in front of him he measured the distance, calculated her swiftly moving body, the direction of her panic, and then smashed her slightly below the cheekbone, aiming at her faintly luminous teeth.

He could not see what became of her. In the darkness she sank back against the bed, plucking soundlessly at her face, turning on her side, thrashing and trying to creep away from the bed. He leaned over, located her head, and systematically battered her with his open hand. She snarled, a hoarse grunt of hatred and pain, and clawed viciously up at him.

"Crazy!" she spat saliva and blood. "You're a crazy *beast*!" She threw up her hands and shuddered away from him; her voice became aimless, a random jumble of terror. "Beast . . ." He followed after her.

When he was done he opened the door and stepped out into the frigid, silent night air. The woman on the bed didn't stir; she lay facedown, convulsively clutching the covers of the bed. The door closed after him, and cut off the sight.

It took five minutes to warm up the frozen motor of the Studebaker. He slammed it into low, turned it around, and drove vigorously out the gate, past the darkened office, onto the road beyond. There were no lights or cars in sight, no motion of any kind as he shifted into high and slammed down the gas pedal. The car roared up the hill and plunged down the far side; with a wrench of the wheel he turned left, passed the dark cluster of buildings, and hurtled onto the freeway. He made a wild, bucking plunge through a gap in the dividing strip, and came out on the far side.

When he reached Cedar Groves he turned off the freeway, into the town. The streets were dark and deserted. He reached his own apartment house without incident, parked his car with the motor still running, and hurried up the steps and down the corridor.

Ellen was asleep when he entered. Soundlessly, he passed through the bedroom to Pete's bassinet. With a jagged sweep he gathered up the baby along with his blankets: he carried the bundle back out, through the living room, and into the corridor.

A moment later he climbed back into the Studebaker. He carefully wrapped Pete in the wool blankets and placed him on the backseat. The baby stirred fretfully; a few dismal wails bubbled from between his wet lips. Hadley slammed the car door and started it forward. He turned the corner and headed for the downtown section.

At the first bar he pulled to a halt; he parked on a deserted side street, by the rear loading platform of a locked-up grocery store. Cautiously rolling up the windows and locking the doors, he left the car and strode down the sidewalk. His heels clicked loudly in the gloomy night silence; lettuce leaves, bits of boxes, and strewn debris littered the pavement. He turned the corner and plunged into the bar.

Hunched over at the counter, he got out his wallet and examined the contents. He had left a ten-dollar bill on the dresser for Marsha. . . . He wondered if she would grasp the intended irony. Only thirteen dollars remained in the wallet; it was nearing the end of the month and his paycheck was just about due.

"What'll it be?" asked the bartender, a stubbled gorilla of a man. The only other patrons were two hulking Negro laborers and a demure pimpish-looking youth in a black leather jacket, a bottle of beer before him, a toothpick between his lips.

"Scotch and water," Hadley said, pushing a dollar bill forward. "No ice."

Thirteen dollars wouldn't carry him far. Enough for this evening, perhaps; but it wouldn't last beyond that. And he could not possibly get his plan into motion tonight; he would have to wait until Saturday night.

Sooner or later he would have to stop at the store. He needed his paycheck. . . . The thought stuck in his mind, lodged there as he accepted his drink and gulped it down, methodically, systematically. The first of a series.

Jim Fergesson was busy sweeping out O'Neill's place when Jack White phoned to give him the news. It was ten o'clock Saturday morning; the August day was not yet hot. Cool, damp sunlight filtered down over the highway and parked cars and shopping people.

"Call his home," Fergesson said angrily. An ominous chill settled into his bones; it stayed there. "He probably overslept. He was working until past nine last night."

White's calm, almost pleased voice came back in his ears. "I called his home; he isn't there. He didn't come home after work last night. His wife's a mess; she doesn't know what she's saying. Something about the kid being gone. Apparently Hadley sneaked in late last night and took the baby with him on his binge."

Fergesson hung up and dialed Hadley's number. A moment later he was talking to Ellen.

"Where is he?" Fergesson demanded. "He didn't come to work, and this is Saturday."

"He's not here," Ellen answered bleakly. Her voice wavered and receded, then returned, disciplined but vacant. "He never came home except to pick up Pete. I was asleep; it must have been in the middle of the night. I woke up and the baby was gone."

"How do you know it was Stuart?" Fergesson demanded suspiciously.

"His key was still in the door . . . I found it standing wide open." Her voice gained momentary strength. "If I had any sense I'd leave him. But I'm not going to. It isn't his fault; it's your fault and everybody else's. He's only trying to live. He just wants his life."

"If he doesn't show up sometime today," Fergesson said, "he's finished. I'm not going to have him around the store. Tell him that."

She flared up wildly. "You and your damn store. And you wonder why he's the way he is. He's not a person to you—you never cared about him. Maybe he's dead; maybe they're both dead."

Gripping the phone Fergesson said: "He's sleeping it off in some jail, more likely. Being manager was a little too much for him. I'll give him until noon and that's it." He slammed down the receiver and stalked away, trembling with rage.

It hadn't taken long: just a few days. If Hadley could have waited one more day for his binge . . . Shakily, Fergesson lit a cigar and stood in the entrance of O'Neill Appliance gazing sightlessly out at the flow of traffic moving along the highway. Blind rage hung over him like a cloud. Just a few days. He reached for the phone and called Jack White at Modern.

"If he comes in, call me," Fergesson instructed. "Better yet, have *him* call me."

"All right," White said; he sounded harassed. In the distance the sound of people and TV sets was audible.

"Can you and Tampini hold it alone?"

"I suppose so."

"I'll see you tonight," Fergesson said. "You're playing with us, aren't you?"

"Sure," White said. "Whatever you say."

"I'm not calling off our game," Fergesson said grimly. "Not for anything Stumblebum does. I'll see you after dinner, at the regular time. I've got the chips here; they'll do."

"Are we going to play here?" White asked.

"We always do, don't we? Why should this time be any different?"

"I'll get the big display room cleaned up, then," White said. "Say, Tampini probably wants to play."

"Fine," Fergesson said. "Let's see what he's like; I can tell a lot about a man by the kind of poker he plays." He hung up the phone and returned to his work.

By noon Hadley had not come in. At two o'clock Jack White showed up at O'Neill's in the store truck, on his way back from a delivery. He and Fergesson talked briefly out on the sidewalk.

"Maybe the bastard's dead," White said, unperturbed. "His wife calls every fifteen minutes. She called the police, the jail, the hospitals, everything she could think of. Friends, relatives, bars—the whole works."

"Any sign of him?"

"None at all."

Fergesson kicked a bit of trash from the sidewalk into the gutter. "He's finished. If he comes in send him around here and I'll pay him off. I don't want to have anything more to do with him."

"You're being a little rough," White observed.

"It's my business. You think a man who'd do this could manage a store?"

White shrugged indifferently. "He's had a lot on his mind. This whole stuff, the sudden load—" He broke off and started up the truck. "But do what you want; you're the boss."

By four o'clock Hadley had not appeared and there was no reason to think he would. Fergesson's tension mounted; by five thirty he was too upset to work. Ignoring customers, he phoned Modern and got hold of Joe Tampini; White was too busy to come to the phone.

"Any sign of him?" Fergesson demanded.

"No sir," Tampini said dutifully.

"His wife still calling?"

"Yes sir. All the time."

"All right," Fergesson said, stonily resigned. "He's not coming in. It's too late."

He hung up the phone and didn't call again. There was no point to it; the inevitable had happened.

That evening he gulped down a hurried dinner, grabbed his blue serge coat, waved good-bye to his stricken wife, and drove swiftly down the darkening street to Modern TV Sales and Service. He ignored the people roaming everywhere and concentrated on parking his car. From the car he lugged a heavy card table, four decks of cards, and two huge packages of chips. Balancing everything against his knee he unlocked the front door of the shop and disappeared inside.

It was seven thirty. The store had been shut an hour and a half. The interior was dim and silent as he quickly made his way downstairs to the storeroom where all the immense cardboard cartons of television sets were carefully stacked on each other. He was starting to set up the card table when the first insistent rap sounded on the door and he had to hurry back upstairs.

"Hi," Ed Johnson puffed. "Who's here?"

"Just me, so far. Stay up top and let the rest in."

"Need any help with the chairs?"

Fergesson accepted the case of beer from Johnson and took off with it. "Stay up here and watch; send them down as they come. The key's in the lock."

"Who the hell are all those people wandering around out there?" Johnson said. "The streets are full of them."

"Some kind of nut cultists," Louis Garfinkel said, pushing into the store. "Los Angeles type. There's a lecture going on or something."

"Niggers," Henry R. Porter said as Johnson admitted him to the store. "A nigger revival cult. I saw the posters; some big buck nigger."

"What the hell does it?" Garfinkel asked as they clustered leisurely around the door. "Is it the climate down there?"

"My theory," Johnson said, "is that it's the smog. The smog is from factories; it's man-made and it's full of metallic wastes. The metallic wastes get in their brains by being snuffed up through the nasal passages, and that's why they're so nutty."

"I would say," Garfinkel disagreed, "that the smog works its way up their ass."

Jack White arrived, wiping the remains of his hurriedly gulped meal, served across the counter to him at the Golden Bear Cafeteria. A few minutes later Joe Tampini came trailing shyly along; this was the first time he had been permitted to play in the monthly poker game.

At the top of the stairs Fergesson and White met briefly. "Any sign of him?" Fergesson murmured.

"I was going to ask you," White said. "No, nothing."

"The damn fool," Fergesson said bitterly. "He had everything in the world, and he tossed it away."

Everybody having come, the front door was locked and they all trooped expectantly downstairs into the basement. Fergesson had busily set up things; everything was ready to go. Rubbing his hands together and frowning he paced around until they were all seated. Then he took his own place at the head of the table and grabbed up a deck of cards. He riffled them, shuffled them, passed them around for cutting, then remembered to appoint a banker.

"You're banker this time," he said to Jack White. The flat stained notebook was passed to White, who began making entries under the various names. Chips were distributed. The men unfastened their belts, accepted initial beers, belched happily, rubbed their hands and wrists, exchanged insults, grinned, and turned abruptly ruthless as the first hand was dealt.

"Naturally," Fergesson muttered tensely, "this is draw. Jacks or better to open. Christ, get the antes in. Come on, White. One from you."

"Anything wild?" Johnson asked, already tightly absorbed in his hand.

"Nothing this time."

"Give me three," Garfinkel said.

"We bet first, you horse's ass. Hold your damn water."

"Up yours."

"Cut the farting and bid," Porter grumbled.

The game took its usual course for half an hour. Down in the cellar of the television shop, below street level, surrounded by solid concrete and steel walls, the six men played tensely and vigorously. Around eight fifteen they paused and passed one by one into the next room to relieve themselves at the filth-stained toilet.

Johnson lit a fresh cigar and leaned back in his chair peacefully. "Good game," he said to Fergesson, who was gloomily contemplating his dwindling stack of chips. "Right?"

"I'm losing heavy tonight."

"Christ, you'll get it back Monday. Sell an extra TV set."

Fergesson got up and stretched. He took off his tie and crammed it in his pocket. After a moment he removed his vest and unbuttoned the top buttons of his shirt.

While he was moving his chair around to make himself more comfortable there was a dull distant thud that vibrated through the room. After a time it came again . . . louder.

"What's that?" White demanded, coming out of the lavatory with his trousers still unzipped.

"Those marching morons—heading for that Society hall. That bunch of nuts going to the lecture." Garfinkel seated himself and swept up a deck of cards. "Hot dog, I'm really greased tonight! Look at those stacks." He indicated his twin heaps of chips. "Bigger than Marilyn Monroe's tits."

"Where'd you get that picture in the crapper?" Porter asked Fergesson. "Boy, I'd like to throw one into that babe."

"Ever seen her in a movie? She sure as hell can't act worth a damn."

"Act, hell. She knows which side of bed she's buttered on. Guess how that snatch got to the top of the ladder."

"Man, that's a barrel of honey waiting to be opened!"

Spirited talk continued, but Fergesson wasn't listening. He was hearing something else, the continual shuffling tramp of feet above him, the disturbing roll and boom.

"It gets under my skin," he muttered as he finally picked up the deck and went through the automatic motions of shuffling. "Goddamn it, I can't play with all of them up there!"

"They're going inside," Johnson pointed out. "The meeting's beginning."

"How do you happen to know?" Fergesson accused.

Johnson colored. "Well, my wife's going."

Calmly counting his pile of chips, Jack V. White said: "I wouldn't be surprised if that's where Stumblebum is. He went to the last one, I know."

The deck of cards almost dropped from Fergesson's hands; he grabbed it and began cutting slowly, wrathfully. "That's right. I remember. Ellen told me."

"Sure," White said easily. "Stumblebum's one of the faithful. Some dame's been coming in the store after him, one of the Society's little ladies."

"A coon?" Fergesson shouted.

"A tall skinny gal. She left off some literature for him."

Memory came to Fergesson. "A magazine . . . I saw it." He shook his head, dazed and disconcerted. "It's terrible; I can't believe it. But I should have known . . . I saw the goddamn thing myself. He was standing there reading it, on my time." Convulsively, Fergesson slammed down the deck in front of shy, silent Joe Tampini. "Deal!" he shouted, his voice hoarse. "For God's sake, let's get going!"

In the gloomy darkness of the car, Stuart Hadley sat holding a wad of blankets and baby clothing in his lap. Beside him, Pete wailed and twisted; his tiny arms waved futilely as he groped for something, grasped the cold empty air that swirled through the car from the parking lot outside.

Presently it entered Hadley's mind that he had been in the process of changing the baby's clothing. He sorted through the soggy, contaminated heap of garments; everything had been soiled at least once. Puzzled, he smoothed them out and started over again, hoping to find something clean, something he could use. Beside him on the seat, Pete shivered and wailed.

In the end, Hadley opened the luggage compartment of the car and rummaged inside. He found a crumpled, greasy automobile blanket and pulled it up front with him. The blanket came apart easily; soon he had a pile of ragged cloth, not clean but at least usable. He wrapped Pete up in one of the squares, closed the giant safety pin, and then wound the blankets around him. The blankets smelled sourly of urine; Pete gazed up at him wretchedly, sick and hungry and helpless.

Getting from the car, Hadley crossed the dark parking lot to the garbage can of a cheap café. He dropped the bundle of contaminated garments into the can and crunched back to the car. For a time he stood undecided; the baby dozed fitfully, breathing through his mouth, his round face pulled together into a tight frown. He should be fed, obviously. And soon.

Making sure the air vents were open, Hadley rolled up the windows of the car and locked the doors. He left the parking lot and stepped up onto the deserted sidewalk. It was becoming evening; the sun was setting. He began to walk, hands shoved deep in his pockets.

When he came to a little square of park among the hulking warehouses and factories, he stopped and threw himself down on a bench, to rest and ponder.

His plan was firm, clear, and completely final. It had emerged as he drove Marsha along the freeway; into his mind the plan had come full-grown, completely developed, as if it had always existed. It was the only solution; all that remained was to put it into effect.

He could not go back to Beckheim because he was not good enough. For him it was too late. He was worthless; he couldn't be saved. But it was not too late for his son. The plan was as simple as that. Beckheim would take Pete and raise him and Pete would be saved; he would become what Hadley had not become, he would do and be all the things Hadley had not done and not been, reach the things he had failed to reach. For Hadley, everything was over; for his son the world was just beginning.

For an infinite period Hadley sat watching the evening sun lower itself into the hazy rim of the Bay. It wasn't until the streetlights came on and a chill wind whipped through his trouser legs that he got stiffly to his feet and began to walk.

His clothes were rumpled and dirty from having slept all night in the car. He needed a shave; his chin was an unhealthy gray-blue. As he walked he was conscious of his uneven gait; his bones ached and he had trouble seeing.

He came to a drugstore, entered, and selected a candy bar from the front rack. In his coat pocket he found a dime. . . . That was all he had left—a few bits of change in his pockets.

Eating the Hershey's bar, Stuart Hadley wandered through town, oblivious of the strolling Saturday evening crowds. Gradually he became aware that a different group of people milled around him. He had reached the center of town; he was moving among the Watchmen of Jesus, the faithful on their way to the Society hall. Eagerly, he joined them.

The flow of people carried him along, and presently he found himself facing the familiar squat yellow structure, with its glowing lights and fluttering cloth signs streaming everywhere. He held back for a while and then allowed the surge of murmuring men and women to carry him up the steps and into the barren foyer. The crowd divided and was processed into the hall itself.

At the inner door, Hadley was stopped by a towering Negro wearing a shiny black suit and an armband. "Your card, sir," the Negro repeated, his hand out. "Your membership card, sir. This is for members of the Watchmen of Jesus Society, sir."

"What?" Hadley said stupidly.

One massive hand was clapped over his arm; he was stopped dead in his tracks. "This is not an open lecture, sir," the Negro repeated, firmly and insistently. Behind Hadley people pushed impatiently, wanting to get past and find seats: there weren't many left. "Do you have a card, sir? You have to have either a white or a blue card, sir."

Stunned, Hadley turned and shoved his way out again, down the steps and onto the sidewalk. The murmuring voices faded away as the people around him filed up the steps and into the hall. Those who were turned back gradually dispersed; in a short while Hadley was alone.

He sat down on a square metal trash box and waited. For a time he considered going back for the car; he had parked in a twenty-four-hour lot and in a few hours somebody might start checking around. Vaguely, he wondered if it was time to feed Pete again. He had lost track of time completely; had he been going to feed him, or had he already fed him? Searching his pockets he brought out twenty-three cents in change. Enough for a quart of milk. But that wouldn't do. And he needed to buy clean diapers for him; cereal, diapers, another blanket . . . Hadley's mind blurred off in a chaotic swirl, and he gave up trying to think. Instead, he sat blankly waiting.

The next thing he knew, the lecture was over. People swarmed everywhere; he was surrounded by people. The night was colder; it was much later. He got awkwardly to his feet and began to push among them; in his mind there was nothing but the need of getting into the hall, an insistent desire to make his way past the door to Theodore Beckheim. He knew that if he could reach him, the great black man would accept Pete; of that Hadley was certain. If he could once get to Beckheim everything would be all right. The hall, of course, was empty; the crowd had left it. He stood gazing in as people edged past him, bemused by the vacant stage and podium on which Beckheim had certainly just now stood.

"Where's Beckheim?" he said to a large middle-aged woman passing with an armload of pamphlets.

She shook her head. "I really don't know."

Hadley hurried urgently back down the steps; suddenly he was sure that Beckheim had already left. He reached the sidewalk and peered everywhere, searching desperately, moving this way and that, unconscious of the dense crowd around him.

At the curb waited a long oyster-yellow Chrysler four-door sedan. As soon as he saw it he knew it was Beckheim's: excitement stirred him and he raced toward it. A knot of people, white and Negro, was making its way toward the car; one of the doors was opened, and an elderly woman in a heavy fur coat climbed in.

Behind the woman came Beckheim.

People pushed and shoved around Hadley, but he didn't notice; hunching his shoulders he forced his way among them, toward the curb and the long yellow Chrysler. Terror filled him; the motor was on and the car was going to start. A white man got behind the wheel; he honked the horn and waved the people from the street, out of the way. The headlights came on in a blinding clap of billiance; Hadley winced, ducked his head, and shouldered his way forward.

A figure directly in front of him refused to move. Hands clutched at him; in his ear shrill voices screamed and yelled. He shook the hands away; tearing himself loose he shoved against the figure. It refused to budge.

"Stuart!" it shrilled. It was Laura Gold. Her face wild, hair disheveled, she blocked his way, arms raised, lumpy body planted against him. "Stuart, what are you *doing* here? Ellen's looking everywhere for you—we *knew* we'd find you here!"

From behind Laura, Dave Gold came scurrying. He grabbed hold of Hadley's coat and dragged him away from the curb, back toward the building, out of the conglomeration of people clustered around the Chrysler. "Where the hell have you been?" he was saying. "Hadley, you're out of your mind—what's wrong with you? Where's the baby—is he all right? What the hell are you doing?"

Hadley tore away. "Let go of me," he said thickly.

Dave Gold kept tugging impatiently at him. People were yelling and stepping on each other; they were shoving angrily. Cars had begun to start up on all sides. Horns honked as they drove through the throngs that milled out into the street. The darkness was slashed violently by shafts of headlights. Over the murmur and shouting rumbled the motors and the swish of tires.

"What's the matter with you?" Dave Gold shouted at Hadley. "You damn fool—stop acting this way!"

Laura was trembling with apprehension. "Let go of him," she chattered, glassy-eyed. "Be careful, Dave. Something's going to happen."

"Shut up," Gold grunted at her. "What's eating you, Hadley? Are you coming with us or not?" He yanked at Hadley's sleeve. "Let's get where we can breathe. I want to talk to you."

"Get your kike hands off me," Hadley said, in a voice not his own.

Gold's face dissolved and then slowly re-formed. "Are you under the spell of that shithead?" he said.

254 II PHILIP K. DICK

Hadley hit him blindly. Laura screamed as Gold's glasses flew off and he stumbled backward, arms flailing. "Get out of here, Dave!" she shrieked.

Gold fell, rolled, then scrambled up. He charged bull-like directly at Hadley, head down. His wiry body smashed into Hadley and for an interval the two of them struggled together. Gold's hot, slobbering breath panted in Hadley's face; he struck out wildly at whatever he could reach. Hadley was choked, buried under the struggling infuriated body. He kicked, rolled away, fought desperately. He saw nothing. There were only billowing shapes, massed shadows around him. . . . His breath ached in his throat and lungs.

Hands plucked. Somewhere far off sirens wailed. Hadley stumbled back and was dragged down to the moist pavement. His head struck something hard; sparks flew as from an anvil. A numbing *clang* echoed and reechoed through his mind; for a limitless period blackness dropped over him and he was only dimly aware of remote shapes and sensations. A foot kicked him; an arm punched into his face. He caught at it, managed to get halfway up. Blinded, blood running down his cheeks, his hands cut and damaged, he staggered away, hit against something, and then broke through the circle of forms.

After that came a vague period of running and stopping to gasp for breath and listen. There were no more people around him. Dark streets, stars overhead. Silent houses and stores. A few cars. He sat down on a curb and got out his handkerchief to wipe the blood from his smashed nose.

He was a mess. His head still rang, and his right side ached violently. A broken rib, probably.

He came to a filling station and got himself into the men's room. Taking off his coat he washed his face in the shiny bowl. He blotted at his hands and arms with paper towels, then sat down on one of the toilets to rest and collect himself.

When he had regained sufficient energy he dried his face and pushed his damp hair back. He crawled into his dirty, torn coat, smoothed down his shirt as much as possible, and left the men's room.

Cold night air knifed at him as he made his way along Freemont Avenue. Ten minutes later he unlocked the front door of Modern TV Sales and Service and headed for the basement stairs.

The six men playing poker peered around in shocked amazement as Hadley appeared. Fergesson lowered his hand of cards and got to his feet. "Where the hell have you been?" he demanded, taking in the sight of Hadley's ruined face and clothing.

Hadley held on tight to the doorjamb. "I want my money."

Fergesson pushed through the gray-fogged room up to Hadley. "Are you drunk?" He blanched as he saw blood leak from Hadley's demolished nose, down his jaw and onto his collar. "Good God, what happened?"

"Somebody must have rolled him," Jack White said softly. They all got up and came quietly over.

"Give me my money," Hadley repeated. He started back upstairs. "I earned it. It's mine."

"He means his check," Jack White said.

Fergesson followed Hadley up the stairs. "Look here, Hadley—you can't come in here like this. Get out of here and go home. If you have any sense you'll go sober up and stay out of trouble. I ought to fire you for not coming in today, but in view of what's happened to you I'm willing to give you—"

"Shut your fucking mouth," Hadley said, heading toward the cash register. "Get this thing open."

Fergesson blinked. For a moment emotion swept across his face, a tide of dismay and pain, as if he were going to weep. Then his face closed hard and mean, without feeling, an impassive wall. "You stupid lush," he said. "I'll give you one more chance to get out of this store."

"Fuck you." Hadley tore and punched at the cash register until it finally wheezed open. He pawed at the bills.

Fergesson grabbed the calendar and located the date. Fingers flying, he counted out a hundred dollars, slammed in the register drawer, pushed Hadley away from it, and threw down the bills on the counter. "All right, Hadley; here's your money. I'm paying you for two weeks. You're fired. I'll mail your bottle of celery extract to your house."

Hadley took the money and stuffed it in his coat pocket. "Fuck you, Fergesson," he repeated, opening the front door and stepping out on the sidewalk. "And all your friends and relatives and your stores and all your TV sets and your poker game." The door slammed and he was gone.

A moment later he entered the neon-lit bar around the corner and threw himself down on a stool. "Scotch and water," he said as the bartender turned from dice shaking and came slowly over. "No ice."

"Sure, Stu," the bartender said. He began to fix the drink, eyeing Hadley nervously. "How's the kid? Everything all right?"

"Fine," Hadley said.

"You look kinda knocked around." The bartender served his drink and took a twenty-dollar bill from Hadley's crabbed fingers. "You sure you're okay? Your nose is bleeding bad."

"I'm okay."

The bartender rang up change and came slowly back with it. A couple of the patrons were gazing at Hadley with horrified curiosity. "You really got banged around," the bartender repeated. "What's the other guy look like?"

Hadley gulped down his drink and didn't answer. As the bartender moved off, Hadley dragged the rest of his money out and began arranging it in careful, even piles. Trying to assemble, on a microscopic scale, some fragments of his shattered plan.

It was dark. But not completely. Sound and motion all around him. He was moving. A great shape loomed up ahead; its blinding orbs bored into him and he ducked his head. The shape came nearer, then turned off to one side. A wave of sickening stench billowed around him. He began to choke; he floundered and twisted and spat.

Another beast loomed, studied him balefully with yellow, unwinking eyes, roared and boomed loudly, and then swept past him. Again he gasped and choked in the cloud of foul-smelling wind it had released from its great behind.

A hand pulled at him. He tugged away; Dave Gold was trying to hold on to him. The hand returned. Voices. Close and loud in his ear. Lights winked overhead, evenly spaced circles of yellow set in the darkness. The fumes were gone; but new shapes loomed in place of the old.

"The poor bastard," a voice said. A man's voice, close to him. He tried to make out the speaker, but he couldn't. He groped in the gloom; shapes flickered and winked around him. They dodged and shifted cunningly; they operated with incredible swiftness and intelligence. He moved a few steps, stumbled, and half fell.

"Look at him." A woman's voice.

"Would you, if you were a man?"

"No."

Hadley peered. Squinted. Circles of light, even-spaced above . . . stars at last in order, pattern and design. Darkness all around, black and thick. Dim shapes less dark that moved as he came near them. Keeping away from him. Cold air licked at his clothing; he shivered violently.

"Come here," he grunted, holding out his arms to catch a shape. But it retreated warily. It was like a game; he was within a circle, blindfolded, trying to catch someone. Anyone. To pass the blindfold on. So he wouldn't have to keep wearing it. He was tired of wearing it. All at once he couldn't stand wearing it any longer.

"Come here!" he shouted. His voice rolled off and was gone in echoing shadows. Dim metallic peals that vibrated and danced around him. He was shocked by the continuing racket; he set his teeth and tensed his body, but still the racket boomed. And still the shapes kept their distance.

"Look at him. Look at his clothes."

"You see very many of them?"

"Once in a while. Saturday night, especially."

"What'll happen to him?"

"Hard to say."

"You think maybe somebody should—"

"No. He'll be all right."

"He better get out of here." A new voice. Hard and ominous. Hadley stopped moving and became rigid. Fear shivered through him. He turned clumsily and began to hobble through the darkness. The circles of light passed obediently by overhead.

"Look at him go."

"The poor bastard."

"Maybe we better—"

"No. Let him go. His own fault. Look at his clothes. Look at him. Look."

The voices faded. Hadley ran on, blindly, his hands out. Suddenly he struck violently against something hard. A great clang and waves of brightness flashed over him. He slid to his knees, and his chin struck something hard and cold. Teeth shattered and hot blood spurted into his mouth; it dribbled down his chin as he lay gasping. He moved feebly; everything wheeled around him.

Dave Gold had hit him. He had to get up and hit back. Or was it Fergesson? Fergesson had hit him. There were shapes around him again. Maybe it was all of them. All of them hitting him at once. Taking a circle up, a ring on all sides.

"He fell."

"He bumped into this pole here."

"Maybe we better—"

"No. He'll be all right. Leave him alone. He'll be okay. It's his own fault."

Hadley groaned. He managed to sit up. With great effort he shook his head and pushed his hair back from his eyes. His hands hurt; his whole body ached. His mouth was bleeding. He spat out bits of teeth and saliva and blood. The darkness began to clear slowly; the spinning lights came to rest. His hands were cut and scratched; bits of ugly black gravel were embedded in the skin. When had it happened? Recently, or a long time ago . . . one or the other. And his clothes were torn and filthy.

He took a deep shuddering breath and concentrated. The curtain of darkness wavered, retreated, then abruptly lifted. He was in a bus station. A Greyhound bus station. It was late at night. He was outside, on the loading platform. A few buses, silent and empty, stood in their stalls. On the other side a few more were loading. Men and women stood in groups here and there. The platform was bleak. Almost deserted. Frigid night wind swept around him. Above, stark yellow lights set in the metal and concrete girders glared harshly down.

A handful of commuters stood nearby, watching him with dull interest. An elderly man with a rolled-up newspaper, in a faded blue business suit. A heavyset man, well dressed, vest and silk tie. A young woman in a heavy coat. A couple of sailors. A Negro workman. None of them moved as Hadley got painfully to his feet. He caught hold of an upright girder for support and hung on tight, his eyes shut, breathing deeply and choking down blood.

His head ached and pounded. He reeked; his clothing was mud-soaked and filthy. Nausea swept him. He was dizzy. He staggered a little and vomited on the pavement, over his shoes and the cuffs of his trousers.

A bus came rumbling in loaded with people, a great lit-up object that roared and thundered and flashed its immense headlights menacingly. Automatically, he moved back, away from the monster and into the shadows. And then he saw the illuminated slot above the windshield of the bus.

SAN FRANCISCO

Terror seized him. A numbing rush of panic that whipped and jerked him like a puppet on a wire. He was in the city. The terror increased until it blotted out everything; he was a speck tossing in an endless sea of fear. He choked, gasped, fought his way up, struggled to breathe, as the waves of terror lapped and rolled around him. At last he managed to push it down; he threw it back and emerged.

He had come up the coast to San Francisco. He was alone; he had left the car back in Cedar Groves with Pete in it. Time had passed, how much he didn't know. It was late—probably past midnight.

He crossed the loading platform and entered the waiting room. It was virtually deserted. Lights blazed down on the dismal benches, suitcase lockers, gum and cigarette machines, drinking fountains, discarded magazines. He located the ticket window and headed toward it.

Halfway there he stopped and got out his wallet.

Fifty dollars were left. Two twenties and a ten. He searched all his pockets. Ticket stub for the bus ride up the coast. Handkerchief, blood-soaked.

Five or six match folders, from Cedar Groves bars. One pocket sagged with silver. Quarters and fifty-cent pieces, dimes and nickels. With numb despair he counted it all out. The whole thing added up to fifty-three dollars and twenty-two cents. That was all he had left from the hundred. He had lost the rest—or spent it.

He approached the ticket window. "When's the next bus back to Cedar Groves?" he asked hoarsely.

"Thirty-five minutes."

Hadley bought a ticket and wandered miserably off. The waiting room was cold. He found a large wall clock and read it. One fifteen.

He knew, of course, why he had come to San Francisco. He was still looking for Theodore Beckheim, retracing his steps back into the past, trying to find the big black man the way he had found him before. But Beckheim was no longer at the apartment on Hayes. He had left Marsha; he would not be there.

Yet deep inside Hadley the yearning subrational need remained.

Again he searched his pockets; gazing with fascination at his moving hands he wondered what they were after. It was a long while before he understood: abruptly he stopped and stood limp and immobile, a wave of hopeless futility sweeping him.

He didn't know Marsha's address.

The phone book was no help. No Marsha Frazier was listed. of course; that wasn't her real name. She had kept the name Frazier, but it was not legal. God only knew what it really was. He gave up and wearily left the phone booth.

After that he paced wretchedly around the waiting room. He couldn't sit still; something kept him moving, an inner ache that made his arms and legs work in spite of his overpowering fatigue. He wanted to do something— but what? What was there left?

Finally he went across the street to an all-night café and ordered coffee. He sat hunched over at the counter, sipping the scalding coffee and rubbing his damaged mouth. His mind was dull. Now, no thoughts came. He was conscious only of his broken teeth, his ruined nose and clothing, his overwhelming sickness and fatigue and misery; nothing else.

Two bus drivers came in and sat down a few seats from him. Young men, big and good-looking. They glanced at him with curiosity, faintly critical and contemptuous. "You get in a fight, buddy?" one of them asked.

Hadley shook his head. "No."

"Celebrating?"

Hadley turned away without answering. They laughed and ordered hotcakes and ham. The café was warm and brightly lit. It smelled of coffee and frying ham. The jukebox began to play over in the corner; one of the bus drivers had put a nickel in it. Glenn Miller's "Anvil Chorus." The sound blared out and mixed with the genial murmur of voices, the bus driver's and the waitress' as she stood in the back, arms folded, talking to the fry cook as he fried the ham.

It was like Jack's Steakhouse and his own kitchen all mixed together. Suddenly Hadley got to his feet and left. He wandered rapidly up the sidewalk, hands in his pockets. The cold night San Francisco wind whipped at him. He hunched over and half shut his eyes, face turned down. He crossed Mission and headed toward Market Street, his mind blank, walking mechanically forward.

Presently he reached Market Street. Only a few cars moved along. Here and there an occasional bus. The night was clear. The great street stretched out for miles, disappearing finally in a tangle of glowing signs and street-lights. On all sides of him were theaters, huge neon signs winking and blinking and buzzing. Men and women hurried past him and through the squares of blinding white in front of each theater. Cafés, parked cars, closed-up bookstores, clothing stores, vast drugstores, all shut for the night. Only the theaters were still open. He avoided the glare of their signs and crossed Market Street to the far side. He plunged into the darkness of a side street.

For an endless period he roamed aimlessly, along silent, deserted streets, past huge office buildings. No lights showed. Only the darkness. On and on he walked. An occasional gas station glowed, then faded behind him. His heels rang in the stillness. Finally he came to Kearny, hesitated, then turned to his left.

He entered the first bar he reached. A small place, off to one side.

THE BRASS RAIL

He pushed his way through a laughing, chattering horde of young men that blocked the doorway, and over to the bar. The bar was made of old wood. Wood tables were scattered around. Sawdust on the floor. An old-fashioned upright piano in the corner. On the black-paneled walls were modern prints, and a few modern originals. The place was dim and opaque; he slumped over on the stool and automatically got out his silver.

"What'll it be?" the bartender asked, a small mean-looking man with close-cropped blond hair. His voice was thin and raspy.

Hadley studied the ancient wood paneling; he rubbed his forehead and muttered, "Bourbon and water."

The bartender went to get it. Up and down the bar were young men, well dressed, most of them in sweaters and slacks. A few were in jeans and dark turtlenecked sweaters. They laughed and chatted; their excited voices rose in a high-pitched concord all around him. A great swarm of bees. It was as bad as the Health Food Store. He tried to ignore them as he counted out silver for his bourbon.

The young man on his right was gazing at him with interest. A slender youth in a sports coat, sweater, and silk tie. Gray slacks. Two-tone shoes. Through a haze of cigarette smoke Hadley made out two intense brown eyes, fixed on him intently, a half-smiling mouth.

"Did you hurt yourself?" the youth inquired politely, in a lilting tenor.

Hadley nodded dully.

"Shouldn't you put something on it?" The youth's hand flew to his cheek. "Good heavens, you're *bleeding*!"

"What's the matter?" Three or four more of them appeared and crowded anxiously around Hadley. "Is he hurt?"

"Did he fall down?"

"Did he hurt himself?"

A whole group of them pressed around Hadley. Inquiring hands fluttered at his face and neck like moths. "Oh, the poor thing!"

"Look at him!"

"Oh, the dear!"

"Somebody hurt him. Look at his clothing! Somebody has just done *awful* things to him."

The murmuring voices, the warm presences, the clouds of pale, anxious hands that billowed and rubbed against him, made Hadley drowsy. Confused, he pushed at them. "Get going," he muttered. "Goddamn fairies." But the hands went on fluttering, and the shapes remained. He tried again feebly, then sank down against the bar in weary despair. Everything, the sights, the sounds, blurred and ebbed. He closed his eyes and rested his head gratefully. The warmth of the place made him sleepy.

"Don't die!" voices whispered anxiously.

"Look at him, he's dying!"

"No, he's just sleeping. Poor little sweet, he's all tired out."

"We'll have to take care of him."

"Has he got a place to go?"

Warm fragrant breath blew against his ear. A voice sang: "Where do you live, sweet?"

Hadley grunted.

"Look in his wallet." Hands felt at his jacket; his wallet was slid cunningly out and examined. He could hear them exclaim and whisper among themselves.

"He lives far from here."

"He's lost."

"The poor sweet got lost. Here's his bus ticket."

"But it's too late. He can't go back now—it's been too long. He'll have to stay here."

An intense, protracted conference followed. Hadley dozed. Arguments, angry words, a sudden flurry of spitting and slapping. He went on sleeping; it all came from a vast distance. Finally a decision was reached.

"I'll take him with me."

"You bitch, you're always favored."

"Doesn't she always get the breaks?"

A gentle, insistent hand touched Hadley on the neck. "Come on, sweet. Time to go. The Rail is closing."

Other hands helped rouse him. "Go along with her. She'll take care of you."

"Come along, sweet."

Hadley opened his eyes. A tiny brown-haired youth stood close to him, waiting excitedly, eyes bright, lips twitching avidly. "Come with me, sweet. I'm going to take care of you."

"And how," voices agreed.

Hadley slid from the stool unsteadily. Hands guided him; the tiny brown-haired boy had firm hold of his arm. He was led from the bar, among the hordes of well-dressed youths. At the door he abruptly halted.

"No," he said.

A flurry of excitement and dismay. "What is it?"

"Don't be afraid," others put in quickly. "Tommy'll take care of you. He'll feed you and make you well."

"Yes, he'll make you."

"He'll put you to bed and take good care of you."

"He'll put you to bed and you can eat candies and sleep and grow fat and you won't have to do anything ever again."

"No," Hadley repeated. "Get your goddamn kike hands off me."

"What's he saying?"

"What's the sweet saying?"

Hadley stood his ground dully. Did he hear right? Were they really saying what he heard? He shook his head, but it didn't clear. Everything was misty and uncertain. The slender, pretty shapes flickered and wavered. The faces, the walls of the bar, all receded and dimmed, then came reluctantly back. He tried to lock them into hardness, but they stayed agonizingly insubstantial. Even the floor under him was soft, like jelly. It flowed and dissolved.

"Get away," he grunted, flinging himself around and pulling his arms loose. "Let go of me!"

His violence terrified them. They retreated in fluttering, squawking flight to form a safe circle a few feet away. Eyes gleaming, they waited watchfully. Voices whispered. Pale hands flitted and were never still.

"Don't let him go," voices said. The youth named Tommy was shoved forward. "Don't let him get away from you. He's cute. Look at his sweet face. Look at his blond hair. His little mouth. Look at his blue eyes. Tommy, he'll get away! Your lover's going to get away!"

"He's not pretty," other voices contradicted. "He's puffy. Look at his eyes. Red eyes. Like a hen."

"But such a nice little plump hen."

"Too plump. He's too soft."

"Like dough. He's *sticky*."

The pitch of voices rose angrily. "He isn't!" protests came. "Stop saying that! It's not true!"

"He's too much like a girl. He's nothing but a nasty dirty girl."

"He's lazy," others chimed. "Stupid and lazy."

"And he left his wife."

"Yes, he ran off with a whore. He lost his job and he left his wife and he hit his best friend. And he left his poor little baby locked up in a car."

"He's all washed up. He couldn't keep an awful little salesman's job."

A voice protested: "He quit!"

"He couldn't keep even a dirty little job like that. He wasn't good enough for that."

"He was *too* good. He wasn't made for a job like that. Look at his hands. He's an artist. Look at his face. He's not a common person. He's noble. He has a noble face and hands. He was made for greater things."

"He can't earn a living and support his wife."

"That bloated toad! Who wants to support her?"

"She was a millstone around his neck. He must rise to better things. He wasn't made for that."

"What was he made for?"

"Tommy, see what he was made for. See if you can make him for better or worse."

"Until death."

"Until death does him part."

Hadley found the door and pushed through. A blast of frigid night wind struck him in the face and he gasped. The wind blew around him furiously as he hurried away from the door, down the gray, silent sidewalk.

A crowd spilled out after him. Luminous shapes that glowed faintly white. Pale and waxen. They drifted around him, darting, touching, and blowing away, like bits of leaves. Like phosphorescent night leaves.

"Don't go!" one cried faintly.

"Come back!" voices wailed plaintively.

"Stay with us!"

"You belong with us!"

". . . belong . . ."

The bits of light danced and were swept away by the night wind. Fairy wands in the frigid darkness, lost behind him as he turned a corner and ran blindly. He was the only living thing. Empty, deserted streets. Great abandoned buildings. A vacant sky above. Remote stars. The wind lashed at him as he raced, mouth open, eyes half shut, gasping for breath.

He ran crazily, around another corner and down the center of the street. Faster and faster he raced. Behind him a great sound swelled. A vast booming sound that grew with frightening suddenness. Without warning he was illuminated. Etched in shadow against the side of a building.

He halted, bewildered. The roar beat against his ears. A vast thundering rumble, mixed with a shrill whine. And the light. He was blinded. He moved in a dazed half circle, hands over his eyes. . . .

Something hit him. Weightless, he flew soundlessly through the night sky. A tiny cinder, drifting through the darkness, caught up by the wind. He felt nothing. There was no sound, no weight, no sensation.

Even when he hit, there was no feeling. Only a dim realization that he was no longer moving. And then the darkness dissolved what remained of him. There was only an empty void, an infinite formless gloom, where he had been.

He woke up slowly. Everything was strange. With a flashing stab of panic he hunted his own identity. Who was he? Where . . .

He managed to focus his eyes. He was in a small room; a strange, unfamiliar room. It was day; bleak, gray midmorning light filtered in the window. The sky was overcast; it was raining. Cold, moist fog lay over a dripping wood fence, a backyard littered with rusty beer cans and weeds. The room itself was ancient. An incredibly high ceiling. Yellow paint. An old-fashioned iron chandelier, hanging at the end of a twisted mass of black wiring. A chipped, white-painted wood dresser, tall and stern. Round china knobs. The floor was covered with faded, cracked linoleum. The bed was iron, wide and high off the floor. A narrow window. Tattered shades.

Dusty lace curtains torn and heavy with age. A heap of ancient leather-bound books was propped up in a row; they filled the corner of the room in a wall-to-celling bookcase. Beside the bed was a cane-bottom chair. And his clothing.

While he was gazing blankly at his clothing, he became aware of the man and woman peering into the room at him.

It was a little old couple; two withered, fragile people huddled together, staring at him with anxious black beady eyes. The woman wore a cotton lace shawl and a shapeless dress, covered with the remains of a housecoat. The man was dressed in a brown shirt, red suspenders, baggy dark trousers, and some kind of slippers. Their hair was thin and gray, spidery wisps clinging drily to their wrinkled skulls. Paper-thin skulls, weathered, aged . . .

The old woman spoke first. Her voice was thick, guttural, heavily accented. They were German; their faces were straw brown, noses large and red, lips prominent. German peasants, with large hands and feet. "Bitte," the old woman muttered, "es tut uns fruchtbar leid, aber . . ." She broke off, coughed, glanced at her husband, and continued: "How do you feel, mister? How are you?"

"I'm all right," Hadley said.

The man coughed, wiped his mouth with the back of his hand, and said gruffly: "We hit you with our truck. You were standing in the street."

"I know," Hadley said.

Rapidly, the old woman added: "It wasn't our fault; you were just standing there. Selbstmord . . ." She glanced apprehensively at her husband. "Er wollte selbst vielleicht—" Back to Hadley she asked: "Why were you there? What were you doing?"

"You're lucky," the man grunted. "No bones broken. We were driving home from the country, back from Point Reyes Station. My brother has a grocery store up there." The ghost of an uncertain smile, the faint trace of shared, covert knowledge, twitched his thick lips. "Ah, you were drunk, nicht wahr? Getrunken, mein lieber junge Mann."

"That's right," Hadley said impassively. He felt nothing, only a dull emptiness.

The old man sucked in his breath excitedly; he turned to his wife and jabbed his finger at her. A flow of German followed; both of them spluttered at once, gesturing and waving their hands. Triumph glowed on both ancient, seamed faces: a weight had been lifted from their shoulders.

"Drunk," the old man repeated proudly. "You see? You were drunk." Pointing his finger at Hadley he cried meaningfully, "It was your fault!"

"Sure," Hadley said listlessly. "My fault."

The tension was broken. Amiable pleasure flooded the old couple; they burst into the room and came gratefully around the bed, faces radiant with joy. "You see," the old man explained to his wife, "I told you. Saturday night, junge Leute freuen sich—Ich erinne mich ganz." He winked at Hadley. "You were lucky, mister," he repeated. "Next time you might not be so lucky. Yes, we picked you up and brought you here. We took care of you; we fixed you up."

Hadley knew they had been afraid to call the police, afraid to do anything but pick him up, put him in their car, and drive home with him. But he said nothing. It didn't matter. . . . Neither their previous terror nor their present good humor mattered to him. He was thinking about Pete in the back of the Studebaker. It had been twelve hours.

"Now look here," the old man was saying to him. "You can't make any trouble for us; you could be arrested for being drunk. Verstehen Sie? Ha," he muttered, nodding wisely, with the eternal cunning of peasants. "We were very good to you; we brought you here and fixed you up. We took care of you. . . . Look at your face—we bandaged you. Yes, my wife's a trained nurse. We took good care of you."

They both watched him intently, waiting for him to say something. They were confident; they no longer had anything to fear.

Hadley explored his face cautiously. His lips had been painted with some kind of salve. And his palms. He was bruised all over. His whole body ached, and felt alien. His clothes, heaped on the seat of a chair near the bed, were an unfamiliar bundle of rags. Were they really his? He wished suddenly he could see his face in a mirror. He started to ask the old woman for a mirror, but he found it difficult to speak. He tried and then gave up. Instead, he lay back against the metal head of the bed and ran his fingers lightly over his ruined nose. It had been washed and partly repaired. Pain flashed to his temples, and he let it alone.

"Do you want something?" the old man asked. "What do you want?"

"I want something to eat," Hadley said.

The two of them exchanged glances and then conferred. "What do you want to eat?" the old man asked suspiciously. "We don't have much on hand; this is Sunday, you know."

Hadley hesitated and considered a long time. "I want a peanut butter and jelly sandwich," he said finally, with solemn conviction.

Their eyes widened in astonishment. "A what?"

"Please." He started to go on, but he couldn't think what to say. He remained silent and waited hopefully.

"Wouldn't you rather have a bowl of hot chicken soup?" the old woman asked.

He shook his head.

Again the two of them conferred. "All right," the old woman said begrudgingly. They moved slowly toward the door. "You know, you can't stay here very long," the woman said warningly. "We can't afford to feed you; people like us don't have very much money."

"I realize that," Hadley said.

The old man licked his puffy lips; his tiny eyes flickered. "If you stay here we'll have to charge you," he said hoarsely.

"That's fine," Hadley agreed.

Together, the old couple moved out into the hall. "Don't you have a family?" the old woman asked bluntly. "Eine Frau, und—entschuldigen, bitte—wir haben das Bild deinem Sohn in dem—" She cackled apologetically. "A fine-looking boy; ist deiner?"

"Yes," Hadley said. He would have answered anything to get them out of the room. "Yes, he's my son."

"Do you play chess?" the old man asked as the woman disappeared down the corridor toward the stairs. His wife yelled sharply to him, and his head ducked away. "I'll talk to you later," he promised Hadley. Loudly, he yelled back: "Ich komme!"

Hadley lay listening. He heard them going downstairs, a muffled sound that diminished and died. Then presently, a long way off, opening and shutting sounds. Dishes. Silverware. The low mutter of arguing voices.

Quickly, Hadley pulled himself upright and threw the bedcovers back. With a violent effort he swung his legs out of bed and onto the floor. His body was stiff as iron; he almost shrieked when he tried to pick up his clothing. His arms and hands burned like fire; he could hardly move his fingers.

He dressed as rapidly as he could, all but his shoes. Sticking his shoes in his coat pockets he limped to the window. It was locked. Easily, he disengaged the elaborate, rusty lock and tugged at the corroded metal handles. It wouldn't open; it was rusted and painted shut. He tugged with all his strength. All at once the window gave; with a protesting groan it slithered up. Expertly, he got his forearms under, knelt down, and strained upward, his hands knotted together. The window rose halfway. Enough.

He scrambled out onto a narrow iron balcony. Damp mist, cold and biting, settled over him. A slowly descending blanket of acrid water. Over the rubbish-system yard, the fences, the rotting garage. He climbed over the railing and leaped from the balcony to the ground.

His naked feet struck with stunning force. He had missed the soft grass and landed on the concrete. Sickening agony crawled up his shattered legs. He fell in a heap and lay twisting, trying to hold back the sounds choking his throat. For a long time he stayed there, fighting off the rolling touch of darkness, waiting for some feeling to return to his feet. Above him at the window there were sounds, a flurry of excited motion. Faces peered out and were instantly withdrawn. Shrill shouts. Running.

He had to hurry. Painfully, he managed to get up and hobble a few steps. Holding on to the side of the house he reached a wrought-iron gate.

Hadley's cold, numb fingers plucked and tore at the gate. Finally he managed to swing it back and limp by it. A narrow concrete walk led between two towering old wooden apartment buildings. He hurried along, toward the street beyond. A few cars swished wetly past. He could see more houses, concrete front steps, a vast hill of apartments rising up into the swirling clouds of mist. The concrete walk seemed to go on forever. One of his shoes fell out of his pocket and he had to stumble back for it.

He squatted down and began to put on his shoes. His fingers wouldn't work well enough to tie the laces; he left them untied and hobbled on. The street came closer with agonizing slowness. He was almost there. He had to bend over to pass below the jutting lip of a window ledge. One more step, then another, another . . .

A gigantic figure loomed up and cut off the street ahead of him. A man in undershirt and dirty trousers, a vast whisker-stubbled face, rolls of red flesh, bad teeth, tiny red-rimmed eyes, expressionless slack mouth. Behind the man scampered the little old German peasant couple, voices shrill and commanding.

"Fang ihn an!" they screeched to the man. "Hurry!"

A huge hairy paw reached out for Hadley. Hadley turned and awkwardly stumbled away. The hand groped, brutish and slow, as he agilely sneaked past it. Bending almost double he scuttled by a second window projection; the giant figure mutely turned and followed. It reached the projection, bending slightly to reach for Hadley. The point of the wooden support beam caught the giant just above his temple.

"Ugh," the man said. A look of surprise settled over his face. He turned slowly toward the projection, his arm up, first clenched. Hadley fled. He reached the sidewalk and dashed down the street.

A bus came lumbering cautiously down the slippery wet surface of the hill. Hadley ran breathlessly, his skin wet with mist. Waving his arms, he shouted at the bus; it began to slow down, belching acrid fumes of carbon monoxide. The driver, a brown-faced middle-aged man, pointed sternly at the bus stop down at the end of the block. Shifting gears, he increased the velocity of the bus slightly.

Hadley continued to run after the bus. The passengers watched, some with amazement, others shocked, a few of them amused. At the stop the bus slowed to a halt; the doors flew open and three girls leaped down. Hadley clambered inside, panting and gasping, pushed past the driver, and sought the first empty seat.

"A dime, mister," the driver said patiently.

Panic seized Hadley. He threw himself down on the seat and began searching his pockets. He didn't have a dime; all he had was a crumpled five-dollar bill. Clumsily, he leaped up and ran to the back door . . . but the bus had already started. Foolishly, he stood in the well, not knowing what to do, knowing only that he did not have what the driver demanded he have.

"Where do you want to get off, mister?" the driver asked with urbane weariness. "Here, mister?"

Hadley couldn't answer. He gripped the pole and hung on tight; houses and cars flashed wetly past outside. The passengers craned their necks and peered at him with fear and curiosity, wondering what he was going to do, wondering how his torment might affect them.

At the next stop the bus halted and the doors slid automatically back. Hadley bounded down onto the pavement; after a pause the bus started and rumbled on, up the steep hill beyond. It disappeared, and the smell and sound of it died.

Taking a deep, shuddering breath, Hadley began walking. To his right was the downtown business section, the expanse of closed-up shops along Market Street. Somewhere beyond were Mission and the slums, the tiny hovels and dives of the Tenderloin. And the Greyhound bus depot.

He turned that way.

It was two in the afternoon when he stepped off the Greyhound bus at Cedar Groves. Hostile, silent rain drifted down on the houses and streets; hunched over, he again began walking.

It took only a moment to reach the factory district; the bus depot was directly at its edge. He located the familiar warehouse and the bleak, deserted parking lot behind it. There, in the far corner of the lot, was the wet gray Studebaker, where he had left it.

But something was wrong. The windows had been rolled down . . . and he had left them up. On the rain-swept asphalt something glinted; a fragment of glass. It came to him instantly: the windows had been broken and the car opened. Somebody had noticed Pete.

Cautiously, he walked on past the parking lot. At a cheap café he entered and ordered a cup of coffee. Sitting at the counter by the blaring jukebox, he sipped the coffee and tautly watched the parking lot. It took a while, over half an hour, but eventually what he expected occurred. A policeman in a dark Army raincoat detached himself from an opposite doorway and crossed the street to the parking lot. Out of the shadows another policeman appeared; the two of them spoke a few words and then separated. They returned to their posts and melted into the drab landscape.

Hadley pushed away his coffee cup and got to his feet. He had lost Pete; and the police were out looking for him. Shoving open the door, he emerged from the warm yellow café onto the bleak rainy street. Quickly he walked off to his right, without looking back. Nobody followed him.

There were three one-dollar bills in his pockets, change from the Greyhound bus fare. Searching carefully he brought up a fifty-cent piece, a quarter, and two dimes. Not far ahead was the dour outline of a cheap transient-class hotel. He headed toward it.

"How much?" he asked the clerk leaning against the flyspecked counter. "A single—without bath."

The clerk studied him thoroughly before answering. He was a tall young man with sallow, pimply skin, a shock of thick, greasy black hair tumbling down around his ears, wearing a dirty pale blue shirt and food-stained slacks. "Looks like something happened to you," he said languidly.

Hadley didn't answer.

"Three dollars," the clerk said. "No luggage?"

"No," Hadley said.

"In advance."

It was more money than he had expected. But he signed the register and handed over the bills. Elaborately, the clerk gave him the key with its heavy square of red plastic, stamped with the name and address of the hotel and the number of the room. With a contemptuous twist of his body the clerk pointed to a flight of wide wooden stairs; he eyed Hadley all the way up, until the lobby was lost behind and Hadley emerged on the second floor.

His room was large, drab, and not clean. Immediately, he pulled open the window and let the damp afternoon air billow in. The gray, stringy curtains fluttered dismally. Outside the hotel a few trucks moved noisily along the wet road, their tires swishing mournfully. The day was dark, leaden gray. Only a few people were out; they ducked along in heavy raincoats and umbrellas. The damp chill made Hadley's jaw ache; around one of his broken teeth the gum was slowly swelling and festering.

He couldn't stand the room.

Getting to his feet, Hadley hurried out into the corridor. He slammed the door after him and descended to the lobby. Only the desk clerk was visible. A yellow plastic portable radio screeched Western steel guitar on a shelf over his head; he slumped over a pocket book spread out on the counter. Hadley wandered in an aimless, desperate circle and then threw himself down on a dilapidated wicker chair near the window of the lobby.

He wondered what he was going to do. He wondered where he was going to go, and how. There was nothing left to his plan. There was nothing left to anything.

For a time he eyed the cigarette machine in the corner of the lobby. He got out the change, but then he put it away. All the money he had would have to go for dinner; already his stomach had begun to growl sickishly. But what could he get to eat for seventy-five cents?

Rain beat against the plate-glass window of the hotel lobby. The tramping splash of men walking past echoed through the open door. Hadley hunched over miserably, beginning to feel the tireless probings of panic.

While he was sitting and meditating, a man came and sat down on the sagging couch across from him. A bald, middle-aged man with a heavy black mustache, wearing a rumpled brown coat and a gray sweatshirt, cord trousers, and black leather dress shoes.

The man nodded. "Afternoon."

"Afternoon," Hadley muttered.

"You hurt your jaw, my friend," the man said solemnly.

"Yes," Hadley answered.

The man got out a cigarette case, bent and imitation gold. He took a cork-tipped cigarette from the case and then held it out to Hadley.

"Thanks," Hadley said gratefully, accepting one.

"Look," the man said; his voice was faintly accented. He leaned forward and lit Hadley's cigarette from the side of the case: it was a combination case and cigarette lighter. With a broad, toothy smile the man settled back and lit his own. "Pretty neat, don't you think?"

"Sure," Hadley said listlessly.

The man looked around the lobby. His eyes grew large and round; his mouth fell open in an expression of wonderment. "Pretty terrible-looking hotel," he said in an awed voice.

Hadley nodded.

The man sagged. He grinned wryly, and shrugged. "I own it." He held out a large, soft hand; there were two gold rings embedded in the flesh of his fingers. "You've heard of me? I'm Preovolos. John Preovolos." He jerked his head. "I own the cigar store and the used-furniture store over that way."

He jerked his head again. "The restaurant on that side . . . serves the hotel. Isn't that something?"

"Sure," Hadley said, a little amused by the fleshy Greek.

"Listen," Preovolos said tensely, leaning forward, his face close to Hadley. "This place is run-down, isn't it? Give me your opinion."

"It is," Hadley admitted.

Preovolos sighed. "I thought so." He accepted the news with philosophical calm. After a moment he inquired ruefully: "The rooms, too? They're the same, you would say?"

"I'm afraid so," Hadley said. "Maybe worse."

Preovolos slumped. "That's what I thought. As I came in the door I said to myself, 'The rooms are even worse.'" He glanced up expectantly at Hadley. "You look like you come from a good family. Would you say that?"

"Yes," Hadley agreed. "I come from a good family. They live in New York. Lots of money."

"Your father is in business?"

"He was a doctor," Hadley said.

"A professional man." Preovolos nodded, pleased. "I thought so when I saw you. 'That young fellow's family is in business or a profession such as medicine or law.' Look here," Preovolos said seriously, "I'll tell you something. This hotel is nothing." He dismissed it with a wave, frowning angrily. "I'm telling you something that I was thinking all this morning. This town is dead. Finished. You know where something's really going on?"

"Where?" Hadley asked.

"Milpitas."

"What's going on in Milpitas?" Hadley asked, grinning in spite of himself.

Preovolos became violently agitated. "Listen," he gasped. "Up in Milpitas a big corporation—I can't give you the name—is buying up ground. Thousands of acres, out in the nothing. A big corporation is out of its mind? That will be the frosty Friday. This corporation—I can't give you the name—is going to set up operations one of these months. Milpitas is going to be big. Milpitas is going to grow."

"And you're going to be in on it?" Hadley asked. "You're going to move this hotel up there?"

Solemnly, his face massive with satisfaction, Preovolos said: "This hotel is nothing. Already I have bought land for my new hotel. When I open that I'm tearing this one down. I'm not even selling it; I'm burning it up for scrap. I'm giving the boards away. Nothing, I don't want ever to see it again." A look of rapture appeared on his face, a spiritual trancelike ecstasy. "My Milpitas hotel," he whispered, his eyes closing. "What a place. When I get that built . . ." Without warning he leaped to his feet and patted Hadley on the knee. "I'm glad to have met you," he said briskly. "I'll see you again. Let me know if there's disrespectful service or anything I can do to make your stay more pleasant."

He swept off and disappeared into a back office. The lobby was empty, except for Hadley sitting on his wicker chair, and the desk clerk behind the counter, reading his Mickey Spillane pocket book.

After a time Hadley got to his feet and wandered from the lobby out onto the gloomy, dripping sidewalk. A measure of lightheartedness had crept back into him because of John Preovolos. He passed Preovolos's café; it was seedy and run-down, like his hotel, like everything the Greek owned, in all probability. He wondered where Milpitas was. He wondered why the Greek had picked that as his illusionary dreamworld. . . . It didn't sound very exciting.

Hadley stepped into a Standard gasoline station and said: "What sort of maps do you have? Let's see the works."

The attendant eyed Hadley with distaste, then indicated a wall rack. "Help yourself."

For a moment Hadley thumbed through them. He found a map of the Bay Area, a map of San Mateo County, a street map of Cedar Groves. "Is this all?" he asked.

"What do you want?" the attendant asked morosely, "a pirate map?"

"I want," Hadley said, "some state maps. Got a map of Mexico? Canada?"

"Not even California," the attendant said, and climbed to his feet as a car pulled up by the gasoline pumps.

Hadley left the station and strolled around. At High Street he turned right. A short way ahead a big Buick four-door was parked, pale blue and white, its windows rolled down. In the back on the window ledge lay a heap of maps. Hadley continued on, gazing into each parked car. When he came to one that had a Maryland license plate he stopped and tried the door handle. The door opened and he slid quickly inside; it was an old-fashioned Oldsmobile, at least twelve years old. Rummaging in the glove compartment he found a fistful of greasy, creased state maps.

Closing the car door, Hadley hurried back the way he had come, the maps clutched tightly. He mounted the stairs of the hotel two at a time, entered his room, and slammed the door after him. A moment later he had the maps spread out on the bed.

His heart labored painfully as he studied them. Maps of Colorado, Utah, Texas . . . states he had never seen, areas a prewar Olds had reached and crossed.

His excitement was too much for him. Trembling, he got to his feet and paced around in an eager, nervous circle. In the mirror over the dresser he examined his face. A line of bluish gray showed around his damaged jaw; he needed a shave. And his hair was soggy and uncombed. There was nothing he could do about the state of his clothing; his suit was torn and his shirt was ragged and stained. His lips were still swollen, his cheeks lined with cuts; but that couldn't be helped. In any case, he could still clean himself up.

Getting his money together he hurried downstairs and out onto the sidewalk. At the drugstore on the corner he purchased a cheap safety razor and a ten-cent package of blades. What did that leave him? Nineteen cents . . . He bought a bar of perfumed soap and left the drugstore.

In the community bathroom down the hall from his room he took a long, luxurious bath. Cold rain hammered on the window and oozed around the sill as he lay half dozing in the immense iron tub, up to his chin in boiling hot water. The ceiling was high above him, strung with cobwebs, remote. The fixtures were archaic and ornate. Over the rack hung a yellowed towel, threadbare from continual use. He had heaped his clothing on the single chair.

When he had finished bathing, the bathroom was dim with steam. Letting the plug out, Hadley clambered from the tub and cautiously began drying his pain-sensitive body. The heavy, warm air smelled of the soap, a pungent woodsy scent that made him relaxed and sleepy. He shaved, standing naked, crouched over the bowl, the hair of his body damp with steam and perspiration. Then he carefully splashed his face with cold water, hurting his jaw as little as possible. He combed his hair and dressed. He straightened and smoothed his clothes as best he could, being careful of his injured rib. Wiping the mirror with the towel, he saw that all things considered, he did not look too bad.

As he passed the desk, the clerk glared suspiciously at him. Hadley grinned starkly back and continued on his way across the lobby and out into the rain. It had let up; only a faint mist drifted here and there across the dismal sidewalks and parked cars. With long strides he walked along the street, toward the railroad track and the rows of buildings beyond.

The first car lot was closed; a sagging chain had been strung from one post to the next, and the squat stucco office was locked up tight. In the mist, the rows of cars stood silent and dully gleaming, metallic animals lasting out the weekend. Hadley lingered to examine the vast shape of a red and cream Cadillac; then he crossed the street to the far side, to a second lot.

The chain was down at this lot; a man and woman were stepping gingerly among the rows of parked cars, touching them and murmuring heatedly. The man kicked tires, peered at mileage indicators, squatted down and ran his hands over fenders and bumpers. The woman, her arms folded, strode sullenly after him. A few feet away stood a redheaded man in his shirtsleeves, watching with detached cheerfulness. His face was tanned and peeling; he was the salesman.

Hadley stepped onto the lot and approached the first car he saw, a pale blue Mercury. The size of the car amazed him; he walked all the way around it, touching the smooth hood, wiping drops of water from the side-view mirror, peering in, awed, at the upholstery and the mass of dials and knobs and levers that made up the dashboard.

He tried to imagine how much it cost. Lettered in poster paint on the windshield were streaked words:

DREAM CAR SPECIAL!!

The door handle was unlocked. It seemed impossible to him that so many huge, gleaming cars could be crowded together in one lot. With their doors unlocked . . . and he could see the keys in the lock. The car was ready to go. It was miraculous.

Drifting down the line of cars he examined a Buick, a Ford, two more Buicks, an Oldsmobile, a green DeSoto, and finally a bulging tanklike Hudson. The Hudson was a flashing gunmetal; its sides dripped and gleamed as if it had risen from some river, a grinning sea monster of steel and chrome and glass. Timidly, he opened the door and gazed at the dashboard, at the steering wheel, the glittering dials and buttons. He had never seen so many buttons in his life.

While he was bent over peering into the Hudson, the redheaded man strolled up and stood a few feet away.

Hadley backed awkwardly out of the Hudson. "Sure a fine car," he said, embarrassed.

The man nodded in tolerant agreement. "It is." He leaned against the fender of a Chrysler convertible, arms folded, shirt moist with mist, his face vacant and benign, unbothered by Hadley's damaged appearance. The couple had gone off down the street to argue; Hadley was the only customer.

"How much?" Hadley asked in a strained voice.

The man rubbed his chin with his thumb, as if making a computation on the spot. Instead of answering he began to walk around the car. "He kept good care of the tires," he said.

"Who's that?" Hadley asked uncertainly.

"The fellow that owned it. Vice president down here at the Bank of America. He used it once in a while to go out in the country. The bank gave him a Chevrolet to use; gave him an expense account for it." The man reached his reddish, hairy arm inside the cabin of the Hudson and pressed a button. The hood came up and the man raised it to the lock position. "Of course, when he got this Hudson he didn't know they were providing him with a company car. He kept it around a year or so and then turned it over to us. Look at the oil filter, there."

Hadley looked.

"You see that?" the man said, pointing down into the intricate maze of machinery. "And the fuel pump's perfectly clean." Disgusted, he said: "Imagine owning a car like this and parking it away in a garage. It's criminal."

Hadley followed him obediently around as he explained various portions of the car.

"Hydramatic, of course," the man said, dismissing the clutch. "Safety-seal tubes, radio, heater, all that. A man like him had them put on and never noticed the difference." He slammed the hull with the palm of his hand. "Underseal. You planning on using this in town?"

"No," Hadley said hesitantly. "More for sort of highway travel."

The man accepted this without comment. "You'll get good pickup on this. It really takes off . . . like a scalded cat." Without special intonation he continued: "Hop in and drive it around. Go ahead; the key's in it."

Hadley felt weak. He pushed open the door and seated himself behind the wheel, facing the flashing panel of controls. "No," he said hoarsely. "Thanks, anyway. What—does a car like this go for these days?"

The man concentrated. He stared up at the sky; frowned; finally moved his lips. Hadley strained, but he failed to catch the sum. "How much?" he asked again.

"Oh, say four hundred down. Around forty-five a month." The man did not volunteer the price of the car; he stood waiting.

Hadley fooled and plucked at the controls. "It's sure a nice car," he said finally. "Damn fine car."

"It'll get you where you want to go," the man agreed mildly, and they both laughed at the audacity of his understatement.

Smiling wanly, Hadley climbed out of the car. "Okay," he said. "That gives me an idea of what I want. I'll have to think it over. I'll come back."

Without batting an eye the man said: "This car won't be here when you get back."

"No?" Hadley said, wondering why not.

"Oh, no," the man said. "Not this car. I have a couple coming back for it sometime this afternoon." He looked around as if expecting to see them coming. "This is a hot item."

"I'll have to take the chance," Hadley said. How many times had he told customers the same thing? Every word, every inflection of the man's little speech had been straight out of the book; Hadley had gone through the routine six days a week for years. But he wanted the car. He wanted it terribly. He licked his swollen lips and moved reluctantly toward the edge of the lot.

"I'll be back," he promised fervently.

The man nodded; withholding his contempt, he waved and turned his back, moved over to the far side of the lot, and stood a long way from Hadley.

Hadley hurried down the sidewalk. Where would he take it first? Nevada, Oregon, maybe all the way to Canada. The world lay open; a car like that could go anywhere. There was no limit. But he couldn't be sure of getting enough money for the Hudson; he slowed down, his excitement dwindling. Four hundred down . . . The whole price probably ran eighteen hundred dollars.

It all depended on how much money there would be.

He tried to remember how Fergesson worked it. . . . At least some of Saturday's receipts were taken home over the weekend, but at the very worst, there would be four or five hundred dollars in the store safe.

At a corner he got out his wallet and peered into it. The store key, brass and minute, lay with the keys to Marsha's car. He got it out and walked holding it clenched in his fist. The closer he got to the store, the better he felt. By the time he turned onto Cedar Street he was almost running. His breath whistled in his nose; his heart pounded.

The streets were deserted. He paused a moment to glance around; there was no one watching him. And anyhow, it didn't matter. They were used to seeing him go into the store. Briefly he glanced up at the familiar old-fashioned front, at the display windows and darkened neon sign.

MODERN TV SALES AND SERVICE

The combination of the safe was clear in his mind; he had known it for years, since the first time he had watched over Fergesson's shoulder as he was putting the money away.

Through the plate glass of the window the interior of the store was a dim expanse of cloudy shapes. Inertly, the television sets stretched out all the way to the back. The night-light flickered a ghostly blue. Stuart Hadley bent down and skillfully inserted the key in the lock.

The key did not turn. It did not go all the way into the lock. He stood for a long moment, dazed and uncomprehending. Then finally, unbelievingly, he understood . . . and his stupefaction turned to incredulous outrage.

Fergesson had changed the lock. A rim of clean new wood, freshly exposed, was visible around the lock panel. The lock itself was shiny, metallic, newly installed. Fergesson must have done it Saturday night after the poker game, before going home.

He couldn't get inside. He was locked out. In a spasm of frustrated wrath he turned and hurled the key violently away from him, into the gutter. It bounced and then lay with the trash and weeds carried along by the dark trickle of water moving toward the sewer.

Stricken, Hadley moved away from the door. He was turning his back, starting mindlessly down the street, when a flicker of motion caught his eye. He whirled, jumped to the window, and jammed his hand against it. Sitting in the upstairs office was Jim Fergesson, heaps of sales tags spread out in front of him. He watched Hadley stonily, his face hard and impassive. Saying nothing. Doing nothing. Presently he got to his feet and stood by the desk with an armload of bills and papers, still watching Hadley.

Outraged, in a haze of baffled, mounting fury, Hadley began pounding on the glass. "Let me in!" he shouted. He ran into the well and pounded on the door. "Come on—open up! Let me in!"

But Fergesson did not stir.

A little after noon that Sunday, Jim Fergesson had come down alone to Modern TV Sales and Service. As he unlocked the front door and entered, the awful silence hit him full force; he had almost turned around and gone back out.

He hated the way his shoes echoed. He hated the night-light. Bending down, he plugged in the luxurious Walco needle display, and then he straightened up painfully. He was getting old. He turned on a small table-model radio and in a moment had the ball game going shrilly.

From the cardboard box under his arm he got out the new Yale lock. He found a hammer and screwdriver under the counter; in a moment he was at work on the door. It took only fifteen minutes to get the old lock off and the new lock on. He tried each key of the set, both from outside and from inside. Satisfied, he locked the door after him, threw the old lock in the trash basket under the counter, and then made his way slowly upstairs.

The office was littered, filthy. Dust lay over everything; there were heaps of cups and glasses, dirty dishes, wadded-up waxed paper; the wastepaper basket had spilled over and was surrounded by trash. The desk was covered with pencil shavings, ashtrays full of cigarette butts; there were trade journals and bills, memos stacked up under the telephone, cards and papers and books and scrawled telephone numbers.

He swept everything to one side and got out the accounts-receivable drawers.

Outside, cold rain poured down; inside the store the air was dank and faintly chill. It never really got light or dry in the store: it was an old building with only a single skylight and the display windows and door at the front to let in the sun. Fergesson's throat ached for a cup of hot black coffee.

In the corner, under the typewriter table, was Hadley's bottle of celery extract and his bottle of fizz water. Both were dusty and cobwebbed; they had been there since Hadley first showed up with them. There were other things of Hadley's around the store; final traces couldn't be erased. His sales book was in a desk drawer somewhere. Heaps of tags that he had made out lay on the desk. In the closet were a pair of rubbers and a tie he had left. Downstairs in the medicine cabinet in the crapper was a bottle of Arrid, some nose drops, some Anacin, and a tube of toothpaste that he used to brush his teeth after lunch. And all the endless little projects of Hadley's: little repairs, little heaps of wires and bolts he was working on, continually, eternally. Tinkering, inspecting, improving.

Reminders were everywhere. Hadley had worked for him for years. In that time a man's imprint is left all over a small retail store. Fergesson grabbed up the two dusty bottles and tried to squash them down into the wastepaper basket, but the basket was too full. Finally he grabbed it up, stuck the bottles under his arm, and carried everything down into the basement to the huge trash cartons.

The basement was cold and frightening. The service department lay in complete gloom; a single overhead yellow light winked feebly as Fergesson emptied the trash, washed his hands, and started back upstairs. Darkness and decay and silence. The primordial chaos was creeping back into his creation. Filth and rubbish were everywhere; the service bench was surrounded by old radio batteries, wiring, piles of discarded tubes. The storeroom was heaped with empty crates, excelsior, boards, bent nails, bottles of polish, old instruction sheets, hammers, screwdrivers. Nobody had time to clean up. Nobody had time to keep the store really running right, as it should have been.

Fergesson carried the broom and dustpan upstairs and began to sweep the main display room. The television sets were covered with dust; high school kids had traced their names and obscene words here and there. Traced across a huge RCA combination were two bloated female breasts. The primordial dust had been stirred by abortive creation, not his own. He savagely wiped the outlines off; they had never lived or stirred. Finding a greasy rag he began vigorously polishing the sets.

Somewhere in his desk upstairs, lost in the litter of papers and notes and tags, was the name of a TV salesman the RCA people had sent around from time to time. A tall thin dull-faced man who looked as if he had a perpetual cold. Sloppy and slow of speech, mechanical smile and bobbing Adam's apple. Just what RCA could be expected to send. A snail, a tortoise, creeping around with a silly grin. A mediocre man with no possibilities. A few tricks, infinite patience, impervious to insult: the perfect modern salesman. The replacement to take the job of Stuart Hadley.

There was Joe Tampini. But Tampini didn't have it. He wasn't a born salesman. He was too shy, too retiring with people. Tampini had no push. He couldn't wade in and *get* people. He didn't have the ability to spin grandiose tales, manipulate the customer in body and mind; Tampini wove no magic spells around his prey. He'd never be more than a tag book and a pencil: he'd let the customer make up his own mind.

Stuart Hadley, somewhere down deep inside him, had something. There had been a possibility there. If Fergesson had got him early enough . . . if he had been able to train him his own way, really bring him up right, all the way from the bottom . . . But four or five years wasn't enough. A whole lifetime was needed.

Fergesson thought how it would have been if he could have got Hadley at, say, fifteen. When he was in high school, a kid in jeans and white shirt. Or younger—say, ten. When he was in grade school, still just a boy. Supervised his whole training as he grew up. Set him on the right path. Made sure he didn't pick up the goofy notions kids today picked up.

Hadley was twenty-five years old. Born in 1927. If only he could have got hold of him before Franklin Delano Roosevelt . . . before the New Deal. All during those crazy years of starry-eyed liberalism, all those years the pinks were running the country. And they still ran it. Sidney Hillman, that Russian Jew. Morgenthau, another Jew. And the worst of all—Harry Hopkins.

Memory of Harry Hopkins swam up before Fergesson and the big Philco TV set he was polishing. The stooped, angular body. The crooked smile. The sunken cheeks, fever-ridden eyes. The painful gait of the "half man." Something like the TV salesman RCA had sent over. They were coming in that way more and more. Tall, vacant-eyed men, smiling foolishly, good-naturedly, turned out by the Roosevelt mold. The shrewd, mean, small men were gone. The earlier race, the men who had come before and built up the country. The cigar-smoking men. The little hard practical men who had fathered these empty-eyed dreamers.

If he had had a son, would he have come out this way? Fergesson polished furiously. No, his son wouldn't have been like this. His son would have turned out different. If he had had a son he would have come out *right*.

Finished with polishing, Fergesson tossed the greasy rag under the counter, turned off the ball game, and made his way upstairs to the office. He pulled the cover from the adding machine and began running a tape on the accounts receivable. As he was sitting down at the desk to check the tape, there came a faint, echoing click, metallic and sharp in the silence of the store.

Somebody was at the door. Fergesson glanced up, his pencil poised over the tape. A form loomed up in the doorway, dark and opaque. It took him a moment to recognize it; at first he thought it was some blundering customer, trying to get in, wanting a radio fixed, tubes checked. Then he realized, with a thrill of pain, that it was Stuart Hadley.

For a moment he rose to his feet and stood watching Hadley try the lock futilely, saw him flush with rage and hurl the key off into the gutter. He saw Hadley start away from the door, then turn abruptly and move back to press his hand and face against the window.

The sound of Hadley's voice came, muffled and dull, blurred by the thick shatterproof glass. *"Let me in!"*

A ghostly sound. Fergesson listened, heard the words, then pushed the adding-machine tape up on his desk . . . it had begun to slither off. He tried to ignore Hadley; he tried to pretend that nobody was out in the street shouting and pounding. The leaden thumps of Hadley's fist against the glass echoed through the store; more ominous thunder to disturb his work and make his routine impossible.

The pounding ceased. Hadley stood glaring stupidly into the store, inert and helpless. The sight made Fergesson nervous; didn't the damn fool understand he couldn't get in? He tried to go on with his work, but it was hopeless. Outside the locked door the opaque shape remained, cutting off the sight of the gray sidewalk and the parked cars.

"Let me in!" Hadley shouted.

Fergesson winced; the tape slid from his hand and he sat immobile, head bent down, waiting for the next blast. He realized it was coming; he prepared himself and stiffened his body.

He had not known there was such hostility in Hadley. He had never comprehended the real extent of Hadley's rage; now all of it was coming to the surface. Fergesson was amazed, and frightened. Again he tried to resume his work, but it was futile. There was no possibility of ignoring what was happening outside his store; there was no way he could pretend it was not out there.

Booming reverberations rolled through the store; Hadley had thrown his entire weight against the glass. Shocked, Fergesson glanced involuntarily up. The expression on Hadley's face was dark and ugly, a baffled, animal frenzy that clouded his eyes and made his cheeks puffy and unhealthy. He was pressed tight against the door, staring blindly in, seeking some living thing to fasten his attention on.

He was not going away.

Fear touched Fergesson, and shame. Not for himself but for Hadley. Behind the man, a handful of people had collected, passersby who had been attracted by the noise. They darted quick, amused looks. . . . Fergesson turned away, humiliated, wondering if he could endure what was going to happen. Wondering if there could be any sense or meaning to a world in which such things were permitted.

"Let me in!" Hadley screamed.

There was no point in saying no. It did not need to be said; it was evident. Fergesson did not bother even to look up; he concentrated on the glass paperweight at the edge of his desk. The paperweight was a hollow globe, in which a miniature scene lay, a tiny house, a tree, a gravel path. Bits of white lay over the roof of the house: particles that swirled through the liquid of the globe when it was revolved.

Silence.

Fergesson peered up warily. Hadley had disappeared. Had he gone away? Had he given up? Did he finally understand that he could never get back in, that he had forfeited his right to admittance, by his own acts, with his own hands?

As Fergesson began breathing again, Hadley reappeared. He had something in his hands. A brick.

Fergesson found himself on his feet. He snatched up the telephone and dialed. "Send a cop," he said to the answering switchboard operator at the city hall.

"Yes sir," the male operator said quietly. "What is the address?"

Fergesson gave him the address and slammed down the phone. He was halfway down the stairs, almost to the main floor, when the brick crashed through the glass door. He heard it instead of seeing it; he heard the shattering burst of glass as the door flew apart. When he reached the front of the store he saw that Hadley had succeeded in making a hole the size of a basketball in the glass. Through the hole Hadley's face peered, furious and distorted, streaked with thin bloody trails from the splintering glass.

As Fergesson watched, Hadley reached through the hole and groped around for the inside door handle. It made no difference; the lock was thrown and the key was in Fergesson's pocket. Hadley continued to explore the inside of the door, plucking and examining the jagged shards of glass blocking his way. Then, abruptly, he put his shoulder to the hole and shoved.

Glass tumbled in, spilling noisily onto the floor. A whole section gave and collapsed inward; the hole expanded to the proportions of a gaping diagonal slot, two feet long and a foot wide. Hadley's coat was ripped; it hung in shreds around his arms and shoulders. Behind him the knot of people had grown to a good-sized crowd. Nobody stirred; nobody made any attempt to approach the crazed man. White-faced they watched, fascinated and terrified, as Hadley stepped back from the door and stood with his legs planted apart, gasping and wiping blood from his cheek.

"Let me in!" he pleaded. His voice came through clearly, a raw and agonized sound, not particularly human. But Fergesson made no move to open the remains of the door. Listening tensely, rigidly, he wondered where the police were, and why they hadn't come.

He knew what Hadley was going to do even before the man began to move. For an instant Hadley stood poised on the balls of his feet, swaying and trying to get his balance. Then, head down, shoulder forward, he lumbered straight at the jagged hole in the door. He struck with stunning force; the glass burst everywhere, raining down on Fergesson, slashing into the floor, the TV sets, the counter. Outside, the crowd gasped in horror.

Hadley was wedged in the hole. Mangled, a grotesque, bleeding thing, he struggled aimlessly. His body flopped at random, a mindless conglomeration of reflexes and muscles, without a central intelligence. His broken fingers traced their way around the remaining glass; his body shuddered and then gradually began to ooze its way inward. Shards of glass stuck from his back and arms, embedded in his flesh. The shocking white of his cheekbones glistened moistly. His left eye hung by a thread on his cheek; part of his lower jaw had been sheared away.

As the flapping, struggling thing plunged head forward into the store, the police ambulance wailed dismally up to the curb. Police appeared; the crowd pulled aside for them, and they quickly approached the doorway.

Fergesson made his way forward and opened the door. He managed to get it all the way aside before he was sick, terribly sick, off in a corner by the end of the counter, where the ghostly blue of the night-light flickered forlornly. The medical team shoved inside the store and clustered around Hadley. After a prolonged interval they got him onto the stretcher and back across the sidewalk to the ambulance. A moment later the siren growled back into existence and the ambulance nosed its way out into traffic.

"You put in the call?" a policeman was saying to Fergesson. "You're the owner of this store?"

"Yes," Fergesson managed. He sank down on the window ledge, among the cardboard displays and dust rags, beside the staple gun. "How hurt is he? Will he live?"

"He'll be all right," the policeman said. "They'll patch him up. Most of him, anyhow." He had his notebook and pencil out; another policeman was clearing away the crowd of frightened, curious people. "You know the individual?"

"Yes," Fergesson said. "I know him. I know the individual."

"You want to prefer criminal charges? Or you want to let it go?" The policeman turned a page in his notebook. "Maybe you ought to let it go."

"I'll let it go," Fergesson said. "I don't want to prefer any charges."

"You're insured?" the policeman asked, indicating the ruins of the glass door. One of the policemen was clumsily trying to close the frame.

"Yes," Fergesson said. "I've been insured twenty years."

Through the torn, gaping hole of the door filtered sounds, the whirr of cars and the hushed voices of people. Uneven sounds, carried by the night wind, the mixed voices, human and mechanical, from the street.

"I'll call his wife," Fergesson said, getting unsteadily to his feet.

"We can call her," the policeman said.

"It's my fault," Fergesson answered, going to the phone and taking hold of it. "So I'll call her."

PART FOUR
Night

In the front seat of the Hillman Minx, Dave Gold sat gripping the wheel and solemnly scrutinizing the street ahead. He drove cautiously, conscious of his responsibility. He avoided holes and ruts; the diminutive English car glided through traffic, over the railroad tracks, past factories and dingy stores, past towering wooden houses drab with age and decay.

"Does your rib hurt?" Laura asked anxiously, turning around in her seat to face Stuart Hadley.

"It's fine," Hadley answered.

Beside him, Ellen squeezed his hand. "We're almost there. I hope you're not too disappointed—it isn't anything like the place we had. It's a little—" She gestured nervously. "I mean, it's all run-down, darling. But it can be fixed up; it could be really lovely."

Laura Gold still peered intently at Stuart Hadley. "How does your jaw feel?" she demanded.

"Fine," he answered, grinning slightly. "It'll be all right."

Satisfied, Laura sank back into her seat and turned her attention on the street. "It's hot," she said. "Dave, turn on the cooling system. I'm baking."

"I don't know how to work it," Dave answered. "Look in the dashboard compartment; that book is there somewhere."

"What'd you buy it for if you can't work it?" Laura demanded. Sniggering, she turned to face Stuart and Ellen. "He got all the extras. He went out of his mind. The schlump!"

"I have to have a car," Dave said doggedly. "I have to drive around."

"He won't let me drive it," Laura said. "It's too good for me to drive. It's his car, not mine." She winked coarsely at Ellen. "The lion asserts himself." She winked at Hadley. "Some lion."

He didn't see the house at first. It was on the left side of the street, his blind side. Ellen watched anxiously, holding on tight to Pete, as Hadley climbed painfully from the car and onto the sidewalk. The heavy late-September sun glared down on him and he stood blinking and adjusting. Then he reached out to take Pete, and Ellen followed after him.

"What do you think of it?" she asked quickly, eyes bright and searching.

While Hadley was studying the ramshackle building, the Hillman Minx coughed into activity and hurried off past him. Dave and Laura waved frantic good-byes; the little car rapidly disappeared into traffic and was gone. Stuart and Ellen stood by themselves on the sidewalk.

"Why did they go?" Hadley asked, with mild curiosity.

"They'll be back later on." Ellen took his arm lightly. "Want to go in? Ready?"

"Sure," Hadley said. He forgot the Golds and started stiffly toward the house.

The ancient wooden structure had once been a respectable, imposing mansion; when this portion of town was new the house had dominated the block. Its ornate turrets indicated that the turn of the century had been its brightest period. Dark shingles covered its sides like rough brown hair; stained and broken, the shingles stretched in uneven rows up to the roof itself. The house stood three stories high. A rusty iron fence surrounded the large lot; a vast dirty palm tree squatted in one corner, by what had once been a garage. Tattered curtains hung in the upstairs windows. The asphalt roofing was a dull, corroded red. Around the cracked gray concrete path grew wilted geraniums. The massive front porch was a series of chipped, sagging boards, a faded blue expanse on which a wicker chair and a potted plant rested; in one corner stood a heap of moldy newspapers.

"A coat of paint," Ellen said hopefully, "would certainly fix it up." She guided her husband up the three cement steps to the heavy gate and stood waiting while he dutifully fumbled with the catch. "I guess it's sort of old."

"Which is our part?" He held the gate aside for her and closed it after. Frail and uncertain, he started toward the porch; Ellen stopped him and led him gently around the side of the house.

"We don't go in that way; we have our own entrance." As they walked she explained briskly: "The woman who owns it, Mrs. Nevin, lives upstairs on the top floor. She has her floor stuffed full of furniture; I saw it the day I answered the ad. The second floor, according to her, is filled with trashy young people from Los Angeles; he's an ad writer and the woman has men friends over when he's away. The people on the ground floor are very quiet, although once in a long while they have a party, but it doesn't last very late, except that once Mrs. Nevin had to go down and ask them please to pipe down."

"And us?" Hadley asked.

"We're on the bottom. In the basement." Ellen stooped and turned the handle of a low door. "It's locked." She got out her key and unlocked it. "Anyhow, this is us. We go in here, like Mister and Mrs. Mole. Do you mind?"

He didn't mind. The two of them stepped into a dark, moist interior; Ellen yanked back a dust-thick curtain and sunlight streamed in. The ceiling bulged with furnace pipes, huge tunnels of metal covered with spiderwebs and soot. Water and gas pipes ran up the wall; the room was long, gloomy, low-ceilinged, silent. There was no furniture. Two walls were without windows; and beyond a third one grew the vast old palm tree. At the far end of the room a door opened into a second room; Hadley gave Pete to his wife and walked toward it.

Beyond the long, low living room was a tiny cramped kitchen. A massive icebox was jammed into one corner; a sink and corrupted black gas stove filled the balance of the room. "No cupboards?" Hadley asked, amused.

"They're in the next room," Ellen said, coming after him.

Beyond the kitchen branched out a series of tiny cells, a labyrinth of passages that ended in a dinette, two bedrooms, a bathroom, a shower stall, and finally a laundry room. There was an additional room still unclaimed from the original cellar; its floor was heaped, wet dirt. The plasterboard walls were stained and yellowed. Over the apartment hung the smell of dampness and mold. Somewhere in the walls a mouse scampered; beyond that there was no sound. The palm tree cut off noises from the street. The ceiling above them was thick, impenetrable. They were totally isolated.

"I guess," Ellen said wistfully, "it's a sort of dungeon."

"It's fine," Hadley said. "And let's not talk about dungeons."

Ellen flushed guiltily. "I'm sorry. I mean, you don't think of it that way, do you? This isn't really so barren; we can fix it all up."

"I think we can," Hadley said. He roamed about, his hands in his pockets, examining each room. In a closet he came abruptly upon himself; from the fragments of a broken mirror stacked in a shoebox his reflection gleamed up, shattered and twisted. It was a shock; he closed the door and stalked out of the room, into the pantry.

"I know one thing," he said wryly to Ellen. "I'm not going to be the nice-looking young man behind the counter again. That's over and done with."

"Is it?" Ellen said, not understanding. "That's good; I'm glad."

Hadley indicated the empty socket where his left eye had been. "I mean this." He touched his bandaged, misshapen jaw. "And the rest."

Ellen busied herself at the sink. "This all has to be fixed up; my God, it's filthy." She tore down some newspapers tacked to the wall. "All this will have to be scoured; the whole place."

"Let's get busy," Hadley said.

"No!" Ellen turned quickly, her face anxious, pleading. "You can't do anything; you're supposed to rest for another two months, at least. Your rib—" She put her hands on his shoulders and gazed up earnestly into his face. "Please."

Hadley walked over to the door and bent down to fix it open. He kicked a square of broken cement against it and stood for a time in the open doorway, his back to his wife. Pete, sitting in the corner of the room, began to wail; his face swelled and blackened and he waved his arms furiously.

"What's the matter?" Hadley asked, turning toward him.

"He pinched his hand." Ellen pulled something away from the baby. "This, whatever it is. A cupboard hinge, I suppose." She slipped out of her jacket and tossed it over the windowsill. For the task ahead she had put on an old pair of faded jeans, a paint-splashed canvas shirt; briskly, she kicked off her shoes and began gathering together the items that had been brought over earlier in the week.

"Here we go," she announced. She carried the zinc bucket to the kitchen and sprinkled soap dust into it; as hot water roared after the soap, she tore cotton rags from a discarded sheet and began tying her hair up with a bandanna. "You sit down," she instructed Hadley, "or go outside. I'm going to do the walls first."

She lathered the heavy scrub brush and searched for something to stand on. "I can't quite reach the ceiling," she said plaintively. "Can . . . you think of anything?"

From the dilapidated garage Hadley found her a wooden crate to stand on. Ellen climbed gratefully onto it and began scouring the ceiling; dirty water dribbled down her bare arms into her rolled-up sleeves and dripped into her face. She grinned happily down at him, eyes wide and hopeful.

"Am I doing any good?" she asked.

"You're doing fine," Hadley told her. "But I think it's about time to knock off and have a beer."

"We're going to have to get ice," Ellen reminded him. "For the icebox . . . And I think it should be cleaned out first." She wrinkled her nose. "It doesn't smell so good."

Cautiously, Hadley seated himself on the doorstep, his knees apart, hands clasped together. Warm autumn sunlight beat down on his face; he squinted and turned his head away. A faint breeze stirred the palm tree, a metallic rustle, heavy and ponderous, like a very old bird shifting fitfully in its sleep.

The sun made him feel good. He enjoyed it; his body relaxed, and some of the dull ache drained out of his joints. Every part of him hurt to some degree; the constant pain had become a background, a distant presence that had gradually waned below the level of consciousness. The vacant darkness of one side of his brain . . . that was the worst of all. Artfully, he focused on a cat making her way among the parked cars on the far side of the street. He could see well enough, though. He could still make his way around. And his rib would eventually heal.

Most of him would heal. If he sat long enough in the sun perhaps even his eye would return, grow back in place, very tiny at first, then larger and larger until it was full sized. But that did not really seem likely. The more he thought about it the more he doubted if such a thing could happen. The idea rapidly dwindled away; regretfully, he allowed it to leave. What had happened to him had left a permanent mark; whether for better or worse, he was not the same Stuart Hadley.

In fact, in many ways, he was not Stuart Hadley at all. Once, he had wondered who or what Stuart Hadley was. Now it did not matter, because he had only a remote, detached relationship to Stuart Hadley. The name stirred nothing; it was an echo that aroused very little in him, in spite of its appearance across the papers in his wallet. It was something to answer to; he could tolerate it to that extent.

Sleepily, he got out his cigarettes and matches. He lit up and cautiously stretched out his legs. Some children passed beyond the iron fence, pushing a bike. They glanced at him; their voices ceased as they made out the destroyed portions of his face. He said nothing; and presently they went on, but not as loudly as before.

It was going to be that way. He was marked, and marked where it showed. No old lady would ever come again, carrying her radio, wanting to have it fixed. There would be no kidding with the dark-haired girl at Woolworth's soda fountain. But he felt no resentment at the realization; the warm sun made him relaxed and at peace.

"Can I have a cigarette?" Ellen gasped, stepping off the box and pushing her hair back out of her eyes. She came over to him and crouched down; dirty water clung to her face and arms. As he handed her his cigarette she leaned forward and kissed him on the back of the neck.

"I'll be able to help you soon," he said. "By the time we move in."

"We'll be moving in the day after tomorrow," Ellen contradicted practically. "I'm just getting it clean enough to live in; you can fix it all up later on."

"How much stuff do you want brought over from your family's place?"

"Just our beds. And our clothes. Dishes—personal things." She straightened up. "You don't mind staying there a couple of days, do you?"

"No," he answered. He could stand anything now.

"We could stay with the Golds."

"It doesn't matter. You kept the living-room furniture? That was paid for."

"Yes," Ellen said. "The living-room furniture and the beds, and that big lamp, and the rugs, and the silver. All the small stuff; it's stored. Everything but the refrigerator and the stove and the television set. I let them take those back . . . It wasn't worth paying them off."

"You mean we didn't have a choice."

"Did—you want them?"

"No," Hadley said. "We can use the icebox." Five weeks in the prison ward of the county hospital had taught him to go without a lot of things.

Ellen moved back to her bucket and rags. "We still have the electric toaster and the electric coffeemaker and the Waring blender. All the kitchen gadgets . . ." Her voice trailed off forlornly. "I couldn't give them up . . . and anyhow, we could have got only a few dollars apiece."

"Fine," Hadley said genially.

"I guess we could use the money, though."

"We'll be all right," Hadley said. He blew a cloud of smoke out into the yard, among the geraniums and candy tuft; he wondered idly if there was any way one man could saw down a full-grown palm tree.

He spent the next month resting and recovering, and puttering around the basement apartment. His body was mending slowly; gradually his strength came back. He had been very sick. It took a long time to recover what he had lost; and not all of it came back. At last, he gave up waiting. He knew there was no more on the way; what he had was all he was ever going to have, the rest of his life.

Before he painted the apartment, he scoured the walls with a steel brush. He chipped the old paint off the woodwork and made arrangements to restore the stain. The wood, under its cheap white enamel paint, was a lovely old walnut; slowly, reluctantly, the original grain and color emerged. He labored patiently at it. . . . The job was a long one.

While he scraped and rubbed and cleaned, Ellen hurried back and forth to her job; while Hadley recovered she was working as a typist and stenographer at a downtown business office. Hadley took care of Pete and the apartment. For the first time in his life he had the long empty mornings in which to think and become familiar with himself. During the weekdays there was no sound except distant radios booming out soap operas, and the squeak of brakes as milk and bread trucks raced along the streets.

As his rib mended, he was able to begin painting. He spent all day Saturday in the paint stores, going over colors and grades, high-gloss, enamel, flat-coat, oil- and water-based, the new rubber-based, brush and roller paints, spray guns, turpentine, sandpaper, everything related to house painting. When he purchased he chose calmly, solemnly. What he carried home was a cardboard box of simple colors, basic materials to build with.

Carefully, step by step, he built his way up. It was slow and painful; he stood all day on a stool, sanding and cleaning and caulking, getting the dust and grime of years off, scraping down to the real substance beneath, the genuine material that had been covered over, buried beneath stale, artificial layers. Plain, unassuming tints began to emerge as he built up from the solid subsurfaces. He worked over each square foot at a time, his attention completely on what his hands were doing, putting everything of himself into the work.

After the cleaning and painting came new fixtures. He ordered plain overhead fluorescent tubing from a wholesale house; one whole day was spent assembling the units, wiring up the starters, ripping out the old decayed wiring and putting in solid aluminum BX cable. At night the apartment smelled of paint, and gas from the kitchen stove. Through the open windows drifted the smell of autumn grass drying in fields and gardens. Ellen sat on the bed, mending moth holes in a spread, as Hadley worked patiently, repairing the plunger mechanism of the toilet.

He wanted to put in better heating. But that could wait; it was still some time before winter. He proceeded cautiously, step by step; he learned all over again, from the ground up. He felt his way along as a weak man should, as a man recovering from a terrible illness had to. He understood how sick he had been; he took his time about coming back.

In an old pair of torn, stained trousers, and tennis shoes, sweatshirt, his neck sunburned, arms perspiring, he squatted in the garden, pounding out frames for new concrete steps. It was something he knew nothing about; he failed, and for a while he put the job aside. He could not expect to do it all at once. . . . He returned to the apartment and restudied the plumbing situation.

One afternoon, while he was laboring over the flue of the stove, Olsen and Joe Tampini dropped by.

"It's looking pretty good," Tampini observed shyly, moving around the apartment. The sight of the store truck parked outside gave Hadley a strange feeling; he ignored it and poured beers for the two men.

"Shit-lousy neighborhood," Olsen muttered, accepting his beer. "Thanks." He threw himself down self-consciously on the couch and crouched forward, bent over and nervous. "Long time no see," he said finally. "How's it going?"

"Fine," Hadley said.

"You sure got banged up," Olsen observed, studying him briefly. "I was the one had to put up another door."

Hadley nodded without answering.

"You gave old man Fergesson the scare of his life," Olsen continued, rubbing beer foam from his hairy upper lip. "He almost crapped in his pants. . . . He's never been the same since. You really jolted him."

Tampini agreed. "He's sort of quiet. He doesn't yell at everybody all the time now."

"Glad to hear it," Hadley said vaguely. He did not mind hearing about the store, but it was difficult for him to concentrate on it. "How's business?"

"Shitty," Olsen answered heartily. "Fergesson fired Jack White; he's got somebody else in, some half-assed goon from Meyberg's."

"I'm on the floor," Tampini said. "I sold a Zenith combination today; that's what we're out delivering."

"Fine," Hadley said, smiling. "How's your girl?"

"We're married," Tampini managed to answer, overcome with shyness. Under his Arrow shirt his chest swelled with pride. "Say, drop over sometime and have dinner with us; Virginia's a swell cook."

"I will," Hadley promised.

The two men lingered. "Good to see you again, Stumblebum," Olsen said abruptly. "The joint isn't the same." He didn't look directly at Hadley. "Sorry you're gone, but I'm glad you told that fat-assed Fergesson off. Do it again for me sometime."

Hadley said nothing.

"I always thought you didn't belong in a crummy joint like Modern," Olsen continued. "If I had anything but crap in my pants I'd tell him to go shove it and get the hell out of there. But I guess I won't. I guess I'm too chicken-shit."

"I never thought of it that way," Hadley said.

"Well," Olsen said, belching, "maybe it wasn't worth it." He gestured toward Hadley's face. "You look pretty damn awful with that missing peeper; why don't you get a glass one? I know a guy, a buddy of mine, he lost an eye in the war and got a glass one. Anyhow, I'm glad you did it. You look all right, considering. You seem to be doing all right."

Thoughtfully, Hadley answered: "I feel okay. A little tired."

The two men got to their feet. "We have to go," Joe Tampini said earnestly. "We'll drop by again sometime."

"Can I come over for a feed?" Olsen asked bluntly. "I can stand some broad-cooked food for a change. Those goddamn hash houses are ruining my gut."

"Sure," Hadley said, grinning. "Anytime. I'll give you a call on the phone." As they wandered out the door, he said: "You think Fergesson will care if you visit us?"

"Fuck him," Olsen bellowed as he strolled down the concrete walk, hunched over, head turned like an enormous crab.

"I think he's sorry," Tampini said, blushing. "I mean, I think he feels it was his fault. He knows—" He broke off, confused. "It's none of my business. I think he feels responsible."

Hadley nodded.

"He's having trouble finding people to run both stores," Tampini said hurriedly. "I think—"

"Come on!" Olsen squalled from the truck. "Get your ass out of the sling—we have to deliver this pile of shit and get back to the store."

The truck drove noisily off, and Hadley reentered the apartment to resume his work. For a little while he thought about Fergesson and the store. Then the images faded; he was glad to get rid of them. They ceased dancing around him, and he turned his attention back to the corroded stove.

The message itself came through Alice. As Hadley and his wife were laying squares of asphalt tile in the kitchen, Ellen said: "I have something to tell you. I don't know what you're going to say; maybe I shouldn't even mention it."

Hadley laid down the glue pot and seated himself at the kitchen table. It was late, almost midnight; the windows were wide open to the heavy night air. Up and down the street there was only darkness and immobility. A few tubby insects bumbled and fluttered around the overhead light.

"I think I know what it is," Hadley said. "Tampini said something when they were over."

Continuing with the tile laying, Ellen said: "Alice Fergesson came down to the office today; she found out where I work from my mother. She stayed a couple of hours." She glanced up anxiously at her husband. "Do you mind if I talk about it?"

"I don't mind."

"She wanted to know how we were getting along. She asked about Pete. And about you, of course. Do you remember her coming to visit you at the hospital?"

"Vaguely," Hadley said. The whole period at the police hospital, the interviews with the judge, the activity of the lawyers, the legal arrangements, were blurred and uncertain in his mind. "How is she?"

"She's fine. She—" Ellen hesitated. "Well, she says that Fergesson says if you want, you can come back to work."

"I know," Hadley said after a pause. "I figured that out."

"She didn't know how you'd feel. . . . Neither did I, because I never thought about it. I just—considered it a closed book. You know what I mean?"

"Yes," Hadley agreed. "I know what you mean."

"It took me completely by surprise. . . . I told her I'd tell you." Ellen grabbed some tiles and worked feverishly, intently. "So that's what she said. She didn't really say much. . . . That's what she came by for, of course. There weren't any details. . . . I guess it would be the same as it was."

"I knew it was going to be brought up," Hadley said. "Is she waiting for an answer?"

"I'm supposed to call her."

"Tell her to thank Fergesson and tell him I'm not coming back."

Ellen let out her breath with a rush. "Thank God."

"It means you have to keep on working awhile. Until I line up something."

"You shouldn't be working yet anyhow!" Ellen protested.

"I'm well enough," Hadley said firmly. "I can begin looking for something."

Presently Ellen said in a tiny voice: "What sort of thing, darling? What are you going to do?" Wanly, she said: "I've been wondering . . . I know you want to do something new, I guess. Different."

"I'll see," Hadley said. "I've been doing a lot of thinking about it. I've almost decided . . . but I want to take my time." He got up and settled down beside his wife to continue the work. "I don't want to rush into anything."

The job he took was not particularly impressive. In a local pipe factory he perched daily on a bench in an elongated storage room, handing out tools to workmen from midnight to nine in the morning. The job paid well; he joined the union and rode back and forth on the bus, a lunch pail under his arm, and wearing sailcloth pants and a sweatshirt. After a few months, a little after Christmas, he quit that job; after careful deliberation, he took a job with the city, operating the equipment that maintained the seven or eight miniature city parks.

Between the two jobs he learned something about heavy machinery. He learned to operate and repair basic mechanical implements; he learned to keep tools clean and oiled, and to put them away where they belonged. The discipline of tool maintenance was taught him. In the early spring he quit his job with the city and went to work for a local ice rink, tending and operating the freezing equipment, keeping it in repair and keeping it functioning.

Working with machinery interested him. For the apartment he bought an old Westinghouse belt-driven refrigerator and began tinkering with it. For a little while he toyed with the idea of taking a course in refrigeration; but he decided against it, partly on the grounds that he could learn more by actual work, and partly because there seemed to be no such course.

As he had expected, refrigeration repair was not something he could learn from a book, or by thinking about it. Or even, he discovered, by talking about it. For days he sat with the contents of the refrigerator spread out around him, examining and studying it, putting it together and taking it apart. He learned a lot about refrigerators.

The job he had quit, the job with the city, remained in his mind. During May, while he thought about it, he tore up the floor of the apartment and installed radiant heating. The hot-water pump and pipes were put together with his own hands—and those of Olsen. Olsen came by and supervised.

"For a guy with only one peeper," Olsen commented, "you're doing okay." Morosely, he added: "But you'd sure be up shit creek if you lost the other."

The two of them replaced the floor and inspected the thermostat of the pump. The pump wheezed and clattered as it ejected hot water into the rings of pipe under the floor. After a fashion, it worked.

"You'll probably burn down the whole joint," Olsen said that evening at dinner as he sat across from Ellen and Stuart, self-consciously spooning up lamb stew and biscuits. "These old firetraps go like kindling once some jackass gets them started."

Hadley and his wife smiled at each other; Ellen reached out and touched her husband's hand.

"You think," Olsen demanded, "maybe you ever want to go back to Modern? Fergesson sure as hell would like to have you back." He added: "The old fart's going to sell O'Neill's place. He can't run both of them; he's too damn old and broken-down."

"I'm sorry to hear that," Hadley said, suddenly perturbed.

"Well?" Olsen shouted, spitting food across the table. "Then why don't you come back?"

"I don't want to come back," Hadley said slowly. "No, I'm not coming back. It's too bad about O'Neill's place. . . ." For a time he sat frowning intently down at his plate. He said nothing; his face was wrinkled and solemn.

"What do you think you'll do?" Olsen asked, slopping down coffee and wiping his chin. "You're not going to stay with that ice rink, are you?"

"No," Hadley agreed.

"And you're not coming back to Modern? You really mean it?"

"I've been thinking," Hadley said. "That job I had with the park . . . I liked working like that, outdoors."

"What are you going to be," Olsen raged, "a goddamn horse?"

After dinner, they sat around the living room. Pete was sound asleep in his bedroom; in the unused room the hot-water pump labored fitfully. "Here's what I've been thinking," Hadley said. "A lot of people are doing things for themselves now, things they used to pay to have done. They paint their own houses, they lay their own flooring, they do all the plumbing, they do their own wiring. Who has a man come in and sand the floors these days? You sand your own floors . . . if you can get hold of a sander."

"People always did that stuff," Olsen disagreed. "Guys always jigsawed little birdhouses out of plywood on their workbench in the garage."

"I don't mean that," Hadley said, "that *Popular Mechanics* stuff. Hobbies on Saturday afternoon, knickknacks around the house. I mean the basic services of construction and maintenance . . . like pouring concrete. Two years ago nobody would have poured his own concrete . . . now everybody does."

"If they can get hold of the mixer," Ellen said quickly.

His hands clasped tightly together, Hadley went on: "A lot of that stuff takes equipment. To do a fifty-dollar job you need two thousand dollars' worth of power-driven tools. If people had access to the tools, they could do almost anything . . . fix their own cars, pour their own roofing asphalt, lay concrete, sand their floors—Christ, they could build their houses and everything inside them. Practically weave their own clothes."

"The women could do that part," Ellen said. "And make bowls to eat out of. All you need is a revolving wheel and lots of clay."

"Okay," Hadley said. "So you want to make a bowl out of clay. You need a potter's wheel—where are you going to get it?"

"I don't know," Ellen said; "I never tried."

"There isn't any place," Hadley informed her. "Contractors own all the stuff; their own crews use them. Try to rent a mixer, a floor sander, heavy-duty paint sprayers, and they laugh at you. They have to laugh—if they loaned you the stuff they'd go out of business. There's no end to what a man can do for himself if he has the tools."

"I suppose you're going to fix your own goddamn TV set," Olsen said bitterly.

"If I ever get one again," Hadley said mildly, "which is doubtful, I'll build it. All you need for that is a two-dollar soldering iron and a pair of pliers."

Olsen lapsed into gloomy silence. "Then what happens to me?"

Hadley leaned toward him. "Here's what I want to do. I want to set up a place where people can rent all these tools. I sat in that pipe factory handing out tools to workmen all day long. . . . When I worked for the city I drove power lawn mowers and compost grinders; I operated electric hedge clippers and sprayers—every kind of damn thing. At the ice rink I have a whole building full of pumps and coils and pulleys to take care of."

"So?" Olsen said.

"I think I know what I'm doing. I need a little place near the center of town, some store, maybe with a lot for people to park and load stuff in trailer carts. I'll rent out tools for everything; people won't have to buy any tools at all. Everything from screwdrivers to pneumatic drills. Blasters, scrapers, power lathes, grinders—the works. Whatever work you want to do, I'll have the tools to rent. By the hour, the day, whatever people want."

"You'll have to know a lot about tools," Olsen said doubtfully. "You'll have to service them all. It'll be a bass-ackward headache."

"I think I can do it," Hadley said. He glanced up. "Don't you think I can?"

"No, you haven't had enough experience," Olsen said bluntly. "You'd go broke. And it'll take plenty of loot to get hold of those power tools; they cost like hell."

"What do you think of the idea itself?"

"It's great," Olsen said. "It'll eventually put me out of business, of course. Nobody'll hire TV servicemen once this damn thing gets going."

"Why don't you come in with me?" Hadley asked. "You've had the experience . . . You know what you're doing. All during the war you were operating a turret lathe—while I was sitting around wasting my time in college."

Olsen's face writhed with pain. "Damn it, I wish I could. It sounds wonderful." He glanced wretchedly at Ellen. "I sure wish I could, but I can't."

"Why not?" Hadley asked. "You don't have to put up any of the money; I can write back east and get it from my mother."

"What, then?"

"Just your experience and common sense."

Olsen reflected. "No," he said emphatically.

"Why not? What are you risking?"

"I'm a bum," Olsen said simply. "I've stayed at Modern too long . . . I have to be getting on, out of this town. You know that. I can't stay in one place . . . I'd go in with you for a while, and then I'd pull out. It isn't right; I'd leave you holding the bag."

"You don't think you'd find this satisfying?"

"I'm restless. I always was; I always will be." Olsen got to his feet and paced unhappily around the room, a huge hunched-over man, his jaw blue and stubbled, his hair a tangled, weedy mass. "I'm sorry as hell. But I'm not dependable. I just can't stay put."

Hadley said thoughtfully: "Neither could I."

"That's different. You were looking for something; you wanted something better than a two-bit salesman job. That wasn't for you. . . . You've got something on the ball. But not me. I don't have anything. If I had half the mind you've got." He shrugged. "But I don't."

Ellen got to her feet and hurried into the kitchen for coffee.

In an old Chevrolet that Joe Tampini had helped them patch up, Hadley and Ellen drove out into the country. Ellen sat behind the wheel; Hadley gazed out the window at the dry brown fields and mountains. It was late July; the air was hot and breathless. A few cars moved here and there. A steady, unmoving blue haze hung over the coast range. In the fields, cows lay dozing under clusters of ancient oak trees.

"It's peaceful out here," Ellen remarked.

The road climbed a long range of hills; the valley lay spread out behind them, a checkerboard of brown and gray-blue, squares that were farms and pastures and fruit orchards. Ahead of the car a small country town squatted by the road. Decrepit, massive barns made up the bulk of the town. To the right stood a towering grain and feed store. To the left jutted a dilapidated hotel, a barbershop, a general supply store. At the far end of town was a modern shopping center: a supermarket, a drugstore, a soda fountain. Further on was a Shell station and a rotting garage. On the hills overlooking the stores were dotted gray and white houses.

Ellen parked the car. She and Hadley and Pete got out and roamed around. They crunched along a narrow gravel road; hot sunlight beat down on them and the expanse of brown fields.

"It's hot," Ellen said.

"We're a long way from the city." Hadley made out a sign on an old-fashioned yellow train depot; freight cars lay immobile on a siding.

WOODVALLEY STATION

"That's what it's called," Ellen said, examining the map. "Woodvalley Station, elevation twelve feet. The nearest big town is Petaluma."

Nobody stirred. The town was quiet, unmoving, sound asleep in the midday summer heat. To the right of the gravel road stood a small white and green bungalow; bushes grew up its sides, and in the backyard were gnarled apricot trees. A vast old woman sitting in a rocker on the front porch watched them mildly as they passed.

"That's like back home," Ellen said. "You see old women sitting around on front porches everywhere."

"You don't see that everywhere," Hadley said, indicating the backyard. Tied up among the fruit trees was a goat. The goat raised his head and glared belligerently at them until they were gone. Then he suspiciously resumed eating.

"If we lived out here we could have a goat." Hadley set Pete down for a minute to light a cigarette. Pete, in his red and white summer suit, began staggering back toward the fence, back to the yard where the goat stood. "Pete would like that. He could drive the goat out into the forest every day and load him up with faggots."

"Is that how we'd live?" Ellen asked, smiling. "That would be the problem. . . . They don't have very many ice rinks around here."

After a moment Hadley said: "They don't have anything. No shops of any kind, only groceries and farm supplies."

"And the barbershop. And gas."

"What happens when things break down? What do they do when their radios blow out tubes?"

"Maybe they don't have radios," Ellen said.

"All farmers have radios."

"Then maybe that garage over there fixes them."

Next to the drugstore was a tiny real estate office. Hadley and his family entered and seated themselves in front of the old-fashioned oak desk.

"What sort of property did you have in mind?" the scrawny dried-up old realtor asked, fitting on his glasses and scrutinizing them. He unscrewed his fountain pen and pushed aside papers on his desk. "This isn't resort country, you know. That's higher up, around the Russian River. I've got a wonderful cabin right on the river; city people like it up there, with all the redwoods."

"I'm not interested in that," Hadley said. "I want something here in the farm country."

There was enough money in the bank for a lot, and nothing more. They left the realtor's office clutching the deposit receipt, feeling awed and foolish.

"What are we going to do with it?" Ellen asked. "It's just an empty lot—nothing but weeds and one old oak tree. We can't live up here, can we?" Wistfully she took her husband's arm, and he shifted Pete to the other side. "Can you build a house? You can't build a house by yourself."

"I can if you help," Hadley answered.

"When?" Wildly, Ellen hurried to keep up with him as he strode back toward the car. "Right away?"

"Not for a while," Hadley answered. "There's no hurry. I want to find out what kind of services they lack here. . . . I want to find out what this town needs that it hasn't got." He halted to peer around. "Did you see any sign of an ice plant?"

"An ice plant!"

"I'm just thinking," Hadley said as he opened the car door. "Where do you suppose they go when they want shoes repaired?" On his face, on his ruined eroded face, was an expression of great seriousness.

"You can't fix shoes," Ellen said gently.

"It's not up to me to decide. It depends on what they want."

"Doesn't it depend on—what you want? I think that's important, too." She added, "It is to me."

"I should find out what they need," he repeated, with conviction. "We'll come back up here now and then. . . . There's no hurry. I'll talk to people and find out. We'll take our time."

Ellen started up the motor and they sat listening to it, waiting for it to smooth itself out. Beside her, Stuart sat with Pete on his lap, his hands resting on the baby's stomach. The serious expression remained; it had not gone away. Probably it was not going away. It was part of that face, part of that damaged bone and ruined tissue that Stuart Hadley had become.

Gently, she reached up and smoothed his blond hair back, away from his ears. The warm country wind had blown it there, disorganized it, undone the careful combing that he patiently practiced each morning of his life. Stuart smiled at the pressure of her fingers.

"Thanks," he said.

"Can I kiss you?" she asked hopefully.

"Sure." He bent down a little, still holding the baby. She leaned up toward him, steadying herself with one hand, turning her face up to his. For an interval her lips touched his; against her, his mouth was calm, not withdrawn, but almost without emotion.

Troubled, she sank back. "You're not very—I mean, you seem so far away."

"No," he said. "I'm right here."

And then she remembered what she had found there, that morning, as she bent over him in the instant of awakening. The terror that had risen then, the timid fright that had quivered across his mouth as she kissed him. The fear was gone now.

"You're not afraid anymore," she said wonderingly. "I didn't realize."

"It's gone," he agreed. "Finally."

"Do you—," she began haltingly. It was hard to say; she was afraid of the answer. "Do you really think you'd be happy here? Away from the city?"

The dreadful answer came without hesitation. "Yes," he said.

In anguish, she protested: "There wouldn't be much to do! There isn't anything here. . . . There's nothing. It's just a drab little country town." Gazing fearfully up into his ruined face, she demanded: "Don't you want more? Your ability—"

"Wrong," Hadley said. "There's plenty to do here."

But she could see it there. And he did not seem to know or understand. That was the terrible part, the part she couldn't bear. He did not seem to know that nothing of him had survived. None of the dreams, the driving fury that had made him strike out, frenzied and irrational, against the indestructible glass wall of the world. He had broken himself against that wall; the world had remained. And he didn't even know it.

"Is there?" she asked wildly. "Is there really something for you here? You'd be satisfied?"

He took her hand; around her flesh his fingers were strong and hard. There was no bitterness in the pressure, only total certainty. He was without rancor. He blamed nobody, not himself, not her, no one and nothing. He was content.

"It isn't anybody's fault," he said. "A thing like this is—" He grinned. "The result of natural law. You put your hand on the stove and you get burned. You bump into a door in the dark and you get a black eye."

Blindly, Ellen released the brake and the car moved forward.

Gazing out the window, Hadley intently watched the tumbledown garage slide past. "A whole lot of things," he said, preoccupied, absorbed, reciting something learned, repeating something cut into the deepest matrix of his mind. "A whole bunch of things to get done."

Reader's Guide

Voices from the Street || Philip K. Dick

"The word 'primordial' pops up frequently in *Voices*, and it's tempting to read this early book as a Dickian urtext. Most fascinating is how Dick's major theme—a playful, terrifying disjuncture between realities—has leaked into this seemingly solid, realistically rendered setting.... He reworks the territory of soured domesticity (à la Richard Yates and John Updike) in a working-class milieu anticipating Raymond Carver. Decades later, his oeuvre (like Philip Roth's) is lovingly enshrined in our national pantheon."

—*Los Angeles Times*

About *Voices from the Street*

Twenty-five-year-old Stuart Hadley is a television salesman for Modern TV Sales and Service (echoing one of the jobs Dick himself held as a struggling writer) in Cedar Groves, California. He and his pregnant wife, Ellen, are struggling to make ends meet in their two-room apartment, and although he comes from a wealthy background, Stuart is reluctant to ask his family for help. But his boss, Jim Fergesson, wants to expand by buying O'Neill Appliance, and is weighing the notion of promoting Stuart to manager of Modern while he takes over the new store himself.

Stuart is dissatisfied with this seemingly complete life, his restlessness initially manifesting itself in weekly drunken binges, during which his violent temper occasionally earns him a night in jail. At the home of his friends, Dave and Laura Gold, Stuart meets Marsha Frazier, who publishes a "high-type quarterly," *Succubus,* and flatters Stuart by remembering that he used to be a painter. He finds himself inexplicably drawn to attend the meetings of an apocalyptic religious group, the Society of the Watchmen of Jesus, which is led by a charismatic black man, Theodore Beckheim.

Gradually, as sexual tension grows between them, Stuart becomes more involved with Marsha, and through her arranges a personal meeting with Beckheim, who urges him to join the Society. But he also begins to uncover some surprising truths, such as the fact that *Succubus* is actually "a racist, neofascist tract," and that Marsha's relationship to Beckheim is far from casual in nature. Ultimately, his interactions with Marsha and the Society will propel the increasingly unbalanced Stuart into an escalating series of events that threaten to shatter what little grip on reality he has.

Topics for Discussion

1. A native of Chicago, Philip K. Dick lived most of his life in California, and set much of his work there. How do the setting of Cedar Groves and its proximity to the distinctive yet differing cultures of Los Angeles and San Francisco inform *Voices from the Street?*

2. This novel was completed and set in 1952, the year Dick sold his first short story, yet it remained unpublished until a quarter-century after his death. Had it appeared at the time, what effect do you think the book and its critical reception would have had on his career?

3. Dick is best known as a science-fiction writer. How does *Voices from the Street,* despite being mainstream fiction, explore such common Dickian themes as the nature of reality, the threat posed by nuclear weapons, the effects of materialism, and religious obsession?

4. "I'm an intellectual," Stuart tells a police sergeant at the start of the novel. "I'm a thinker. A dreamer." Is that how he truly sees himself? Do you agree with this self-assessment?

5. Casual bigotry—against blacks, Jews, gays, and others—is pervasive in *Voices.* Do these appear to be Dick's own biases, exclusively those of his characters, or simply the tenor of the times? Are such attitudes more acceptable when encountered in a historical context?

6. Classified as 4-F due to liver trouble, Stuart is unable to serve in the Korean War. How have his feelings about war changed since World War II? Has the Bomb affected them?

7. How does Stuart react to Ellen's pregnancy and the eventual birth of Pete? How much of what happens, and what Stuart does later on, is a result of his feelings about fatherhood?

8. Stuart is visited by his sister, Sally, who says that she had made him "weak." What can we infer about the history of their relationship, and about Stuart's feelings toward Sally?

9. Initially skeptical that religion is "just another business," Stuart then becomes fascinated with Theodore Beckheim, head of the Society of the Watchmen of Jesus. Is he genuinely thirsting for spirituality, merely looking for someplace he can belong, or something else?

10. Stuart's violent sexual encounter with Marsha is brutal and shocking. Does the reader get the impression that she in any way "deserved" what happened or brought it upon herself?

11. Stuart's plan for Pete leads him into new depths of self-destructive behavior and violence. Do your feelings about the character change any as a result? Are his actions forgivable?

12. Fergesson blames himself for what happens to Stuart. Why? Is this self-blame justified?

13. Near the end, Dick refers to "the whirr of cars and the hushed voices of people. Uneven sounds, carried by the night wind, the mixed voices, human and mechanical, from the street." How do these voices function on a metaphoric level? How do they affect Stuart?

14. The conclusion finds Stuart reunited with his family and full of plans for the future, yet Ellen feels that "nothing of him had survived." Is this ending happy, sad, or ambivalent?